PRECIOUS BANE

MARY WEBB

Precious Bane

WITH AN INTRODUCTION BY
STANLEY BALDWIN

AND A NEW PREFACE BY
MICHELENE WANDOR

The Dial Press
New York

Published by
The Dial Press
1 Dag Hammarskjold Plaza
New York, New York 10017

First published 1924 by Jonathan Cape
Preface copyright © 1978 by Michelene Wandor
All rights reserved.
Manufactured in the United States of America
First printing

Library of Congress Cataloging
in Publication Data

Webb, Mary Gladys Meredith, 1881–1927.
Precious bane.

(A Virago modern classic)
I.   Title   II.   Series.
[PR6045.E2P7   1982]   823′.912   81–12437
ISBN 0-385-27216-2 (pbk.)   AACR2

To my dear H.B.L.W.

Contents

BOOK ONE

BOOK TWO

BOOK THREE

1

BOOK FOUR

Introduction

MARY MEREDITH, the author of *Precious Bane*, was born in
the little village of Leighton, near Cressage, under the
Wrekin, on March 25th, 1881, and died at St. Leonards,
October 8th, 1927, and was buried at Shrewsbury. She
was the daughter of George Edward Meredith, a school-
master of Welsh descent, by his marriage with Sarah Alice
Scott, daughter of an Edinburgh doctor of the clan of Sir
Walter Scott. She was the eldest of six children and spent
her early girlhood at The Grange, a small country house
near Much Wenlock; from 12 to 21 she lived at Stanton-
on-Hine-Heath, six miles north-east of Shrewsbury, and
for the next ten years at The Old Mill, Meole Brace, a mile
from Shrewsbury. In 1912 Mary Meredith married Mr.
Henry Bertram Law Webb, a Cambridge graduate and a
native of Shropshire. After two years at Weston-super-
Mare, where Mr. Webb had a post in a school, Mr. and
Mrs. Webb returned to Shropshire, living at Pontesbury
and Lyth Hill, working as market gardeners and selling the
produce at their own stall in Shrewsbury market. Mrs.
Webb had written stories and poems from childhood, but
it was at this period that she seriously turned her mind to
writing novels. A volume of essays on nature, *The Spring
of Joy*, and three novels, *The Golden Arrow*, *Gone to Earth*, and
The House in Dormer Forest, had been published before she
came to live in London in 1921. *Seven for a Secret* followed
in 1922 and *Precious Bane* in 1924. It was awarded the
'Femina Vie Heureuse' Prize for 1924–5 given annually for
the best work of imagination in prose or verse descriptive of
English life by an author who had not attained sufficient
recognition.

I am indebted for these biographical particulars to Mr.
Webb, to whom *Precious Bane* is inscribed. I never met Mary
Webb and knew nothing of her work until I read *Precious*

Bane at Christmas, 1926. I am glad to think that I was in time to send her a few words of appreciation.

The stupid urban view of the countryside as dull receives a fresh and crushing answer in the books of Mary Webb. All the novels except *Precious Bane* are set in the hill country of south-west Shropshire, between the Clee Hills and the Breiddens, and between Shrewsbury and Ludlow. The scene of *Precious Bane* is the country of north Shropshire meres – the Ellesmere district, but the dialect is that of south Shropshire. It is the country of the Severn lowlands and of isolated upland ridges where Celt and Saxon have met and mingled for centuries. For the passing traveller it is inhabited by an uncommunicative population dwelling among places with names like Stedment and Squilver and Stiperstone, Nipstone and Nind. There are of course the old castles and timbered black and white houses for the motoring visitors. But to the imaginative child brought up among the ploughlands and pools and dragon-flies there is 'a richness on the world, so it looked what our parson used to call sumptuous.' It is this richness which Mary Webb saw and felt as a girl and remembered with lyrical intensity as a woman.

She has interlaced with this natural beauty the tragic drama of a youth whose whole being is bent on toil and thrift and worldly success only to find himself defeated on the morrow of the harvest by the firing of the cornricks by the father of his lover. The dour figure of Gideon Sarn is set against that of his gentle sister, Prudence, who tells the tale. She is a woman flawed with a hare-shotten lip and cursed in the eyes of the neighbours until her soul's loveliness is discerned by Kester Woodseaves, the weaver. And so there comes to her at the end of the story the love which is 'the peace to which all hearts do strive.'

The strength of the book is not in its insight into human character, though that is not lacking. Nor does it lie in the inevitability with which the drama is unfolded and the sin of an all-absorbing and selfish ambition punished. It lies

4

in the fusion of the elements of nature and man, as observed in this remote countryside by a woman even more alive to the changing moods of nature than of man. Almost any page at random will furnish an illustration of the blending of human passion with the fields and skies.

'So they rode away, and the sound of the people died till it was less than the hum of a midge, and there was nothing but a scent of rosemary, and warm sun, and the horse lengthening its stride towards the mountains, whence came the air of morning.' (p. 107.)

One reviewer compared *Precious Bane* to a sampler stitched through long summer evenings in the bay window of a remote farmhouse. And sometimes writers of Welsh and Border origin, like William Morris, have had their work compared to old tapestries. But while these comparisons suggest something of the harmonies of colour they fail to convey the emotional force which glows in these pages. Nature to Mary Webb was not a pattern on a screen. Her sensibility is so acute and her power over words so sure and swift that one who reads some passage in Whitehall has almost the physical sense of being in Shropshire cornfields.

Precious Bane is a revelation not of unearthly but of earthly beauty in one bit of the England of Waterloo, the Western edge, haunted with the shadows of superstition, the legendary lore and phantasy of neighbours on the Border, differing in blood and tongue. This mingling of peoples and traditions and turns of speech and proverbial wisdom is what Mary Webb saw with the eye of the mind as she stood at her stall in Shrewsbury market, fastened in her memory, and fashioned for us in the little parcel of novels which is her legacy to literature.

STANLEY BALDWIN.

10 Downing Street, S.W.1.
October, 1928.

5

Foreword

To conjure, even for a moment, the wistfulness which is the past is like trying to gather in one's arms the hyacinthine colour of the distance. But if it is once achieved, what sweetness! – like the gentle, fugitive fragrance of spring flowers, dried with bergamot and bay. How the tears will spring in the reading of some old parchment – 'to my dear child, my tablets and my ring' – or of yellow letters, with the love still fresh and fair in them though the ink is faded – 'and so good night, my dearest heart, and God send you happy.' That vivid present of theirs, how faint it grows! The past is only the present become invisible and mute; and because it is invisible and mute, its memoried glances and its murmurs are infinitely precious. We are to-morrow's past. Even now we slip away like those pictures painted on the moving dials of antique clocks – a ship, a cottage, sun and moon, a nosegay. The dial turns, the ship rides up and sinks again, the yellow painted sun has set, and we, that were the new thing, gather magic as we go. The whirr of the spinning-wheels has ceased in our parlours, and we hear no more the treadles of the loom, the swift, silken noise of the flung shuttle, the intermittent thud of the batten. But the imagination hears them, and theirs is the melody of romance.

When antique things are also country things, they are easier to write about, for there is a permanence, a continuity in country life which makes the lapse of centuries seem of little moment.

Shropshire is a country where the dignity and beauty of ancient things lingers long, and I have been fortunate not only in being born and brought up in its magical atmosphere, and in having many friends in farm and cottage who, by pleasant talk and reminiscence have fired the imagination, but also in having the companionship of such a mind as was my father's – a mind stored with old tales and legends that did not come from books, and rich with an abiding love for the beauty of forest and harvest field, all the more intense, perhaps, because it found little opportunity for expression.

In treating of the old subject of sin-eating I am aware that William Sharpe has forestalled me and has written with consummate art. But sin-eaters were as well known on the Welsh border as in Scotland, and John Aubrey tells of one who lived 'in a cottage on Rosse highway,' and was a 'lamentable poore raskell.'

My thanks are due to the authors of *Shropshire Folk Lore* for the rhymes of 'Green Gravel' and 'Barley Bridge,' and for the verification of various customs which I had otherwise only known by hearsay, and to the Somerset weavers, who recently let me see both hand looms and spinning wheels in use.

MARY WEBB.

May, 1924.

Preface

'For you canna write a word even, but you show yourself – in the word you choose, and the shape of the letter and whether you write tall or short, plain or flourished. . .'

These are the words of Prudence Sarn, narrator of *Precious Bane,* telling the story of her life from the contented perspective of a happy old age. They are poignant words because they represent Prue's attempt to tell a story of hardship and prejudice; but they are also encouraging words, indicating the importance of written material – fact and fiction – in the difficult process of constructing a picture of the ways women have perceived and lived their lives.

Precious Bane was the fifth of Mary Webb's six novels. She was born in 1881 and died in 1927; she spent most of her life in Shropshire, where her novels are set, and from which she drew inspiration for her poetry and essays on nature. Her education was respectably minimal – as the eldest of a family of six, she was expected, after finishing school, to help with the studies of her siblings. In 1912 she married a teacher, and her first novel was written in 1916. Although she didn't start writing seriously till she was in her thirties, she had written poems and stories since she was very young, encouraged by her father.

During her lifetime she was a relatively minor literary figure, gathering respect from some fellow writers, but with little commercial success for her work. Rebecca West wrote of her second novel, *Gone to Earth,* that she thought it was the novel of the year, and its author 'a genius'. It was not till a year after her death, in 1928, that a collected edition of her work was published by Jonathan Cape, with introductions by various illustrious contemporaries, such as John Buchan, G. K. Chesterton and Prime Minister Stanley Baldwin.

Precious Bane was first published in 1924, and was considered by some critics as a 'masterpiece' *(sic)*. It was awarded the Prix Femina Vie Heureuse in 1925, a prize

8

given for the 'best imaginative work in prose or verse descriptive of English life by an author who has not gained sufficient recognition' – the same prize was won in 1927 by Radclyffe Hall for her novel *Adam's Breed*, a year before the scandal around her lesbian novel *The Well of Loneliness*. Not that Mary Webb could be compared directly with Radclyffe Hall in subject matter, style or political intentions, but it is interesting that two women writers who are being read with renewed interest today should have shared the same literary award.

Her reputation till now has been mainly that of a 'nature' writer, with her work being compared to that of A. E. Housman (also a Shropshire writer) and Thomas Hardy. Certainly her prose-landscape descriptions have a vibrant quality which combines acute observation of rural detail with a love of the varieties of country life. But this is not enough to explain why there should be a revived interest in her work. Her brand of pantheistic philosophy, when she expressed it as such, is transformed by a real empathy with the day-by-day experience of peasant life, viewed through the experience of women. There are very few novels about the rural poor, and scarcely any which depict the life of a working woman against the backdrop of religion, superstition and ignorance, which are the framework of this novel. Some of this empathy is perhaps due to Mary Webb's personal circumstances – she was something of an invalid, and, like Prue Sarn, had a harelip. This may help account for her sympathy for the emotional isolation of other women, even someone like Prue who came from a very different class; Thomas Moult, in his 1932 biography of Mary Webb, describes how for her wedding 'she chose for her guests the inmates of the women's ward of the workhouse she visited; an old herbalist who had endeared himself to her by his knowledge of plants. . .'

Precious Bane is set in the early nineteenth century, just after the Napoleonic wars, in a period of industrial and agricultural unrest in Britain. These events scarcely touch on the story in any overt way, and Prue remarks disingenuously that 'though a deal happened out in the world,

9

nought has happened to us'. Although national events appear to be outside the concern of the isolated, rural and largely illiterate community, the backdrop to Prue's story is the three centuries of intense and virulent witch-hunting all over Europe. This backdrop belies the apparently true-story romance flavour which a crude summary of the story might carry: ugly duckling woman, exploited by ruthless brother, meets gentle Prince Charming – the kind weaver Kester Woodseaves, who at the end of the story quite literally gallops in on a horse and carries Prue away to love and safety. However, the danger from which he saves her is no dragon or mythical being, but the material forces which shape myth and superstition, and which, in the history of witch-hunting, focused with murderous misogyny on women.

There are a number of reasons why Prue is thought to be a witch, and why she comes to be the scapegoat for a series of harsh and frightening events. First she has a physical blemish – a harelip – her 'bane'. Superstition has it that children with harelips were born to women who were frightened in pregnancy by the devil in the shape of a hare. Local rumours say that Prue 'took shape as a hare on dark moonless nights and went loping across the hills'. Her bodily blemish is also a blemish on her womanhood, and everyone assumes that she is not as other, normal women. Prue as an old woman comments with hindsight on the belief that 'if there was something wrong with a person's outward seeming there must be summat wrong with their mind as well', and for Mary Webb this is one of the destructive aspects of myth.

The second reason local people believe Prue to be a witch is related to the fact that she can read and write – taught by Beguildy, an aggressively atheistic and much mis-understood man, known locally as a wizard. The double-edged value of literacy then is difficult for us to grasp today. But literacy and the consequent access to written knowledge it provided was largely a tool of the ruling class; and in the witch-hunts of the seventeenth and eighteenth centuries women thought to be witches were often accused of pos-sessing knowledge which they applied as healers. A woman such as Prue would normally not follow the privileged path of the small number of bourgeois class women who learned to read and write, and would therefore be viewed with suspicion. For Prue herself, literacy is solace, the channel whereby she can communicate with Kester, as well as a way of managing the family farm. She keeps a diary – almost unheard of for a woman of her class, though a common form of occupation for 'ladies', as we know from the other fiction of the period. Her courtship with Kester is indirect and poignant; as the family scribe, she writes her brother's love letters to Jancis, Beguildy's daughter, while Kester returns letters in Jancis's name. In fact they are writing the love letters to each other.

Underlying the fear of women as witches was a terror of women as sexual beings. The classic fifteenth-century handbook *Malleus Maleficarum* on witch-hunting is quite unequivocal on the matter: 'All witchcraft comes from carnal lust, which in women is insatiable.' In *Precious Bane* one of the most extraordinary and erotic scenes represents Prue's awareness of her own sexual potential, concealed as it is by her harelip from the eyes of those around her. She is not pretty, therefore supposedly she cannot be a sexual woman. She does not want to face Kester for the same reason – afraid he will be repulsed by her. But when she offers to replace Jancis in Beguildy's phoney Venus-raising ceremony and realises afterwards that Kester has seen her naked, she is quite unashamed of her body. It is a section of the book which is powerfully suggestive and erotic at the same time – and seen completely from the woman's point of view.

Prue's nonconformity to the rural female image (which had little of the refined femininity of the gentry's ladies, but still saw women as secondary to men) is exacerbated by the fact that she works hard alongside her brother – and is dubbed the 'barn-door savage of Sarn'. She revels in the hard work, and again is conscious of the contradictory position in which she is placed: 'It was strange to think that while I went about my housework and outdoor work tomorrow, slaving like a man, at men's jobs, I should be in my own soul the bride of the weaver'.

Precious Bane is the most powerful and direct of Mary Webb's novels. It is worth reading for its undoubted literary qualities; 'Once a white owl came by, like a blow feather for lightness and softness. Mother said it was Father's spirit looking for his body.' But it is also worth reading for the insights it gives us into the potential for women's self-realisation and for the way it demonstrates how myth and material circumstances combine so powerfully to affect individual female destiny.

MICHELENE WANDOR.

July, 1978.

12

BOOK ONE

Chapter 1: *Sarn Mere*

IT was at a love-spinning that I saw Kester first. And if, in these new-fangled days, when strange inventions crowd upon us, when I hear tell there is even a machine coming into use in some parts of the country for reaping and mowing, if those that mayhappen will read this don't know what a love-spinning was, they shall hear in good time. But though it was Jancis Beguildy's love-spinning, she being three-and-twenty at that time and I being two years less, yet that is not the beginning of the story I have set out to tell.

Kester says that all tales, true tales or romancings, go farther back than the days of the child; aye, farther even than the little babe in its cot of rushes. Maybe you never slept in a cot of rushes; but all of us did at Sarn. There is such a plenty of rushes at Sarn, and old Beguildy's missus was a great one for plaiting them on rounded barrel-hoops. Then they'd be set on rockers, and a nice clean cradle they made, soft and green, so that the babe could feel as big-sorted as a little caterpillar (painted butterflies-as-is-to-be, Kester calls them) sleeping in its cocoon. Kester's very set about such things. Never will he say caterpillars. He'll say, 'There's a lot of butterflies-as-is-to-be on our cabbages, Prue.' He won't say 'It's winter.' He'll say, 'Summer's sleeping.' And there's no bud little enough nor sad-coloured enough for Kester not to callen it the beginnings of the blow.

But the time is not yet come for speaking of Kester. It is the story of us all at Sarn, of Mother and Gideon and me, and Jancis (that was so beautiful), and Wizard Beguildy, and the two or three other folk that lived in those parts,

13

that I did set out to tell. There were but a few, and maybe always will be, for there's a discouragement about the place. It may be the water lapping, year in and year out – everywhere you look and listen, water; or the big trees waiting and considering on your right hand and on your left; or the unbreathing quiet of the place, as if it was created but an hour gone, and not created for us. Or it may be that the soil is very poor and marshy, with little nature or goodness in the grass, which is ever so where reeds and rushes grow in plenty, and the flower of the paigle. Happen you call it cowslip, but we always named it the paigle, or keys of heaven. It was a wonderful thing to see our meadows at Sarn when the cowslip was in blow. Gold-over they were, so that you would think not even an angel's feet were good enough to walk there. You could make a tossy-ball before a thrush had gone over his song twice, for you'd only got to sit down and gather with both hands. Every way you looked there was naught but gold, saving towards Sarn, where the woods began, and the great stretch of grey water, gleaming and wincing in the sun. Neither woods nor water looked darksome in that fine spring weather, with the leaves coming new, and buds the colour of corn in the birch-tops. Only in our oak wood there was always a look of the back-end of the year, their young leaves being so brown. So there was always a breath of October in our May. But it was a pleasant thing to sit in the meadows and look away to the far hills. The larches spired up in their quick green, and the cowslip gold seemed to get into your heart, and even Sarn Mere was nothing but a blue mist in a yellow mist of birch-tops. And there was such a dream on the place that if a wild bee came by, let alone a bumble, it startled you like a shout. If a bee comes in at the window now to my jar of gillyflowers, I can see it all in clear colours, with Plash lying under the sunset, beyond the woods, looking like a jagged piece of bottle glass. Plash Mere was bigger than Sarn, and there wasn't a tree by it, so where there were no hills beyond it you could see the clouds rooted in it on the far side, and I used to think they looked like the white water-lilies that lay round the margins of Sarn half the summer through. There was nothing about Plash that was different from any other lake or pool. There was no troubling of the waters, as at Sarn, nor any village sounding its bells beneath the furthest deeps. It was true, what folks said of Sarn, that there was summat to be felt there.

It was at Plash that the Beguildys lived, and it was at their dwelling, that was part stone house and part cave, that I got my book learning. It may seem a strange thing to you that a woman of my humble station should be able to write and spell, and put all these things into a book. And indeed when I was a young wench there were not many great ladies, even, that could do much more scribing than to write a love-letter, and some could but just write such things as 'This be quince and apple' on their jellies, and others had ado to put their names in the marriage register. Many have come to me, time and again, to write their love-letters for them, and a bitter old task it is, to write other women's love-letters out of your own burning heart.

If it hadna been for Mister Beguildy I never could have written down all these things. He learned me to read and write, and reckon up figures. And though he was a preached-against man, and said he could do a deal that I don't believe he ever could do, and though he dabbled in things that are not good for us to interfere with, yet I shall never forget to thank God for him. It seems to me now a very uncommon working of His power, to put it into Beguildy's heart to learn me. For a wizard could not rightly be called a servant of His, but one of Lucifer's men. Not that Beguildy was wicked, but only empty of good, as if all the righteousness was burnt out by the flame of his fiery mind, which must know and intermeddle with mysteries. As for love, he did not know the word. He could read the stars, and tell the future, and he claimed to have laid spirits. Once I asked him where the future was, that

15

he could see it so plain. And he said, 'It lies with the past, child, at the back of Time.' You couldn't ever get the better of Mister Beguildy. But when I told Kester what he said, Kester would not have it so. He said the past and the future were two shuttles in the hands of the Lord, weaving Eternity. Kester was a weaver himself, which may have made him think of it thus. But I think we cannot know what the past and the future are. We are so small and help-less on the earth that is like a green rush cradle where mankind lies, looking up at the stars, but not knowing what they be.

As soon as I could write, I made a little book with a calico cover, and every Sunday I wrote in it any merry time or good fortune we had had in the week, and so kept them. And if times had been troublous and bitter for me, I wrote that down too, and was eased. So when our parson, knowing of the lies that were told of me, bade me write all I could remember in a book, and set down the whole truth and nothing else, I was able to freshen my memory with the things I had put down Sunday by Sunday.

Well, it is all gone over now, the trouble and the struggling. It be quiet weather now, like a still evening with the snow all down, and a green sky, and lambs calling. I sit here by the fire with my Bible to hand, a very old woman and a tired woman, with a task to do before she says good night to this world. When I look out of my window and see the plain and the big sky with clouds standing up on the mountains, I call to mind the thick, blotting woods of Sarn, and the crying of the mere when the ice was on it, and the way the water would come into the cupboard under the stairs when it rose at the time of the snow melting. There was but little sky to see there, saving that which was reflected in the mere; but the sky that is in the mere is not the proper heavens. You see it in a glass darkly, and the long shadows of rushes go thin and sharp across the sliding stars, and even the sun and moon

16

might be put out down there, for, times, the moon would get lost in lily leaves, and, times, a heron might stand before the sun.

Chapter 2: *Telling the Bees*

MY brother Gideon was born in the year when the war with the French began. That was why Father would have him called Gideon, it being a warlike name. Jancis used to say it was a very good name for him, because it was one you couldn't shorten. You can make most names into little love-names, like you can cut down a cloak or a gown for children's wearing. But Gideon you could do naught with. And the name was like the man. I was more set on my brother than most are, but I couldna help seeing that about him. If nobody calls you out of your name, your name's like to be soon out of mind. And most people never even called him by his Christen name at all. They called him Sarn. In Father's life it was old Sarn and young Sarn. But after Father died, Gideon seemed to take the place to himself. I remember how he went out that summer night, and seemed to eat and drink the place, devouring it with his eyes. Yet it was not for love of it, but for what he could get out of it. He was very like Father then, and more like every year, both to look at and in his mind. Saving that he was less tempersome and more set in his ways, he was Father's very marrow. Father's temper got up despert quick, and when it was up he was a ravening lion. Maybe that was what gave Mother that married-all-o'er look. But Gideon I only saw angered, to call angered, three times. Mostly, a look was enough. He'd give you a look like murder, and you'd let him take the way he wanted. I've seen a dog cringing and whimpering because he'd

17

given it one of those looks. Sarns mostly have grey eyes – cold grey like the mere in winter – and the Sarn men are mainly dark and sullen. 'Sullen as a Sarn,' they say about these parts. And they say there's been something queer in the family ever since Timothy Sarn was struck by forkit lightning in the times of the religious wars. There were Sarns about here then, and always have been, ever since there was anybody. Well, Timothy went against his folk and the counsels of a man of God, and took up with the wrong side, whichever that was, but it's no matter now. So he was struck by lightning and lay for dead. Being after awhile recovered, he was counselled by the man of God to espouse the safe side and avoid the lightning. But Sarns were ever obstinate men. He kept his side, and as he was coming home under the oak wood he was struck again. And seemingly the lightning got into his blood. He could tell when tempest brewed, long afore it came and it is said that when a storm broke, the wildfire played about him so none could come near him. Sarns have the lightning in their blood since his day. I wonder sometimes whether it be a true tale, or whether it's too old to be true. It used to seem to me sometimes as if Sarn was too old to be true. The woods and the farm and the church at the other end of the mere were all so old, as if they were in somebody's dream. There was frittening about the place, too, and what with folk being afraid to come there after dusk, and the quiet noise of the fish jumping far out in the water, and Gideon's boat knocking on the steps with little knocks like somebody tapping at the door, and the causeway that ran down into the mere as far as you could see, from just outside our garden gate, being lost in the water, it was a very lonesome old place. Many a time, on Sunday evenings, there came over the water a thin sound of bells. We thought they were the bells of the village down under, but I believe now they were nought but echo bells from our own church. They say that in some places a sound will knock against a wall of trees and come back like a ball.

18

It was on one of those Sunday evenings, when the thin chimes were sounding along with our own four bells, that we played truant from church for the second time. It being such a beautiful evening, and Father and Mother being busy with the bees swarming, we made it up between us to take dog's leave, and to wait by the lych-gate for Jancis and get her to come with us. For old Beguildy never werrited much about her church-going, not being the best of friends with the parson himself. He sent her off when the dial made it five o'clock every fourth Sunday – for we had service only once a month, the parson having a church at Brampton, where he lived, and another as well, which made it the more wicked of us to play truant – but whether she got there early or late, or got there at all, he'd never ask, let alone catechize her about the sermon. Our Father would catechize us last thing in the evening when our night-rails were on. Father would sit down in the settle with the birch-rod to his hand, and the settle, that had looked such a great piece of furniture all the week, suddenly looked little, like a settle made for a mommet. Whatever Father sat in, he made it look little. We stood barefoot in front of him on the cold quarries, in our unbleached homespun gowns that mother had spun and the journeyman weaver had woven up in the attic at the loom among the apples. Then he'd question us, and when we answered wrong he made a mark on the settle, and every mark was a stroke with the birch at the end of the catechizing. Though Father couldn't read, he never forgot anything. It seemed as if he turned things over in his head all the while he was working. I think he was a very clever man with not enow of things to employ his mind. If he'd had one of the new-fangled weaving machines I hear tell of to look after, it would have kept him content, but there was no talk of such things then. *We* were all the machines he had, and we wished very heartily every fourth Sunday, and Christmas and Easter, that we were the children of Beguildy, though he was thought so ill of by our parson, and often preached against, even by name.

19

I mind once, when Father leathered us very bad, after the long preaching on Easter Sunday, Gideon being seven and me five, how Gideon stood up in the middle of the kitchen and said, 'I do will and wish to be Maister Beguildy's son, and the devil shall have my soul. Amen.'

Father got his temper up that night, no danger! He shouted at Mother terrible, saying she'd done very poorly with her children, for the girl had the devil's mark on her, and now it seemed as if the boy came from the same smithy. This I know, because Mother told it to me. All I mind is that she went to look very small, and being only little to begin with, she seemed like one of the fairy folk. And she said – 'Could I help it if the hare crossed my path? Could I help it?' It seemed so strange to hear her saying that over and over. I can see the room now if I shut my eyes, and most especially if there's a bunch of cowslips by me. For Easter fell late, or in a spell of warm weather that year, and the cowslips were very forrard in sheltered places, so we'd pulled some. The room was all dim like a cave, and the red fire burning still and watchful seemed like the eye of the Lord. There was a little red eye in every bit of ware on the dresser too, where it caught the gleam. Often and often in after years I looked at those red lights, which were echoes of the fire, just as the ghostly bells were reflections of the chime, and I've thought they were like a deal of the outer show of this world. Rows and rows of red, gledy fires, but all shadows of fires. Many a chime of merry bells ringing, and yet only the shadows of bells; only a sigh of sound coming back from a wall of leaves or from the glassy water. Father's eyes caught the gleam too, and Gideon's: but Mother's didna, for she was standing with her back to the fire by the table where the cowslips were, gathering the mugs and plates together from supper. And if it seem strange that so young a child should remember the past so clearly, you must call to mind that Time engraves his pictures on our memory like a boy cutting letters with his knife, and the fewer the letters the deeper he cuts. So few

20

things ever happened to us at Sarn that we could never forget them. Mother's voice clings to my heart like trails of bedstraw that catch you in the lanes. She'd got a very plaintive voice, and soft. Everything she said seemed to mean a deal more than the words, and times it was like a person fumbling in the dark, or going a long way down black passages with a hand held out on this side, and a hand held out on that side, and no light. That was how she said, 'Could I help it if the hare crossed my path – could I help it?'

Everything she said, though it might not have anything merry in it, she smiled a bit, in the way you smile to take the edge off somebody's anger, or if you hurt yourself and won't show it. A very grievous smile it was, and always there. So when Father gave Gideon another hiding for wishing he was Beguildy's boy, Mother stood by the table saying, 'Oh, dunna, Sarn! Hold thy hand, Sarn!' and smiling all the while, seeming to catch at Father's hands with her soft voice. Poor Mother! Oh, my poor Mother! Shall we meet you in the other world, dear soul, and atone to you for our heedlessness?

I'd never forgotten that Easter, but Gideon had, seemingly, for when I remembered him of it, saying we surely durstn't take dog's leave, he said, 'It's nought. We'll make Sexton's Tivvy listen to the sermon for us, so as we can answer well. And I dunna care much if I *am* leathered, so long as I can find some good conkers and beat Jancis, for last time she beat me.'

Conkers, maybe you know, are snail shells, and children put the empty ones on strings, and play like you play with chestnut cobs. Our woods were a grand place for snails, and Gideon had conker matches with lads from as far away as five miles the other side of Plash. He was famous all about, because he played so fiercely, and not like a game at all.

All the bells were sounding when we started that Sunday

21

in June – the four metal bells in the church and the four
ghost bells from nowhere. Mother was helping Father
with the bees, getting a new skep ready, down where the big
chestnut tree was, to put the play of bees in. They'd
swarmed in a dead gooseberry bush, and Mother said,
with her peculiar smile, 'It be a sign of death.'

But Gideon shouted out—

'A play of bees in May is worth a noble that same day.
A play in June's pretty soon.'

And he said –

'So long as we've got the bees, Mother, we're the better
of it, die who may.'

Eh, dear! I'm afraid Gideon had a very *having* spirit,
even then. But Father thought he was a sensible lad, and he
laughed and said –

'Well, we've got such a mort of bees now, I'm in behopes
it wunna be me as has the telling of 'em if anybody does
die.'

'Where be your sprigs of rosemary and your Prayer
Books and your clean handkerchers?' says Mother.

Gideon had been in behopes to leave them behind, but
now he ran to fetch them, and Mother began setting my
kerchief to rights over my shoulders. She put in her big
brooch with the black stone, that she had when George
the Second died, and while she was putting it in she kept
saying to herself – 'Not as it matters what the poor child
wears. Deary, deary me! But could I help it if the hare
crossed my path? Could I help it?'

Whenever she said that, her voice went very mournful
and I thought again of somebody in a dark passage, groping.

'Now then, Mother! Hold the skep whilst I keep the
bough up,' said Father, 'they've knit so low down.'

I'd lief have stayed, for I dearly loved to see the great
tossy-ball of bees' bodies, as rich as a brown Christmas
cake, and to hear the heavy sound of them.

We went through the wicket and along the tow path,

because it was the nighest way to the church, and we wanted to catch Tivvy afore she went in. The coots were out on the mere, and the water was the colour of light, with spears in it.

'Now,' said Gideon, 'we'll run for our lives!'

'What's after us?'

'The people out of the water.'

So we ran for our lives, and got to the church just as the two last bells began their snabbing '*Ting* tong! *Ting* tong!' that always minded me of the birch-rod.

We sat on the flat grave where we mostly sat to play *Conquer*, and the church being on a little hill, we could watch the tuthree folks coming along the fields. There was Tivvy with her father, coming from the East Coppy, and Jancis in the flat water-meadows where the big thorn hedges were all in blow. Jancis was a little thing, not tall like me, but you always saw her before you saw other people, for it seemed that the light gathered round her. She'd got golden hair, and all the shadows on her face seemed to be stained with the pale colour of it. I was used to think she was like a white water-lily full of yellow pollen or honey. She'd got a very white skin, creamy white, without any colour unless she was excited or shy, and her face was dimpled and soft, and just the right plumpness. She'd got a red, smiling mouth, and when she smiled the dimples ran each into other. Times I could almost have strangled her for that smile.

She came up to us, very demure, in her flowered bodice and blue skirt and a bunch of blossom in her kerchief.

Although she was only two years older than I was, being of an age with Gideon, she seemed a deal older, for she'd begun to smile at the lads already, and folks said, 'Beguildy's Jancis will soon be courting.' But I know old Beguildy never meant her to get married. He meant to keep her as a bait to draw the young fellows in, for mostly the people that came to him were either young maids with no money or old men who wanted somebody cursed cheap. So at

23

this time, when he saw what a white, blossomy piece Jancis was growing, he encouraged her to dizen herself and sit in the window of the Cave House in case anybody went up by the lane. It was only once in a month of Sundays that anybody did, for Plash was nearly as lonesome as Sarn. He made a lanthorn of coloured glass, too, the colour of red roses, and while Jancis sat in the stone frame of the window he hung it up above her with a great candle in it from foreign parts, not a rushlight such as we used. He had it in mind that if some great gentleman came by to a fair or a cockfight beyond the mountains he might fall in love with her, and then Beguildy planned to bring him in and give him strong ale and talk about charms and spells, and offer at long last to work the charm of raising Venus. It was all written in one of his books: how you went into a dark room and gave the wise man five pound, and he said a charm, and after awhile there was a pink light and a scent of roses, and Venus rose naked in the middle of the room. Only it woüldna have been Venus, but Jancis. The great gentleman, howsoever, was a long while coming, and the only man that saw her in the window was Gideon one winter evening when he was coming back that way from market, because the other road was flooded. He was fair comic-struck about her, and talked of her till I was aweary, he being nineteen at the time, which is a foolish age in lads. Before that, he never took any account of her, but just to tell her this and that as he did with me. But afterwards he was nought but a gauby about her. I could never have believed that such a determined lad, so set in his ways and so clever, could have been thus soft about a girl. But on this evening he was only seventeen, and he just said, 'Take dog's leave oot, Jancis, and come with us after conkers.'

'O,' said Jancis, 'I wanted to play "*Green Gravel, Green Gravel.*" '

She'd got a way of saying 'O' afore everything, and it made her mouth look like a rose. But whether she did it for that, or whether she did it because she was slow-witted and timid, I never could tell.

'There's nought to win in *Green Gravel*,' said Gideon, 'we'll play *Conquer*.'

'O I wanted *Green Gravel*! You'll beat me if we play *Conquer*.'

'Ah. That's why we'll play.'

Tivvy came through the lych-gate then, and we told her what she'd got to do. She was a poor, foolish creature, and she could hardly mind her own name, times, for all its outlandishness, let alone a sermon. But Gideon said, so long as she got an inkling of it he could make up the rest. And he said if she didna remember enough of it he'd twist her arm proper. So she began to cry.

Then we saw Sexton coming across the ploughed field, very solemn, with his long staff, black and white in bands, and we could hear Parson's piebald pony clop-clopping up the lane, so we made off, and left Tivvy with her round chin trembling, and her mouth all crooked with crying, because she knew she'd never remember a word of the sermon. Tivvy at a sermon always used to make me think of our dog being washed. He'd lie down and let the water souse over him, and she did the same with a sermon. So I knew trouble was brewing.

It was a beautiful evening, with swallows high in the air, and a powerful smell of may-blossom. When the bells stopped, ours and the others, we went and looked down into the water, to see if we could get a sight of the village there, as we did most Sundays. But there was only our own church upside down, and two or three stones and crosses the same, and Parson's pony grazing on its head.

Times, on summer evenings, when the sun was low, the shadow of the spire came right across the water to our dwelling, and I was used to think it was like the finger of the Lord pointing at us. We went down into the marshy places and found plenty of conkers, and Gideon beat Jancis every time, which was a good thing, for at the end

25

he said he'd play *Green Gravel*, and they were both pleased. Only we were terrible late, and nearly missed Tivvy.

'Now, tell!' says Gideon. So she began to cry, and said she knew nought about it. Then he twisted her arm, and she screamed out, 'Burning and fuel of fire!'

She must have said that because it was one of the texts the Sexton was very fond of saying over, keeping time with tapping his staff the while.

'What else?'

'Nought.'

'I'll twist your arm till it comes off if you dunna think of any more.'

Tivvy looked artful, like Pussy in the dairy, and said – 'Parson told about Adam and Eve and Noah and Shemamanjaphet and Jesus in the manger and thirty pieces of silver.'

Gideon's face went dark.

'There's no sense in it,' he said.

'But she's told you, anyway. You must let her go now.'

So we went home, with the shadow of the spire stretching all across the water.

Father said –

'What was the text?'

'Burning and fuel of fire.'

'What was the sarmon about?'

Poor Gideon made out a tale of all the things Tivvy had said. You never heard such a tale! Father sat quite quiet, and Mother was smiling very painful, standing by the fire, cooking a rasher.

Suddenly Father shouted out –

'Liar! Liar! Parson called but now, to say was there sickness, there being nobody at church. You've not only taken dog's leave and lied, but you've made game of *me*.'

His face went from red to purple, and all veined, like raw meat. It was awful to see. Then he reached for the horsewhip and said –

'I'll give you the best hiding ever you had, my boy!'

26

He came across the kitchen towards Gideon.

But suddenly Gideon ran at him and bunted into him, and taking him by surprise he knocked him clean over.

Now whether it was that Father had eaten a very hearty supper, after a big day's work with the bees, or whether it was him being in such a rage, and then the surprise of the fall, we never knew. However it was, he was taken with a fit. He never stirred, but lay on his back on the red quarries, breathing so loud and strong that it filled the house, like somebody snoring in the night. Mother undid his Sunday neckcloth, and lifted him up, and put cold water on his face, but it was no manner of use.

The awful snoring went on, and seemed to eat up all other sounds. They went out like rushlights in the wind. There was no more ticking from the clock, nor purring from the cat, nor sizzling from the rasher, nor buzzing from the bee in the window. It seemed to eat up the light, too, and the smell of the white bush-roses outside, and the feeling in my body, and the thoughts I had afore. We'd all come to be just part of a dark snoring.

'Sarn, Sarn!' cried Mother. 'Oh, Sarn, poor soul, come to thyself!'

She tried to put some Hollands between his lips, but they were set. Then the snore changed to a rattle, very awful to hear, and in a little while it stopped, and there was a dreadful silence, as if all the earth had gone dumb. All the while, Gideon stood like stone, remembering the horsewhip Father meant to beat him with, so he said after. And though he'd never seen anyone die afore, when Father went quiet, and the place dumb, he said in an everyday voice, only with a bit of a tremble –

'He's dead, Mother. I'll go and tell the bees, or we met lose 'em.'

We cried a long while, Mother and me, and when we couldna cry any more, the little sounds came creeping back – the clock ticking, bits of wood falling out of the fire, and the cat breathing in its sleep.

27

When Gideon came in again, the three of us managed to get Father on to a mattress, and lap him in a clean sheet. He looked a fine, good-featured man, now that the purple colour was gone from his face.

Gideon locked up, and went round to look the beasts and see all well.

'Best go to bed now, Mother,' he said. 'All's safe, and the beasts in their housen. I told every skep of bees, and I can see they're content, and willing for me to be maister.'

Chapter 3: *Prue takes the Bidding Letters*

In those days there was little time for the mourners to think of their sorrow till after the funeral. There was a deal to do. There was the mourning to make, and before that, if a family hadn't had the weaver lately, there was the cloth to weave and dye. We hadn't had the weaver for a good while, so we were very short of stuff.

Mother told Gideon he must go and fetch the old weaver, who lived at Lullingford, by the mountains, and went out weaving by the day or the week. Gideon saddled Bendigo, Father's horse, and picked up the riding whip with a queer kind of smile. As soon as he was gone, Mother and I began to bake. For it wasn't only the weaver that must be fed, but the women we were going to bid to the funeral sewing-bee. They would come for love, as was the custom, but we must feed them.

It seemed lonesome that night without Gideon. He had to bait and sleep in Lullingford, but he came back in good time next day, and I heard the sound of the hoofs on the yard cobbles through my spinning. We were hard at it, getting yarn ready for the old man. He came riding after

Gideon on a great white horse, very bony, which put me in mind of the rider on the white horse in the Bible. He was the oldest man you could see in a month of Sundays. He hopped about like a magpie, prying here and there over the loom, looking at his shuttle for all the world like a pie that's pleased with some bright thing it's found. I had to take his meals up to the attic, for he wouldna waste time leaving off for them. It was a good thing the apples were all done, so he could hop about the loft without let or hindrance. 'Now you must take the bidding letters for the sewing, Prue,' Mother told me.

Can I take one to Jancis, Mother?'

'No. We munna spend money paying for a bidding letter to Jancis. But she can come, and welcome.'

'I'll go and tell her. She sews very nice.'

'But not so well as you, my dear. Whatsoever's wrong, thee sews a beautiful straight seam, Prue.'

I ran off, mighty pleased with praise, which came seldom my way. I met Gideon by the lake.

'Taking the biddings?' he said.

'Ah.'

'Jancis coming?'

'Ah.'

'Well, when you be there, ask Beguildy to lend us the white oxen for the funeral, oot?'

'To lug Father to the church?'

'Ah. And when we've buried Father, you and me must talk a bit. There's a deal to think of for the future. All these bidding letters, now, you met as well have written 'em and saved a crown.'

I wondered what he meant, seeing he knew I couldna write a word, but I knew he'd say in his own time, and not afore, that being his way. Nobody would have thought he was but seventeen, he seemed five-and-twenty by the way he spoke, so choppy and quick, but ever so quiet.

When I got to Plash, Jancis was sitting in the garden,

29

spinning. She said we could borrow the beasts, that were hers by right, being a present from her Granny, though she never had the strength to control them in a waggon nor to drive plough with 'em like I had in the years after. But she got a bit of pin money by hiring them out for wakes, when Beguildy didna pocket it. They dressed up beautiful with flowers and ribbons after they'd been scrubbed.

I went in to speak to Beguildy.

'Father's dead, Mister Beguildy' I said.

'So so! What's that to me, dear soul?'

He was a very strange man, always, was Beguildy.

'Tell me what I knew not, child,' he said.

'Did you know, then?'

'Ah, I knew thy feyther was gone. Didna he go by me on a blast of air last Sunday evening, crying out, thin and spiteful, "You owe me a crown, Beguildy!" Tell me summat fresh, girl – new, strange things. Now if you could say that the leaves be all fallen this day of June, and my damsons ripe for market; or that the mere hath dried; or that man lusteth no more to hurt his love; or that Jancis looketh no more at her own face in Plash Pool, there would be telling, yes! But for your dad, it is nought. I cared not for the man.'

And taking up his little hammer, he beat on a row of flints that he had, till the room was all in a charm. Every flint had its own voice, and he knew them as a shepherd the sheep, and it was his custom when the talk was not to his mind to beat out a chime upon them.

'I came to see if we could borrow the beasts for our waggon. Jancis said yes.'

'You mun pay.'

'How much, mister?'

'The same as for wakes, a penny a head. So you be taking the biddings? Now who did your mam pay to write 'em?'

'Parson wrote 'em for us, and Mother put a crown in the poor-box.'

30

'Dear soul! The bitter waste! I'd have wrote 'em very clear and fine for half the money. I can write the tall script and the dwarf, round or square, red or black. Parson can only do the sarmon script, and a very poor script it be.'

'I wish I could write, Mister Beguildy.'

'Oh, you!'

He laughed in a very peculiar way he had, soft and light, at the top of his head.

'It's not for children,' he said.

But I thought about it a deal. I thought it would be a fine thing to sit by the fire, in the settle corner, and write bidding letters and love-letters and market bills, or even a verse for a tombstone, and to do the round or the square, tall or little, red or black, and sermon script too if I'd a mind. I thought when anybody like Jancis angered me by being so pretty, I'd do her letters very crabbed, and with no red at all. But I knew that was wicked of me, for poor Jancis couldna help being pretty.

Then Beguildy went off to cure an old man's corns, and Jancis and I played lovers, but Jancis said I did it very bad, and she thought Gideon would do it a deal better.

Chapter 4: *Torches and Rosemary*

IT was a still, dewy summer night when we buried Father. In our time there was still a custom round about Sarn to bury people at night. In our family it had been done for hundreds of years. I was busy all day decking the waggon with yew and the white flowering laurel, that has such a heavy, sweet smell. I pulled all the white roses and a tuthree pinks that were in blow, and made up with daisies out of the hay grass. While I pulled them, I thought how angered Father would have been to see me there, trampling it, and I could scarcely help looking round now and again to see if he was coming.

After we'd milked, Gideon went for the beasts, and I put black streamers round their necks, and tied yew boughs to their horns. It had to be done carefully, for they were the Longhorn breed, and if *you* angered them, they'd hike you to death in a minute.

The miller was one bearer, and Mister Callard, of Callard's Dingle, who farmed all the land between Sarn and Plash, was another. Then there were our two uncles from beyond the mountains.

Gideon, being chief mourner, had a tall hat with black streamers and black gloves and a twisted black stick with streamers on it. They took a long while getting the coffin out, for the doors were very narrow and it was a big, heavy coffin. It had always been the same at all the Sarn funerals, yet nobody ever seemed to think of making the doors bigger.

Sexton went first with his hat off and a great torch in his hand. Then came the cart, with Miller's lad and another to lead the beasts. The waggon was mounded up with leaves and branches, and they all said it was a credit to me. But I could only mind how poor Father was used to tell me to take away all those nasty weeds out of the house. And now we were taking him away, jolting over the stones, from the place where he was maister. I was all of a puzzle with it. It did seem so unkind, and disrespectful as well, leaving the poor soul all by his lonesome at the other end of the mere. I was glad it was sweet June weather, and not dark.

We were bound to go the long way round, the other being only a foot road. When we were come out of the fold-yard, past the mixen, and were in the road, we took our places – Gideon behind the coffin by himself, then Mother and me in our black poke bonnets and shawls, with Prayer Books and branches of rosemary in our hands.

32

Uncles and Miller and Mister Callard came next, all with torches and boughs of rosemary.

It was a good road, and smoother than most – the road to Lullingford. Parson used to say it was made by folk who lived in the days when the Redeemer lived. Romans, the name was. They could make roads right well, whatever their name was. It went along above the water, close by the lake; and as we walked solemnly onwards, I looked into the water and saw us there. It was a dim picture, for the only light there was came from the waning, clouded moon, and from the torches. But you could see, in the dark water, something stirring, and gleams and flashes, and when the moon came clear we had our shapes, like the shadows of fish gliding in the deep. There was a great heap of black, that was the waggon, and the oxen were like clouds moving far down, and the torches were flung into the water as if we wanted to dout them.

All the time, as we went, we could hear the bells ringing the corpse home. They sounded very strange over the water in the waste of night, and the echoes sounded yet stranger. Once a white owl came by, like a blown feather for lightness and softness. Mother said it was Father's spirit looking for its body. There was no sound but the bells and the creaking of the wheels, till Parson's pony, grazing in the glebe, saw the dim shapes of the oxen a long way off, and whinnied, not knowing, I suppose, but what they were ponies too, and being glad to think, in the lonesomeness of the night, of others like herself near by.

At last the creaking stopped at the lych-gate. They took out the coffin, resting it on trestles, and in the midst of the heavy breathing of the bearers came the promising words –

'*I am the resurrection and the life.*'

They were like quiet rain after drought. Only I began to wonder, how should we come again in the resurrection? Should we come clear, or dim, like in the water? Would Father come in a fit of anger, as he'd died, or as a little boy running to Grandma with a bunch of primmyroses? Would Mother smile the same smile, or would she have found a light in the dark passage? Should I still be fast in a body I'd no mind for, or would they give us leave to weave ourselves bodies to our own liking out of the spinnings of our souls?

The coffin was moved to another trestle, by the grave-side, and a white cloth put over it. Our best tablecloth, it was. On the cloth stood the big pewter tankard full of elderberry wine. It was the only thing Mother could provide, and it was by good fortune that she had plenty of it, enough for the funeral feast and all, since there had been such a power of elderberries the year afore. It looked strange in the doubtful moonlight, standing there on the coffin, when we were used to see it on the table, with the colour of the Christmas Brand reflected in it.

Parson came forrard and took it up, saying –

'I drink to the peace of him that's gone.'

Then everybody came in turn, and drank good health to Father's spirit.

At the coffin foot was our little pewter measure full of wine, and a crust of bread with it, but nobody touched them.

Then Sexton stepped forrard and said –

'Be there a Sin Eater?'

And Mother cried out –

'Alas, no! Woe's me! There is no Sin Eater for poor Sarn. Gideon gainsayed it.'

Now it was still the custom at that time, in our part of the country, to give a fee to some poor man after a death, and then he would take bread and wine handed to him across the coffin, and eat and drink, saying –

I give easement and rest now to thee, dear man, that ye walk not over the fields nor down the by-ways. And for thy peace I pawn my own soul.

And with a calm and grievous look he would go to his own place. Mostly, my Grandad used to say, Sin Eaters

34

were such as had been Wise Men or layers of spirits, and had fallen on evil days. Or they were poor folk that had come, through some dark deed, out of the kindly life of men, and with whom none would trade, whose only food might oftentimes be the bread and wine that had crossed the coffin. In our time there were none left around Sarn. They had nearly died out, and they had to be sent for to the mountains. It was a long way to send, and they asked a big price, instead of doing it for nothing as in the old days. So Gideon said –

'We'll save the money. What good would the man do?'

But Mother cried and moaned all night after. And when the Sexton said 'Be there a Sin Eater?' she cried again very pitifully, because Father had died in his wrath, with all his sins upon him, and besides, he had died in his boots, which is a very unket thing and bodes no good. So she thought he had great need of a Sin Eater, and she would not be comforted.

Then a strange, heart-shaking thing came to pass.

Gideon stepped up to the coffin and said –

'There *is* a Sin Eater.'

'Who then? I see none,' said Sexton.

'I ool be the Sin Eater.'

He took up the little pewter measure full of darkness, and he looked at Mother.

'Oot turn over the farm and all to me if I be the Sin Eater, Mother?' he said.

'No, no! Sin Eaters be accurst!'

'What harm, to drink a sup of your own wine and chumble a crust of your own bread? But if you dunna care, let be. He can go with the sin on him.'

'No, no! Leave un go free, Gideon! Let un rest, poor soul! You be in life and young, but he'm cold and helpless, in the power of Satan. He went with all his sins upon him, in his boots, poor soul! If there's none else to help, let his own lad take pity.'

35

'And you'll give me the farm, Mother?'

'Yes, yes, my dear! What be the farm to me? You can take all, and welcome.'

Then Gideon drank the wine all of a gulp, and swallowed the crust. There was no sound in all the place but the sound of his teeth biting it up.

Then he put his hand on the coffin, standing up tall in the high black hat, with a gleaming pale face, and he said –

'I give easement and rest now to thee, dear man. Come not down the lanes nor in our meadows. And for thy peace I pawn my own soul. Amen.'

There was a sigh from everybody then, like the wind in dry bents. Even the oxen by the gate, it seemed to me, sighed as they chewed the cud.

But when Gideon said, 'Come not down the lanes nor in our meadows,' I thought he said it like somebody warning off a trespasser.

Now it was time to throw the rosemary into the grave. Then they lowered the coffin in, and all threw their burning torches down upon it, and douted them.

It was over at long last, and we went home by the shortest way, only Gideon going by the road with the waggon. We were a tidy few, for all that had been at the church came back for the funeral feast. There was the smith, and the ox-driver from Plash Farm, and the shepherd from the Mountain, and the miller's man and a good few women, as well as those I spoke of afore.

Mother had asked Tivvy to mind the fire and see to the kettles for making spiced ale and posset, for the air struck chill along the water at that time of night.

When we raught home there was Missis Beguildy as well, and Jancis. They had a nice gledy fire, and the horn of ale set upon it all ready. She was a kind soul, Missis Beguildy, but sorely misliked through being the wife of a wizard, a preached-against man. She was never invited to weddings nor baptisms. But at a burying, when the harm's on the

36

house already, what ill can anybody do? Missis Beguildy dearly loved an outing. She'd have liked to live in Lullingford and keep a shop, and go to church twice of a Sunday, and sing in the choir. She'd no faith at all in her goodman's spells, though she never said so, except to me and a tuthree she knew well. Once, a long while after this, when there'd been trouble at the Stone House, which you'll hear of in good time, when she'd quarrelled with Beguildy, I went in by chance and found her with Lady Camperdine's bottle (in which he said he'd got the old lady's ghost), shaking it as if it was an ill-mixed sauce, so that I thought the cork would come out, and shouting, 'I'll learn ye! I'll learn ye? Lady Camperdine indeed! Plash water! That's what's in this here bottle. Plash water and naught else.'

It was seldom anybody saw Missis Beguildy. She was always out with the fowl or the ducks, or digging the garden, or fishing. She was a good fisherwoman. If it hadna been for her, they'd have clemmed, for Beguildy never reckoned to do anything but wizardry. She'd baked us a batch of funeral cakes in case we hadna enough, and she was so kind and comely, being fair, like Jancis, and plump, and the posset she made was so good, that everybody forgot she was the wizard's wife, even Parson.

'I'm to take back the cattle, my dear,' she said to Mother; 'hay harvest, we use 'em a deal.'

'Bin you started?'

'Ah. Bin you?'

'I start to-morrow,' said Gideon.

Everybody looked at him, tall in the doorway, with a kind of power in him. And it seemed to me that everybody drew away a bit, as if from summat untoert.

Parson got up to go.

' It's to-morrow now, young Sarn,' he said. See you do well in it, and in all the to-morrows.'

'To-morrow! O to-morrow!' said Jancis. 'It be a word of promise.'

She yawned, and all in a minute her mouth was a rose, and I knew I couldna abide her.

'One song!' Sexton spoke very solemn. 'One holy song afore we part.'

So we stood up about the table, where the twelve candles were guttering low, and we sang –

> *With a turf all at your head, dear man,*
> *And another at your feet,*
> *Your good deeds and your bad ones all*
> *Before the Lord shall meet.*

There being a sight more men than women, the song sounded deep, like bees in a lime-tree. Jancis and Tivvy sang very clear and high, and cold too, as if they didna mind at all that the poor corpse lay out yonder with only turfs for company.

Then there was a trampling and a traversing, and they all went out, Mother standing by the door the while, doling out the funeral cakes. These were made of good sponge, with plenty of eggs, coffin-shaped and lapped up in black-edged paper.

By this the birds were singing very loud and clear, with a ringing, echoing noise. Our chimneys lay in the mere, which meant that it was sunrise. There was a cuckoo in the oak wood, and the first corncrake spoke up from the hay grass, very masterful.

Gideon said –

'It be too late for sleep now. To-morrow be come. Let's go down into the orchard. I want to tell you what I've planned out.'

Little did I think, as I followed him down into the orchard, where was neither blossom nor fruit, what those plans were to mean for us all.

Chapter 5: *The First Swath Falls*

WE climbed up into the old pippin trees where we had a favourite place between the boughs. Looking at Gideon's face among the bright leaves, I thought it was very queer to think of all those sins being on him. Ever since Father was a little baby, roaring and beating on his cot of rushes, on through the time when he was a lad, taking dog's leave from church; and after, when he went cockfighting and courting, all the evil he did, Gideon had got to carry. All his rages were Gideon's rages.

'Now, Prue,' says Gideon, 'listen what I be going to tell ye. You and me has got to get on.'

'And Mother?'

'Oh, well, Mother too. But she's old.'

'She'd like to get on though, sure.'

'That be neither here nor there. If we get on, she will. You and me ha' got to work, Prue.'

'I amna afeered of work,' I said.

'Well, there'll be a plenty. I want to make money on the place – a mort of money. Then, when the time's ripe, we'll sell it. Then we'll go to Lullingford and buy a house, and you shall hold up your head with the best, and be a rich lady.'

'I dunna mind all that about being rich and holding up my head.'

'Well you *must* mind. And I'll be churchwarden and tell the Rector what to do, and say who's to go in the stocks, and who's to go in the almshousen, and vote for the parliament men. And when any wench has a baby that's a love-child, you'll go and scold her.'

'I'd liefer play with the baby.'

'Anybody can play with a baby. None but a great lady can scold. And we'll buy a grand house. I hanna put my eye on one yet, but there be time enow. And a garden with a man to see to it, and serving-wenches, and the place full of grand furniture and silver plate and china.'

'I dearly like pretty china,' I said. 'Can we get some of them new cups and saucers from Staffordshire, with little people on 'em?'

'You can get anything you like, and a gold thimble and a press full of gowns into the bargain. Only you mun help me first. It'll take years and years.'

'But couldna we stop at Sarn, and get just a little bit of new furniture and china, and do without so many maids and men?'

'No. There's not enow of folks at Sarn, saving at the Wake, and that's only once a year. What's once a year? And what use being chief if there's nobody to be chief of? "Chief among ten thousand." That's a good sounding text. I'd lief be chief among ten thousand.'

'I wonder if it be the lightning in you,' I said, 'makes you feel like that?'

I always used to think he looked as if he'd got it in him when there was anything out of the common going on. His eyes would be all of a blaze, but cold too. And he'd make you feel as if you wanted what he wanted, though you didna. Times, when he wanted to look for badger-earths in the woods, he made me think I did too. And all the while, what I wanted in my own self was to go and gather primmyroses.

'Well, it'll take a deal of lightning in the blood to do what I'm set to do,' he said. 'The place never did more than keep us, Mother says. And Father left naught – not but just enough to pay the weaver and Sexton and buy the wax candles and gloves and that for the burying.'

'Whatever shall we do, if we'd only just enough afore,' I wondered, 'and Father to work for us? We can never put by money, lad.'

'I shall do what he did and a deal more beside.'

'You never can.'

'I can do all as I've a mind to do. I've got such a power in me that naught but death can bind it. And with you to give a hand—'

He stopped a bit there, and pulled a leaf, and tore it. 'Being as how things are, you'll never marry, Prue.'

My heart beat soft and sad. It seemed such a terrible thing never to marry. All girls got married. Jancis would. Tivvy would. Even Miller's Polly, that always had a rash or a hoost or the ringworm or summat, would get married. And when girls got married, they had a cottage, and a lamp, maybe, to light when their man came home, or if it was only candles it was all one, for they could put them in the window, and he'd think 'There's my missus now, lit the candles!' And then one day Mrs. Beguildy would be making a cot of rushes for 'em, and one day there'd be a babe in it, grand and solemn, and bidding letters sent round for the christening, and the neighbours coming round the babe's mother like bees round the queen. Often when things went wrong, I'd say to myself, 'Ne'er mind, Prue Sarn! There'll come a day when you'll be queen in your own skep.' So I said —

'Not wed, Gideon? Oh, ah! I'll wed for sure.'

'I'm afeerd nobody'll ask you, Prue.'

'Not ask me? What for not?'

'Because — oh, well, you'll soon find out. But you can have a house and furniture and all just the same, if you give a hand in the earning of 'em.'

'But not an 'usband, nor a babe in a cot of rushes?'

'No.'

'For why?'

'Best ask Mother for why. Maybe she can tell you why the hare crossed her path. But I'm main sorry for ye, Prue, and I be going to make you a rich lady, and maybe when we've gotten a deal of gold, we'll send away for some doctor's stuff for a cure. But it'll cost a deal, and you must work well and do all I tell you. You're a tidy, upstanding girl enough, Prue, and but for that one thing the fellows ud come round like they will round Jancis.'

I thought about it a bit, while the water lapped on the

banks at the foot of the orchard. Then I said I'd do all Gideon wanted.

'You mun swear it, Prue, a solemn oath on the Book. Maybe, if you didna, you'd tire and give over soon. And I'll swear what I promised, too.'

He went into the house to fetch the Book. I sat still and listened to the rooks going over to the rookery at the back of the house, beyond the garden and the rickyard. They were coming back from their breakfast in the fields away towards Plash. I wanted my breakfast, too; for whoever's dead, we poor mortals clem. And as I listened to the sleepy sound of the cawing, and the flapping of their wings when they came over low down, I thought it seemed a criss-cross sort of world, where you bury your Father at night, and straightway begin to think of breakfast and housen and gold with the first light of dawn; where you've got to go cursed all your life long because a poor silly hare looked at your mother afore you were born; where a son, eating his Mother's batch-cake and drinking of her brewing, loads his poor soul with all his Father's sins.

Gideon came running back with the great Book in his hands, very heavy, and fastened with a silver clasp.

'Come down, Prue, and swear,' he said. 'Now hold the Book.'

I asked him if he was sure Mother would give us leave to do it.

'Give us leave? It's not for her to give us leave. She canna hinder me. The farm be mine. Didna you hear her say so when I took the sin upon me?'

'But will you make Mother abide by that?'

'Will folk pawn their souls for naught? Is another's sin sweet in the mouth that I should eat it safe at a price? The farm be mine for ever and ever, until I choose to sell it. Now swear! Say –

'I promise and vow to obey my brother, Gideon Sarn, and to hire myself out to him as a sarvant, for no money, until all that he wills be done. And I'll be as biddable as a prentice, a wife, and a dog. I swear it on the Holy Book. Amen.'

So I said it. Then Gideon said –

'I swear to keep faith with my sister, Prue Sarn, and share all with her when we've won through, and give her money up to fifty pound, when we've sold Sarn, to cure her. Amen.'

After we'd done, I felt as if Sarn Mere was flowing right over us, and I shivered as if I'd got an ague.

'What ails you?' says Gideon. 'Best go and light the fire if you be cold, and get the breakfast. We can talk while we eat. Mother's asleep. There's a deal to say yet.'

So I went in and lit the fire, and set the table as nice as I could, for it seemed a bit of comfort in a dark place. I wondered if it would be unfeeling to pull a few rosebuds to put in the middle. And seeing that it wasna unfeeling to eat and drink, I thought it wouldna hurt to pull a rose or two.

When Gideon came in from the milking, we sat down, and he told me all that was in his mind. First, I was to learn to make cheeses as well as butter. Then he was going to make some withy panniers for Bendigo, and every market day he'd ride to Lullingford with butter and eggs, cheeses and honeycomb, fruit and vegetables and even flowers.

'Them roses, now,' he said, 'you could bunch 'em up, and they'd bring in a bit.'

Times there'd be dressed poultry and ducks, rabbits, fish, and mushrooms.

'You'll see, Prue, we'll make a deal,' he said.

'But what a journey! Thirty mile in the day.'

'I'll plough a bit of land to grow corn for Bendigo. As for me, I'm never tired.'

When we'd saved a bit, we were to buy another cow. She'd calve in the spring, and then there'd be two cows milking when one was dry. That ud mean more market butter. After that, we were to buy two oxen to plough and turn the flail and lug manure, and save hiring Beguildy's beasts. When our sow farrowed, we were to keep all the piglets and turn them loose in the oakwoods, and Mother was to take her knitting and mind them. Then there'd be

43

a deal of bacon for market, over and above what we could eat. We'd only got five sheep, but Gideon said we'd mend that by keeping all the lambs, and so have wool to sell and a big flock of sheep next year. Mother and me were to spin yarn all winter, and he'd sell it at the draper's or change it for things we were bound to have at the grocer's, such as salt for curing, yeast and sugar. Soap we made ourselves out of lye. Rushlights we made too, out of fat and large dry rushes. Rye we had, and one small field of wheat. Father used to take a few sacks at a time to be ground at the mill where Tivvy's uncle lived.

'I shall grow more corn, acres of corn,' he said, 'and take it to the mill in the ox-wain. Whatsoever the French do, corn wunna come amiss. And though it's cheap now, it wunna be if they tax it, which I hear tell is more than likely. It'll be better, a power, to have one acre under wheat then than to be coddling about with twenty acres under aught else. We'll grow hops as well, and never be short of a drop of good ale, for though I mean to work you, Prue, I wunna clem you. Good plain food, as much as you can eat, but no fallals. The rough honey after we've put by the best for market, fruit when it's cheap, bacon and taters and bread, and eggs and butter when the roads are too bad for market.'

'I shall put up a prayer for bad roads,' I said.

Gideon looked at me very sharp, but seeing it was only my fun, he laughed.

'A' right, but it'll take the Devil's own weather to stop me.'

He'd got a plan that I should learn to do sums and keep accounts and write. I was glad, for I dearly loved the thought of being able to read books, and especially the Bible. It always werrited me in church when Sexton read out of the Bible, for no matter what he read, it all sounded like a bee in a bottle. It didna matter when he was reading – 'And he took unto him a wife and begat Aminadab . . .' for it was naught to me if he did. But when there were things to be read with a sound in 'em like wind in the aspen tree, it seemed a pitiful thing that he should mouth it over so, being very big-sorted at being able to read at all. I wanted to be able to read

'Or ever the silver cord be loosed'

for myself, and savour it. It would be grand to be able to write, too, and put down all such things as I wanted to keep in mind. So when Gideon said I was to learn, I was joyfully willing.

'But if Mister Beguildy learns me, how can I pay?' I said.

'You can dig taters for 'em, and give a hand in the hay, and drive plough for 'em now and again. Beguildy's so mortal lazy, and so big-sorted with being a wise man, there's not a hand's turn of work in the man. Mooning, mooning! A salve for every sore, he's got, saving for idleness. You be strong. You can pretty near dig spade for spade with me. Pay that way. And if you've a mind, you can put on your black and go and ask him this evening.'

He went off to the hay meadow with his scythe, and I set about my work with a will, and should have sung a bit, but called poor Father to mind. It made me gladsome to be getting some education, it being like a big window opening. And out of that window who knows what you metna see?

When I took Gideon's nooning, going through the rookery, I called to mind that we'd never told the rooks about a death in the place. It's an old ancient custom to tell them. Folk say if you dunna, a discontent comes over them, and they fall into a melancholy and forget to come home. So in a little while there are your ellums with the nests still like dark fruit on the sky, but all silent and deserted. And though rooks do a deal of mischief, it's very unlucky to lose them, and the house they leave never has any prosperation after. So I remembered Gideon of this, and we went to the rookery.

They were the biggest ellum trees I've ever seen, both common and wych ellums. Under them it was all dimmery with summer leaves. The ground was green with celandine, that had just left blowing, and enchanter's nightshade, not quite in blow. The leaves were white with droppings. It was a very still, hot day, with only a little breeze rocking the very tops of the trees, and a sleepy caw coming down to us time and again. I used to like to come to the rookery on days like this, after tea, when I'd cleaned myself. And on Ascension Day in special I liked to come and watch if they worked. For they say no rook'll work on Ascension Day. And sure enough I never saw them bring even a stick on that day, but they seemed very thoughtful and holy in their minds, sitting each in his tree like Parson in pulpit.

'Ho, rooks!' shouted Gideon, 'Father's dead, and I be maister, and I've come to say as you shall keep your housen in peace, and I'll keep ye save from all but my own gun, and you're kindly welcome to bide.'

The rooks peered down at him over their nests, and when he'd done there was a sudden clatter of wings, and they all swept up into the blue sky with a great clary, as if they were considering what was said. In a while they came back, and settled down very serious and quiet. So we knew they meant to bide.

When we were back in the field, Gideon laughed a bit, while he was whetting his scythe on the hone, and he said – 'I'm glad they mean stopping. I be despert fond of rooky-pie.'

With that, he swept the scythe through the grass, thinnish and full of ox-eye daisies, and sighing with a dry sound. And because the grass was so thin, you could watch the scythe, like a flash of steely light, through the standing crop before the swath fell. And it seems to me now that it was like the deathly will of God, which is ever waiting behind us till the hour comes to mow us down; yet not in unkindness, but because it is best for us that we leave growing in the meadow, and be brought into His safe rickyard, and thatched over warm with His everlasting loving-kindness.

46

Chapter 6:

'Saddle Your Dreams before you Ride 'Em'

So soon as I'd milked, Gideon being still hard at it in the meadow, I went upstairs and put on my black, and my mob-cap. I never wore it to work in, to save washing, and folk thought I was a heathen, pretty near, what with no mob-cap and no shoes or stockings most of the time, but bare feet or clogs. Gideon could whittle a clog right well, and they be grand for doing mucky work like I did. I'd made me a sacking gown, too, short to the knee, for cleaning the beast-housen in. I know everybody called me the barn-door savage of Sarn. But when I remembered the beautiful house at Lullingford that was to be, and the flowered gowns and dimity curtains and china, I didna take it to heart much.

I was very choice of my homespun gown with the cross-over, and the new mob-cap trimmed with little sausages made of sarsnet, very new-fangled. So I did my hair in ringlets – one on each side and two at the back, down to my waist.

I was comfortable in my mind, thinking how we were going to send away for simples to make me as beautiful as a fairy. While I milked I thought about it, and while I cleaned the sties, and while I scrubbed the kitchen quarries.

Mother winnocked a bit, to hear I was off to Plash, for she was low and melancholy from abiding under the shadow of death. She'd been so used to humouring a tempersome man that she felt as restless as you do when you've just cast off the second stocking-toe of a pair. She'd sit quiet a bit in the chimney corner, and you'd hear the wheel whirring softly, like a little lych-fowl. Then suddenly she'd give over spinning, and wring her hands, that always made me think of a mole's little hands, lifted up to God when it be trapped. And she'd say, 'Sunday was a week, he had no bacon to his tea ! Sunday was a fornit, he didna like the dumplings, and no wonder, for they were terrible sad, Prue. Twice I o'er-boiled his eggs in that last week, and the new smock, Prue—'

At that, she'd cry a long while.

'I hivered and hovered over it, Prue, so he died afore it was done. Oh, my dear, to think on it ! It wanted but the shoulder pieces and the cuffs, and it would ha' been the best smock ever I made. But I hivered and hovered, and he couldna bide any longer. He heard the mighty voice, child, calling among the ellums out yonder, and he couldna tarry for his smock, poor soul. All my stitches for naught.'

'Now, Mother, you mun finish it for Gideon,' I said. 'It'll fit Gideon right well, for he's a fine big man, though not so broad as Father. But he'll fill out. Come his eighteenth birthday, I shouldna wonder but he'll look right well in it. So you'd best hurry up.'

'Well,' she said, 'well, there's sense in that, child. He took the sin, to wear all his life long. He shall have the smock.'

She fetched Gideon's Sunday coat, and took the smock out of the dresser drawer, to measure it.

I sent up a wish that they might be enough of a size to content her. And so they were, and she quieted down again, and set off once more, whirring like a little lych-fowl.

But it wunna for long. She gave me a look, time and again, while I was putting on me mittens, and said –

'The ringlets be right nice, Prue.' And then : 'You've got a very tidy figure, child.'

And all in a minute she bent two-double over the wheel and began the old weariful cry –

'Could I help it if the hare crossed my path: could I help it?'

'Oh, Mother, Mother!' I beseeched her, 'give over crying for what we canna mend. I canna bear to hear you cry, my dear. Mother! Look ye! I dinna mind at

48

all. There, there now, my lamb!' (I was used to call her that, because she seemed so little and so lost). 'There, dunna take it to heart. Listen what I'll tell you! *I'd as lief have a hare-shotten lip as not!*' With that, I ran out of the house and through the wicket and up the wood path, roaring-crying.

I cried so loud that there was a whirr of wings on this side and on that, and far up the glade a coney heard me, and sat up in the middle of the path like a Christian, with one paw held up, just as Parson does, giving the blessing. Only it was a curse that his cousin, the hare, gave me.

I wondered why it cursed me so. Was it of its own free will and wish, or did the devil drive it? Did God begrutch me an 'usband and a cot of rushes, that He's let it be so? In the years after, it did often seem a queer thing that I should be obliged to work weekdays and Sundays so as to earn enough money to put straight what a silly hare had put crooked. And I knew it would take a deal of money to cure a hare-shotten lip. There was a kind of sour laughter in the thought of it. It called to mind the blackish autumn evenings, when grouse rise from the bitter marsh and fly betwixt the withered heather and the freezing sky, and laugh. Old harsh men laugh that way at the falling down of an enemy. And the good ladies of the town, big with stiff flowered silks and babes righteously begotten, laughed so behind their fans when they went to the prison to see a lovely harlot whipped. With that kind of bitterness a man might laugh when he was dying of a wound gotten in the king's cause, and one came busily in while the Parson was reading the prayer for the dying, and cried out, 'The king doth give you an earldom, and send you a bidding letter to his palace.'

Ah! Those be the ways grouse laugh, and that was how I laughed in those days. But now I sit here between the hearth and the window, with the tea brewing for one that will be home afore sundown, and the clouds standing upon the mountain, and when I laugh, I laugh easy, like the

49

woodpecker in spring. He was ever a laugher, was the woodpecker, and a right merry laugher too. He'll fly into an ellum tree, and laugh to see it so green. And he'll fly into an ash, and laugh to see it so bare, with only the black buds and no leaves. And then he'll fly into an oak, and laugh fit to burst to see the young brown leaves. Ah, the woodpecker's a good laugher, and the laughter's sweet as a sound nut. If we can laugh so at the end of long living, we've not lived in vain.

But that evening I laughed like the grouse, and my heart was rebellious within me.

Yet I could not but be pleased to think of the writing. I was glad also because it would give me a hold over Gideon, since if he was too harsh with Mother and me, I could be a bit awkward about the writing. I ran along by the water, feeling light and easy in my best sandal shoes, thinking how I'd work to get the stuff that was to make me as beautiful as a fairy, and how in a while there'd come a lover, and the axings would be put up in church, and in another while I'd sit in my own house place with my foot on a rocker and with a babe, grand and solemn, on my knee, better than all the French wax dolls they told of, that I'd never seen, but wanted very bad.

I was contented to see the coots swimming about with a trail of coot chickens after them, for all the world as if they were on a string. And I laughed to see the heron that lived on the far side of the water, and had got a missus and a nest there, standing knee-deep among the lilies, fair comic-struck. In after days I saw Gideon look like that, time and again, when he'd lief talk to Jancis and couldna call to mind a single word, or when he'd put his best cravat on and couldna get it to his liking, looking in the glass that he bought out of his second wool money, after he'd seen Jancis under the rosy light.

I met Jancis afore I got to the Stone House. She was bringing the oxen in, because they were ordered for a fair and the people were coming for 'em early in the morning.

Betwixt the two white beasts, with a hand on each, with all that gold hair shining, and a face like a white rose, she looked like the ghost of a beautiful lady that died a long while ago and came again every midsummer and fled at cockcrow.

'Oh!' she said, 'you've gotten ringlets, Prue. Shall I have ringlets for Sarn Wake?'

'As you please,' I answered, very snappy. For she was pretty enough without ringlets, and her mouth more a rose than ever. I thought how rich the ringlets would look, hanging down like ripe yellow bunches of white currants when they be traced very thick on the boughs, and she saying 'O!' and the fellows wanting to kiss her.

When she'd fastened the beasts in the trevis, we went indoors. 'Mister Beguildy!' I called out, 'I want you to learn me to read and write and sum, and all you know. I'm to pay in work. Gideon and me's going to get rich, and buy a place in Lullingford, and have maids and men, and flowered gowns for me, and china –'

Beguildy looked at me over the rim of a great measure of mead. 'Saddle your dreams afore you ride 'em, my wench,' he said.

'How mean you, Mister Beguildy?'

'The answer's under your mob-cap,' says he. 'If I be to learn ye, there's to be no argling, no questions and no answers. I say the saying, but you mun find the meaning. Now you come back to me a week to-day and tell me what I meant, and then for a bit of a treat I'll show you the bottle with the old Squire in it, old Camperdine, great-grandad to this un, him as came again so bad every Harvest Home, and sang a roaring bawdy song somewhere up in the chancel, only none could see un, so none could catch un.'

'Saving you.'

Beguildy smiled. He'd got a very slow stealing smile, that came like a ripple on the water, and stayed a long while.

'Ah. Saving me. I caught un proper.'

'What way did you?'

'If I told you, Prue Sarn, you'd know as much as me.'

'But so tell how you got him into the bottle!'

'Dear to goodness! You've forgotten the bargain. No questions.' He picked up the hammer and beat upon the row of flints, making out a little tune. And with that, in came Missis Beguildy, like the dancing woman at the fair comes in when they sound the drum. She'd got a basket of trout and a couple of fowl she was going to dress for the Wake the oxen were going to. She'd got on an old bottle-green hat of Beguildy's, tall in the crown, such as gentle-men of the road were partial to then, and it looked very outlandish atop of her frizzy grey hair.

'Did you hear tell?' she said to me.

She'd got a deep, solemn voice, and as she was too busy to speak often, everything she said seemed very weighty, as if the Town Crier said it, standing on the steps of the market in his braided coat.

'I heard as the Devil was dead,' said Beguildy, 'but it inna true, for I met un yestreen, and very pleasant spoken he was indeed, and right pleased to have your Feyther's company, Prue.'

'Now hush your gabble,' said Missis Beguildy, pulling the feathers out of the fowl in handfuls, so that the room was like a snowstorm. 'Did you hear tell, Prue, as poor John Weaver strayed off the road going through the woods in the dark of the moon last night, and was drownded in Blackmere? Death's very catching, poor soul.'

'Why it wanted but an hour to dawn when he left,' I said.

'Time enow, time enow. It's dark as Egypt in the woods down yonder.'

'Who'll take his place?'

'They seyn there's a nephew learning the trade. But he's bound 'prentice for a year or two. They'll make shift with a hired mon, I reckon.'

'And it ud be better, a power,' burst out Missis Beguildy, 'if *you* took that sort of job.'

52

She took the poker from the fire and singed the fowl very shrewdly, as if it met have been Beguildy.

'Woman, I've better things to think on than weaving weeds to cover the poor dying body. Dunna I snare souls like conies, and keep 'em from troubling the lives of men? Canna I bless, and they are blessed, curse, and they are cursed? Canna I cure warts and the chin-cough and barrenness and the rheumatics, and tell the future and find water, though it be in the depth of the earth? Dunna the fowls I bless beat all the other fowls in the cock-fighting? Ah, and if I chose, I could make a waxen man for every man in the parish, and consume them away, wax, men, and all. Canna I do all that, woman?'

'So you say, my dear.'

Missis Beguildy set the fowl's legs to rights and ran a skewer through, to make all safe.

Seeing that the Wizard was becoming very angry, I told his missus how I was going to be his scholar, and he was to learn me to spell and write.

'Will your headpiece stand it, child?' she asked. For she always thought, in common with many people, that if there was anything wrong with a person's outward seeming, there must be summat wrong with their mind as well. By that measure, Jancis, who was so silly that oftentimes she appeared to be well-nigh simple, would be a very clever woman.

'Ah. Prue's headpiece be right enow,' said Beguildy. 'Only I do think there be too many questions in it. But her'll fettle into a good scholar, will Prue. We'll start to-day 's a week, Prue. Jancis, you can get the besom and sweep out my room a bit. Put the tuthree books together, gather me some quills, and be very careful of all my bottles, for you never know who's in 'em. We dunna want any frittening about the place. Oh, and you met as well turn them toads out from behind the locker; they be all dead.'

'Prue,' says Jancis, when I went out, 'if yo'll tell me the way to make ringlets like that, I'll tell you what Feyther's

53

old riddle-me-ree means. I know, because he's said it over and over, and I've heard un tell the answer.'

'I made 'em round and round the poker, my dear,' I said. 'Not too hot, and give it a good clean first. But you needna tell me the answer to the riddle-me-ree, for I'd liefer find it out.'

The dew came showering on to my gown as I went past the bushes of wild roses at the wood gate, spilling out of the hearts of the blossoms. It was so quiet that I could hear the sheep cropping across the corner of the mere in the glebe, and the fish rising out in the middle, and the water lapping against the big, stiff leaves of the bulrushes.

I felt like a lady, walking out in my best on a weekday. It wasna often that I could be spared, and it was to be a deal less often now. So I was glad Gideon wanted me to be a scholar, for once every week I should get the afternoon and evening off.

When a breeze came, the leaves lapped up the silence like the tongues of little creatures drinking. Up in heaven there were clouds like the bit of lace on Mother's wedding-gown, and a setting moon as green as a young beech leaf. And down under the polished water was another moon, not quite so bright, and other clouds, not quite so lacy, and the shadow of the spire, very faint and ghostly, pointing across the water at us.

Chapter 7: *Pippins and Jargonelles*

MOTHER looked up when I went in. She was stitching the smock.

'What a big girl you look coming in, Prue,' she said. 'And you are not near sixteen yet!'

54

I asked where Gideon was.

Cutting by moonlight. Such a lad I never saw! Labours and sweats as if summat was after un.'

'Well, the moon's setting down behind the church croft now, Mother,' I said, 'so he'll be bound to give over.'

I went to the meadow. He'd got as much cut as a full-grown man could ha' done. He was rubbing the scythe-down with a handful of grass, and honing it for putting away, as I came over the field. I thought it sounded nice, coming over the wet, dimmery swaths, and sad as well. When I called to mind all the things he'd taken on shoulder, I was sorry for un.

'Come thy ways in to supper, Gideon,' I said.

'By gum! You look like a ghost, stealing out from under the dark hedge, all in your blacks, with that white face.'

Then he seemed to remember him of all we'd got in hand. He began to cross-waund me about the work.

'Shut the fowl up?'

'No.'

'Be quick about it, then; it should ha' bin done this hour. Looked the traps?'

No. I thought you would.'

'When I'm mowing, I canna do aught else, saving the jobs that are too heavy for you.'

'There binna many of them.'

'When you've done the fowl and the traps, you can set a tuthree night-lines in the mere. I've got some sawing to do yet.'

'It'll take a terrible long while, and I'm no good at setting the night-lines,' I said, nearly crying, being tired already, and it late, and another day's work beginning, seemingly.

'Did you make a bargain, or didna you?'

'Ah, I did, Gideon.'

'Then abide by it.'

Wandering about the place when Mother was abed and Gideon in the fields, I felt lonesome. I wished there was

55

some shorter way to be as beautiful as a fairy. Then a thought came to me all of a sudden. I wonder it didna come afore, but then I'd never much minded having a hare-lip afore. It seems to me that often it's only when you begin to see other folks minding a thing like that for you, that you begin to mind it for yourself. I make no doubt, if Eve had been so unlucky as to have such a thing as a hare-lip, she'd not have minded it till Adam came by, looking doubtfully upon her, and the Lord, frowning on His marred handiwork.

Now my thought was this: why shouldna I, that was in sore need of healing, do as the poor folk did here at Sarn in time past, and even now and again in our own day. Namely, at the troubling of the waters which comes every year in the month of August, to step down into the mere in sight of all the folk at the Wake, dressed in a white smock. It was said that this troubling of the water was the same as that which was at Bethesda, and though it had not the power of that water, which healed every year, and for which no disease was too bad, it being in that marvellous Holy Land where miracles be daily bread, yet every seventh year it was supposed to cure one, if the disease was not too deadly. You must go down into the water fasting, and with many curious ancient prayers. These I could learn, when I could read, for they were in an old book that Parson kept in the vestry. Not that he believed it, nor quite disbelieved it, but only that it was very rare and strange.

The thing I misdoubted most was it being such a public thing. I had need be a very brazen piece to make a show of myself thus, as if I were a harlot in a sheet, or a witch brought to the ducking-stool. And sure enough, when I spoke of it timidly to Mother and Gideon, they liked it not at all.

'What,' says Gideon, 'make yourself a nay-word and a show to three hundred folk? You met as well go for a fat woman at the fair and ha' done with it.'

'Only I amna fat,' I said.

'That's neither here nor there. You'd be making yourself

a talked-about wench from Sarn to Lullingford and from Plash to Brampton. Going down into the water the like of any poor plagued 'oman without a farden! Folk ud say, 'There's Sarn's sister douked into the water like poor folk was used to do, because Sarn's too *near* to get the Doctor's mon, let alone the Doctor.' And when I went to market they'd laugh, turning their faces aside. Never shall you do such a brassy thing! It ud be better, a power, if you took and made some mint cakes and spiced ale for the fair when the time comes, like Mother was used to do. You'd make a bit that way.'

'Yes, my dear,' said Mother, 'you do as Sarn says. It'll bring in a bit, and you'll see all as is to be seen, which you couldna, saving in the way of business, for it'll be scarce two months from Father's death. And come to think of it, what an unkind thing it would be for a poor widow to have it flung in her face afore such a mort of people that her girl had got a hare-shotten lip.'

She began to wring her little hands, and I knew she'd go back to the old cry in a minute, so I gave in.

'You've got to promise me you'll never do such a thing, Prue,' ordered Gideon.

'I promise for this year, but no more.'

'You've got a powerful curst will of your own, Prue, but promise or no, you shanna do such a thing, never in life shall you!'

'And in death I shanna mind,' I said. 'For if I do well and go to heaven I shall be made all new, and I shall be as lovely as a lily on the mere. And if I do ill and go to hell, I'll sell my soul a thousand times, but I'll buy a beautiful face, and I shall be gladsome for that though I be damned.'

And I ran away into the attic and cried a long while.

But the quiet of the place, and the loneliness of it comforted me at long last, and I opened the shutter that gave on the orchard and had a great pear tree trained around it, and I took my knitting out of my reticule. For it was on Saturday after tea that I had spoken of the troubling of the water, and the week's work being nearly done, I had my tidy gown on, and the reticule to match. Sitting there looking into the green trees, with the smell of our hay coming freshly on the breeze, mixed with the scent of the wild roses and meadowsweet in the orchard ditch, I hearkened to the blackbirds singing near and far. When they were a long way off you could scarcely disentangle them from all the other birds, for there was a regular charm of them, thrushes and willow-wrens, seven-coloured linnets, canbottlins, finches, and *writing-maisters*. It was a weaving of many threads, with one maister-thread of clear gold, a very comfortable thing to hear.

I thought maybe love was like that – a lot of coloured threads, and one maister-thread of pure gold.

The attic was close under the thatch, and there were many nests beneath the eaves, and a continual twittering of swallows. The attic window was in a big gable, and the roof on one side went right down to the ground, with a tall chimney standing up above the roof-tree. Somewhere among the beams of the attic was a wild bees' nest, and you could hear them making a sleepy soft murmuring, and morning and evening you could watch them going in a line to the mere for water. So, it being very still there, with the fair shadows of the apple trees peopling the orchard outside, that was void, as were the near meadows, Gideon being in the far field making hay-cocks, which I also should have been doing, there came to me, I cannot tell whence, a most powerful sweetness that had never come to me afore. It was not religious, like the goodness of a text heard at a preaching. It was beyond that. It was as if some creature made all of light had come on a sudden from a great way off, and nestled in my bosom. On all things there came a fair, lovely look, as if a different air stood over them. It is a look that seems ready to come sometimes on those gleamy mornings after rain, when they say, 'So fair the day, the cuckoo is going to heaven.'

Only this was not of the day, but of summat beyond it.

I cared not to ask what it was. For when the nut-hatch comes into her own tree, she dunna ask who planted it, nor what name it bears to men. For the tree is all to the nut-hatch, and this was all to me. Afterwards, when I had mastered the reading of the book, I read –

His banner over me was love.

And it called to mind that evening. But if you should have said 'Whose banner?' I couldna have answered. And even now, when Parson says, 'It was the power of the Lord working in you,' I'm not sure in my own mind. For there was naught in it of churches nor of folks, praying nor praising, sinning nor repenting. It had to do with such things as bird-song and daffodowndillies rustling, knocking their heads together in the wind. And it was as wilful in its coming and going as a breeze over the standing corn. It was a queer thing, too, that a woman who spent her days in sacking, cleaning sties and beast-housen, living hard, considering over fardens, should come of a sudden into such a marvel as this. For though it was so quiet, it was a great miracle, and it changed my life; for when I was lost for something to turn to, I'd run to the attic, and it was a core of sweetness in much bitter.

Though the visitation came but seldom, the taste of it was in the attic all the while. I had but to creep in there, and hear the bees making their murmur, and smell the woody o'er-sweet scent of kept apples, and hear the leaves rasping softly on the window-frame, and watch the twisted grey twigs on the sky, and I'd remember it and forget all else. There was a great wooden bolt on the door, and I was used to fasten it, though there was no need, for the attic was such a lost-and-forgotten place nobody ever came there but the travelling weaver, and Gideon in apple harvest, and me. Nobody would ever think of looking for me there, and it was parlour and church·both to me.

The roof came down to the floor all round, and all the beams and rafters were oak, and the floor went up and down like stormy water. The apples and pears had their

59

places according to kind all round the room. There were codlins and golden pippins, brown russets and scarlet crabs, ciffins, nonpareils and queanings, big green bakers, pearmains and red-streaks. We had a mort of pears too, for in such an old garden, always in the family, every generation 'll put in a few trees. We had Worcester pears and butter pears, jargonelle, bergamot and Good Christian. Just after the last gathering, the attic used to be as bright as a church window, all reds and golds. And the colours of the fruit could always bring my visitation back to me, though there was not an apple or pear in the place at the time, because the colour was wed to the scent, which had been there time out of mind. Every one of those round red cheeks used to smile at poor Prue Sarn, sitting betwixt the weaving-frame and the window, all by her lonesome. I found an old locker, given up to the mice, and scrubbed it, and put a fastening on it, and kept my ink and quills there, and my book, and the Bible, which Mother said I could have, since neither she nor Gideon could read in it.

One evening in October I was sitting there, with a rush-light, practising my writing. The moon blocked the little window, as if you took a salver and held it there. All round the walls the apples crowded, like people at a fair waiting to see a marvel. I thought to myself that they ought to be saying one to another, 'Be still now! Hush your noise! Give over jostling!'

I fell to thinking how all this blessedness of the attic came through me being curst. For if I hadna had a hare-lip to frighten me away into my own lonesome soul, this would never have come to me. The apples would have crowded all in vain to see a marvel, for I should never have known the glory that came from the other side of silence.

Even while I was thinking this, out of nowhere suddenly came that lovely thing, and nestled in my heart, like a seed from the core of love.

BOOK TWO

Chapter 1: *Riding to Market*

In telling this story I take little count of time. For when the heart is in stress, what is time? It is naught. Does the bridegroom, that has clemmed for his love a long while, hearken to the watchman's voice telling over the hastening hours? Does he that dies in the dawn care to what hour the dial points when the sun arises, that rises not on him? And when we poor beings take up our stand against all the might of the things that be, striving to win through to our peace, or to what we think is our peace, when we are dumbfounded like a baited creature in the bull-ring, then we forget time. So four years went by, and though a deal happened out in the world, naught happened to us.

Rumours came to us of battles over sea and discontents at home. The French went to Russia and never came back, save a few.

At last, one golden summer evening, there came one riding all in a lather to tell of the great victory of Waterloo. But the news Gideon liked best, which came in the same year, was the news of the corn tax.

'Fetch me a mug of home-brewed, Prue,' he shouted, when he raught home from market and told me. 'it's the best news ever we had. We'll be rich in a tuthree years. We must get more land under corn. I *thought* corn would never come amiss, but I didna hope for anything like this'll be. When Callard came up to my stall with the tidings, I was fair comic-struck. "Dang me!" I says. "What?" I says. "Make the furriners pay to lug their corn to us?" "Ah, that's the size of it," says Callard. "And that'll make it scarce, seesta, and that'll make it dear, seesta!" "Why, mon, I've seen that this long while," I says. "But I never thought they'd do it." And what d'ye think I did then, Prue? Why, axed un to the *Mug of Cider* and stood un a drink! So you can tell how comic-struck I must ha' bin. And now all we've got to do is to drive plough, both of us.'

So there was a prospect of living harder than we had in the four years gone, when we'd slaved from daybreak to dark, and in the dark too, by the wandering light of the horn lanthorn. It wouldna have come so hard to me, if it hadna been all for the money, if I could have been a bit house-proud, and if Gideon had taken a pride in fettling the farm. But there was none of that. It was just scrat and scrape to get the money out of the place and be off.

I grew as lanky as a clothes prop, and Mother began to show signs of wringing her hands about that too. For being little herself, and Missis Beguildy and Jancis and most of the women about being little, it seemed meet to Mother that a woman should be small. So when I grew and grew, and was very slender also (for indeed, with such a deal of work and little time to eat, anybody would be slender) she said I was like a poplar in an unthinned woodland or an o'er tall bulrush in the mere, and I got used to being ashamed of my tallness as well as the other trouble, until – but I munna be too forrard with the tale.

Gidéon wore his smock and looked right well in it. He was two-and-twenty now, a man grown, very personable, broad in the shoulder, with a firm, well-knit figure. As his body set, his mind set with it, harder than ten-days' ice. He'd no eye for the girls at market, though there was a many looked at him. And once at market when he was wearing Father's blue coat with the brass buttons, Squire Camperdine's daughter (not the squire in the bottle, but his great-grandson) came riding past his booth, and smiled at him. But Gideon would only laugh when I questioned him, and stroke his chin, and look at me warily. There was no doubt he was a very comely man, and it used to seem to me unfair that it was me, and not Gideon, that was born after the hare looked at Mother. For Gideon could have grown what they call a *moustachio* and looked very well, and none need have known he'd got a hare-shotten lip. But with me it was past hiding.

As to the farm, it was doing pretty well. We'd got a big flock of sheep, so that the shearing took us above a week. We'd got a herd of pigs that kept Mother busy all the time the acorns lasted, tending them in the oakwood. The grass-meadow by the orchard was under wheat, but we had no good of it the first year, for the wheat sprouted and acker-spired in the ear, it being a very wet season.

There was enough saved to buy two oxen for ploughing and other heavy work about the place. Being a bit out of fashion, they were not very dear. Gideon said that when he went to buy them I could go too and give a hand driving them back. And I could look in the shop windows while he haggled over the beasts, and then we could look at the house he'd set his mind on buying when it should come into the market. But Mother must know naught about the house, or she'd tell folk. 'And if they thought I have such a thing in mind, they'd bant all my prices and double all their own, and where should we be then?' said Gideon.

You may guess I was glad to be going pleasuring, for I'd scarcely been away from Sarn since Father died, and Lullingford always seemed a wonderful place to me.

I was in the cornfield, leasing, when Gideon said it, he being just back from market, coming across the field in the last light of evening; and the shadows of him and Bendigo stretched away over the grass from the far gate to the orchard as I watched them come.

'But how'll I go!' I asked. 'I canna ride pillion, for there be the panniers.'

'If you'll do a bit extra leasing, I'll hire the mill pony when I take the next corn to be ground. Going to Plash for a lesson to-morrow?'

'Ah.'

'Then fetch back the beasts, oot, and I'll go with corn Saturday.'

63

'But I've leased till there's scarce an ear left any part in of this field or the other,' I said.

'Ask Beguildy to let you lease his. I saw them lugging their corn.'

'But Jancis and Missis Beguildy –'

'Now you know very well Jancis is too bone-idle to pick up as much as an ear. Though I like her right well, and as for looks –'

He stopped and stood, with his hand on Bendigo's neck, gazing away to where Plash shone like bright honey in the long light, dreaming.

It was but seldom Gideon sat still, and very seldom he gave his mind to any thought but the thought of making money. But the name of Jancis would often quieten him, and when he fell into one of his silences he would make me think of a tranced man that was once brought to Beguildy to be awakened. And he made me think of a brooding summer tree on a windless day, minding its own thoughts above the water. He was like the lych-gate yew that dreams the year long, and keeps its dream as secret as it keeps its red fruit under the boughs. Gideon had been used to fall into a dream like this ever since he saw Jancis under the rosy light. Times, he'd mutter 'No, no!' and shift his shoulders as though from a weight, and bestir himself, and be more of a driver than ever. For Gideon was a driver if ever there was one, and what he drove was his own flesh and blood. It seemed a pity to me that a young man should be so set in his ways, and have no pleasant times, for I was mighty fond of Gideon. I knew well where he went of a Sunday, when he took off his smock and put on the bottle-blue coat. He was a deal more regular at Plash than ever he was at church. The rosy light started it, but it would have likely been the same, anyway. Missis Beguildy told me how he'd come and knock, and Jancis would run to the door in her best gown and ribbon or a flower in her hair, and go red and white by turns. And I saw for myself too, when she came to our

64

place, how she would pant under her kerchief, and I wondered how this might be. For Gideon was just Gideon to me, but to her he was fire and tempest and the very spring, and his voice was as the voice of the mighty God.

He'd come in, Missis Beguildy said, with no word, and he'd sit down, and Beguildy would scowl, having no mind for Jancis to marry. He'd scowl from the inner-most chimney corner, for he felt the cold very bad, living in such a damp place and being a very stay-at-home man. And Gideon would scowl back.

Jancis blushed and trembled over her spinning, taking sideways looks at Gideon as a wren will. And Missis Beguildy set her face like a flint, and laid plans to get her good man out of the kitchen. She dearly loved to see a bit of lovering going on, being short of summat to think of and talk of. She wanted to be a granny too. So she'd go to any length, but she'd get Beguildy out of the room. Once, when Gideon was glowering more than common, being very desirous to kiss Jancis because she'd put on some new ribbon or what-not to set her off, and when Missis Beguildy had called her man and come back and argufied, and gone out and called again, but still he'd only sit there like a goblin in the dark of the fire, she even went so far as to set a light to the thatch on the barn. Ah! She did! She was a very strong-minded woman. And she kept the poor man, who couldn't abide any work with his hands, running to-and-agen with buckets all evening. When he'd nearly douted one place, she set light to another while he was dipping water from the lake.

'I kept the flint and tinder right hot, my dear,' she said to me. And she laughed! I never saw a woman laugh more lungeously over anything than she did over that. She said she took a peep at the window, just to encourage her, and she could see through the clear bits in among the bottle-glass that they were sitting side by side on the settle.

65

'Very right and proper!' she says, and runs back to her work.

Another time she loosed the sow, and it made straight for our oakwood, she having taken it there afore. Beguildy liked his rasher, and the sow meant many a bacon-pig, so for fear she should come to harm, he took stick and went after her, cursing considerable. After a bit he began to be suspicious, because any ill that came, came on a Sunday, and he liked his day of rest, though he *was* a heathen man. So he said to Gideon, 'There's no luck with you. When you come, harm brews. Keep off.'

So he had to give over going. Then he wiled Jancis into the woods, and I'd see them going up the dim ways, rainy or frosty was no matter, she with her face like a white rose, shining, and he looking down at her, loving, and angered to be loving. When they were in the woods, Missis Beguildy was so interested in the wizard's bottles with the ghosts in them (so he said) that he'd have hard work to answer her questions. And she'd give him such a tea that it lasted nearly to supper. But he found out. He began to wonder why Jancis had taken such an affection for Tivvy, it being Tivvy she said she went to see. And as he couldn't speak to Sexton, being at daggers drawn, he followed her one evening unbeknown. And when she got home, he leathered her so that her eyes were red for weeks, and she came running to Gideon all bedraggled with tears. He was in a rage with Beguildy, and he told Jancis he'd lief wed with her, only not till he'd won through, and was rich. For how could he get along, he said, with a helpless one like Jancis clinging to him, and a tribe of children, very likely? But he was moody and troubled in mind, for he could see Jancis but seldom, Beguildy being so watchful. I thought maybe the plan to show me the house he wanted was to comfort himself and strengthen his will, because he was afraid of giving in. He wanted to give in, mind you, for he was sore set on Jancis, only he was fixed, and when

66

he was fixed he couldna let himself give in, not if it was ever so.

It turned out that we couldna borrow the mill pony for a good few weeks, because she'd gone lame. So the harvest was long over, winter upon us, and Christmas drawing nigh, when they sent a message to say we could have the loan of it for the Christmas market, for they'd just bought one of the old horses from the Lullingford and Silverton coach, and they would drive that to market themselves. I may say I was very pleased to think of the outing, and watched the weather very anxious, for it boded snow.

I was up at four on market day, setting the place to rights for Mother and getting the things together for market. Eggs and dressed fowl we had in plenty, and greens and apples and a bit of butter. Polishing the apples in the attic, peace came upon me, as it ever did up there, since the time I told of. While the rushlight flickered in the cold air, and the mice scuttled, I stood at the open window that was like an oblong of black paper. No sound came in. Naught stirred outside. Even the mere was frozen round the edges, so that the ducks must go skating every morning afore they could come at the water. The world was all so piercing still that it was almost like a voice crying out. It was used to seem to me that when the world was so quiet, it was like being along of somebody as knew you very well, ah! like being with your dear acquaintance.

Down in the dark barn the cock crew, thin and sweet, and I thought it sounded like no earthly bird; but maybe that was because I was in the attic, where things were always new. You may think it strange that a woman like me should think such things, being one that worked with my hands always, at poor harsh tasks, whereas you'd expect such thoughts to come to fine ladies sitting at their tapestry work. But I was so lonesome, and had such a deal of time for thinking, and what with that and the book-

67

learning I was getting, all sorts of thoughts grew up in my mind, like flowering rushes and forget-me-nots coming into blow in a poor marshy place, that else had nought. And I can never see that it did much harm, for the thoughts seldom came but in the attic, and they did never make me dreamy over my work.

So now, hearing the clear sound of our game-cock crying out upon the dawn, that was yet more than two hours away, I ran downstairs all of a lantun-puff to get the breakfast. When Gideon came in, it was all ready, and a great fire roaring, for we need never stint of wood at Sarn, which was much to be thankful for at a time when many poor families in England must herd together six or seven in one cottage to boil their kettles all on one fire. I was always thankful for our plenteous wood, that cost naught, and need not take up too much of Gideon's time neither, for if I burnt more than he cut I could make shift to chop it myself.

We were as snug as could be, sitting in the merry fire-light with a red glow shining on the quarries and the ware and the spinning-wheels in the corner. I was pleased to think Mother wasna to be lonesome, for I'd asked Tivvy to come and keep her company, since I never could enjoy anything if one I loved was lonesome or sad. Shaking the cloth out of the door after it got light, I could see her red cloak coming along under the dark woods; for as Tivvy never did anything nor thought anything, she had all her time to herself, as you met say, and so she had no cause to be late.

Gideon had roughed Bendigo and the mill pony over-night, so all being ready and the sun just risen, we set off.

All the lake was full of red lights, as if our farm was on fire, reflected in the water. The black pines stood with their arms out, dripping with hoar frost, all white-over, so that the tips of their drooping branches were like your fingers when you take them from the suds. The rooks were very contented, cawing soft and pleasant, as if they

68

knew their breakfast was ready as soon as our ploughland thawed a bit, and in the stackyard there was a great murmuration of starlings.

'Bring me a fairing!' screams Tivvy from across the water.

Gideon looked sullen, and I knew the only fairing he'd a mind to bring was one for Jancis. So I called out – 'I will. What shall it be?'

'A bit of cherry-coloured sarsnet to tie up my hair,' she calls. For though she was a foolish piece in most things, she knew very well she'd got pretty curls, bright brown and thick. She'd toss them ever so when Gideon was there, and take every chance to miscall Beguildy, though she durstna say anything against Jancis, for fear Gideon might blaze out. But she was clever enough in this, as oftentimes a stupid girl is when she's in love, and she could always make it seem a very poor, ill-liking sort of thing to be sweet on a wizard's wench, and a grand thing to be in love with the sexton's daughter, whose dad could mouth texts as fast as the wizard could mouth charms.

It was a grand morning, very crispy underfoot, with moor-fowl about, especially widgeon. We were riding to the hills. Across the far woods and the rough moors beyond, and the bits of ploughland here and there, and the frostly stubble where partridges ran from the noise of the trotting, we could see the hills, as blue as pansies. Promising hills, they seemed to me. There was a clatter in the spinney, and a flock of wood-pigeons got up and took their flight, with wings flashing blue in the sun, for the same hills. It was as if some wonderful thing was there, as it might be a healing well, or some other miracle, or a holy person such as there were of old time.

I said as much to Gideon, but he was looking away over shoulder to Plash and the long spire of blue smoke going up from the Stone House. He began to whistle below his breath, for he'd never whistle outright, even at the merriest, but always very quiet and to his mommets.

So I said no more, and in a while our old road ended, and we came into the main road where it was bad going, for whatever the weather was, the road the Romans made was good going, and even better than the turnpike. In a little we passed the mill folk going soberly along, and then a tuthree more, and soon we were riding up the hill into the town, with the plovers crying about us in their winter voices.

So we rode to Lullingford to look upon a dream. For the house we were about seeing was woven into the dream of Gideon's life. The house, that is, along with what it meant, the maids and the men, the balls and the dinners with the gentry at the *Mug o' Cider* at election time.

When we were going through the ford as you come into the lower part of the place, Gideon said –

'I wish Jancis was riding pillion with me.'

'Why, so she shall,' I said, 'the very next time we come. Why shouldna she come every time?'

'There be Beguildy.'

'Oh, Beguildy! I'll wile un with his own spells and charm un with his own charms,' I said, and I laughed as we went up the narrow street, so that heads came out of windows here and there to see what it might be.

'Husht now, girl!' says Gideon. 'Laugh quiet. Not like a wild curlew.'

'But a curlew's very good company, and a pleasanter voice I seldom heard, and I'm pleased with the compliment, lad.'

And indeed I was pleased with the world and all. For there was summat about Lullingford, as if a different air blew there, and as if there was a brighter sun and a safer daylight. I knew not why it was. It was a quiet place, though not near so quiet as now. Folk go off to the cities these days, but when I was young they gathered together from many miles around into the little market towns. Still, it was quiet, and very peaceful, though not with the stillness of Sarn, that was almost deathly, times.

70

There was one broad street of black and white houses, jutting out above, and gabled, and made into rounded shop windows below. They stood back in little gardens. At the top of the street was the church, long and low, with a tremendous high steeple, well carved and pleasant to see. Under the shadow of the church was the big, comfortable inn, with its red sign painted with a tall blue mug of cider. It had red curtains in the windows, and a glow of firelight in the winter, and it seemed to say, in being so nigh the church, that its landlord's conscience was clear and his ale honest, and that none would get more than was good for him there. But of the last I a little doubt.

Of a Sunday the shops had each a bit of white canvas stuff hung afore the window like an apron, which made it seem very pious and respectable. There were few shops, and only one of each kind, so you could never run from one to another, cheapening goods.

There was the Green Canister, where they kept groceries and spools and pots and pans, and there was the maltster's, and the butcher's and the baker's, for Lullingford was well up with the times, since it wasna all towns could boast a baker in days when nearly everybody baked at home. Then there was the leather shop, for boots and harness, and the tailor's which was only open in winter, for in summer he travelled round the country doing piecework. There was the smithy too, where the little boys crowded after Dame-School every winter dusk, begging to warm their hands and roast chestnuts and taters. It was a pleasant thing to see the sparks go up, roaring, and to feel the hearty glow about you, warming you to the heart's core, with nothing to pay or to do, like love. Near by the smithy was the row of little cottages where was the weaver's. Like the tailor, he went abroad over the country-side in summer, and sometimes to a village in winter, if it was open weather. But in hard weather he stayed in his snug slip of a house and heard the wind roaring over from the mountains north to the

71

mountains south. I never could tell why this cottage drew me, even from a child. It had a narrow garden and a walk of red brick, an oaken paling, and bushes of lavender on either side the walk. Three well-whitened steps led up to the door, and there was a window of many little panes, not bottle-glass. Above was another window. At the back, a patch of garden ran down to the meadows, and there was a second window in the living-room that looked over this garden and the meadows, to the mountains. This I knew, because I went there once with a message in the old weaver's time. Upon the front of the house was a vine, very old and twisted. This was a rare thing in a place of such hard winters, but the town was sheltered by the mountains, and the weaver's house faced south, so the vine throve, and though in cold seasons the grapes didna always ripen, in some years they ripened very well. What with the vine and the lavender and the pleasant shadows on the strip of green lawn, and the lilac tree that stood beside the door, and what with the great weaving frame in the living-room, which was comfortable with firelight shining on brasses and copper vessels, and very well kept; what with it all, I could never pass it without a look of longing. I was used to envy the fat thrushes hopping on the lawn. It drew me as heaven draws the poor sinner, weary of his miry wanderings.

So to-day, as we rode by, I said –

'Gideon, what is it makes that house different to the other housen?'

'It inna different.'

'Oh, but it's as different as if it was builded of stone fetched from another world!' I cried out. 'It's as different as if the timbers were falled in the forests of the Better Land.'

'Dear to goodness, girl, you bin raving,' says he. 'Husht, or the beadle'll put you in pound.'

So I hushed, and we came to the *Mug of Cider*, and after turning our beasts in among the rest, we set out our goods in the market.

72

Chapter 2: *The Mug of Cider*

THE market was in the open, in a paven square by the church. Each had his own booth, and the cheeses stood in mounds between. There were a sight of old women in decent shawls and cotton bonnets selling the same as we had, butter and eggs and poultry. There was a stall for gingerbread and one for mincepies. There was a sun-bonnet stall and a toy stall, and one for gewgaws such as strings of coral and china cats, shoe buckles and amulets and beaded reticules. It was a merry scene, with the bright holly and mistletoe, the cheeses yellow in the sun, and the gingerbread as brown and sticky as chestnut buds.

The butcher stood at his door, which gave on to the market-place, shouting his meat, and holding up a long, shining knife, enough to make you think the French were coming. There was a woman selling hot potatoes and pig's fry and a crockman who put up his wares to auction, and every time the clock chimed he broke summat, keeping some '*seconds*' in readiness, which served to amuse the people. Then the mummers came along and gave us a treat, and in one corner the beast-leech was pulling teeth out for a penny each, and had a crowd watching. What with them all shouting, and the mummers mouthing their parts, and the crash of broken china, and beasts lowing and bleating from the fair ground close by, and the chimes ringing out very sweet at the half-hours, you may think there was a cheerful noise.

When we'd got rid of our goods, we went into the *Mug of Cider* for a snack. Ten or a dozen old men sat without, though the air was so nipping that they must have bin starved. Each one was holding a great pewter tankard, and they were roaring out at the top of their voices –

'*The Lord's my shepherd, I'll not fear.*'

Each one went his own way and made his own tune, and I

73

thought how angered Mister Beguildy would be if he could hear 'em making such an untuneful sound, for he was very particular over his row of flints, and when he struck them he was troubled if they didna strike the note true.

But when we were come by these old ancients, every one held his mug where it was, and stopped in his singing, and so sat with his mouth open and his eyes fast on me. They were like those new-fangled mommet-shows with the little dolls that stop all together when the showman unhands them. There they sat, with the inn behind them and the frosty sunshine on their old, red, veiny faces, and a kind of frittened look. As we passed the bench, every head of them came round slow, and the score or so of eyes stared slantwise over the rims of their cups, as young owls will stare and turn their heads, watching you over their feathers.

As we went through the dark doorway, with its door studded with nails like a prison, and came into the inn parlour, where sat the more genteel, I saw their looks fasten on me too, but more shyly. The farmers and their ladies and two or three folk that had come by the early coach and were baiting here, and the Squire's son, who was a parson in Silverton and was on the way home for Christmas and was taking some refreshment because his nag had cast a shoe, all of them looked up, quiet and careful but very curious, at me. All on a sudden I knew that all these folk, the grand ones within and the old fellows without, were staring at my hare-shotten lip. They were thinking, according to their station and their learning –

'Here's a queer outlandish creature!'

'This is a woman out of a show, sure to goodness!'

'Here be a wench turns into a hare by night.'

'Her's a witch, an ugly, hare-shotten witch.'

Maybe in the tuthree times I'd come to Lullingford in the past they'd stared so, but then I was but a child and didna see.

74

I could hear the old men without croaking like a lot of rooks, and one said –

'Dunna drink while she's by. It'll p'ison yer innards.'

Another said –

'Dunna look upon the baigle. Her'll put the evil eye on you. You'll dwine and dwine away.'

The folk inside looked each at other, and I wished I could die. For all the bitter cold and my thin gown and us being far from the fire, I was all in a swelter. For indeed I loved my kind and would lief they had loved me, and I felt a friendliness for the drovers and for the gentry, and the host and his missus. For they were part of my outing and part of Lullingford and of the world, that ever seized my heart in its hands, as a child will hold a small bird, which is both affrighted and comforted to be so held. I would lief have ridden forth and seen new folk, new roads, new hamlets, children playing on strange village greens, unknown to me as if they were fairies, come there I knew not whence nor how, singing their songs and running away into the dusk; old folk wending their way along paths in meadows of which I knew not so much as the name of the owner, to churches deep in trees, with all the bells a-ringing, pulled by men I never saw afore. Ah, I should dearly ha' liked that. Only the gist of it must ever be that the old folk looked kind as they saw me go by, and the children smiled or threw me a blossom, and that when I came to inn or tavern they'd say, 'Draw in to the fire now, dear 'eart, for night thickens.' Ah, I'd dearly ha' liked that!

This made it all the more of a shocking thing to me that the real world was thus towards me, for living so apart I had not truly felt my grief afore. But now I knew that I was fast bound in misery and iron, as the Book saith. Ah, prisoned beyond a door to which the great nailed door of the inn was but paper!

As I was bending over my plate so that my bonnet met hide the tears, a lady came in. She was a handsome piece if ever there was one! She was lissom as a wand, dressed

75

in a long scarlet riding coat and a highwayman hat to match with a great swath of chestnut hair tied in a bow. She'd got black eyes with no human soul in them, but sparkles instead, like a cat's eyes on a frosty night. Gauntlets on her little hands, spurs on her boots, she came in laughing from a talk with the old men on the bench.

'A besom, host!' she says. 'We want a besom here.'

Everybody smiled and sniggered a bit. I knew well what she meant, for once when Mother was talking to me she said that if folk began to speak of besoms I'd best go, since it was their way of saying I was a witch.

But Gideon never noticed, for not being afflicted like me he never thought of such things, and being used to me he didna have it in mind that other folk met not be. And he was very deep in considering over whether Jancis or the big house and the maids and men were best, so it all went by him.

The lady ran to the Squire's son and clapped him on shoulder, which made him frown because of his dignity, and she says –

'So you've come Christmasing like a good lad! Who's the woman with the hare-shotten lip?'

He made a sign to warn her to talk soft, and nodded towards Gideon ever so little.

'Why, if yonder isn't young Sarn of Sarn!' she says, flushing a bit and coming running across to where Gideon sat, very handsome in the blue coat with the brass buttons and the black band for Father on the arm, and his eyes darkling over the thought of Jancis. I nudged him, and he stood up, and looked all the better for it, being such a fine figure.

She held out her hand, for the gentry were always friendly to the farmers, in especial to voters about election time, and she sparkled at him out of her black eyes and said –

'There's to be an election soon, and Father's got some work for you, Sarn. So you'd best come and see us one day, and take bite and sup, if your sweetheart can spare you.'

76

She looked very spitefully at me. Seemingly she thought Gideon was an only child, and so she chose to take me for his acquaintance, or else she chose to mock him – lashing him into her slavery by making him look a fool.

Now Gideon was altogether with the Squire as to politics, because of the corn tax, but he hadna made up his mind in good sadness whether he meant giving all those things up and settling down contented with Jancis and a crowd of little uns till death them parted. So he hummed and hawed a bit, and not being used to hiver-hover from a common man, she lost her temper. 'So! So! You've no time, Sarn. You've no time, I see,' she says. 'You'll be dancing on Diafoll Mountain next Thomastide no doubt. Oh, fine you'll look, Sarn, with your missus here, and broomsticks all round and the moon shining!'

She laughed like a tinkle of jangled bells, and Gideon came to the knowledge of what she meant. He was ever slow, but sure. Eh, terrible sure.

That was one of the times I spoke of when I saw Gideon angered. His face had gone dark and his eyes had the look as if the mere was running behind them, cold, and bitter cold. He looked down at her so that she blenched, and he said very slow –

'Ma'am, this be my sister. If I've a mind to dance on the Diafoll Mountain along of witches, I ool. And if I've a mind to dance upstairs at the 'unt ball along of the gentry, I ool. But I wunna ask *you* for a partner. And I doubt I wunna be able to vote for Squire neither, for can a man govern the land as canna govern his own womankind, but lets his girl go about like a ripstitch-rantipole? He should ha' give you more stick, ma'am.'

'Dorabella!' calls her brother, very much put about at her being in such a brawl.

They went out, and Gideon sat down and went on with his victuals. Nor did he eat a bit less hearty for it all, though I could scarce touch a morsel. So soon as he went off to buy the oxen, I made haste to go from the place.

77

There were plenty of errands to do, what with malt and sugar and tea to buy, and boots for us all, and Tivvy's present, and a bit of baccy for Gideon, for he never bought any himself, since, if he was near with others, he was near with himself also. When I'd finished, and bought a tuthree extras for Christmas, and packed all into the panniers, Gideon was ready to go and see the house. He was pleased with the cattle. Brindled longhorns they were, and very strong. With so few people using oxen for farm work they were cheaper, a power, than they used to be. So he was cheerful, since neither then nor at any other time did he seem cast down by my sorrow. How could he know, indeed, that my heart was bleeding because of Miss Dorabella and the old men on the bench? He was angered because he thought it disgrace to himself that a hare-shotten lip should be cast up against one of his family, and a scent of witchcraft into the bargain. But for me he took no thought, any more than if I was one of the new-bought oxen that somebody prodded in passing by. He whistled under his breath as we went along the by-road that led to the house he'd set his mind on. I'd never been along that way, for it lay outside the town on the other road from ours, and when we did come in we hadna much time for gadding about. We soon left the coach road and were in a lane with deep frozen ruts in it, and high hedges white-over with rime.

The evening was closing in a bit, but Gideon said never mind, we'd manage the beasts all right, for it ud be light as day when the moon rose. He was very wrought-up about the house, I could see, so I agreed to all he said, for I never liked to dampen down anybody's pleasure. Lord knows there's little enow in the world, and Gideon was ever one that took life hard. So when it turned out that he'd planned to treat me to a dish of tea after, at the *Mug of Cider*, and have a chat about all we meant to do, seeing we couldna when Mother was by, I said naught agen it, though I thought I'd liefer have gone into Hell's mouth than face

78

it. But Gideon wanted to talk while the holiday feeling was on him, afore the dumbness of Sarn got the better of him agen. For it was a most peculiar thing how you couldna speak your heart out at Sarn, and I never knew whether it was the big trees brooding, or the heavy rheumaticky feeling of being so close to the water, or the old ancient house full of the remembrances of old ancient people, or that there was summat foreboded. So Gideon kept his thoughts and turned them over and over in his mind like a snowball, till at last the snowball was too much for six strong men to shift, and nigh big enough to bury anybody.

We went through a gate into an avenue like a carriage drive. At the end there was another gate, with balls on posts, very grand. Within was a carriage sweep and flower knots, trimly kept.

We stood there, looking through the wrought-iron gates at the place that Gideon said was to be ours. It was new, built since Queen Anne died, and it was a despert big house, very solid, with four windows each side the door, and over the door a porch of stone. Above the eight windows were eight more, and over them dormer windows that Gideon said would be the windows of the men-servants and the maid-servants. There were steps up to the door, and a stone mounting-block with steps also, and a walled garden at one side, and a round pigeon cote.

No light showed, and the place had a melancholy look, so still it was, so dark, in its dark still trees.

'I'd lief there was a light,' I said.

'Dear to goodness, a light? It wunna be dark this hour, to call dark. What do they want with a light? The housekeeper can spin by firelight, I hope, and an old chap can sit in the chimney corner and set his mind on a better world without wasting tallow, let alone wax!'

Gideon had taken over the management already, seemingly, and I was bound to laugh.

'You seem pretty anxious the poor gentleman should set his mind on a better world,' I says.

79

'Why, so I am, but not too soon. It ud never do for the old chap to go out all of a lantun-puff afore we've got the money together. Say in about ten year.'

'So he's to order his coffin in ten years' time, poor gentleman.'

'You be very sharp to-day Prue,' says he. 'But he's bound to go some day, no danger. We mun bide our time.'

'He's Miss Dorabella's great-uncle, inna he?'

'Ah.'

'Wunna they want it for young Mister Camperdine?'

'Laws, no! He's after a bishop's palace.'

'Nor yet his cousin?'

'Dear no! He'll never bide long in a place, that lad wunna. A rolling stone, he be, and a caution. No, it'll be put up to auction when the old man goes, and you and me must mind to get the money ready.'

'Why, look ye, a light!' I says.

'Where?'

'Why there, in that lower window on the garden side.'

I saw it as well as could be, a large pale light wandering from window to window downstairs and then sliding up, in a long window that seemed to go down the stairs, and beginning over again in the upper story. One window would shine for a minute and then go black, and another shine. It had a very strange, uncontented look, wandering like that. There's nothing so contented as a steadfast light, but a flickering light going to and agen in a void is a sad thing to see. It went on like that a long time, and the cold strengthened. There was no sound at all. We stood there like beggars outside the gate, and the unquiet light wandered in the dark. All of a sudden it went out.

'Oh, it's gone out!' I says. 'Oh, deary, deary, me!'

'What of that?' says Gideon.

'I wanted it to steady and come to rest in a window, and shine out with a heartening glow,' I said. 'But now it's gone out.'

It distressed me mightily that it should go out, so that

80

I wrung my cold hands together, though why it should hurt me thus I couldna say.

'It was but the housekeeper looking for her knitting-needles or old Camperdine seeking his snuff-box. And now they've found it, they've douted the light. Very sensible too.'

'No!' I said. 'No! It was love, lad, wanting to steady and shine. But the house was too much for it. The dark's closed in now. The light's douted.'

And I began to cry, which was a foolish thing to do. But Gideon wasna so angered as he met have been, for he was in a good temper about the oxen and the house.

'You're sickening for summat,' he said, 'for you be no cry-baby, Prue. Come on to your tea now, while I tell you all that's in my mind. I've a deal to say, for that little vixen of Camperdine's has changed my mind for me, so I must tell you the new plans as well as the old.'

We turned away from the shut gate, as dumb as stones, and we left all the twenty-four windows with no light in them, and the dark trees with no breath of air in them lying there in the vast of night.

Chapter 3: *'Or Die in 'tempting It'*

IT wasna near so bad as I'd feared at the inn, for the old men were gone with their droves, and the Camperdines were by this at their dinner. It is often so, if you are in a heavy dread of summat and yet brave it, and behold! it is nought. The landlord and his missus, thinking little of us, sent the maid-servant to wait on us – a frightened, simple creature, like Miller's Polly, and nothing to be feared of. We had the parlour to ourselves, for folk go

1ome early from Lullingford market in the winter, seeing
what the roads are even to this day. I was glad of the red
ire, and the steaming tea, after the sadness of that house
with its dead light.

Gideon began to talk after a while, very slow, and as if
the words cost gold.

'Now, Prue, I've gotten a deal to say, and if we dunna
want to be benighted, I'd best start. You know as me and
Jancis have taken up together in good sadness?'

'Ah.'

'I didna think to care about any wench like I do about
that girl, Prue. Catches at a chap's vitals, she do. I never
meant to go furder than a bit of fun. I didna reckon to
marry, nor yet I didna mean lawless love. I meant fair
by Jancis, and so long as we had our Sunday evenings it
was all right. When there's no gainsaying there's no burning
in the blood. Gainsay, and the blood's on fire. Afore old
Beguildy found us out we were contented enow and as
innocent as two pinks on a stem.'

'And still be that last,' I says.

'Ah.'

He looked strangely on me for a while, and said –

'You've got the second sight, seemingly, our Prue.'

'No. Only a bit of sense.'

'Well, now as the old man's given me the go-by, I did
hunger and thirst after Jancis pretty near as much as I do
after the place yonder, and the money and all as goes with it.'

'Not more?'

'Laws, no!'

'Then you dunna love Jancis in good sadness, Gideon.
You do but lust after the girl in carnality.'

'Dear to goodness! It met be Parson preaching. That's
what the book-learning does to a woman.'

He laughed a bit, awkward like, and began stuffing baccy
into his pipe. But I knew that if I'd got any wisdom it was
never book-learning as gave it me, but just the quietness
of the attic.

82

'Well, big words or not it's no matter,' he said. 'I want the wench. I want her so bad that I'd very near set my heart to give up all and bring her to Sarn and order one of them rush cradles off Missis Beguildy. So then, to conquer the longing, I planned to bring you to see the place, and talk about it, and maybe begin to buy some bits of things agen we furnish.'

'To harden your heart the more.'

'Ah. And I planned to get some education off you after a while, and gather power to me at election times, and be so well thought of that I could even put my heart on a squire's girl.'

'Miss Dorabella!'

'No less. What be she, after all, but a woman? She hanna got more to give than any other woman, and what would any man, even the Lord of the Manor, do more for a girl than get her with child?'

'Husht! They'll hear in the kitchen and be angered at such wild talk.'

'True talk.'

'Maybe true. But nobody'd like it the better for that.'

'Ever since she threw me that first saucy look I've had it in mind. She angered me and pleased me both. So I thought if so be I could bring myself to give up Jancis – for either I mun give up Jancis or I mun give up all thought of the other – then Jancis met have taken up with Sexton's Sammy.'

'It would nigh kill the girl, Gideon, and Sammy's no woman's man, and he's pretty well crazed with learning texts, into the bargain.'

'Oh, he'd take her if I'd let un. She stirs him to anger with her flighty ways and being a wizard's wench and all. I see a look in Sammy's face time and agen. Wed with her and tame her, that's what Sammy ud do.'

'But that would be a cruel thing, Gideon.'

'Well, I'd a mind for it when we set out for market. I

83

thought to throw Jancis at the fellow's yead like I throw a crust to Towser, for it mun be one thing or other. And she'd have been contented enough when the children came. Though, Lord help 'em, they'd ha' had Sammy's scowl and bin born with their mouths full of texes. But she'd have seen nought wrong with 'em. Anyway, that's what I'd settled in my own mind.'

'Dear to goodness, what a God Almighty!' I says, mocking a bit, though I knew he could ha' done it if he'd a mind. He was ever a strong man, which is almost the same, times, as to say a man with little time for kindness. For if you stop to be kind, you must swerve often from your path. So when folk tell me of this great man and that great man, I think to myself, Who was stinted of joy for his glory? How many old folk and children did his coach wheels go over? What bridal lacked his song, and what mourner his tears, that he found time to climb so high?

'But now,' said Gideon, 'my mind's set, and I shanna change agen. I wunna give up either Jancis or the place at Lullingford here; I'll have both. And I'll lead Jancis out in a gown as would stand of itself, with her bosom bare as a lady's, at the 'unt ball, in front of Miss Dorabella. Not only that neither. But when you and Jancis be at the grand place, and the gentry calling in their carriages –'

'And Mother! You've missed out Mother.'

'And me a man of standing, more looked up to than Squire, and not yet old, nor near it, then –'

He was quiet a long while, thinking.

'Well, Gideon,' I says, 'what then?'

'Why then, if Dorabella Camperdine comes across my path with them black eyes and that red smile, let her look to herself. I'll take her. Out of wedlock, I ool, for what she said to you and me to-day. And when the poor wizard's wench is my lawful missus, I'll make Squire's girl a w'ore.'

With that word he banged down his fist on the table so that the tankard of ale rolled on the floor.

84

'If you be so set in your ways,' I says, 'there'll be more than a flagon of ale spilled, my dear.'

'You talk like an old ancient woman, Prue. I be as I was made. None can go widdershins to that.'

I can hear Gideon say that now, gruff and short and with a kind of broken-hearted sound. It was as if he'd give all to be as he could never be; as if his soul in that hour, away from Sarn and all its ancient power, wrostled mightily to be free of itself. Maybe you've seen a dragon-fly coming out of its case? It does so wrostle, it does so wrench, you'd think its life ud go from it. I've seen 'em turn somersets like a mountebank in their agony. For get free they mun, and it cosses 'em a pain like the birth pain, very pitiful to see. But in our Gideon it was worse to watch. There he sat, by the comfortable fire, with the spilled beer gleaming on the quarries like dark blood, and he said no word for above an hour. I know it was that, for when he went into his trance I heard the missus of the inn call to the maid-servant to turn the spit and hasten on the meat, for supper must be served in an hour. Then all was still, and I sat with folded hands, seeing Gideon's dark face there opposite when the fire blazed up. I sat as mum as a winter blackbird. It seemed to me that the mighty hand was upon him, striving with him to make him go widdershins to what he was, to what Father had made him, and Grandad, and all of them, back to Timothy, that had the lightning in his blood. I could see in mind Lullingford New House, and the light wandering, as if it wanted to steady and shine. I wished it might be well with Gideon, and that he met take Jancis, not for vengeance but for love, and because she was the candle of his eye, and his dear acquaintance, and not for lust. And I wished he might take thought for Mother, and even for me, that I be not like his dog or his bought slave.

After a long lapse of time I heard a voice outside say,

'Is all finished?' And another voice answered, 'Ah, all's

85

done.' It had a solemn sound, though I knew it was only the dinner they meant.

Gideon stirred and muttered to himself.

'Or die in 'tempting it,' he said.

So I knew we were all set out on a dark road, Gideon and Mother and me, and now Jancis.

We went out and saddled the nags, and set forth for home through a world as stiff as a rock, driving the oxen afore us. The dumbness had come back upon Gideon. The outing was over. The road puddles were gone beyond crackling-stiff, and were iron. And the hedges were even as the wrought-iron gates of Lullingford New House. It was the middle of the night when we came past Sarn Mere, and saw the ice a deal further out, and the lily leaves frozen under.

'Well, it's bin a very costly day,' says Gideon, 'and I'm in behopes you've enjoyed yourself.'

I knew it hurt the lad sore to spend. It was a crust in pocket and a sup of water mostly, on market days. So I put the old men and Miss Dorabella out of mind, and only said –

'Ah, it was grand, and thank you kindly, lad.'

'And you'll agree to all?'

'Ah, didna I vow it?'

'But that was afore Jancis.'

'I agree to Jancis. But it ud be all one if I didna.'

'Not if you wouldna work.'

'Oh, I'll work. I never was afeard of work.'

All of a sudden a sweet scattered whistling came falling from the dim moony sky.

'Hark!' he says. 'The Seven Whistlers.'

But I said I thought it was only some magpie-widgeon we'd disturbed at the end of the mere, being mortally afeard to think of those other ghostly birds.

'No,' he says. 'No. It be the Seven Whistlers, sure enough. It bodes no good.'

This was a strange thing for Gideon to say, for he mostly

86

laughed at signs and bodings, and I could not but think of it, up in the attic after.

Mother and Tivvy were sitting up for us, and seemingly Mother had seen us in the tea leaves, drownded in Sarn. She'd scarce believe in us for a long while, but cried and wrung her hands and said, 'They binna real. It's only the *know* of them.' So I was bound to give her one of my Christmas presents to comfort her. She was ever a child in heart, was poor Mother. She was so simple and trustful that I always thought it would be as wicked to hurt her as to hurt a babe in swaddling clothes, or a poor moth flittering in the dusk. Ah, an evil thing, a devil's trick, to betray such a trusting heart, such trembling, praying little hands!

'I be to lie in your chamber, Prue,' says Tivvy. 'I be glad, for it's cold lying alone, in black frost weather.'

She looked slanting at Gideon, and I could see she was nearly wild with jealousy of Jancis. And indeed Gideon did look a proper fine man, with his face all frosty red and his eyes lit up with the day's doings. He'd but to nod, and Tivvy ud follow. But he was never one to chop and change, and his mind was made up, so I knew it was Jancis or none. I didna want Tivvy in my bed, she did so snore and snoffle in her slumber. So I waited till she was fast, and then I took the lanthorn and Father's old sheepskin coat that lapped me up feet and all, and I went to the attic and wrote in my book. It was always my custom, if things grieved me or gladdened me, to write them down in full. Also I had much need of the peace that was in the attic, after such a bitter dose of the world beyond Sarn. Because I had no lover, I would lief have been the world's lover – such world, that is, as I could reach. I was like a maid standing at the meeting of the lane-ends on May Day with a posy-knot as a favour for a rider that should come by. And behold! The horseman rode straight over me, and left me, posy and all, in the mire.

Chapter 4: *The Wizard of Plash*

CHRISTMAS went by us and nought stirred the quiet, unless you count killing the pig. Nobody came Christmasing, for there was nowhere for them to come from, and nothing for them to come for. Mother was very middling with a cough, and took to her bed, so I didna go for a lesson till the New Year. But on New Year's Day I went, and, as I ever liked to pay first, I took the oxen straight away to the field I was ploughing for Beguildy. He couldna abide ploughing, so for every lesson I did so many furrows. I could plough nearly as well as most men, though not so well as Gideon. He drove the straightest furrow I ever saw. It was impossible to him to do anything ill. What he did, whether it was to be seen or not, whether it was done once in a way or every day, must be done as if his life was on it. He'd have no makeshifts. He'd thatch the ricks, even though they were to be cut into straight away, as well as if he was working for the thatchers' medal. Working by his lonesome in the fields, hedging or binding sheaves, with only the tall clouds for watchers, and the woods, floating on the summer mist, he'd still labour like a man showing his mettle at a hiring fair. Times, I thought it was pitiful, the way he'd give himself no rest. And times I could almost see the crowd of folk, the farmers watching, the judge sitting in his waggon or trotting to and agen on his cob. I could almost hear the muttering of the folks, the jeering when Gideon bungled, the roar of cheering when he did well, and the judge saying in his loud voice, 'I give the prize to Gideon Sarn, best man in the hedging, the binding, and the ploughing.'

Then I'd come to myself and see only the tall clouds, that hadna stirred, the tall hedges with meadowsweet below, the woods and the hills and the sweet blue air with larks hanging in it as if them above had let them down on threads, and shaking so with their joyful song that they threatened to break their threads. Not a bit did they care who won the prize, nor which of them sang best or loudest, so long as all sang, so long as none lacked nest or cropful, drink of dew and space to sing in.

These things I thought while I was ploughing the five-acre field at Plash with the white oxen, that looked yellow in the deathly white of the hoar-frost which lay over the earth like a shroud, though not too hard for ploughing.

As the share went onwards, the reddish, turned earth shone richly, and the rooks followed, for they were sore clemmed, poor things, walking stately in the furrows.

In a while Jancis came running across from the house with her mother, all agog to tell me of the handfasting of her and Gideon and of how angered Beguildy was. Jancis did truly look as lovely as a fairy with her rosy face and yellow curls. Missis Beguildy came panting after, apron flying, and loaded with news, like one of the French frigates folk tell of.

'But we wunna starve here like crows,' she said. 'Come you in and have a sup of tea. Sarn brought me a pound canister, no less!'

I knew he must be very deep in love to bring more than a quarter, but I said naught, only finished my furrow and unspanned the cattle.

'We can have a nice chat, for Dad's busy in his room, curing Miller's Polly,' says Jancis.

'What's to do with Polly?'

'It's what *inna* to do with the child,' says Missis Beguildy. 'First she got the chin-cough and now she's got the ringworm. She's always got summat. He's put her in a chair with a string of roasted onions round her neck, and I'm sure I cried quarts getting em ready. Dunna you ever be wife to a wizard, Prue. It's like what it says in the good book, and I wish I could go to church Christian and hear it, it be like it says, 'I die daily.' Ah, it's like that, being wife to a wizard. If it inna onions it's summat else. I'm sure I near broke my neck fetching bletch from the church bells for this very child, to cure the chick-pox, the maister being a deal too bone-idle to fetch it himself.'

'Never you mind, Mother, when I'm married I'll look after you,' says Jancis.

I couldna but sigh to think what a many plans they were all making, and each plan cutting the throats of the others. I put the oxen in the shippen and came in. There was a good fire and a pleasant scent of tea, and I was bound to feel a bit glad that Polly was such a measly child, though it *was* unkind, for I knew Beguildy ud be a long while curing her. Mother always said the mill children were measly because the water-fairy in the pool under the mill-race put her eye on their mother afore they were born, but Gideon said it was because they were fed on the flour the rats got into, and Missis Beguildy said it was because they sent em to Beguildy to be cured.

'A dose of brimstone and treacle, that be what she wants, and some good food. But the mill's no place for good bread, no more than the farm's a place for good butter, seeing it means cash, and the home folk get the leavings.'

Just then Beguildy popped his head in, and looking dreamily at his missus said –

'I want some May butter.'

'May butter! You met as well ask for gold. How dun you think I've got any May butter, nor June nor July butter neither, when we sell every morsel of butter we make almost afore it be out of the churn, and never taste nought but lard?'

'I'm bound to have May butter or the charm wunna work,' says Beguildy in his husky voice.

'What be it for?'

'To fry the mid bark of the elder and cure the chin-cough.'

'Well, for all the butter, May or December, as she'll get in our place, she may die of the chin-cough!' shouts Missis Beguildy. And with that, a loud roaring came from the inner chamber, because poor Polly thought she was at death's door.

'Go and read in your old books, and find summat easier,' says Missis Beguildy. 'I've summat better to think of than charms.'

"You be above yerself, woman. You think to see our Jancis wedded and bedded and rounding to a grandchild all in a lantun-puff. But I tell ye not every troth ends in church, not every ring holds wedlock, not every bride-groom takes his vargin, and I dunna like the match! Owd Sarn still begrutches me that crown, though he be where crowns buy nought. And I tell you young Sarn was born under the threepenny planet and 'll never keep money. Sleeps on his face, too. And them as does that drowns. My gel's not for Sarn. You may ride rough-shod over my wish and will. You may send out bidding letters for a love-spinning, which is all to the good. But still I'll bide for a higher bidder. Why, she be as white as a lady and as sound as a well-grown tater! No squire nor lord even but ud take it kind to be asked to lie beside her.'

'But not to wed with her.'

'What of it? He'd pay, wouldna he?'

By this, Jancis was roaring-crying as well as Polly. Beguildy popped into his room again, and we set to work to comfort her. We drew close in to the fire with our tea and planned for me to write the bidding letters for the love-spinning.

'And a caking into the bargain,' says Missis Beguildy.

'You make money by a caking. And weaver shall come and stop a tuthree days and make up all we've spun.'

Jancis clapped her hands.

'Oh! I dearly love a Do,' she said.

'Ah, so do I.'

'But the caking be the best of all. Oh, I love Gideon dearly for asking me to wed!'

All the while as we talked we could hear poor Polly coughing and whooping sore, and Beguildy shouting –

'Quiet now, hush yer noise, I say! Curse ye! Ye're cured!'

Then Missis Beguildy asked me to write down the biddings for them to see. So I did, and they were mighty pleased, for all they couldna read what I'd written any more than two butterflies in the hedge can read the mile stone.

'Put down,' says Missis Beguildy, 'as Jancis, only daughter of Mister Felix Beguildy and Hepzibah his wife, is promised and trothed to Mister Gideon Sarn, farmer, living on his own land at Sarn. And put down as they'll be wed as soon as maybe, and that Jancis invites em to a love-spinning.'

'And put down,' says Beguildy, popping his head in again, 'that you're a parcel of fools, and that this marriage shall not be till Sarn Mere goeth into the earth whence it came. For I've seen in a glass darkly a young squire that rides this way with his pockets full of gold.'

When Polly was gone, coughing as bad as ever, and I went into the other room for my lesson, I gave Jancis a little pat on shoulder, for I was sorry for the child. She looked more than ever like a petal of the may on a day of cold rain.

'Well, well now,' says Beguildy, 'I make no doubt you've ploughed a tidy bit?'

'Ah.'

'Well, what'll I learn ye?'

'Learn me to write "*Marriages be made in heaven*," Mister, and "*Whom God hath joined together let not man put asunder.*"'

He chuckled a bit.

'Clever wench! Clever wench! But you'll not get the better of me. Rather shall you write, "*Intermeddle not with high matters*." Dunna a wizard, as knows the fortunes of a parish, know what be best for his own?'

'Leave be, Mister! There's enough agen the poor child, what with Fate and such a pigheaded man as Gideon.

If you meddle, maybe you'll do harm as you canna mend.'

'Namore, namore! I've said me say. Dunna weary me.'

He beat lightly on his little music, which was a sign that his patience was over. As the notes tinkled out, I knew it was useless to argle any more. For as there was no power or sweetness in his flinty music, such as there is from harp and fiddle, so there was none in his soul. It gave a small and flinty music because it was a small and flinty thing. He'd got no pity because he'd got no strength. For it inna weaklings and women that pity best, but the strong, mastering men. They may put it from them as my brother Sarn did. But even so it will come upon them some day, and the longer they deny it the stronger it will be when it comes. Ah! It met even be such an agony as will make a man hate his life.

Chapter 5: *The Love Spinning*

IT took a long while to get ready for the Do, it being a caking as well. A good few of the religious sort held that cakings were wickedness, being in the nature of gambling. But for us women, leading such lost-and-forgotten lives, they were a bit of enjoyment, and even Sexton's wife said she'd come and bring Tivvy. She got Missis Beguildy to fix it on a day when Sexton was going with Parson to a place a long way off to look into the case of a woman taken in adultery. She knew Sexton ud stay till the bitter end, and wouldna be raught back till the small hours. And even if he found out, he'd be so contented at the punishing of a sinner that maybe he'd not be more than grumbling-angry.

The name *caking* was given because we played cards for cakes. To tell the sober truth, it was real gambling. The woman who gave the Do made a big batch of cakes, saffron or rich sponge, and sold them to the guests at a penny each. Cakes were what we played for, and the losers were bound to buy more, whereas a good player could go away with a big basketful, or she could sell them to the losers at twopence each.

Mother was not to hold or to bind, but she must come. Gideon promised to look after our jobs for the day, so we set out early. We were to make a day of it, spinning all the forenoon and then, after the noon-spell, settling down to cards.

It was a fine fresh morning with a damp wind full of the scent of our ricks. There's no scent like it for bringing summer in winter. When I smell it now I see the long gleamy waves of grass like green silk, and the big red clover bobs, and corncrakes running low in the thick grass, dark with dew.

But at that time the first thing it put me in mind of was how hard-got it was, how we'd sweated and laboured by moonlight, and got up agen afore we'd had time for a dream, to sweat and labour once more. Still, it smelled pleasant, and so did Gideon's bonfire of old hedge-brushings, and the deep floor of leaves in the wood, and the pine-trees where there were always canbottlins cheeping and playing.

Mother looked well in her big poke bonnet and frilled tippet, like a bright bird with her quick brown eyes and red cheeks. We only took the little spinning-wheels, seeing we were to spin flax and hemp and not wool, so I could carry them easy. The mere was a bit cruddled with ice at the north side still, but you could tell that spring was afoot though it was but February, by the mating-games of the water-ousels and the nesting caw of our rooks. There were green tongues on the woodwind sprays too, so bright, they minded me of the tongues of flame that

94

came down from heaven. In that dead time, coming so quick and fresh, they always seemed more to me than all the honeysuckle blossoms of the summer.

When we came through the oakwood Mother smoothed her mittens very complaisant and said –

'I binna tending swine this day. I be a lady.'

'Indeed to goodness you be,' I said. For I did dearly like her to enjoy herself. I said I made no doubt she'd win enough of cakes to keep us all for a week of nine days.

'Will Jancis be a good daughter to me, think you, my dear?'

'I make no doubt of it, Mother,' I said.

'Will she leave me my own place by the fire and speak kind?'

'Ah, she ool, I know. But you needna fret, for it'll be many a long day afore those two are shouted in church.'

'I'd lief not. I'd lief be a granny, Prue. Will the babe favour Gideon or her, dun you think?'

I said, not having the second sight I couldna tell, but I thought it ud be the very spit-and-image of its dad.

'Maybe, maybe. It ud be better, a power, that it should favour us than the Beguildys. It's bad for a babe to have a preached-against grandad.'

'Oh, there's not much harm in Beguildy, nor yet good,' I said. 'He be just a pleasant painted show like a blown egg.'

'I be glad he'll be away to-day.'

Missis Beguildy had sent a message by Gideon to her cousin at Lullingford to tell her to send for Beguildy on that day to come and cure her man's toothache. For seemingly he'd had one taken out by the beast-leech, and he parted so hard with it that the beast-leech, being a terrible man when his blood's up, loosened all the others lugging it out. So he got the toothache shouting-bad, and it was a good amusement for Beguildy to go

95

and cure it. He was always very proud of that charm
beginning –

'*Peter sat a-weeping on a marble stone,*'

and he'll go on saying it over and over till the person cries
for mercy. Then he claps on a bagful of salt, fire-hot, and
whether it's the salt or the charm, the person most always
says he's cured.

'They'll keep him late, not to spoil our sport,' says
Mother, clapping her hands softly like a child.

We came out into the open fields, and I thought no day
had ever looked so fair, yet knew not why. The hills
Lullingford way were blue as a summer sky, a deep promising blue, and there was a richness on the world, so it
looked what our Parson used to call sumptuous. There
were the red ploughlands and the old yellow stubble in
the sun and Plash Pool, glassy blue, and the mill roof in
the valley, red. All the grassland was clear green like
the green in church windows, or like the green hill far
away where no herb grows but the Calvary clover. Even
a summer day can seldom match such a day as that, when
the snow is but just gone and the waters freed, and when
there is a clear shining above and below. You could tell
there was summat out of the common at the Stone House,
by the great blaze of firelight in the window. Jancis came
running to the door and made her obedience to Mother
very prettily. We were the first, saving for Miller's Polly
and her mother. They were always first everywhere, for
they said an hour from home was an hour in heaven.
They wouldna explain more, only if you drove them hard
and asked them for why, was it the Mill-'us or the water
or what? Then they'd say, 'The Miller.' And if you said
why, what ailed the man? they'd say, 'Was he ever known
to smile, leave alone laugh?' And indeed he never was.
He'd got a lattance in the speech as well, and what with
the two things he was very disheartening to live with.
There was a foolish tale that he'd had a bogy out of the

96

water for sweetheart, and that when he got married she put silence on him for a curse.

Missis Miller was a poor creature, like a mealworm, but very pleasant-spoken. Sexton's missus was just the opposite. She always made me think of a new-painted coach, big and wide, with an open road, and the horn blowing loud and cheerful, and full speed ahead. She was as gay in her dress as a seven-coloured linnet, and if she *could* wear another shawl or flounce or brooch, she would. She wore so many petticoats it was a wonder she could walk, and once Tivvy said to me that to watch her mother undress was like peeling a big onion down to the core. Tivvy wasna one ever to make a joke, so it shows what a great thing it must ha' been to watch. I was used to think myself, seeing her and Sexton together, that she was like a big hank of dyed wool, and he was the thin black distaff it was to be wound off on to. When she and Tivvy were come, we were eight, and our wheels made a pleasant humming in the warm room the while we talked. The ox-driver's wife from Plash Farm came next with two tall girls, very quiet and meek for all their size. Folk said their father tied them to the ox-trevis every Saturday night and beat them to keep them in mind of their manners. They'd always stand up if their mother spoke to them, and bend their long necks like meek swans. The twelfth was the shepherd's wife from the moors beyond Plash. She was a strange creature, but fair to look upon, enough to make a man's mouth water. She'd got sloping shoulders and long hips, and her hair was like a blackbird's wings. Her eyes were clear green and her face was flushed like a ripe peach, and she'd smile in secret to herself like a fairy. It was said, but whether with any truth I know not, that the shepherd paid no money for the moors that belonged to a tavern-keeper in Silverton, but that every midsummer Felena, which was his wife, went up to the rocks at the hilltop and spent the night with the tavern-keeper. There were wilder tales too, about her being seen dancing by moonlight in a ring of cattle and sheep, mother-

97

naked, and how a shaggy creature with ram's horns that could only have been Satan, came and danced along with her, mopping and mowing, while the ring of beasts made a low moaning. But to me she seemed a pleasant, harmless creature, and very handy in all she did.

I could see that the ox-herd's wife didna care for her girls to be spinning with Felena. She was so respectable and highminded that she never spoke of anything between banns-up and baptism if she could help it, and took no notice of young couples during that time. She said nought to Felena, and it was Mother, ever kindly, who said –

'You spin like a fairy, Missis Felena.'

'There's nought else to do in the mountain,' said Felena in a low, singing voice, 'but spin and spin and spin, morning, noon and night.'

'Save on Midsummer night, my girl,' raps out Missis Sexton, 'and then I'm told you've enough to do and plenty!'

Felena turned scarlet and hung her head, and suddenly Moll and Sukey burst out, as if they'd wanted to say it for years and years –

'Oh, Missis Felena, is it true as you lie with the tavern-keeper and dance on the yeath mother-naked?'

Never did I see any woman so angered as their mother was. 'Sukey and Moll!' she says.

'Honoured ma'am?' says they, all of a twitter.

'Out with yer hands!' says she.

And stooping down she took off her sandal shoe, which she wore because it was a party, and slippered em both on the hands right soundly, till they roared agen.

I heard after that one married a farmer and the other a retired coachman, and both did well: it wasna for lack of correction if they did ill.

They went on with their spinning, meek as mice, snoffling over their wheels. Missis Beguildy was very put-about, for it seemed like being a melancholy party. So I asked Jancis to sing *Green Gravel* to liven us up. We all joined in, even Polly, whooping the while. Felena sang in a cool-sounding voice, and Sexton's missus sang very loud, and Mother quavering, and Missis Miller like a bird new come from the cage.

So what with the singing and the whirring, the kitchen was like a tree full of starlings. It was getting on for time to stop spinning when Mother said should we sing –

'*The Lord's my Shepherd,*'

and afterwards I spoke for having –

'*He brought me to His Lordly House,*
His Banner it was Love,'

And just as we were singing that, and the wheels going like churn-owls, there was a quick footfall without, and a rush of fresh air, and a long ray of sunshine from the door to me, and he stood there in the light looking upon us.

'He,' I say, as if you'd know him out of the world as I did.

He stood in the doorway, and I rose up from my seat in the shadows at the back of the room, as if he was my own bidden guest.

Chapter 6: *The Game of Costly Colours*

How did he look? What like was he? Was he well-favoured? It be hard to say. There are no looks in love, no outward seeming, no telling over of features. When you are but a moth in the candle of his eye, can you tell his stature, or if he be dark or fair? Did Magdalene, that was like Felena, know, when she lay at the feet of the only man she ever loved yet never loved, whether the carpenter's Son featured His mother or not, whether He was big or little in stature?

99

Shall we know, when we be come into His presence that made us, what outward seeming His majesty has? No. Only our hearts will tremble in the light. I could never tell you how he looked as he stood there; but I can tell you how the women looked that glassed him.

Tivvy and Polly gaped in wonder, finger on lip. Moll and Sukey leaned forrard as you lean to a fire in winter, and their mother gathered them to herself jealously. Missis Sexton spread her flounces, and Jancis coloured up and said 'O!' and set one of her ringlets straight, and said 'O!' again. Mother smiled at him, and Felena—well, Felena's eyes settled on him as a brown owl drops to its prey.

I sat down farther in my corner, and a faintness came over me. For here was my lover and my lord, and behold! I was haie-shotten.

The room was all so still, you could hear the drip of water off the roof.

All of a sudden he laughed out, and indeed it must have been a comical thing to see us all like mice when Pussy goes by, and to hear us one minute making such a to-do and the next making no to-do at all.

He off with his hat and made us a little bow and said –

'Sarvant, ladies! The weaver, if you please.'

If we pleased! As if we wouldna be pleased with anything he met say! So he was the weaver! Well, it made no manner difference to me. If he'd said he was the king of Fairyland or a murderer with the bloodhounds after un, it would ha' been all one to me.

'Kester Woodseaves, if *you* please, missus,' he says in a kind of merry mockery, looking towards Missis Sexton, she being the biggest, both in tallness and roundness.

Then Missis Beguildy brought him to the fire and made him take bite and sup. But I kept out of sight.

'Be you from far, sir?' asks Felena in her lingering way. Her lips were red and pleasant, though not kind.

Lullingford, missus,' he made answer, with a measuring look. 'Neither very near nor very far.'

'As the crow flies, near,' she said, as if she pleaded.

'Only we bain't crows, missus.'

'I live on the mountain over yonder,' she says; 'and I'm nigher to Lullingford, a power, than these.'

'A longish ride.'

'Not far! It be on your road to – a'most everywhere.'

I thought, 'She says all I'd like to say.'

'By gum, missus, I doubt it's on the way to hell,' he made answer.

They were like folk wrestling, but we did not know their quarrel.

'Oh, I be glad it's you that's to weave my wedding linen, and not the ugly hired man,' said Jancis.

'So you're to be wed, child?'

'Ah. To Gideon Sarn, sir. Dun you know Gideon?'

'I've heard tell of him.'

I wondered what he'd heard of Gideon. All in a minute it was more to me that he should like Gideon and Mother and me than that I should master the reading of Revelations, which beat me still, because of the strange words and the roundabout way of the telling. I'd laboured over it a long while, and labour brings a thing near the heart's core. Above and beyond that, I wanted to know the mind of John, he being lonesome on his bylet in the sea as we were at Sarn, and having many thoughts in his mind, both deep and bright. Now one like Tivvy had no thoughts at all, and you soon tire of looking in an empty porringer. And Mother had two thoughts or three, and Gideon two. So the mind of John had drawn me as none other did afore, but now the book of Revelations was but a windlestraw to this man's whim.

'Oh, Mister Woodseaves, will you come to my wedding if Prue writes you a bidding-letter?' asked Jancis.

'Maybe I ool,' he made answer, looking at her mother as much as to say that she could give him the go-by if she would. 'And who's Prue, that can write bidding-letters?'

I was in a swelter, but just as Jancis was going to rush on

me and drag me out of hiding, Sukey and Moll, who could never be quiet for long, burst out –

'Please, mister, ool you come to our weddings too?'

Then they giggled mightily, and put their heads together, shaking their curls and bending their long necks. Then they put their hands afore their mouths and ran across the kitchen to him, and one whispered in this ear and one whispered in that, and then they ran back, to their bench, two-double with laughter. Jancis, being near, heard Sukey whisper, 'I'd lief you were bridegroom!' I hoped their mother wouldna get to know, and slipper them again, for they'd saved me from being seen. I couldna bear that he should see me, for fear of a cold look, or scorn. I'd liefer stay down-under, like the daffadilly, lest the weather be winterly. For if she too eagerly comes up, desirous of the sun, she can but stand and shudder in the bitter frost, torn by the fangs of the winds. So she has lost her warmship, and yet hanna won through to summer.

'Sir! Be you wed?' asked Felena, and her voice was pretty and slippery like a grass snake.

'Why, no to that, missus.'

'Nor handfasted?'

'I'm thinking you were an attorney once,' he says, 'and stuck questions into poor men like skewers before you put em out of their misery.'

She took no notice, but only said –

'You be not of this country. You come from afar.'

'Oh, indeed to goodness, he is of this country, Missis Felena,' Mother chirped up like a little bird. 'He came back from being 'prenticed after his uncle was drownded. It was his uncle wove the mourning when my poor maister died, falling down in a fit and dying in his boots on the sabbath the bees did play.'

'And now he's dead and your A'ntie's dead, you live by your lonesome, I suppose,' says Jancis.

'Well, I do and I don't.'

'Dear to goodness, Mister, have you got a kept 'oman?'

This was Felena.

'Your thoughts be all beaded on one string,' says Kester.

Then Sukey and Moll burst out –

'Who cooks for ye?'

'Who sweeps for ye?'

'Who sews yer buttons on?'

'Who knits yer stockings?'

'I do for myself, my dears, and my thoughts be my company.'

He looked round very contented, and I could see he was thankful that none of all these women had a right to come over his door-sill.

'Well, thank you for me, Missus,' he said, putting down his mug and plate. 'And now for work. The loom's in the attic, I suppose?'

'Ah, I'll show you. There's a bed there too. You wunna finish for two days or three. There's a plenty for you to do. But come down and get your supper along with us, for it inna every day we have a randy.'

By the time she came back every tongue was at it. Sukey and Moll were quarrelling as to which of them, if they could do as they willed and go and work for him, should pour his supper ale and fill his pipe. It was enough to make an owl laugh.

'A nice young fellow,' says Missis Sexton, 'and a God-fearing, I'll lay, if the women let un alone.'

She looked very meaningly at Felena.

But Felena was fallen into a muse.

'I like him better than Gideon, a power, though Gideon *be* your brother, Prue,' says Tivvy.

Missis Miller spoke for the first time.

'He's as different,' she said, 'as different as mortal man could be, from the Miller!'

It was the greatest praise she could give.

Polly gave a loud whoop, as if to say that she agreed.

'Well, time goes by, and even a toothache must be cured

103

some day,' said Missis Beguildy. 'So we'd best set to at the caking afore my maister comes back. Thank you kindly for the spinning. We've done enough to keep that young man busy for above a bit.'

She brought out a big willow-pattern dish stacked with cakes, saffron and sponge fingers and gingerbread babies. These last are little men of gingerbread, with currants for eyes.

Sukey and Moll screamed with joy to see them.

'I dunna care about the others, if so be I can win a gingerbread man!' says Sukey.

'I'll win six,' says Moll. 'Six curranty babies for me!'

'You'll need more gumption than you've got then,' says Missis Sexton, 'for there's no game so hard as the game of Costly Colours. I've played it at every randy since I was a maid, and I'll lay that your Ma has too, and Missis Sarn and Missis Miller. Yet it's a difficult game to us still. And for you that have played it seldom or never, it'll go hard, but you'll lose every cake.'

'Tell 'em the way of it,' says Missis Beguildy, 'you've got such a head.'

Though she meant it in good sadness, it made me laugh. For indeed Missis Sexton's head was marvellous to see, with oiled hair in rolls and bobs and bands, and a high comb, and ribbons, and a vasty cap on top of all.

She went across the kitchen like a coach and six, and stood by the fire, telling us about the game of Costly Colours – how you counted, and of the trumps, and how three of a suit was a *prial*, and four of a suit was *Costly*, and how you could *mog*, or change, your cards, and of the deuces and Jacks, and 'Two for his heels,' and how if you made nought of your hand it was called a cock's nest, and you were bound to give a cake all round.

'I canna mind a word!' says poor Tivvy.

'Nor me,' says Polly.

So they stood out and left us ten, and it was only eight we wanted for two tables. So I offered to stand out.

'Why, you be the best player of all,' says Jancis. And the mother of Sukey and Moll settled it, saying –

'Stand out, girls. You can play turn-the-trencher with Polly and Tivvy. But no noise!'

They burst out crying, wanting to win the cakes But their mother said did they want more slipper, so they hushed. Then she bought them each a gingerbread man, and promised them some more at the end.

Felena drew at the same table with me. That is to say, it was the pig-killing bench with a board and a white cloth on it, for they had but one table.

'There's not one of us women but ud like a gingerbread man, is there, Prue Sarn?' she says. 'So us being too old for cakes, shall us make-believe to be playing for the soul of the weaver?'

'As you please,' I says. ' But it seems to me to be none of our business.'

'Why, Prue Sarn, you're as white as a shroud one minute, and as red as a peony the next, and such burning eyes! What ails you?'

I was angry, yet there was a warmship in this one thing, that she seemed to be counting me as one like herself, and not as one that was set aside from the game of love. I suppose, being under suspicion of dancing with the devil, she had a fellow-feeling with me for being mixed up with tales of witchcraft. For they'd even begun to say of me that I took shape as a hare on dark moonless nights, and went loping across the hills, and had a muse running under the churchyard. Such things were first said in idleness or mischief or to scare children, and then, in the loneliness of old farms, full of creakings and moanings on windy nights, they grew. And none can tell what such things will grow into at long last, nor what harm they may do. I didna like it much when Felena took his name on her lips, for all on a sudden it was a precious name to me. And it seemed to me then, as it ever has, that he was not a man to speak of lightly. Watching him out of my darkness beyond the settle, I had thought his wrath would be like a cloud-burst, though his smile was a spring day full of warm gilly-flowers.

Felena drew me farther from the rest.

'A man,' she said, 'whose like I've not seen afore, neither on the roads nor at market. The others are gaubies to him. Did you see the colour of his eyes?'

'No.'

'Nor could I see. His eyelids cut across them so straight, and the candle of his eye is so big and black, you canna see the colour. I'd lief be nigh him, to see.'

Her glass-green eye misted, and a rich, swooning look came over her.

'A man to gamble for,' she said.

'Take your places! Take your places! Cut for first deal in the game of Costly Colours!' cries Missis Sexton.

As I sat down I twisted the words of Felena in my mind, and said in the deeps of myself –

'Not a man to gamble for. A man to die for.'

We gave our minds to the game, and the four girls having been sent into the yard, the room was as silent as a dream. I could hear them singing *Barley Bridge* out there.

> *Shift your feet in nimble flight,*
> *You'll be home by candlelight.*
> *Open the gates as wide as the sky,*
> *And let the king come riding by.*

After a while the singing died away, and I wondered what mischief was brewing. But I'd enough to do, for I was determined to beat Felena, and as Missis Sexton was her partner and Missis Miller was mine, I knew I should have my work cut out.

The fire, mended with pine wood, gave a good, sweet smell and a warm light, enough to play by. It lit up the walls, and the sticky gingerbread men on the blue dish, and Jancis, as fair to see as if she'd been made out of solid

106

gold in old time, for an altar. In the quietness, with *Barley Bridge* in my mind, a sort of waking dream came to me.

I saw a great crowd of people beside the troubled water of Sarn. They were dressed in holiday colours, but their faces were evil. Then one came riding through them on a tall horse, and his face was the face of the weaver. A woman stood forth from the crowd. She had a necklace of green glass beads and green blazing eyes. She cried out –

'My body, my body, for a ride on your saddle!'

But he turned aside from her to one who stood hidden, in a torn, sad-coloured dress, with a hare-shotten lip. He stooped to her, saying –

'Ah, my dear acquaintance!'

And she gave him a sprig of rosemary. She said no word and she supposed he would go by her. But he set his arms about her and gathered her up before him on the saddle, and his right arm was strong around her. So they rode away, and the sound of the people died till it was less than the hum of a midge, and there was nothing but a scent of rosemary, and warm sun, and the horse lengthening its stride towards the mountains, whence came the air of morning.

'Two for his nob!' called Missis Sexton. 'Your deal, Prue.'

So I tucked my legs under the bench as well as I could for her furbelows, and went at it with a will. And may I say that Missis Miller and I won, out and out, to her everlasting astonishment. For she seemed to think it an impertinence on her part to beat Missis Sexton.

'You played like a demon, Prue Sarn,' said Felena.

It was late, so Jancis opened the door and called, 'Supper!' and in rushed the four hoydens, who seemed children to me, though I was nearly of an age with them. They burst out with their doings, though they had better have kept them to themselves.

'We've bin in the attic.'

'We sat on the bed!'

'He can whistle like a throstle.'

107

'He weaves as quick as ninepence!'

'He's got a green coat for Sundays and a Bible with pictures in it, and he can read the Bible.'

'He's got a watch, and a pipe with a silver band, and he won the wrestler's medal at Silverton.'

'He canna abide bull-baiting nor cock-fighting nor shameless women.'

'He likes a good song and home-brewed in reason, and a dance in the meadow, and the sound of bells.'

'He's got a great lump of muscle on his arm, like a frozen snowball.'

'We measured un on the attic door, and round the inches with the weaver's measure.'

'He be thirty-eight inches round the middle and five foot ten inches high!'

'He's got a pair of Wellington boots but he dunna wear 'em much, being above his station and a dommed lot of trouble to clean.'

'*He* said dommed, *we* didna.'

'He likes children and dogs and a quiet life.'

'He wouldna mind a missus of his own if she was biddable. Only he's never seen the woman he'd lief have yet.'

'His eyes be watchet blue, what you can see of 'em for the black middles and the lids and the lashes.'

'And if so be he'd got any sisters he'd like 'em to favour Sukey and me!'

'God bless me!' says the mother of Sukey and Moll, and I could see the slipper threatening, 'God bless me, not a thousand starlings in the reeds make such a din.'

It was lucky for the girls that their mother happened to have won.

'Get your tippets on now, this instant minute!' she said.

'Call un down, Jancis!' they pleaded.

So she called him to supper. The sound of the treddles and the thud of the batten stopped, and he came down.

Sukey ran to him and put summit into his hand. Then they made their curtsies and said –

'Thank you for me,' and followed their mother.

But Sukey put her head in at the door again, and gave a bit of a giggle and whispered –

'I gid him my gingerbread baby!'

'Out, girls!' ordered their mother, and off they went, with a lanthorn to light them, and the ox-goad in case of gentlemen of the road.

I went out to the barn, that Kester Woodseaves might not see me, and when I came back he was gone to the attic again. Felena had gone early, with a luring smile and a word for him.

'If you come our way, Mister, I'll learn you the story of Adam and Eve.'

The two from the mill were very unwilling to part, but at last they went, and we made ready to go also.

'A right good caking!' says Missis Beguildy. 'I've made enough on the cakes to pay weaver, and we've spun a deal. A Love Spinning's a great savation. So now you can tell your son, Missis Sarn, as we shall be ready with the bride and the linen as well, when he give the word to make the bed.'

Beguildy raught back as we set out. He was a bit peart, but not drunk. He said he'd met Miss Dorabella's cousin, and that he wouldna believe Beguildy could raise Venus. So he'd told him to come and see for himself.

'Venus? Where *is* the baggage?' says his wife. 'How can you raise her if she inna here?'

'But he'd only sing –

'Peter sat a-weeping,'

and play, very dot-and-go-one, on his little flints.

Chapter 7: *'The Maister be Come'*

'WELL, Sarn,' says Mother when we raught back, 'we've spun a deal and had a good randy, and now your wedding sheets be on the loom.'

Gideon looked bashful and said it ud be many a long day afore enough of money was gotten together for that.

'Our Prue won at her table!'

'Eh, did she now? Well done!'

He could understand that and respect it, for it was what he liked to do.

'Cakes enough to keep us a week of nine days!' says Mother.

'She was thinking of the savation, I make no doubt.'

'No, I wunna, Mother,' I said.

'Why, what was it then?'

'I dunno. I just wanted – Costly Colours, Mother,' I says, in a foolish way.

'But what use be they if you get no cakes with them?'

I said I supposed they were no use, but all the same I wanted them – the Costly Colours.

'She's sleepy,' says Gideon, 'that's what she is, else she'd talk sense. Best go to bed both.'

'Shanna I bide for the lambs?'

For at lambing-time I was used to sit up part of the nights, to let Gideon get a wink of sleep. But he said no, I'd had a day of it, and I might as well finish in style with a good night.

'I've bin as lazy as a lord all day,' he says, 'being obliged to be about the place to do the little jobs.'

He was a good-hearted lad, in spite of all, and if he missed to do a kindness it was only because he didna think of it, or because his mind was so set on one thing. And times if he'd been callous and it was brought home to him, he'd take it very hard, though often it was a long while after.

'Well, bed then, Prue!'

Mother hopped about with her stick like a robin with the rheumatics.

'It's been a grand day. A day to think on and talk over. Not wrong neither, for if we *be* still in our blacks, it was a kindness we were doing. None can blame for a kindness. Did I demean myself well, Prue?'

'Why, yes, Mother, no danger!'

'Did I spin well?'

'You spun grand.'

She ever had this way of asking, like a child, and she wound herself round your heart like a child, too.

'And such a nice young man, the weaver be, Sarn! A man any woman ud like for a son.'

'Be that Woodseaves?'

'Ah.'

'A fine wrostler, they say. A deal of booklarning for one of our class too. Squire offered un a clerking job at the Hall, but he wouldna take it. Said he'd liefer work with his hands and that he couldna abide politics, for they were all lies and he'd sooner keep clear. 'I'll weave white linen rather than black lies,' he says, and the owd Squire was very huffy. He'd like to have given Woodseaves warning to leave the place, only the house is hisn, willed by his uncle.'

Mother wanted to know if I liked the weaver.

'I thought you didna, my dear, for you never spoke, but went beyond the settle.'

'Like him?' I said. 'Oh . . . like him?'

'Why, lookye, Prue, you be asleep on your feet,' says Gideon. 'Off to bed now, or you'll do no work to-morrow.'

But indeed I was not asleep, but moithered. For it is a strange thing, and very strange, when the maister is come, and you would lief fetch him in and bring out the best, fresh butter and cheese in large dishes, and new milk, even to the top of the big stean, and when you'd put on your Sabbath gown and a posy, and smile at him with a yes for all his askings, and behold! all is nothing, for you have a hare-shotten lip, being under the ban of witchcraft.

'*The Maister be come, and calleth for thee. The Maister be come* . . .'

All night, in the attic, I could hear those words, very triumphing and yet sad. And when the dark thinned and shapes began to steal out from the blackness, and the small of dawn came in, and our game-cock crowed loud and sweet because it was the beginning of spring, I still heard those words, with kindness in them and a shiver of dread –

'*The Maister be come.*'

The words made such a murmuration, and were so piercing-sweet, that I wrote them in my book. Of all I had thought to write of the Love-Spinning and the game of Costly Colours, and of his coming, I wrote little. Yet when I open the book and see those four words in the very best tall script I could do, it all comes back to me so clear, as if it was to-day.

I looked at the loom, and saw him there, weaving. I looked at my copy book and wondered if he could do the tall script and the short, red and black, plain and flourished. And I was very sure that he could do them all, and more.

Next morning Jancis came running down the path, and I wanted to say, 'Is he well?' For it seemed to me that anything might have come to him in the dark hours. But I could only say, 'When does the weaver go?'

'Oh, to-morrow,' she said, as if it was no matter.

Then she cried and begged me to help her, for Beguildy was determined to raise Venus to confound the young squire, come what might.

'And it be me as is to be Venus! Oh dear! Oh dear! And it's the day after to-morrow. And I'm feared, Prue. For if Sarn knew that I'd stood up in a room all naked with a pink light a-shining on me, and a strange man there, never would he speak to me agen.'

'No,' I said, for I knew Gideon pretty well.

'And he'd be bound to find out.'

'Ah, he met.'

'But Feyther's mad about it. Raise Venus he ool. He says young Mister Camperdine laughed so, and clapped him on shoulder and said he'd give un five pound to do it, *whatever* he raised. Five pound, Prue! And when I said no, he beat me. And he says if I wunna do it, he'll put me to the field work, and beat me every Saturday for a year. Oh, Prue, whatever is to be done?'

'How's he going to set about it?'

'Oh, I'm to be in the cellar under his room, and the trap door's to be open, and I'm to have a rope under armpits on a pully to the roof, and Mother's to be in cellar to light the smoky stuff and put the rope round me proper. Then Feyther'll pull the rope in the kitchen, under the door, and I shall come up slow under the red light. He says it ull be too dimmery to see my face, but that's poor comfort. It wouldna be any excuse to Sarn's mind.'

'No. Be you very fond of Gideon, Jancis?'

'Ah, I be.'

'Do ye mind that text, "The Maister be come"?'

'In the Bible? Ah, I mind it.'

'Do you feel that way about Gideon?'

The pretty colour came in her face.

'Oh, yes, indeed, Sarn be maister.'

'And the other . . . goes to-morrow, you say?'

'What other?'

'Why, Mister Woodseaves.'

'Oh, he goes to-morrow.'

'Well, look ye, Jancis, I'll do it for you.'

'*You?*'

Her mouth was so round and so red in her astonishment that I could have hit the girl.

'Yes, me! I know it's a funny thing for me to be Venus,' I said bitterly.

'But Feyther ud know.'

'You say he's to be in the kitchen.'

'And the young man!'

'You say he inna to see your face. It'll be dark and I'll turn aside. And I'll put the muslin off the currant bushes over my head, so as he wunna see my dark hair. He'll see what he's come to see, the gallus young wretch, a naked woman. Then he'll pay the money and you'll go free.'

'Oh, Prue, you be good! I love you, Prue! I'll make it up to you some way. The best of it is that it wunna matter for you, seeing you'll never have a lover.'

So cruel can folk be, and mean nothing. This was the reward for my kind act. But those that say good doings are rewarded are wrong.

I'd like to have strangled her for that saying. The angry blood was roaring in my ears.

'Go away now,' I said. 'We'll talk of it to-morrow. But go quick now out of my sight!'

And with a puzzled and frightened look she went.

Chapter 8: *Raising Venus*

SERIOUS-MINDED folk will need to pass over this raising of Venus, but I will shorten it as well as I can. It seemed a dreadful thing to me, as I set forth when the evening came, that I should be going to show myself stark naked. For though I knew that Miss Dorabella and other grand ladies did take off the tops of their gowns, evenings, and come forth half bare, and think it no shame, yet women of our sort have more chariness of themselves.

As I went in by the garden way, through the door on the low level, not to be seen, I was all of a tremble, and it was only the pitifulness of poor Jancis that made me go through with it. We could hear Beguildy moving about up above, opening the trap-door and putting all ready.

I thought what a silly old man he was, to think anybody believed in his May-games. Then we heard young Mister Camperdine's horse, and there was a shuffling of feet above, and Beguildy pulled on the rope to show all was ready.

Oftentimes it is easier to die for love's sake than to be made a fool for love's sake. So I thought as I was lugged up into the dark room in a cloud of smoke that made me gasp, holding out my hands to keep me from knocking against the sides of the trap, and not knowing whether to laugh at the foolishness of it all, or to cry at the sorrow-fulness of this play-acting, which so mocked me. For here I was pretending to be the most beautiful woman that ever was, and a goddess into the bargain, and yet I was cursed as you know.

All was dimmery in the room. I could but just make out a figure at the far side. Beguildy was singing some queer kind of spell in the kitchen, and the young man's horse was stamping and shaking its bridle outside.

As I came up clear of the trap, and hung there in the rosy light, the young squire started forrard in his chair, and held out his hands like a child at a pastry shop. But I knew he was under solemn oath not to stir from his chair. I thought it must be a strange thing to go through life with men holding out their hands on this side and on that, to be always the pastry cake in the window with hungry eyes upon it. Then all of a sudden I heard a movement on the other side of the room, and turning that way I could have cried aloud, for there sat Kester Woodseaves.

Did ever Fate play such a trick? Here was the one man out of all the world that I must hide from, since already I loved him so dear, and so must never hurt him with my grief. And there he was, so close in the small place that two strides would have fetched him to me. He was leaning forrard like the young squire, and he made to hold his arms out and then drew back and gave a sigh, and I know now that the desire of woman was stirring within him. It came on me then with a great joy that it was my own self and no other that had made him hold out his arms. For in that place he could not see my curse, he could only see me gleaming pale as any woman would. Often since, I have wondered if he'd have been so stirred if it had been Jancis hanging there, crucified in nakedness, instead of me. Was it all of the flesh, as it was with the young squire, or did my soul, that was twin to his, draw him and wile him, succour his heart and summon his love, even, then? For I do think that the spirit makes herself busy about the body, and breathes through it, and throws a veil over it to make it more fair than it is of itself. For what is flesh alone? You may see flesh alone and feel nought but loathing. You may see it in the butcher's shop cut up, or in the gutter, drunken, or in the coffin, dead. For the world is full of flesh as the chandler's shelf is full of lanthorns at the beginning of winter. But it inna till you take the lanthorn home and light it that you have any comfort of it. And I have ever seen that the women with fair mounded cheeks, and breasts like the round pyatt where Felena danced, yet lacking any soul to laugh or weep in them, be not the ones that draw men. The ones that lure men to them by the tuthree, the score, and the hundred, as folk draw towards a lighted church, when the Easter Supper is ready, be often those that care not much for their bodies.

This is a strange thing, as true things are often, but not so strange as this wiling and summoning of a man by a woman flawed and cursed, a woman to whom it was said, 'You'll never have a lover.' Two men would have been my lovers that night if I'd willed it so. And as I saw the squire's shoulders stooped forrard with the weight of his longing I knew for the first time that, whatever my face might be, my body was fair enough. From foot to shoulder I was as passable as any woman could be. Under the red light my flesh was like rose petals, and the shape of me was such as the water-fairies were said to have, lissom and lovesome.

I hadna cared so much, nor been so dismayed, at playing this foolish game afore a stranger. But now I was all one blush from head to foot, and cold as ice as well. Every second was an hour, and I was shamed as if I had gone whoring. Yet I couldna but rejoice to have given my body in this wise to the eyes of him who was maister in the house of me for ever and ever.

I pulled the muslin over my face and looked slanting through it towards this wonder. For indeed he was a wonder to me then and always, not for his looks nor for anything that he did, but for the silent power of what he was, the power gathered up in him, as tremendous as a great mountain on the sky, that you couldna measure nor name, but only feel.

In the thinning smoke I could see him, with his face set beneath the shock of bodily love, for whether or not he loved me after, he did in that hour, and with the wounded look that is ever on the faces of men between the coming of the lust of the eye and its satisfying.

It takes a long while to write down, but I was only in the room as long as Missis Beguildy could count sixty. Beguildy was afraid they'd find him out if he allowed them too long, never dreaming, poor simple fool, that neither of them believed a word of his tales. While I was still faintly from the shock of seeing Kester Woodseaves, Beguildy called from the kitchen –

'Well, well, gentlemen, have I yearned my five pound?'

'Aye, aye!' says Mister Camperdine, with his look heavy on me, 'and more, and more!'

Beguildy began to sing another foolish rhyme, which was the sign for me to be ready to go down. Never was any woman so glad of a cellar as I was when I raught back there. I got into my clothes as quick as might be, for we could hear the squire argufying with Beguildy in the kitchen.

'What now? What now? Speak with a body?' Beguildy was saying. 'Now how can ye speak with Missis Venus,

117

and she dead and gone this thousand year? I fetched her back for ye, through the grave and gate of death, for five pound in cash, but I canna keep her. She comes a-walking on the air, in a cloud, for the time you can count sixty, and then she's gone. For she is but a beautiful bogy, seesta! and she mun be raught home by candlelight.'

There was a great burst of laughter at that, and as Mister Camperdine went out to his horse, he called back –

'I'll have another look at Venus one day, Beguildy. She's got a very tidy figure, by Gad, *wherever* she's from!'

As I crept home under the close net of winter boughs, my heart was all dumbfounded, even as the heart of a bride when first her lover looks upon her beauty. Only there was shame in this, and a great distress, being that I was no bride, and that I had been stared-upon and longed-after by a strange man as well as by him that was the world and all to me, though I had seen him but once afore.

It was strange to think that while I went about my house-work and out-door work to-morrow, slaving like a man, at men's jobs, I should be in my own soul the bride of the weaver. While I ploughed with Gideon, turning up the frosty earth, while I cleaned the shippen in my sacking and clogs, while I stood in the mucky fold giving the ducks and fowls their meat, looking more like a man than a woman, and more like a mawkin than a man, all this time I should be woman to him, dwelling beneath the light of his eyes, warmed by his smile, his banner over me being love. While I strode but half a furrow or so behind Gideon, I should be lying trembling in my lover's arms, fainty as I was at Beguildy's. Though my hands were hard and chapped and my face red and coarsened with weather, I should be, while I thought upon him I loved, a flower and the petal of a flower. For love is a May-dew that can turn the swartest woman to a Jancis. And though I had but the shadow of it, yes! the shadow of a shadow, as when you see the reflection of a water-lily in the mere, not still, but in ripples, so that even the reflection is all distraught and is not wholly yours, yet it had made the world all anew.

I wondered if aught would have happened to me in my outward life by the time the water-lilies came again, lying along the edges of the mere like great gouts of pale wax. There was but a mockery of them now, for amid the frozen leaves lay lilies of ice. Yet as I thought of Kester Woodseaves and what he had come to mean, I seemed to hear and see, on this side and on that, in the dark woods, a sound and a gleam of the gathering of spring. There was a piping call in the oak wood, a bursting of purple in the tree-tops, a soft yellowing of celandine in the rookery. When I was come into the attic, spring was there afore me, though it was so cold that my hands could scarce write. None the less, I put down in my book the words, 'The first day of spring.' And I wrote it in the best tall script, flourished. So I should ever call to mind the second time of seeing him I loved, and the first time of his seeing me. Not only had he looked at me, but he had looked with favour and longing, and though I knew it was only because the truth was hidden from him, yet I was glad of what I had, as a winter bird is, that will come to your hand for a little crumb, though in plenteous times she would but mock you from the topmost bough.

I took my crumb, and behold! it was the Lord's Supper.

Chapter 9: *The Game of Conquer*

IN the morning, ploughing one of the far meadows with Gideon, I saw yellow nut catkins in the hedge, and brought them home and set them in a jug on my locker in the

attic. I plucked them early, and tied a bunch to each of
the ox's horns, so all that day of sad-coloured weather
the white cattle went up and down the red field, which
was white-over in parts, so that they looked yellow, with
nodding gold plumes on their heads, as if it was a fair.
When we unspanned, Gideon said –

'What'n you been after, bedizening the cattle?'

'It's May Day,' I says.

Gideon looked bepuzzled, but he said, well, he supposed
I liked my jokes, and he didna complain so I worked
well.

'When'll this weary old ploughing be done, Gideon?' I
says, for of all things I hated it, not for itself, but because
it spread out over our lives till there was no room for anything else. He was in a fever to plough. Dawn and dark,
frost and rain, he'd be on the land, hard at it, and often
when it did the land more harm than good. All the farm
was to be corn. All the rickyard was to be full of corn.
Only grow enow of corn, he said, and we should be rich
afore we knew it. I couldna abide the new law, which
made it pay so well.

'As soon as we've got enow, off we'll go, Prue, and never
see the place again,' he said.

'I canna understand that, Gideon,' I told un. 'If you
were land-proud, I could. But it do seem so queer to
spend every bit of time and strength on the land, like a
mother with a child, and then not love it. It's as if the
mother cared nought for the child, but only cared to sell it.'

'Ah, that's the size of it, Prue. I dunna care a domm for
the land. Nor yet I dunna care for the money. Not *as*
money.'

'Well, what is it you *do* care for?'

'To get me teeth into summat hard and chaw it. To
play Conquer till there inna a cob nor a conker left but
mine. To be king-o'-the-wik and the only apple on the
bough.'

'But for why, Gideon?'

'You be always asking me for why. Because I was made like that and I canna go agen it.'

We always came back to that.

'The thing is to keep the right men in, so as they canna change the law afore we've made our money,' he said.

It was just as if the country was his mommet, to do his will and put crowns in his pocket.

'Which be the right men?'

'Them as keeps up the price of corn.'

'But the poor folk, that clem, would lief have prices down.'

'They mun grin and abide. Let 'em work. I work, dunna I?'

Indeed to goodness, he did work! He was nought but bone and muscle, and if he was a merciless man, he was merciless to his own self first. I said, would he side with Squire, at elections, in spite of what Miss Dorabella said.

'Ah, 1 doubt I mun. He's got a deal of corn land, he'll never let prices down.'

'And when'll you leave ploughing?'

'Not till we've bought the place, and there's money in bank into the bargain.'

'But when we've ploughed up all the farm, save what grass we're bound to keep for the beasts, then you'll be bound to stop.'

'No. If we hanna got enough of money, I shall start on the woods.'

'Oh, deary, deary me!' I said, for I was like to cry. It was the unkindest thing that he should think of the woods. For now there'd never be any rest for any of us, since the woods were ours all round the farm, and there was work in them world without end. The tears rolled down my face, and I could feel them, cold and slow as the cold evening light.

'Why, what ails ye?' says Gideon. 'Crying? Bless me, what a wench! Look ye, girl, we be working for the future.'

121

'I mislike the future,' I said. 'It's like the bran pie they give the Lullingford children, Christmas. You may get summat, but most likely you'll only get a motto. And if you get summat, ten to one it inna what you want, for what you want inna in the pie.'

'Dear to goodness, what a mort of idle words! The future's as you make it.'

'Why, no,' I says. 'It be like the blue country a traveller sees at dawn, and he dunna know if it'll be a kind country with farms sending up a trail of smoke in the sunset, and a meal for the asking, or if it'll be a wild, savage moor where he'll starve to death with cold afore morning.'

'Why there now,' says Gideon, 'you're starved with cold, that's what's the matter. You want a cup o' strong tea and a good plate of taters and bacon. And hark ye! If that inna Mother banging the tray I'll be dommed.'

Poor Mother set store by the evening time, being one that liked company. She said the days dragged so in the silent place, and she was timid, startled at the fall of a leaf or the creaking of a door. She was used to plead with me, time and agen, to leave ploughing and bide with her a bit. But I was bound to do Gideon's will, so I made up comfortable tales for her of the day when we'd be well-to-do, with men and maids and a kitchen girl and no pigs. She'd brighten up a bit, but soon she'd sigh and shake her head.

'A far cry, a far cry, Prue. Maybe I wunna last. I'd lief things were a bit easier now, my dear. I canna abide tending pigs in the 'oods. My poor legs do ache, and if I set down I get the rheumatics. And the pigs do go daggling about down by the water, so my feet be always wet. I'd liefer less maids and men in the years to come, and less pigs now. I'd liefer less company then and a bit more now. All that's a long way off, and no more satisfying than the many mansions of Paradise. Tell un that, Prue. Tell Sarn, my son, I'd liefer have a few things now, and not so many in the years to come.'

'Ah, I'll tell un, Mother. And you must think of the time when we'll leave ploughing.'

'Sarn'll never leave ploughing. Or if he does he'll do summat else. It's this-a-way with un, he canna rest. He's like a man I heard tell of, riding post across the land with dreadful news, foundering nags and buying fresh uns, with no thought but to get there. So when he got there and told the news he was so fixed in mind he couldna stop, but rode and rode, with no rest, crouching down and cutting the horse by day and by dark, going with no news to nowhere. They seyn he rides still. I tell you, Prue, it ud have been better, a power, for us and for him too, if my son Sarn had bin born an idiot boy, to play with coloured stones and put daisies on a string.'

She looked so strange, standing there in the fold, with her long staff and red cross-over shawl, with her mouth a-tremble and her eyes shining like a prophet's, and the great lean pigs gruntling and snouting around her, and Sarn Mere standing up beyond her like the blue glass round a figure in a church window. I wondered if ever they put pigs in church windows, in pictures of the Prodigal Son, and I couldna help but laugh a bit in a kind of pitiful way, thinking that this here was the prodigal mother, and how glad we'd be if Gideon was a bit prodigal too.

'What ails you, laughing?' she says.

'Only to think as you be the prodigal mother.'

'I dunna understand. I canna understand ever-a-one of my two chillun. Oh, deary me! But I take it unkind in you, Prue, to laugh when I be crying.'

Poor Mother! She said true things, times. She'd put words to my own complaint about the world, that laughed though I cried.

'There, there, I'll tell Gideon,' I said.

It was one of the queer things in our lives that I was the go-between, taking messages from Mother to son. She could never get courage to begin, nor to face his cold, steely look.

Next morning I spoke to Gideon. He was in the field afore me, as always. It was frosty and misty, so the ploughed land looked like tarnished mirrors, or like the mere in overcast weather, sheeny and not solid. Where the frost held and the sun shone, the fields were polished, like lake water with a gleam on it.

Gideon and the oxen came on slow, making a little solid dark picture in the lonesome fields. It put me in mind of the black oak figures carved on the peak of the gables on some of the Lullingford houses, and always looking very dark on the sky. The breath of the oxen and the steam from their bodies stood up about them and hemmed them in, so as they went up and down they seemed like a picture, round and all to itself, that somebody was moving about in the waste of fields.

'Gideon,' I says, 'Mother be very middling. She wants rest. Get a lad to mind pigs in the woods.'

'A lad! Dear to goodness, what lad?'

'There's Miller's Tim. He's not but seven, but he could mind pigs and I'd give un his tea.'

'What! Feed a great lad of seven every day of the week save Sunday? Be you mad, Prue?'

'Mother's very moped and middling. She wants rest and she wants company in the going down of the years, and a bit of comfort.'

'Amna I working for that? Inna she going to have maids and men, the best of good things, a pew in church, and real chaney to eat off?'

'Ah! In the years to come, if she lasts. But she met not. It be now that matters.'

'There's naught ails Mother. She can go on very well. She gets good air minding pigs, and she can croodle over the fire after dark, to ease the rheumatics.'

'And she's moped, lad. She wants me at home more.'

'Well, you will be when we leave ploughing.'

'That's a long day. Any road, you mun get a boy to mind pigs.'

'Mun, mun? Who be you to say that to me? I be maister of Sarn.'

'You've no right to drive Mother to death when she's old and ailing.'

Gideon gave me that withering look.

'Maybe,' he says, very slow and bitter, 'maybe you'd like to get wed and bring a lad to Sarn that-a-way, to tend pigs. That is, if anybody'll have ye.'

He picked up the plough handles and went on down the furrow. It needed a long while in the attic to wash out those words, but the power that was there washed them away in a while. I made allowance for Gideon, since he lost so many nights of rest, it being still lambing time. For lambing time is the shepherd's trial. In the black of night, in the dead of the year, at goblin time, he must be up and about by his lonesome. With mist like a shroud on him, and frosty winds like the chill of death, and snow whispering, and a shriek on this side of the forest and a howl on that side, the shepherd must be waking, though the pleasant things of day are folded up and put by, and the comforting gabble and busyness of the house and the fold are still, and the ghosts are strong, thronging in on the east wind and on the north, with none to gainsay them. So when Gideon was short with me I only took a bit more time in the attic. It was pleasant there when spring drew on, with a dish of primmyroses on the table and a warm wind blowing in. When April came we were still ploughing, and I was so used to it that I'd given over being tired, and enjoyed it, and sang to myself the while. It was grand to go down the red furrow with the share cutting strong into the stiff earth and shining like silver. It was fine to look away to the blue hills by Lullingford, and see the woods of oak and larch and willow all in bud between, as if a warm wind blew from there and called the leaves. It was pleasant, too, seeing the rooks follow in a string at my heels, looking as if they'd been polished with the andiron brush, and to see the birds again that had been away,

125

and to hear the water-ousel sing wild and sweet, and the lapwings change their winter cry for summat warmer. There were violets now to pull for market, and daffadillies in the corner under the ivy hedge, and tight pink buds like babies' little fists in the apple trees.

Mother cheered up a bit, and one day when we were having our tea by the window, with a bunch of gillyflowers on table, she said –

'We'll have the weaver.'

I gave a gasp and a choke, and Mother wanted to know what ailed me.

'Nought, nought, but why not the weaver's man? It ud be cheaper.'

'I like the best weaving.'

I fell into a dream, for if Kester was going to weave for us he'd have to come into the attic, walking to and agen round the weaving frame, looking out of my little window, making the place his place, so I should have him there for ever after. Yet still I couldna abide the thought of him seeing me, and I argufied for having the weaver's man till Gideon thought I was in love with the fellow, though he was said to be simple and had got fourteen children into the bargain. But Mother put on her spectacles and looked at me, and pushed them up and looked again, and settled them in place to look a third time.

'We'll have the weaver,' she said, and that was all.

It was the day after this that Jancis came rushing in, all wild, to say that Beguildy was going to take her to the hiring fair on May Day, unless Gideon could stop it. She came into the dairy where I was churning, and she said –

'Oh, Prue, the young gentleman's been again, and have me he will, leastways you!'

She gave a giggle in the midst of her crying.

'And Father says it's that or the hiring fair. It'll be three years, Prue. I'll be bound for a dairymaid or a kitchen wench for three years, that is, unless Gideon offers to wed with me now.'

'Gideon wunna, my dear, he's fixed in mind about the ploughing. Nought'll turn him from that.'

'But I shouldna stop it.'

'You'd be another mouth to feed. And if you ailed –'

'I shouldna. I be stronger than I look.'

'You canna tell, Jancis. When you wed, you begin a game of Blind Man's Buff that ends you canna tell where. And if little uns came, what about all that money Gideon's set on making?'

'Oh, deary me! Oh, I canna bear it, Prue. I do love Gideon right well, and once parted may be as bad as never met.'

'Well, you talk to Gideon.'

'And will you put in a word wiselike?'

'Ah, I'll put in a word. But what he wunna do for you, that be his dear acquaintance, he wunna do for me, that be nought but his hard-drove sister.'

Just then Gideon came across the fold to fetch the buttermilk for the pigs.

He stood in the dairy door, and I thought it small wonder she was sweet on him, for in his smock and leather breeches, with his black head bare and his eyes blazing on Jancis, he was as well favoured a man as you could meet in ten parishes. And I thought, as I looked round the dairy, that it was as good a place as anybody could wish for asking to wed. The sun shone slanting in, though it was off the dairy most of the day. The damp red quarries and the big brown steans made a deal of colour in the place, and the yellow cream and butter and the piles of cheeses were as bright as buttercups and primmyroses. Jancis matched well with them, with her pretty yellow hair and her face all flushed at the sight of Gideon. She was like a rose in her pink gown. Outside the window, in the pink-budded may tree, a thrush was singing. I mind it all so clear, and should, even if it wasna written in my book.

'You be early,' says Gideon.

'And welcome?'

'Oh, ah! You be surely welcome.'

127

She looked at me mischievously as if she was asking me if I did mind, and stood tiptoe for Gideon to kiss her.

'I've got news,' she says. 'Good news or bad, as you do make it.'

'Me?'

'Ah, it's this-a-way, Sarn, Feyther says I mun —'

She looked at me, helpless like.

'Beguildy wants to sell the child, Gideon. What's the use of mincing words? He wants to sell her to young Camperdine for his pleasure.'

Jancis hid her face in her hands.

'And if so be she says no, she's to go as a kitchen wench to the May Fair and be prenticed for three years.'

'What! Sell my girl? Beguildy'll sell my girl? Dang me, I could drown him dead for that!'

'He's not sold her yet, Gideon.'

'The better for un.'

'But she'll be bound prentice for three years away somewhere beyond Lullingford.'

Gideon stooped and pulled away her hands, looking fiercely on her face.

'Be you a true wench to me?' he says. 'Dang me, if you've lost your maiden'ead to young Camperdine, I'll lay un out with the pole-axe. Ah! And you I'll strangle.'

'No, no, Sarn, I hanna, I hanna,' she cried out. 'I be a good maid to you, Sarn, indeed I be.'

'But what's she to do, Gideon? For unless she'll be the young man's light-o'-love she's bound to go away.'

'I canna abear to go away.'

She burst out crying again. I waited for Gideon to speak, but he said naught.

'There's one other way, Gideon.'

I said it coaxing, for I knew it was his hour of choice for the two of them. The good road for both was in their power to take this day. It was one of the times in Gideon's life when he might choose his blessing, the path of love and merry days where the pretty paigle grew, the keys of

heaven, or the path of strange twists and turns, where was
the thing of dread, the bane, the precious bane, that feeds
on life-blood.

Jancis seemed to know also that their lives in some fashion
hung upon this hour. She stooped down and kissed his
hand, and she said in a soft, hoarse voice –

'O, be my sweetheart, Sarn!'

Gideon gave a kind of groan.

'I know where you be dragging me, Prue,' he said, 'with
your eyes so strongly upon me. You be pulling me down
to poverty and the loss of all I've dreamt of.'

'I'd work double, lad,' I said.

'What use? You know right well what would happen.
Could any man do other with a pretty piece like that for
missus? Mouths to feed, mouths to feed. Never no grand
house nor maids and men, nor pew in church. No money
for you. No 'unt ball for Jancis. No hail-fellow-well-met
with the gentry for me. If ever we make any money it
wunna be for years and years. We shall lose the house and
go pottering on, eating up all we make. A man with a
wife and family never gets on. He mun make his money
first.'

'But wouldna you work better if you were happy, lad,
with Jancis happy too?'

'Why, no. Happiness and idleness be twins. If you want
to work, you munna be happy nor miserable. You mun
just think of work and nought else. Another thing, if I take
Jancis now, in the teeth of young Camperdine's longing
after her, he'll be agen me himself and he'll set all the
gentry agen me. Whatever's made the man so mad in
love, it's done now, and we mun take care.'

He looked at Jancis suspiciously, and she prayed me
with her eyes to explain all. But that I couldna do. I'd
done a deal for Jancis, but that was too much. For I was
afraid that if I spoke at all it would get round to Kester
Woodseaves. Jancis was under promise that none should
know, saving only, in the utmost need, Gideon. So I kept

silence, and I canna see that it made any difference, for speaking would only have put it off, and Beguildy had made his mind up about Jancis, and if it wasna the young squire then it ud be somebody else. It was best for Gideon to decide once for all, then if he chose right he and Jancis could be wed, and it would be out of Beguildy's power to make any more plans.

'It'll only put off the riches for a bit, Gideon,' I said.

'No. It ud put em off for ever and ever. The best thing to put off is getting wed. We'll wait three year. That'll give us time to turn round. Not as I want to put it off.'

He fell silent, looking at Jancis. I could see the longing in his face, and he was all of a tremble. It was strange to see such a great strong fellow shaking like a woman that's seen frittening.

He took a step towards Jancis, and I made to go out, for I thought he'd take her in arms and all be well. But all of a sudden he muttered

'No, no!' and drew back. Then he said –

' There'd be no satin gown for ye to dance Sir Roger in at the'unt ball then, Jancis. You'd be sorry for that.'

'Ah.'

'Well, if you go for a dairymaid or summat you'll be yearning for it as well as me. Three year inna long. By the end of three year all the ploughland should be bearing well, and us'll be reaping what we've sown.'

'Dear Lord forbid,' I says.

Gideon fell into a rage, though why I never could think, and burst out –

'Why that, now? Why that? I'm well content to reap what I sow.'

'But not if its the bane, Gideon? Not if it's the precious bane as I read about in the book the Vicar lent me? You dunna want *that* amid the corn, lad, what grows in hell?'

'*Whatever* it is,' he says, 'if I sow it and it brings me the things I'd lief have, I'll welcome it.'

There came a little sobbing sound from Jancis, and when

I looked at her I saw beyond her golden head the spring day all o'ercast and the thorn tree lashing in a sudden wind.

'You'd best be going home-along, my dear,' I says. 'There's tempest brewing.'

'I shall come on Sunday, and tell your dad what I think on him,' said Gideon.

'No, no dunna anger him!'

'What do I care for his anger?'

'Oh!' she cried out, 'everything's all as I wouldna have it. Why canna folk live quiet and peaceful? Why must you be so fixed in your mind, Sarn? Hark at the wind rising! There's summat foreboded.'

She began to cry again, hiding her face in her apron.

'O, I wanted to send out the biddings and be shouted in church,' she said, just as she used to say, 'O, I wanted to play *Green Gravel*.'

Gideon snatched her to himself and kissed her, but he didna change his mind. Once he'd made it up, nothing ever would turn him.

'I mun go,' she said. 'Come and send me, Sarn.'

As they went, I saw her wring her hands and heard her say –

'Oh, I see a dark road going down into the water. And the sun's gone out. O, Sarn, dunna make me walk that road!'

All in a minute she'd faded away like a ghost in the wild, dark, stormy woods.

BOOK THREE

Chapter 1: *The Hiring Fair*

ON May Day, there being a deal of stuff for market, I borrowed the Mill pony again and set out with Gideon very early, while yet the purple blossom and the green leaves of the lilac trees were all of a grey blur. I'd pulled some lilac overnight for market, so we rode with the sighing of it and the good smell of it all about us. It was a very still morning. Not a breath stirred the young red oak leaves, and even the silver birches, that will shift and shiver in any breeze, like water-weeds at the lake-side, were all becalmed like weeds far down where not a ripple comes. Save for our horse-hoofs on the wet flinty road there was no sound, neither from the grey fields on either side, nor from the water, the woods or the sky. So still! It seemed to me some miracle might come to pass on such a day. The dawn could not hold its breath more if Judgment was to break that eve, and the dead rise. When the colour came in the hedges, the bird's eye, that was in great plenty, looked upon us, very simple and innocent, as if thousands of blue-eyed children watched us go by. The ollern trees that fringed the road dripped with yellow catkins. Beyond stood the hills, mounded out of sapphire stones like the new Jerusalem, and all becalmed under a sky without so much as a cloud. Not a bird nor a trail of mist of smoke stirred in all the plain. It seemed to me, as I rode alongside of Gideon without a word, while he frowned and darkened, thinking of Beguildy, that it was like a great open book with fair pages in which all might read. Only it was written in a secret script like some of Beguildy's books that he never locked away, knowing they were safe. For indeed every tree and bush and little flower and sprig of moss, every least herb, sweet or bitter, bird that furrows the air and worm that furrows the soil, every beast going heavily about its task of living be to us a riddle with no answer. We know not what they do. And all this great universe that seems so still is but like a sleeping top, that looks still from very swiftness. But why it turns, and what we and all creatures do in the giddy steadfastness of it, we know not.

I said to Gideon that it was like a book.

'Book?' he says. 'Why, no, I see no book. But I see a plenty of good land running to waste, as might be under corn.'

So we see in the script of God what we've a mind to see, and nought else.

We came beneath a wild pear tree in early blow, and it put me in mind of Jancis.

'Now I wonder,' I said, 'where Jancis'll sleep this night?'

'At Grimbles'.'

'How can you tell?'

'I can tell because I say it is to be. Missis Grimble is for-ever changing dairymaids, and I hear tell she's after one this year.'

'It's a long ways off, Gideon.'

'None the worse for that, she'll be out of young Camper-dine's way.'

'She'll be terrible lonesome.'

'You can write me a letter to her now and again.'

'And welcome. But how'll she answer?'

'I thought of that.'

Gideon spoke triumphing-like.

'It's such a great big place that they have the weaver every month or two. Weaver can write for Jancis.'

'What?' I says with my breath very short, knowing I was going to say that name, 'what, Mister Woodseaves?'

'No other.'

Why, dear to goodness, here was a queer trick of fortune for me! I was to write love-letters for him I loved to read, and he was to write letters back for me to read, once in

133

every few weeks. I let the pony go her own pace, and we fell behind, for Mill pony was like Mill folk, and took everything sad and quiet, as if she'd been discouraged above a bit.

There'd be letters coming in the summer days, written in his own script, with his own wording and turns of speech. His hand would ha' moved slow along every page, over and over, while he looked down at the lettering with those long-shapen blue eyes that pierced to the heart's core. Of course they'd be letters to somebody else from somebody else, and it ud be all the wrong way round, for his would be in the name of Jancis, to Gideon, and mine would be in the name of Gideon, to Jancis. It would all be moithered and twisted and topsy-turvy like the water-lily shadows in the mere, when I'd lief it met be clear and real. Still, I could speak my heart out. I could say the things I'd thought never to say. I could lay my soul as naked afore him as I myself had been, for no eyes but hisn would read my letters. Not that my soul was anything to show, but yet I greatly desired to show it. This is a very strange thing, and ever to be found in lovers. I couldna help but laugh to think what a figure of fun Gideon would look dizened out in my soul, and how dumbfounded Jancis would be, hearing things read out of Gideon's letters that no power of angel nor devil would ever make Gideon say, and how she'd pucker up her face and wonder if weaver was making game of her, and then think, 'Oh, well, folks inna themselves when they're writing.' I was laughing over it all when I heard Gideon shouting –

'Hi! Hi! Where bin 'e going? Pony'll put fut in the ditch in a minute and break her leg and all the eggs in your basket into the bargain. What ails you, dreaming?'

It was but just in time. Pony and I got out of the ditch as best we might and went on, a bit crestfallen and very mim and careful. Then it came over me on a sudden that I should see the mind of Kester Woodseaves in those letters as open as the sky. I should know him as if I lived along of him. For it inna by the deal that's said, but by what's in the things said, that you can know a person. Just as it inna the extra length or breadth of a gown that keeps you warm, but the quality of the stuff. In all he wrote, I'd find him. For you canna write a word, even, but you show yourself – in the word you choose, and the shape of the letters, and whether you write tall or short, plain or flourished. It's a game of *I spy* and there's nowhere to hide. I thought how Mister Woodseaves would go tramping home, pleased to ha' done a kindness, and very pleased to be unlocking his own door, lighting his own fire, and keeping himself to himself. And all the while he'd have showed himself to me, let me into the house of his mind, bid me to sit down by the fire of his great kindness.

> '*He brought me to his noble house.*
> *His banner it was love.*'

'Prue!' shouted Gideon. 'Dang the girl! Oh, dang the girl! Pony's got her foot in the reins and her teeth in the grass, and here I've been obleeged to come back half a mile. Marketing day and all! Whatever ails you? Be you sickening for summat? Dear to goodness! Anybody ud think you were in love!'

Arter that, pony and I were very careful. We kept our thoughts on the road and the market, and as you always come, at long last, where your thoughts are, so we came to Lullingford and found the Hiring Fair just beginning.

The long row of young folks, and some not so young, who were there to be hired, began near our stall. Each one carried the sign of his trade or hers. A cook had a big wooden spoon, and if the young fellows were too gallus she'd smack them over the head with the flat of it. Men that went with the teams had whips, hedgers a brummock, gardeners a spade. Cowmen carried a bright tin milk pail, thatchers a bundle of straw. A blacksmith wore a horseshoe in his hat, and there were a tuthree of them, for a few big farms would club together and hire a blacksmith by the year. Shepherds had a crook and bailiffs a lanthorn to show how late they'd be out and about after robbers. Though, as Gideon said, having a lanthorn is no more promise that a man'll so much as put his nose out of the bedclothes after dark than it's promise when a chap agrees to the text, 'Thou shalt not covet thy neighbour's house,' of a Sunday that he wunna spend all the week trying to compass it. Which was just what Gideon did himself.

There were tailors and weavers, wood carders and cobblers too, for the farmers clubbed together for them also. The carder had a hank of coloured wool, and the tailors made great game running up and down the line of young women and threatening to cut their petticoats short.

Jancis laughed with the rest, but I could see she'd been crying. She looked a real picture in her print gown and bonnet, with the dairymaid's milking stool. They were a tidy set of young women, the housemaids with broom on shoulder, the laundrymaids with dollies. It was no wonder that many a young farmer, who wanted neither cook nor dairymaid, should linger a bit, and that it should come into his mind that he wanted a wife.

'There's Grimble,' said Gideon. 'I made sure he'd come because of the bull-baiting. He's just got a new dog, I hear tell, as fierce as fire.'

There was most always a bull-baiting after the May Fair, and it was a thing I couldna abide. I looked where Gideon pointed and saw Mister Grimble, a man with a long nose that looked as if he poked it into everybody's business and stirred up trouble.

'Be that his missus?' I said.

Gideon looked at the woman, like a gingerbread doll, flat and baked pale, with curranty eyes, and said it was.

'Very near, and a driver,' I said.

'Well, Jancis'll take a deal of driving. The pretty ones be always the idle ones. And she's used to be clemmed at home. She'll see she dunna clem too much.'

He seemed quite unconsarned.

'She'd be better a power, at a small place with nice folk that ud treat her kind,' I said. 'What for do you want her to go to Grimbles'?'

'More money. They give a better wage than smaller folk. We mun think of that first.'

'The bane!' I whispered. 'The precious bane!'

For indeed this talk of money was beginning to wear on me like a song sung over and over, and a song misliked to start with. Gideon had spoken to Farmer Grimble about Jancis, so, as she never dared to go against his word, she beckoned to Beguildy and said –

'Mister Grimble's missus'll hire me, Feyther, if you please.'

'Oh, 'er will, will 'er? And what'll you give me for the wench for dree year?'

'Eighteen pound.'

'Make it twenty and you shall take her.'

'Nay, nay, it's too much.'

'She can work if she's a mind. She's strong. I give you leave if you make it twenty, to drive if she wunna be led.'

'If you lay finger on my girl it'll be the worse for ye,' said Gideon. 'And *she's* to have the money, not you, Beguildy.'

'Hearken, hearken! Did you ever hear the like! A fellow that was born under the threepenny planet and sleeps on face and'll come to be drowned!'

Gideon fell into a sudden rage and gave him a great clout with the flat of his hand, and Beguildy screamed out –

'I'll pay ye! I'll pay ye for this! Curse ye! The very spit of your dad you be. You owe me a crown,' he says, going by me on a blast of air. 'And you canna leave me and mine alone. Curse ye! In sowing and harvesting. In meadows and housen. By fire and by water. A waxen man! I'll make a waxen man this night, and call it Sarn. Slow, slow, it'll consume away – Sarn, the sin-eater!'

Gideon looked at him, making no sign. The people drew back a bit, fearing they knew not what. Just then, elbowing through the crowd, came the young squire, Mister Camperdine's nephew.

'I heard,' he says to Beguildy, 'that Venus was come to the Hiring Fair. My aunt wants a still-room maid, and I came to see if Venus – '

'If you mean Jancis Beguildy, sir,' says Gideon, speaking quick, 'she's prenticed already.'

'What, so soon?'

'Ah, to a farmer a great way off.'

He looked hard at Mister Camperdine, and Mister Camperdine looked hard back.

'It's a great disappointment,' says Mister Camperdine, 'for my good aunt.'

'Your lady-aunt, sir,' says Gideon very dry-like, 'will soon find another maid. Never faithful to one long, if I may make so bold, your lady-aunt inna, sir!'

The young squire frowned, but looking around and seeing nobody but Jancis, short and plump, he supposed the one he was after had gone already, and so thought further argling but waste of time. He sighed and said to himself –

'So Venus vanishes!' and went away. And very glad I was to see the last of him.

Beguildy and Jancis went to the inn with the Grimbles to sign the prentice paper binding Jancis for three years. She was to drive back with them that night. She was free till then, and Gideon said seeing she was going to work for Lullingford New House, she ought to have a look at it. So off they went, while I minded the stall.

I'd all but done, for the place being fuller than ordinary, the things went off pretty quick. The lines of young people had shrunken till there were only a few left that were wanted by none. These were such as were known to be over-fond of the bottle or to have a base-born child, or to be incurables of some crippling disease, or not to know rightly what was their own and what was other people's. I used to wonder how they felt, poor folk, going jogging along

138

in the evening, back where they came from. I was glad I worked at whome, and had no need to go and be hired, for certain sure nobody ud have taken me. It was a bitter thought, that.

The market-place was emptying fast, for the people were getting some refreshment afore the bull-baiting. But I'd still got some daffodillies to sell, and Gideon didna like anything to go back. So I sat still, in the quiet afternoon, looking down the empty street where the shadows of the lilacs and synty trees lay very dark and pleasant. I noticed that Missis Grimble was there too. She was packing up, and as she put each pat of butter into the basket she gave it a look as much as to say that she'd give it a bit of her mind after, for not being sold. In a while she came across to me.

'You be sister to my new dairymaid's young man, binna you?'

'Ah.'

'I'm in behopes they're serious?'

'Oh, ah!'

'That's right. I like my wenches to be walking out afore they come, and with a chap at a distance. I've got sons, and it's a deal safer. And so long as the chap's at a distance and canna be got at, it dunna hinder the work. Well, I'll be going now. They loose the first dog on the bull in an hour, and I must get a cup of tea first. I never can enjoy anything proper, nor take notice, if I'm clemmed. Whether it's a wedding or a confinement, a baiting or the Lord's Supper, I canna truly enjoy it as it should be enjoyed unless I've got a pint or two of good strong tea inside me. Well, good day. It's a great affliction for ye.'

She went back to her stall to gather her baskets.

There now! Never could I be left in peace. Never could I be let to get away from my misfortune. Here I sat, as peaceful as could be, till she must come up and say that. 'A great affliction.' But afore she said it I'd forgotten it, so I hadna got it. I was out of the cage till she put me in again. I was vexed, and the tears stood in my eyes.

139

Suddenly, along the quiet road, through the shadows, and through the mist on my own eyelashes, I saw somebody coming. A man, it was. And if there be any meaning in that word as I hanna thought on, let them that read put it in. Let them put the strength and the power, the kindness and the patience, the sternness and the stately righteousness of all good men into that word, and let him wear it. For it was himself, Kester Woodseaves, the maister.

He came along without haste, yet as if he had some great business to attend. I saw that he was in his best – the black beaver hat, green coat, flowered weskit, and the Wellington boots.

'Weaver, weaver!' called Missis Grimble. 'When'll you work for me next?'

He looked up, and came our way.

What did I do, I, that knew his smile was my summer? Why, I got up so hasty that I upset the daffodillies. I left all our baskets and butter-cloths, and the jam-pots for flowers, and I ran from the place as if summat was after me. But, being that the market was at the end of the road, and only open in front, there was nowhere for me to go but into the market-keeper's office, which was a dark room at the back of the market, and had a small window with no glass, looking on the stalls. So I couldna help but hear all they said.

'Why, lookye!' Missis Grimble screamed out like a cackling hen, 'her's fled away as if you were the murrain or the Lord or the bailiffs. What ails the wench? Mostly I see em run *to* and not *from* when a young chap comes along.'

'Who *be* she?' asked Kester.

He had ever a very out-of-the-ornary voice. It was like as if, when he spoke, the sound of the speaking made the world new for itself, not caring about the old world. It was like a wide, blossomy thorn-tree on a sweltering day in early June. You could sit down under it and rest you. And it was like the still hearth-fire on a winter night, when with Edric's out in the forest, and the curtains be close, candles snuffed, all fast, and the master of the house raught whome.

'Who *be* she?' he says. And even though it be only a passing thought and three words, I'm a flower that knows the sun.

'Why, her be Sarn's sister from away yonder at the mere. Prue Sarn. The woman with the hare-shotten lip. A very queer creature. But it makes 'em queer, you mind, to be born the like of that. Some say she's a bit of a witch.'

He said nought, but he went across and picked up my flowers, setting them in the jam-pots man's fashion, a bit clumsy and all thumbs, enough to make you cry with love. I could see from the dark at the back of the office.

'A very neat, tidy figure she's got,' he said. And in a minute I knew that he knew I'd heard, and so would ease the wound. Oh, most kind maister, the very marrow of Him that loved the world so dear!

'Be you going to the baiting, Mister Woodseaves?' asked Missis Grimble.

'Why, yes and no to that.'

'Eh?'

'You'll see in good time, Missis Grimble.'

With that he went on his way. And what did I do? I did a thing I never thought to do for any man, so forrard it was. I came out of the dark room, straight into the sunlight, and step by step along the road I followed him, as if I'd no bashfulness at all, such as every girl should have. I kept a long way back, for fear he might turn about and see me, but I never let him out of my sight. It seemed as if I couldna. I was drawn on and on. If I lost sight of his green coat round a turn of the road, I was all distraught till I'd got sight of it again.

The bull-ring was well beyond the town, in a green meadow where a brook ran. And though if you'd gone a-walking in that green meadow any other day in the year, to gather lilies or forget-me-nots, or to walk, beside the water, folk would have thought it a soft thing to do, it was

141

all right and proper to-day, because they were going to kill a creature there.

The people in the road never noticed me, in my plain black, with my face hid in my bonnet. From a good way off I could see the ring, and the bright colours of the gowns and coats all jumbled together, and a deal of sad-colour from the coats of the working men who could seldom afford a best coat save the funeral coat of the family. I could see the bull, a little white one, tied to a staple in the wall of the bull-ring, which was a semi-circle built of rough grey stones. The bright yellow sunshine held them all, as if they were bees in the mid of the honeycombs, and the blue air, the brown water, the green meadow were all so fair, I could not believe blood must be shed on such a day. I wonder to myself, times, if it was fair, clear weather on Golgotha when Mary looked up at the cross, and whether there was some small bird singing, and the bees busy in the clover. Ah! I think it was glass-clear weather, and bright. For no bitter lacked in that cup, and surely one of the bitterest things is to see the cruelty of man on some fair morning with blessing in it.

Chapter 2: *The Baiting*

As I came nearer I saw that, as the custom was, not only all the women of Lullingford were there, but all the children as well. I thought it shame to bring these poor things, that would soon enough know the evil of the world, to see the dogs torn to ribbons and the hapless beast killed. I said so after to Gideon, but he thought nothing of it.

'Why, you'd make 'em as soft as 'ool,' he said. 'They mun be brave and well-plucked.'

142

I said I couldna see that it was soft not to like to see a cruel deed, and that it seemed to me to be braver not to like seeing another's pain.

'Well, well, we canna make the world, for it's made already,' says Gideon.

There it all was, then, the crowd, the shouting and betting, the yapping and snarling of the dogs, people elbowing and pushing, men crying hot taters and chestnuts, apples, spiced ale, and gingerbread, children in their white pinnies watching the bull, very skeered, for it was grumbling to itself. Poor thing, it was thinking of its own big blackberry pasture at the back of Callard's Dingle, I make no doubt. It hated neither men nor dogs, and had no grudge against any if only it could be back there, roving the meadows in the dew. There they all were, and there was Kester. I lost sight of him in the crowd, and hastened my steps, with a wonder in my heart the while what he could be doing in such a place. For I thought him to be a different kind of man from all these. Yet such faith I had in him that I was sure, if he was here, that he was here for good. And something drove me on, so that I must seek him in the crowd, and keep nigh him, as if I was his angel for that day. A poor angel, but God minds not much, I think, what like His angels be, so that they do His work proper. The shepherd's collie that runs home to warn the missus that her man has fallen down the rock is his angel sure enough, though he may be a mongrel of the very worst, with ears as flat as a spaniel.

Blindly and without reason, like the shepherd's dog, I kept close to Kester Woodseaves, yet not so close that he might see me. So it was that I heard all he said to the men who stood round about the ring with their dogs, a bit apart from the crowd. And though they were men of my own countryside, and some of them known to me, yet I must say that there were among them a tuthree very evil faces. The dogs were fierce and ugly, many of em with great jowls, snarling and slavering and showing the red of their eyes.

143

Yet if I had been bound to choose between men and dogs, I'd have chosen the dogs. Mostly they were terriers, but there were a good few bulldogs, and of these Grimble's new one was far the worst, with a grin that sent me cold. There were one or two with a lot of mastiff in them, and there were a mort of mongrels.

The men all turned towards Kester when he came up, and Farmer Huglet, the chief of them, called out –

'Where's your dawg?'

Mister Huglet was a great raw-looking man who seemed as if he'd come together accidental and was made up of two or three other people's bodies. He was a giant, very nearly, and clumsy, with tremendous long arms, and so big round the middle that tailors who brought their own stuff always charged extra for his clothes. He'd got a mouth like a frog, and a round red snub nose, and such little eyes that they were lost in the mountains of flesh that made up his face. Whenever he couldna understand anything, he laughed, and his laugh was enough to frighten you. It came pretty often too. Grimble was hand-in-glove with him, and while Huglet stuck his red snub nose in the air, Grimble kept his long pale one down, so between them they didna miss much. They'd each got two dogs.

'Why, it's weaver,' says Grimble. 'Dunna you know weaver, Huglet?'

'Why, no, we hanna crossed paths afore. My brother-law weaves for me, you mind. Well, weaver, where's your dawg?'

'I've got none.'

' No dawg? Stand aside, then.'

But he stood where he was. It so happened that he was about at the mid of the half-moon of grey stone that made the bull-ring, and the men with the dogs fell away a bit on either hand, so he was alone. Standing there so slim and straight in his green coat, with the airs blowing his hair a bit, so that a lock of it fell o'er his brow, his hat being under arm, he seemed to have nought to do with any there, but

144

to be a part of the fair meadow, that matched his coat. He wore no beard nor whiskers, so you could see the shape and colour and the lines of all his face, which seemed to me to be a face you could never tire of looking on. Times I wonder if heaven will be thus, a long gazing on a face you canna tire of, but must ever have one more glimpse. He had a kind of arrowy look so that though Huglet towered over him he seemed to tower over Huglet. He looked round about and said –

'Chaps, I've come to ask ye to stop this.'

There was a long, bepuzzled silence. Then Huglet laughed and slapped his thigh, and roared again. Grimble looked at his boots and gave a snigger.

'Well, that's a good un!' shouted Huglet. 'Stop the bull-baiting, oot, young fellow?'

'Ah. I'd lief stop it.'

'And what for would you stop it, dear 'eart?' asked Grimble in a soft, sing-song voice.

'Stop it?' roars Huglet, 'he *canna* stop it.'

'I'd lief it was stopped over all England.'

'You'd lief a deal, young man. Why, I tell ye there's bin bull-baiting in England ever since it *was* England! Take away the good old sport and it wouldna *be* England!'

All this he said in the same loud roaring voice.

'I asked ye, what for would ye stop it?' repeated Grimble, soft and obstinate.

'Because it's a cruel, miserable business.'

'It inna cruel. The dawgs like it. They enjoy it. And the bull likes it right well.'

Mister Grimble looked down at the trampled grass for all the world as if he was reading the words there.

'What's it matter if they enjoy it or not? *I* enjoy it!' says Huglet. 'That's enough, inna it?'

The other men drew round. For though it was the ordinary thing to hear Mister Huglet shouting fit to burst, it was out of the common to hear him shouting so long at one person. When Huglet shouted like he was doing now,

145

folk said that the person he was shouting at always gave in and went away quiet.

'What be trouble?' asked Mister Callard, the owner of the bull. Mister Huglet turned round and spluttered out –

'This here borsted fellow wants to stop the baiting. The baiting, mind, as we all come a many weary mile to see.'

'Rising up a great while afore day,' puts in Mister Grimble.

'Dear now! And missus and me at such trouble to bring the beast along bright and early. Whatever ails the mon?'

He looked at Kester as the apothecary will look at a man a long while sick.

'Ah,' says the landlord of the *Mug of Cider*, 'I've heard tell of folks as wanted to stop the long kneeling. I've even heard of a tuthree as wanted to stop wars and rumours of wars, but bull-baiting? Never in life! Whoever, save a few fratchety parsons, did ever want to stop a baiting?'

'He must be going a bit simple, poor fellow,' says Grimble. 'Feel well, weaver?'

The miller came up and had a look, shook his head, and went away, which was a great deal for the miller to do.

'But what *for* do ye want to stop it, like?' says Mister Callard, very puzzled.

'I've told em why. Never mind all that. Look ye, Mister Callard, ool ye sell the bull to me?'

'Sell un?'

'Ah, I wunna argle and bargle over the price.'

'But it wouldna be worth my while. I'll get more, a power, by letting un fight. Win, and I'll be a rich mon. Lose, and I get best butcher's price from the ring owners, seesta?'

'What ud you make if he won?'

'Twenty pound.'

'I'll give you twenty pound, and you can take the beast away.'

'God bless me!' says Mister Callard. 'Oh, God bless me, I'm sure.'

He stared at Kester as if he was spirit-struck.

'Bargain?' says Kester.

Missis Callard, who never spoke but after Callard spoke, and then said the same thing, and never did aught but what she was told to do, came up all in a flusker, leading the bull.

'Take the gentleman's offer, Father! Take it, my dear!' she said, all out of breath. 'Take the twenty pound and us'll lead the darling whome.'

Callard was so astounded at her daring to speak that he could only keep on saying –

'God bless me!'

'God bless ye, is it?' says Huglet, beginning to roar again. 'I'll give ye God bless ye if you do any such thing, Callard. Dang me! Spoil all our sport for twenty pound! I'll larn ye! And you too, young man!'

'Oh, but he mun be worse than sawft or simple, he mun be stark raving mad to offer twenty pound for the little beast and then give back what he's bought,' says Grimble. 'Oh, I could cry! Yet the poor chap was all right Monday was a fortnit, weaving for us as nice as nice. But he's gone wrong in the yead since, surely to goodness! Oh, dear me!'

He wiped his face and seemed quite taken-to.

Kester pulled out his wallet and offered Callard the money. It was pretty well all his uncle left him, I doubt.

By this, Missis Callard had called all the children to her, for they had five children as well as the baby, and she whispered em, and all of a sudden they cried out together, 'Take it, Feyther! Take it, honoured Feyther! We beseech thee to hear us!'

At the surprise of that, Mister Callard seemed to be quite moithered, and he reached out his hand to Kester for the money. But Mister Huglet struck it down.

'I wunna be robbed of my sport!' he said. 'Dunna you dare take it, Callard. We want our sport, I tell ye!'

All the men with dogs looked black and muttered –

'Ah, that's righteous! That's gospel! We want our sport!'

'Chaps,' says Kester, very pleading, 'it be pity on so fine a day to set one poor creature to tear another. Devil's work, it be. If it's fighting you want, why canna you wrostle, or box man to man? Look ye! To make a bit of sport, I'll take any six of ye on, one after other, to wrostle. The one that beats me by most shall take my coat, and the next shall take my hat and weskit. Now then!'

Nobody said anything, only they shuffled a bit, and looked here and there. Everybody seemed to know that Kester was a very good wrostler, and nobody seemed to take to the job. Mister Grimble looked at Kester as if he hated him. And it was plain, by what came next, that he did, in very truth. For now, having made up his mind not to play second any more to Mister Huglet, he up and said –

'The young man speaks well. Now, I'll fall in with all he says and agree to the stopping of the baiting this day, on one condition.'

'Out with it,' says Kester.

'That you take on the dawgs yerself.'

Mister Grimble gave a spiteful cackling laugh, and Mister Huglet roared agen.

'Got ye there, me lad!' he shouted. And Grimble said –
' You may love the dumb creatures ooth yer purse, but ye wunna go so far as to love em ooth yer own blood!'

'Go on with the baiting!' orders Mister Huglet.

'Tie the beast up agen,' says Mister Callard to his missus, who was standing by, eager to hand it over to Kester, so as he could give it back as he said.

'Whose dawg drew first?'

Mister Huglet took no more notice of Kester, but went on with the arrangements.

'Mister Towler's dawg drew first, and *Mug o' Cider* second,' said one of the owners of the bull-ring.

'Come forrard, Towler.'

Kester stood very still, eyeing Mister Grimble till he got quite put about. For he didna seem to want to meet Kester's eye.

'That ud be the best bit of sport ever you had, eh, Mister Grimble?' says Kester at last. 'To see a man baited like a bull.'

'Why, nobody ud be such a fool.'

Kester looked round.

'Chaps!' he says, 'if so be as I agree to Mister Grimble's plan and take on the dogs one by one, not to kill 'em, but to put 'em on chain with nought but my bare hands, and they as savage as you like, if I do this at my own risk, will ye give it me in writing as there wunna be another baiting in Lullingford for ten years? And if I fail to put any dog on chain, I've lost and the baiting goes on.'

Everybody's tongue was loosed at that.

'God bless me!'

'Dear to goodness!'

'Domm it!'

'Well, that beats all, dang it!'

'Daze my 'ouns!'

There was a regular clack of voices.

One or two called out that they wouldna agree to it. But mostly they were very curious to see what would come of it, and as it was known that the parson didna like the baitings and had been writing the squire to put a stop to them, everybody thought they might be stopped soon anyway, and so they might as well have the fun, for this was a chance of rare sport, and the like of it had never been seen in the place.

When Mister Huglet could speak for laughing, he explained to all the people what was doing.

'Hands up for it!' he called out.

All but about a dozen held up their hands.

'Done!' says Mister Huglet. 'And done *for*, my fine feller!'

I caught hold of Miller's Tim and told him to go to Kester and whisper as Grimble's dog was a new one, and extra bad in temper. But indeed I felt that neither this nor anything was any manner of use, and I couldna think of aught to do. But one thing I was determined on, I'd keep nigh him, and when he was down I'd rush in and drag him away, and if Grimble interfered it ud be the worse for un. There's none so fierce as a loving woman, and it always seemed a strange thing to me that the Mother of Jesus could keep her hands off the centurion, and it could only have been because her Son had given orders afore. But indeed if it had been me, I think I should have forgot the orders.

Tim came running back, and I saw those strong blue eyes follow and settle on me for a breath. Then I hid behind Missis Callard.

'He knowed it,' says Tim. 'But ableeged all the same.'

I went to the refreshment booth and stole the carving-knife. But almost afore it was hidden under my flounced skirt I saw that there was to be no need of it, anyway for a while. There was to be summat more like a miracle than anything I've seen afore. This was the way of it.

'Go to the mid of the wall,' says Huglet, 'and fasten the dawgs to the bull chain. And if you fasten either of mine I'll give ye five shillings, me lad! Oh, I could bust a-laughing to see anybody be such a fool!'

'Mister Towler's dawg!' says the head of the ring. 'Ready!'

They loosed Towler's terrier, the savagest little beast in the place.

'At 'im! Bite 'im!' shouts Towler, and I was like to faint. And then it came to pass.

Kester stepped forward.

'Well, Bingo!' he says. 'Good dog!'

Bingo stopped, looked at Towler as much as to say he'd made a mistake, and ran to Kester as pleased as Punch, wagging tail and fawning round.

'We be friends, binna we?' says Kester.

Towler gave a curse, and Huglet looked as black as night. But nobody could say it wunna fair and square, and some of the better sort laughed and said, 'Good for you, lad!'

It was the same with the *Mug of Cider* dog, and the next.

As the owners came up to fetch them when they were on the chain, they looked very old-fashioned and taken aback.

Kester laughed.

'I like a dog,' he says. 'Dumb things be my fancy. You couldna know it, but so it is, and I can only see one dog here as inna friend to me, being new-come to these parts.'

'Ah,' says Grimble, 'you wunna play yer May-games with Toby. Indeed to goodness, if you get off with your life you'll do well.'

All in a minute I thought of a better thing than the carving-knife, though I kept that in case of need. I'd run to the town for the apothecary, there being no doctor in the place, to have him there in case of harm. There were a sight more dogs yet, for they wouldna let him off any. There met be time if I was quick. So, with the carving-knife still under my dress, I edged out of the crowd, got into the road and ran for dear life. But afore I went, I took one look at him I did love, since if I wasna quick enough I might never see him alive again.

He was laughing, and Huglet was leading one of his dogs away. Though Kester didna weave for Huglet, he'd made friends with his dogs on market days, outside the *Mug of Cider*, seemingly. He'd such a way with animals that a tuthree minutes was enough, and they were friends to him for ever.

And as I looked back it seemed to me, though I told myself it must be fancy, that those eyes, so live and bright, dwelt on me, and smiled at me, friended me and pled with me, being as are the eyes of a man when he looks long upon his dear acquaintance, who has given her peace for his, her soul to his keeping, and her body for his joy.

But as I ran I said to myself —

'Nay, Prue Sarn, you be nought but his angel, and a poor daggly sort of angel, too.'

And all the blue bird's eye in the hedge banks went into a mist of tears as I ran, and looked no more like flowers, but like a blue tide of sorrow to drown me.

151

Chapter 3: *'The Best Tall Script, Flourished'*

I MAY say I went over the distance to the town quicker than it's been done this long while. I hid the carving knife in the hedge, for fear of tripping over it. The apothecary's was open, as I thought, for he was churchwarden and couldna go agen the parson. I never saw the big green and red bottles look so beautiful, as if they were full of water from Paradise river. Inside there was a pleasant dusk, for the little window was so close-set with liniments and medicines, drenches for horses, simples for cows, plaisters, cordials, and bunches of yarbs that you couldna see at all. It smelt very pleasantly of peppermint, yarbs and soap, and the apothecary looked at me kindly over his spectacles and asked what the matter was.

'Why, sir, it's murder, pretty nigh,' I says. 'I do beseech you to shut up the shop and come, or such a man as this town never saw afore, nor will again, will be done to death.'

He pulled on his boots, good man, at that.

'What remedies must I bring?' he says. 'You can tell me the rest as we run.'

So I told him summat for dog-bites and summat to bring a man round when he was near death. In a minute he clapped his hat on, and off we went.

'Take a sup of brandy,' he says. 'You're nigh done.'

But I told him, no, only if I fell behind he must hasten on to the bull-ring.

I fell back just afore we got to the carving-knife, and caught up again at the field gate. As we came in I could see an awful struggle going on, for we were only just in time. He'd finished but for Grimble's dog.

As we came up there was a roar. He'd got the dog chained. Then there was another roar, and I saw (oh, my dear love!) that the dog had got him by the throat.

I caught Grimble's shoulder.

'Take yer dog off!' I said.

Grimble never stirred.

A second of that grip and he as I loved so dear ud be dead and cold.

I rushed forrard, I, that had never wilfully hurt any living creature, and as the great beast stood reared with his teeth in my master's throat, I ran him through the heart.

The blood spirted, and the heavy body fell down all of a heap, and Kester with it.

I pulled him away and dragged the dog's jaws apart. There seemed to be no life in Kester.

'Water!' I says to Huglet, who chanced to be nighest. 'Fetch water, you murderer! Brandy, Mister Camlet, please!'

He stooped over Kester.

'I mun burn the bite,' he said. 'Best do it afore we bring him round. But how to heat the iron?'

I stood up. I cared for nobody. They couldna have been more feared if I'd been a savage queen.

'Six men pick up sticks!' I says. 'And quick about it! And you, Grimble, find flint and tinder.'

'I hanna got one,' he muttered.

'Find one!' I screamed like a wild thing, holding up the knife. 'Find one, or – '

The fire was blazing quicker than it takes to tell it. We poured a little brandy down Kester's throat, to keep the spark of life in, then Mister Camlet burnt the bite, and Kester awoke with a shout of agony, for being in a dead swound he hadna been ready for the pain.

'There, there, my dear!' I says. For the shriek went through my heart. 'There, there. It be done now! None shall touch you now.'

Mister Camlet bound him up, and I washed his face with cold water and gave him more brandy.

'Not a deep wound,' says Mister Camlet. 'We were only just in time, though.'

'We couldna help but be in time,' I says. 'I be his angel for to-day.'

And with that the green field swam up afore me and I swounded clean away. When I came to myself there were Gideon and Jancis sitting by me on the grass, and all the folks were gone.

'Where be he?' I says.

'Who? Weaver?' says Jancis. 'He be all right and cared for. They've took him back to Lullingford, and Missis Callard'll stop with him.'

'She's mighty pleased with the little bull,' said Gideon.

'You saved that chap's life, and no mistake, Prue. I never saw the like! We were just coming in at the field gate, and I looked across and saw you. "By gum!" I says. And that was all I did say. I ran, and Jancis ran, but you'd done for the owd dog afore we could come at you. You take the medal, Prue!'

'You canna ride home, Prue. Shall I run and ask Miller to take her, Sarn? And couldna I come back and give her a hand with the work for a day or two?'

'You can ask Miller and welcome. It's a good thought. But as for coming back, you know very well you're Grimble's vessel-maid now, till three years.'

' I didna want to be. It's you and Feyther made me.'

'Well, but you've seen the house, hanna you? You'll be working for that and the 'unt ball and the silver plate.'

'Ah. I've seen the house, and I think it looks a dark, bitter old place, for all it's new, and I'd liefer never go to no 'unt ball than lead the life of a driven slave.'

She was crying, but it made no manner of difference to Gideon.

'You've got to go to Grimble's and you've got to go to the 'unt ball in good time, so why make such a ding-dong?'

'But why must I, Sarn?'

'Because my mind's set.'

It was almost as if he said, 'Because I'm in the stocks.'

154

As if his maid called him to come maying, but, feet and hands, he was fast bound.

When she was gone, they gave me a sup of tea at the *Mug of Cider*, for I was all of a-tremble still, and then Miller helped me up into the gig, and the old coach horse, that had known the merry sound of the horn tooting, and the sudden light and commotion at the turnpikes, when they rushed out in the dead dark to open, laboured into a trot. For indeed he seemed much of Missis Miller's mind, caring not if he never saw home again. Missis Miller had nought to say, Miller as usual had nought also, and Polly was asleep. After a while Missis Miller and Tim went to sleep too. We drove on sadly in the chilly evening. It was dusk, and then it was dark. Gideon was far ahead, for Bendigo was a good trotter, though aged. The mill pony, tied to the back of the gig, clopped onwards with a sorrowful sound.

It suited me, the quiet and the melancholy, for I was sad and quiet too. He that I loved was hurt, and I couldna get to him. There he lay, as weak as a babe, and only Missis Callard to tend him. I forgot that she, having six, was well knowledged in tending helpless folk, for it is the way of lovers to think that none can bless or succour their love but their own selves. And there is a touch of truth in it, maybe more than a touch. We went on and on, through country that was neither hilly nor flat, in a night neither dark nor gleamy, feeling neither glad nor sorry. I thought we were like people bound for some place beyond the world that was neither hell nor heaven. Our six heads, counting the nag's, all nid-nodded, and I think we were all asleep, even the old coach horse, when the miller spoke, out of his sleep, I do believe.

'I canna abide 'em,' he said, with a nod toërts his wife and children. 'I wish they were kit-cats, to drown in mill-pond. I wish the world and all was a kit-cat.'

He said no more. It was like when they say the creed, solemn and choppy. That was all the miller ever said to me, and I do think he said it in his sleep. On we went, till we came to the dark mill, the soundless water, like soft black crape. The others got out and untied the pony, and Miller drove me back to Sarn. The night was full of the smell of water and moss, with a drift of primrose scent now and again. I thought of the weaver's house, that seemed built of a spell, and him, lying there in the kitchen with the loom, his face barred with the shadow of it, cast by the rushlight, his hair all tousled and damp with the sweat of pain.

'If Missis Callard spoke unkind to him, I could slap her babby,' I thought. But I knew she wouldna. She was a good soul, though I always thought she must have had a mind like a shell, hollow, to echo other people as she did.

When we came to our place, there was Mother on the door-sill, very consarned. She said what nobody else had, and what I'd never thought of.

'You met ha' been killed, Prue!'

She sat down and began to cry, so I had to laugh at her and ask for summat to eat, to show I was alive all right. So then she got me such a meal as never was, though she should by rights have been asleep hours. Seemingly Gideon had told her some sort of tale, but she must know more. She wasna to be satisfied, but kept on wanting more. She put on her spectacles and looked at me very attentive, sitting there in the big oak chair. I was quite put-about with her staring so, with that still look of a sitting bird when somebody comes and spies at her, and she never winks nor flinches, but just looks back with sharp brown eyes, as much as to say, 'I'll stand by what's mine.' Mother seemed to be looking past me at summat that threatened me. Maybe it was my Fate, as she thought it to be. It was summat that threatened to do me harm, I'm sure, for after a bit Mother looked very defiant and sat up ever so straight and said –

'We'll have the weaver.'

Just as if somebody forbad her to have him.

She said nought of all I'd told her, never a word about it being a foolish or forrard thing to save a strange young

156

man's life without with your leave or by your leave. She only kept on giving little nods now and again, and saying –
'Ah. Come summer, we'll have weaver.'
Then she said she'd go to bed now, and I went and wrote in my book.
There was no change in our lives, only it was quieter without Jancis coming in of a Sunday. The Stone House seemed very lonesome, lacking her, and Missis Beguildy not half the woman she had been. She seemed to cling to me, and kept talking of the little ways and sayings of Jancis as if she was dead. This made Beguildy very angry, for in truth he was sorry Jancis was gone, not only because of the young squire, but because in her unhandy way she got through a good bit of work. He'd say, 'Now, hush thy noise, woman. The wench'll be back in no time, with twenty pound in hand, dear me. Now, dunna go to talk of her as if she was dead, fool! A gamesome lusty young woman the like of that! Many's the golden pound her'll put in our pockets, when she's learnt her duty, and given over hankering after a man as was born under the three-penny planet, and'll come to be drowned. No offence meant, Prue, and none taken I'm in behopes. You ploughed the gorsty bit right tidy, Prue, and us'll do words of four synnables this day, if you've a mind.'
Oh, there's no doubt Beguildy was a very queer old man. I was used to think if he'd had a good education he met have been one of these great men we all think so much of. A great scholar he could have been, or a music-man, or a rhymer, or a preacher. And maybe if all of his mind had been used proper, he wouldna have brought ruination on hisself as he did. Ah! And on more than hisself. But that we cannot know. We are His mommets that made us, I do think. He takes us from the box, whiles, and saith, 'Dance now!' or maybe it must bow, or wave a hand or fall down in a swound. Then He puts it back in box, for the part is played. It may be a Mumming, or a Christmas or Easter play, or a tragedy. That is as He pleases. The

play is of His making. So the evil mommets do His will as well as the good, since they act the part set for them. How would it be if the play came to the hour when the villainous man must do evilly, and see! he is on his knee-bones at his prayers. Then the play would be in very poor case. There was a mommet once called Judas, and if he had started away from his set part in fear, we should none of us have been saved. Which is all a very strange mystery, and so we must leave it. But it being so, I think we do wrongly to blame ill-doers too hardly. It is a dreadful fate to be obleeged to act in a curst, ugly way, when surely none would choose it. 'Needs be that offences come.' How should Gabriel show his skill with a two-edged sword if Lucifer wouldna fight? 'But woe be to him by whom they come.' Ah! So if the play has a murder in it, or if a good maid is brought to shame, a mommet must be found to do the bad work, though very like, if they could choose, never a one but would say, 'Not me, Maister!' Only they know nought. For I think we be not very different from the beasts, that work deathly harms in the dark of their minds, knowing nothing, weltering in blood, crouching and spring-ing on their prey, with a sound of shrieks in the night, and yet all the while as innocent as a babe. And I think we be not very much other than the storms that raven in the forest, and the hungry fire that licks up lives in a moment, and the lips of the water, sucking in our kin. It is all in the Play. But if we be chosen for a pleasant, merry part, how thankful we ought to be, giving great praise, and helping those less fortunate, and even being grateful to that poor mommet which goeth about night and day to work our destruction. For it might have been the other way.

So, in spite of all, I was always sorry for Beguildy, though, dear knows, he was the villain in our story.

We had a very middling crop that summer, both of grass and grain. Our lives went to the same tune, with no change, saving that Mother was as good as her word and did send for Kester.

I thought she seemed very busy all that June, spinning as if it was ever so, till even Gideon gave a word of praise. Then one day she said –

'There's such a deal spun, I shall be obleeged to send for Weaver.'

But I was settled in my mind not to see him, so the day he was coming, about the end of hay harvest, I took the brummock and went hedging in the far fields where none would find me.

'I'm going hedging, Mother,' I says. 'I'll take some bread and cheese. Can you see to the young turkeys and tell Gideon he must make shift with the milking, for I shanna be back till dark.'

What must she do but begin to wring her hands and keep on saying under breath –

'Oh, the pity, the pity, to be so curst!'

But go I did. And when I raught home, there in my attic were the bits of wool and thread he'd left, and a very pleasant smell of tobacco. For he liked to smoke a bit while he worked. And just by the corner of the loom what should I find but a blue-and-white handkerchief, which I very dishonestly did put in my locker, and turned the key with great satisfaction. I said to myself in a kind of gloating way that some day I'd launder it, and roll it up with a bit of lavender, and send it back. But not yet.

Mother was full of tales about the weaver. Oh, he was such a kind man, and strong, and so considerate! I thought I could have told her that. Like a son to her, he'd been, she said. I should ha' seen him a-sitting on the settle at his tea. I dare say, I thought, and lose my heart worse than ever!

'Wanted to know if I'd any other family besides Sarn.' she said. 'So I told un.'

'Oh, Mother, what did you tell him?' I said.

'I told un I'd got the best girl in the 'orld, and a good daughter to me, and very jimp and slender, with a long, silky plait to the knees, and dark, meltin' eyes, and such pleasant ways, merry and mocking and pitiful. Ah! I told

un! Proper, I did! And I told un you could do the tall
script and the short, and that Beguildy was learning you to
read, and that you could do words of four synnables now.'

'Dear to goodness, Mother,' I said, 'what a tale you made
out!'

'No tale, my dear, for 'tis the truth.'

'Did you say aught of Gideon's letters? I mean, did you
say I wrote 'em?'

'Why, no, my dear. Sarn met not ha' liked it, nor Jancis,
nor you.'

'No. You've got a lot of sense, Mother.'

'It was always said in our family as I had, my dear.'

'So Weaver thinks we're a very well educated family, I
make no doubt, Mother, and he'll take it for gospel that
Gideon writes the letters.'

After, when I was helping her to bed, I took courage to
say –

'Did you tell Weaver I was hare-shotten?'

'No, no, my dear! What for should I do that?'

'Only he met be thinking of me a bit, seeing you said
such things, and then if he met me ever – '

'Well, my dear, if he met you, and he's the man I think
him, he'd be bound to like you right well,' says Mother
roundly.

When I'd tucked her in, she catched my hand.

'Prue, should you care if he'd got but one leg, or one arm,
or was all pitted with the smallpox?'

'Care, Mother?' I cried out all in a minute and never
thinking, 'of course I shouldna care. I should love un the
more for it!'

'I knowed you did, my dear,' says Mother, very contented. 'I knowed you loved the man. And I'm right glad
of it. Now, dunna you hide from him, Prue. Be well
plucked and risk all, like a good player in the game of
Costly Colours.'

'No, no! Never will I. Oh, Mother, it was unkind in you
to catch me like that!'

'I only wanted to know, Prue. I be getting ancient and old, and the time draws nigh when life'll be a burden. I'd lief know as there was good in store for the best girl ever.'

She looked out and away through the little moony window, with the dark round blots that were red roses pressed on the panes, and the silver sky dim, and not starry, but very kind-seeming, and she seemed to be listening to summat. Then she said –

'I do believe all shall be well with you, Prue. It's come to my heart as soft as dew, and as sweet as a red rose, that you'll get love as well as give it. After my time, though, after my time. But no matter for that, so I do know it's to come.'

I felt a shiver of strangeness in the night.

'What is it, my dear?' I asked her. 'Is it the second sight?'

'No. I see nought. But I feel it within me.'

'You be well, be you, Mother?' I said, for I was afraid she might be slipping from me, since the dying are ever so.

But she said, yes, she was in her daily health, and well, and not going to die this many a day, only it came on her at the thought of Weaver, and how he'd said –

'Well, single I am, and single shall stay, I do believe. But if ever I did think of asking to wed, it ud be just such another as that'n.'

At the end of corn harvest Gideon asked me to write his second letter to Jancis.

We were having our suppers on the bench under the dairy window. After, I fetched the ink and said, what should I write? So he said I must write that he was well and hoped she was, and she was to be a good girl and work hard and not ask for any early money for clo'es or boots, but think of all that was to come, and it was a middling harvest, and her father still in the same mind about the young squire, who was about coming back from the Low Countries next year with his pockets full of money, and the big longhorn cow had calved, but dropped her calf like the gwerian she was, and to tell Mister Grimble he could do with a few lambs when he fetched them off the hills for the winter, but no sign of fut-rot, or home they'd come, dang-swang, and so no more from G. Sarn.

Then he said, 'Put in as I'll see her, Christmas market, if Grimbles ool bring her.'

I said I'd do the best I could, and did it matter if I put in a bit more? And I couldna help but laugh, for it did seem such a peculiar letter for a fellow to write to his sweetheart. And Gideon looked up very sharp and said, why did I want to write more? So I said the pen did run away sometimes, and he said he supposed it wunna easy to know quite what you were at when you started writing, and God save him from such foolishness, and so long as I put in all he'd told me I might put in some as well, if I'd a mind.

So I wrote it.

SARN.

September Twenty-six.

MY DEAR SWEETHEART,—

It do seem a long while since your letter, which was a beauty, and I kissed it a good few times. You know very well how to do a love letter. I can see the two of you at it, your golden hair shining and your pretty face bent down, and Weaver smiling a bit, and looking well amused, with those eyes that would 'tice any girl away from her own man, and mind you dunna fall in love with anybody but me, if possible. Maybe I shall see you at the Christmas market. Tell Weaver that all Mother's tales of our Prue be made-ups, for she's very ornary in every way. Tell Mister Grimble I could do with a few lambs. Tell Weaver when he goes nigh Huglet's he might carry a gun as well as not, for Huglet's got an awful dog now, and I hope all's well betwixt Weaver and Grimble. If there's ever any sewing work Weaver wants done, being a lone womanless man, I've got two women in my house, Mother and sister, both glad of a job at a fair price, and red cabbage pickle and damson cheese they maken, which pays them very well to sell at half market price, and a charity to employ them. It's a middling harvest, longhorn's dropped her calf, young Camperdine's expected back next year, and if they've gotten fut-rot, back they'll come, dang-swang, and so good-bye for now, and take all care of self. In the beginning of a cough take a lemon and crushed honeycomb fire-hot, and you be my dearest, dearest love as I'd spend my life for very willing any time, and die for you by bite of dog or any way, my dear, and so good night, from your lover,

GIDEON SARN.

That is a nice text, 'The Maister be come.'

I often wondered as the autumn went on, and the cold nights, what they thought of my letter. We knew they had it all right, for one market day Gideon came back with the lambs that Grimble had put in pen for him at the *Mug of Cider*, and they were good ones, with no fut-rot. But it was drawing on to Christmas when the letter came from Jancis, and I mind it was a wild night, with a lashing of rain on the window, when I read it to Gideon. But it was warm within. It made a good Christmas for me, in spite of work, and Mother very ailing, so as we had to send for the doctor's man all the way from Silverton, for Gideon wouldna hear of the doctor, saying the expense was more than enough as it was. He kept on grumbling and saying she was a burden and Mother would ask me: 'Does Sarn think I be a burden?' So it was very awkward for me. But that letter was as heartening as a platter of good hot soup, and lest Gideon should take it to his own keeping, I made a copy of it, and this is it.

THE HIGH FARM, OUTRACK.

December 1.

MY DEAREST ACQUAINTANCE, –

I am thinking of Sarn as I write this, and of the best of lovers. Mister Woodseaves ud be very glad of the sewing and the pickle and the damson cheese Sarn was so kind as

163

to mention. Perhaps might speak to your sister one day
about it. Mister Woodseaves says that is the best cough
cure ever, and tried it one foggy night after getting back
from here to Lullingford, but thinks it ud take a woman to
mix it proper. Sorry about the harvest and the calf, but no
need to worry about Huglet's dog, not being afraid of any
dog, nor of Huglet neither. But that was a near shave at
the Baiting, by gum, and a plucky woman to rush in the
like of that and save a poor fellow. For Mister Woodseaves
hears tell it was a woman did it, a tall slim woman with
beautiful dark eyes, so they do say. It inna for me to say
anything, as you know, Sarn. But others will talk. Weaver
says if ever he had an acquaintance he'd lief she was that
sort. And so good night, and a merry Christmas from

JANCIS BEGUILDY.

I love you already, and if these things be done in the dry
tree, what shall be done in the green?

Chapter 4: *Jancis Runs Away*

IT was a Christmas Eve again a year and eight months
after Kester stopped the bull-baiting. There'd been no
letters from Jancis a long while, but Gideon never worried
about such things. He said it was only the weather, for the
roads were so waidy round about Grimble's that nobody
could come at them in bad weather. They came to market
seldom in winter, but laid in a store of such things as they
needed, and Mister Grimble would send half a score waggons of grain to be ground at the mill, and then they'd
settle down, the farm and the two labourers' cottages, with
the horses in stable and the cattle in the near pasture and

the sheep in the mangold fields close by, all snug for the winter. They were used to keep a lot of simples and cures at such farms, because no apothecary or doctor could get to them, the roads being past all telling bad, not if it was ever so.

'Woodseaves canna go there, and Jancis canna send to Lullingford, but come a bit of fair weather, we shall hear,' said Gideon.

I used to think of Jancis, mewed up with Missis Grimble, a woman I couldna abide, nor could Jancis. I thought of the high mountains and the sleat storms like a wall of ice between her and us, and the snow, thick and soft, whispering, whispering.

'It goes round the house, and round the house, and leaves a white glove in the window.'

That's what they say of the snow at Sarn.

There were two sons, of course, to liven things up, but one of them was going to wed with the labourer's girl, and the other was very religious and didna hold with any kind of May-games, nor pleasuring, nor even much laughing and talking. So she'd only Missis Grimble, that was a driver and a scold, and Mister Grimble, that was very awkward in bad weather, because of the rheumatics. I used to think of her a deal. For if you thought of anybody at Sarn, you thought of them a deal, it being so quiet, especially in the winter, and time standing still, so it seemed.

And whenever I thought of Jancis I called to mind a thing I saw once in June, when we had strange untoёrt weather and a deal of tempest and sleat, which one day for about an hour turned to snow. And I saw the wild roses, so tender and nesh, and used to nothing colder than dew, with their pale pink petals all full of snow, and seeming to be frozen through and through, gold hearts and all. I thought of her always like that, for I was fond of her, and she seemed a child to me, though she was older. Even in spite of her making me remember that she was pretty and I was ugly, I was fond of her, and the more so when she was in trouble, for I never love folks quite so well when it's bright weather with them. So I wished I could have sent her summat for Christmas, if it was only a hemmed kerchief of plain linen. I'd asked Gideon to inquire after her at Kester's when he went to market, but Kester was away, and the house shut up. That was uncomfortable news, for I liked to think of him by his own fireside, in the little house I knew by sight. It seemed he was nigher then. But it was his custom to go off for a month at a time in the winter to stay at one village or another and do all the weaving there, to save going to-and-again.

It was very quiet in our kitchen. Mother was in bed, being always bed-ridden now in hard weather, and Gideon was in the woods, getting the Christmas grand. For whatever else we were stinted of, we always had that, since it took only labour to get it, and Gideon never grudged that, poor lad. I went to the door to listen if he'd finished chopping, and I could hear the axe barking, and the echo of it coming from across the mere. The trees were mounded up with snow, and the mere frozen till near the middle. The woods, as white as sugar, stood round the water so still as if they were spelled, like folk in some old tale of witchcraft, so deep they were in trusses and bales of snow, and not a breath stirring. You couldna call summer to mind. You couldna think of the mere with lilies on it, and ripples. I held my breath, it was so quiet, till a redshank called from the far end of the mere by the church, very sorrowful, with a sound like 'Mute! Mute!' Then some widgeon went over against the darkening sky, and I heard Mother give a little cough, so I knew she'd be wanting her tea. The sound of the axe had stopped, so Gideon ud be coming soon, and I set about getting the meal.

I was baking, a thing I dearly liked. Most of the work I did was men's work, and baking seemed so light and pleasant after it. I liked to see the dough rising afore the big red fire, and to get the oven ready with burning wood, raking out the ash after, and setting the loaves in rows.

166

It was pleasant to be in the warm, glowing kitchen, full of the good smell of bread, and to look out at the grey-white fields and woods, cold and lonesome, and then to draw the curtain, and kindle the rushlight, setting the table and putting the tater pie to'get hot on the gledes, and knowing that in a little while all those I cared for would be comfortable for the night. The fowl had been shut up since the first dusk, the cows and sheep were folded, Bendigo littered-up, Pussy by hearth, Mother with a bit of fire in her room and the warming-pan in the bed, and now Gideon was on the way back to his supper. The oven being still hot, I put in a batch of mince-pies, for Gideon liked a bit of good fare as well as anybody, though he'd growl times, and talk about ruination, and where'd our house be and the silver plate and all. But though I did as he said all the year round, with a bit of bread and cheese and a tater for a meal, at Christmas time I went by my own road, and we had our merrymaking almost like other folks. And since, after all that came to pass, I've been more glad of that bit of disobedience to Gideon than of anything in our lives then. For I can say, 'Anyway, they had *that*, whatever else they didna have.'

I was singing to myself a bit, and talking to Pussy, who was almost too comfortable to purr, only if I spoke she'd partly get up, and arch herself very polite, and open her mouth to mew, and then be too bone-idle to make any sound. But she looked at me as much as to say, 'I know you made this nice gledy fire to warm me, missus, and I know you've got summat in larder for I, and thank you kindly.'

All of a sudden there came a soft tap at the door. So tiny and timid it was, it might almost have been a poor red-breast tapping with its beak. There was one would come in hard weather, and if I was too long feeding it, it would tap on the window. I went to the door, and it being dark by now, and nobody coming our way in a month of Sundays, I may say I thought of frittening and fairies and Loblieby-the-fire, and all sorts of queer things that were used to happen in time past.

I opened it.

There against the white, dreary stretch of the frozen mere, all woebegone and white in the light of the fire, was Jancis.

No sooner did I pull her in than she fell down dangswang in a heap on the floor. The poor girl! Never did I see such a pickle. Her clothes were all torn, boots broken, hands and face scratched as if she'd been through brier hedges, which it turned out after that she had, and everything wringing wet as if she'd been dragged out of the mere. She'd fainted dead away, and I'd enough to do to get her round. When she came to, she told me she'd had no food for nearly two days, and she'd walked all the way from Grimble's in this weather

To think of it! The long and the short of it was that she'd run away, and she'd no money and no decent boots, and she had to slip away when she could, which chanced to be when she hadna got her shawl.

She cried and cried.

'Oh, I couldna bear it, Prue! Oh, dear Prue, dunna scold! It was more than anybody could bear. And when it came nigh Christmas and there was no news, and all of 'em ten times worse, being mewed up with the hard weather, oh, I *couldna* bear it. And the girl at the cottage told me that the last two dairymaids ran away as well. She said why didna I run away, too? Partly she said it because she was sorry for me, and partly because Alf Grimble, that's her young man, was paying me attentions. So she told me the best time to go, and kept 'em all out of the way, and gave me some bread and meat and a bottle of milk, and promised to tell them some tale to keep them from following me.'

She stopped a bit for breath, and there came from outside the sound of Gideon's cart-wheels creaking along in the snow.

168

'What be you going to say to Gideon?' I asked her.

'Oh, dunna let him be angered with me, Prue! Dunna! I canna bear any more. When I tell you all I've been through, you'll see I canna.'

Gideon came to the door, dragging the great log, that was the Christmas brand, on a chain.

'Dunna turn me out, Prue! Whatever he do say, and however angered he be at me losing the place he settled on, keep me for this night!'

So I said, did she think any creature could make me turn her out at any time, let alone in such weather? And I tucked her up on settle, and said she must rest now, and afterwards she should have a sup of tea, and then to bed, and all her troubles were over. Then she smiled and whispered –

'I love ye, Prue! You bin like the Saviour to me this night,' and so fell asleep.

Times, seeing what came to pass, I'm main glad of that smile and that whisper.

Eh, but Gideon was in a rage!

'Why, she'll lose all the money,' he says, the first minute, 'and she'll not only lose the money for the year and four months to come, but she'll lose the wages for the year and eight months she's been there. If they break their time, they get no money. You know that as well as I do.'

I asked how he could think of the money when she'd come to our door the like of that, all draggled and half dead.

'You always were a fool, Prue,' he says, 'and I suppose you always will be.'

But my patience was out, and I talked to Gideon straight.

'I'd thank you to keep your tongue in leash this evening, Gideon! Here's Christmas, and Jancis come to you out of death's arms, very nearly. For it wanted but a little. If she'd lost her way again, so late, she'd have been done. And seeing I've taken her in and she's to have my bed, and I've cossetted her for ye, she being your dear acquaintance, you'd ought to be humble and grateful to me and to them above for the salvation of the poor child.'

'Dear to goodness! What a spitfire all in a minute!' says he. He laughed a bit, being startled, for I wasna used to breaking out like that. Then he went tramping into the kitchen.

'Well!' he says, very loud, for he wunna used to sick folks, and he always seemed to think they were deaf. When Mother was sick, he'd shout at her summat odd, though Mother had kept her hearing very well.

'Good evening, Sarn!' says Jancis, very small and weak.

'So you've raught back.'

'Ah!'

'Broke your time and all.'

She began to cry.

'Now then, dunna do that!' he says quite taken-to. 'Prue'll give me some more tongue if you cry. I amna to say a word, not to-night. There'll be summat to be said to-morrow, but I'm to leave you be to-night. Well, how bin 'ee?'

He stood in the middle of the kitchen and shouted it at her, so I couldna help but laugh.

'Nicely, thank you kindly, Sarn,' she says.

'You dunna do much credit to your pasture at Grimble's. I'll say that. Seen young Camperdine ever?'

'No.'

'Got an acquaintance over yonder?'

'No, Sarn. You be my acquaintance for ever and ever.'

'Not Alf Grimble?'

'No. But he was sweet on me, a bit, and pestered me. That was why I ran away.'

I never thought Jancis was so clever. But every woman's clever when she's in love, I do believe. She was ever so white against the black settle.

'I ran away because you be the only acquaintance I do want, Sarn.'

'So that was it! I'll break Alf's head for un come cattle-market.'

'No. Dunna, dunna!'

'So you ran way all those miles and miles because you didna like Alf, and because I was your dear acquaintance?'

'Ah.'

'Give us a kiss, wench!'

I ran away into the dairy at that, and Pussy with me, for she was always a bit skeered when Gideon was in. I skimmed and skimmed, and if I cried a bit, who was the worse? For I wished I was on settle with a young man shouting at *me* from the middle of the kitchen, and then saying, 'Give us a kiss, wench!' And if you should ask what manner of young man would I choose, I'd say as he'd wear a coat the colour of a May meadow, and look at you with eyes full of power and knowledge till your soul turned right over.

'I canna have what I want, Pussy,' I says. 'But you can, for your wants be easy got.'

And I gave her a great saucer of cream. I did! What would Gideon have said if he'd known? But he'd got his cream in the kitchen.

'I'm giving you this, Pussy,' I says, 'because I canna get my own cream. It eases me to see somebody satisfied.'

She looked at me, frittened, thinking she must be going to get slapped in a minute, since it was too good to be true. Then she lapped it up.

With that, I heard Mother calling.

'You've had that, anyway, Pussy,' I says. 'And now, Mother, would ye like some cream with your tea?'

'Why, yes, my dear. I do dearly like a drop of cream with my tea. But what'll Sarn say?'

'He's busy lapping cream hisself, Mother.'

'Eh?'

Mother thought I was comic-struck.

'Well, in a manner of speaking. Jancis be come.'

171

'Jancis?'

'Ah. Run away.'

'Dear to goodness!'

'Walked all the way, she did.'

'But why didna she go whome?'

I'd never thought of that. It seemed so natural she should come to us, like a clemmed redbreast.

'She was afraid of Beguildy, I make no doubt, Mother.'

'Ah. You'll have to go and tell Missis Beguildy.'

'Boxing Day, I'll go. Let Jancis have her Christmas.'

'Be they, as you met say, lovering at all?'

'Ah. He was took by surprise, and he gave her a kiss afore he knew it.'

We laughed a bit.

'And now for your tea, Mother. There's getting to be a real Christmassy feeling. Cream all round! And after supper I'll trim the house up with holly.'

'Mind you get some cream yourself, my dear.'

As I went down the stair into the kitchen, where the two were sitting very old-fashioned on the settle, I wondered what would be cream for me. All in a minute, as I was scalding the tea, I knew.

'Jancis,' I said, 'you'd ought to write to Mister Wood-seaves and say you've run away, or maybe he'll be making shift to go over extra early to write a letter for you.'

'A'right, Prue, seeing it's you and not me as writes, I dunna mind. But he wunna go over there again.'

'Not go? For why?'

'I'll tell you all about it to-morrow-day. I be so tired now.'

'All right,' I said, though I did long to hear about him.

'I'll tell about running away to-night,' she said, but I told her 'supper first.'

'Draw up now and take bite and sup. Then you can tell us all about it, and then I'll write.'

I knew it would do her good to tell it. For when you've come through a bad time, to tell of it takes the thorn out. So she told us how she'd timed it to get to Lullingford on market day and ask Gideon to bring her back, but took the wrong road in the hills, all looking the same in the snow, and wandered far out of the way, and was benighted, and slept in one of the huts that they make of furze for lambing time; and how she heard a breathing under the door and thought it was the roaring bull of Bagbury, but she cried out upon the Trinity three times, as loud as she could, and it went away. Then she struggled on to Lullingford, going across fields, not being able to find the road. She was chased by a horse, which was worse than the roaring bull of Bagbury, and that was when she crept through the hedge. When she got to Lullingford, Gideon was gone, for he always started back as soon as he could. She went to Kester's, but he being away, she could get no help there. She was afraid to ask anybody else, for fear they'd send her back to Grimble's, so she started off again. But afore she'd gone far, she was so fainty that she had to creep into a barn and wait till morning. Then when she got to the woods, she thought of a short cut, and lost her way again. And indeed it was no wonder, for in the woods about Sarn it inna all that easy to find your way in summer even.

'Dear to goodness!' says Gideon, 'you want a chap to look after you, seemingly. Such a tale of foolishness I never heard.'

'And what Feyther'll say passes me,' she went on. 'He'll be neither to hold nor to bind. He's very set in his ways now, and if you go agen his plans he's very crousty. If Mother knew, maybe she'd think of a way out.'

'I'll go and see your mother, come Boxing Day,' I said. 'It'll be a funny thing if we canna invent summat to get the better of an old moithered man, hoping you dunna mind me saying it.'

'Mind! You can say the worst you can think of about my

dad, and I doubt I shanna think it's too much. And truly he *be* moethered, book-learning or no.'

'Set your heart at rest now. We'll think of summat to give you time to turn round. Maybe you could get another place. Or maybe Gideon –'

'If you mean, maybe Gideon'll want to get wed, I say, in my own good time and not afore. I've told Jancis if it's a good harvest and we do well I'll be willing to get wed at Harvest Home. And she's willing as well.'

'I'm right glad. Loving's never too early. And if you be fond of a girl, you mun want her to be in your house, by fireside and table, indoors and out.'

I was thinking of a little house not twenty miles away, as different as could be from ours, and one in it as was a very obstinate bachelor, and didna want any woman there, let alone poor Prue Sarn. I thought it was about time I wrote the letter.

'What shall I say in your letter, Jancis?'

She said I was to say what I liked. So I fetched ink and paper and my quill, and wrote it.

Christmas Eve.   SARN.

DEAR MISTER WOODSEAVES,—

I write to acquaint you as I've left Missis Grimble, being very near with the food and a driver, and maister's rheumatics very awkward in sharp weather, and sons awkward also one way or another. I've broke the journey at Sarn. I may say Gideon and me think to be married come Harvest Home. I may say I be very glad, for when you dc love anybody you want to be with them and canna rest nights, wondering where they be, and if all's well, and if they change their stockings when damp, and if they be lonesome ever.

I be more choice of him I love than of all else in the world beside.

He be so kind and so brave, and when he be there I can but say, 'The maister be come.'

174

I love him past telling, and shall to the end, and so good night. Mister Woodseaves, and a merry Christmas, from

JANCIS BEGUILDY.

'You write a pretty tidy letter, Jancis,' I says. 'Would ye like me to read it?'

'Laws, no! What for should ye? You know what's to be said.'

'Ah. I know right well what's to be said. Only I munna say it,' I thought. 'That's the trouble.'

I fastened the letter up and put it on the chimney-piece ready for Gideon to take next market day.

There was a strangeness about the place all that Christmas. It was the best Christmas ever we had, and there was more singing and laughing than there'd bin for many a year. And yet it was in a manner of speaking sad. It seemed to me as if the singing came from a great way off, under the water. And when Jancis sat by the window, with the light falling on her pale gold hair and pale face through the greenish bottle-glass, it made her look as if the water flowed over her.

'Green gravel, green gravel, the grass is so green!
The fairest young lady that ever was seen.
I'll wash you in milk, and clothe you in silk,
And write down your name with a gold pen and ink.'

Ah! I can hear Jancis singing that song now, with her sweet shrilly voice, a great way off, ah, me! a great way off.

Mother let me get her up, Christmas morning, and came into the kitchen, sitting snug in the chimney corner, watching the lovers with a pleased, understanding, merry look such as I've often seen on the faces of old women that have lived their lives and known summat of love. It's as if they said, as they looked at the young lovers –

'Pleased, be ye, my lad? You'll be better pleased yet! . . .

175

All of a twitter, be ye, my girl? Well, I can tell ye, you'll be in more of a twitter later on, a power.'

I could see very well that when we three sang 'As Joseph was a-walking,' and 'Good Christian men, rejoice!' Mother was hearing other voices too, little voices like the Callard children's, lifted up all together, shrilly and sweet. She was seeing other faces, well scrubbed and rosy, lifted up to her as she sat in the dusk of the settle, ready to smile when the solemn carols were done, and shout 'Granma!'

She kept on patting Jancis on shoulder, and saying, 'Pretty thing! Pretty!' and once I heard her cautioning Jancis against hares.

'When your time comes, my dear, dunna you go in the 'oods much, nor yet in the meadows. Keep near whome and you wunna come across one. 'Twould be a sad mischance, so it would.'

'Oh, Missis Sarn!' says Jancis, laughing and colouring up above a bit, 'you do run on so fast! We inna so much as courting yet.'

'And so do time run on, my dear. You munna let the moss grow on the path of love. Dunna give too many naywords. He's a good lad when you dunna vex him.'

'But it's Sarn more than me as wants to wait,' said Jancis.

'Foolish, foolish lad! What matter for the silver plate? What matter for so many maids and men? I'm sure I'd be content without, so as I needna tend swine again, and can have my feet to the fire and a cup of tay.'

'Sarn wants to take me to the 'unt ball,' said Jancis. 'And I be to go in afore Miss Dorabella.'

'That's a mischievous thought. For what dun it matter who's first so long as all be in? And what is it to go to one ball more than another?'

'But I'd like it right well, to go in afore Miss Dorabella!'

'And so thee shall!' called out Gideon from the door, where he was knocking the snow and mud off his boots.

'And so thee shall, my girl, and dressed as shameless as a lady!'

176

He came across the kitchen with the bit of mistletoe he'd clomb the big apple tree to get, and gave her a loud, smacking kiss under it.

Mother clapped hands, as pleased as a child when kitty wakes up and plays. But even when she clapped for joy, her hands still looked like the little praying paws of a trapped mole.

'Not later than Harvest, Sarn?' she pleaded. 'You wunna put it off later than that? I'll last till then, sure. But after – the winter comes, and who knows? I'd lief see you wed afore winter.'

'Oh, we shanna put off, Mother. No danger! What need? For I shall be a rich mon when I've sold the corn, and it'll cost nought to get it, for we can have a love-carriage, and I can pay back with task-work in the winter. And in another tuthree years we can shift, for the old mon at Lullingford wunna last long, and the money'll be ready when the place comes on the market.'

So they were all merry, and when I said, 'The tea's scalded!' Gideon gave me a very affectionate pat on the shoulder and said I was a good wench.

'A right good wench if ever there was one. Now draw up! Draw up to table all! I want me tea cruel.'

But I couldna be as merry as they were. I felt outside it all. Only I took a bit of comfort, now and again, between cutting bread and frizzling rashers and pouring tea, in looking up at my letter on the mantel, with the address on it in very tall script –

> Mister Woodseaves,
> The Weaver's House,
> Lullingford.

Then Jancis told us about Kester, and of the things that had come about through Grimble's spite, which couldna be told in letters. For it seemed that Grimble and Huglet had misliked Kester ever since he stopped the baiting, and the mislike had soon grown into black hatred. They tried to set all the other farmers agen him, saying this and that. They found fault with his weaving, which was the best in all the country round. And they said he was slow, and dear. Not content with that, they must enquire into his religion and his ways of thinking in the matter of the corn laws and the Parliament men. They hob-nobbed with Squire over that, and set him agen Kester too, worse than he was, for they said nought about the baiting, but kept to the corn. Every way they could, they worked against Kester, and very worried they must ha' been that he didna drink or go after women, or do anything that they could have told of to the Parish Constable. But they did their best to make his life a burden, for it irked them so sore to think of no bull-baiting for ten years. So one day when he was weaving at Grimble's and it came to evening, Mister Grimble looked at the cloth Kester had done in the day, and couldna find fault with it, neither with the quality nor the quantity. For he'd worked right well, and Jancis said it was as smooth as silk, and never a lump nor a knot in it. He said nought to Kester, and after supper Jancis fetched the paper and they began to write the letter to Gideon. And it seemed Mister Grimble couldn't abide to see that, for he couldna read nor write, and he thought Kester was above hisself. So when he couldna keep any longer, but mun speak or burst, he says –

'If young Sarn do like damaged goods, he'll get what he wants, and I doubt he'll have you to thank, Weaver. Very comfortable and pleasant you be together, I must say, you and Sarn's girl. It's baby linen you'd best be weaving, young Woodseaves.'

And with that, Kester snatched up his hat and all his things in a fury, but saying nought. And when he got to the door, he turns round and says –

'You may get Huglet's brother-law to weave for ye from now on, Grimble. You'll go without weaving for all me. You bin a foul-mouthed toad and a disgrace to your parish, which is situated in hell.'

178

He flung out, and he never came near the place again.

I was forced to go up to the attic to think about it a bit. I did love Kester so sore for his rage. I thought I'd like to see un in a rage, though not with me, for if he was in a proper rage with me, I'd die.

On Boxing Day I went across to the Stone House, and a windy walk it was, for the snow was drifted deep along the wood path. But it was fair overhead, and mistletoe thrush was singing, and the cuckoo's beads were very bright on all the may-trees. Beguildy was out, for a wonder. Missis Beguildy and me had a good talk.

'Well, well, poor lamb,' she said, 'to think she couldna come to her own Mother because the mester be such a pig-headed fool! Drat the man! Now what's to do? For go back to Grimble's she never shall. But ours'll be roaring-mad to think of all that money gone. Keep her a bit longer till the worst's worn off, my dear!'

'Oh, she can bide, and welcome, as long as she's a mind.'

'May them above reward ye!' she says. For she was a very religious person, in the manner of the church. And though I've no wish to speak ill of her, yet I partly think she was religious, in a measure at least, to spite Beguildy. But maybe this is a wicked thought of mine.

'Gideon was telling us that Callard's girl ran away afore winter,' I said. 'She's by lonesome there all day with the five little uns and the baby. Maybe if we went at it the right way, and made a favour of it, they'd pay the same rate as Grimbles. They'll get nobody else till the spring, for they're all hired now till May, and besides, Callard's Dingle inna a place the girls like. You go and see Missis Callard, and I'll make shift to have a lesson to keep your maister busy.'

'But you've left learning this long while, my dear, for you know as much as Beguildy does.'

'Ah, well, there's summat new I want to learn, but I dunno if it's in the books.'

'What met that be?'

'It's an old ancient charm, Missis Beguildy, and it's called content.'

'Oh, that! It's in no book of hisn.'

'Nor in any book,' I said. But I thought, there's one knows it. Please God, he met learn me. But that he never will.

'Eh, but it be no manner use for me to go, Prue,' she says. 'They'd set the dogs on me, very like. Callard's very religious, you mind. And he canna abide ours. And all *he* thinks, his missus thinks; all *he* says, *she* says, pat like the Sarn echo. Come to that, it'll go hard but they'll take Jancis in at all, whatever, being who her dada is. But maybe if *you* went, and told them on the quiet that Jancis is promised to Sarn, they met think of it, for your brother's beginning to be well spoken of as a man that's bound to be rich.'

So I said I'd go. I couldna abide going, being looked at a bit sideways myself, and spoken ill of time and again. But when I saw Gideon and Jancis so pleasant and merry together in the even, playing beggar-me-neighbour by firelight, I knew I was bound to go.

'Why, Gideon,' I says, 'you're busy at it, I see. Though you canna play conquer with cob-nuts and snail-housen now, being too old, you're beggaring somebody still.'

'Conquer!' says Mother from her corner. 'Ah, what a game that is! He was always very set on it, you mind. He liked to play ooth them big pink-and-white conquers, the Roman snail, they callen it, dunna they, Prue? It was those you went after the night poor Sarn was took in his boots. Poor soul!'

She cried a bit, and went to look very small, which she always did when she was vexed.

'There, there, Mother, dunna fret, he's in peace now.'

'Ah, poor soul! And Sarn's took the sin. My son Sarn. Shumbled it up proper, a did. And I can see as there'll be

180

lads to play conquer in our kitchen yet, with the big pink-and-white uns, of an evening.'

She looked across at the settle. Gideon had just beggared Jancis, and was in very good fettle.

'Ah, boys *and* girls,' says Mother. 'For I see well as he'll beggar her of more than cards.'

She began to laugh at the thought of the grandchildren, and at her joke, and she laughed so much that she gave herself a hoost, and I had to put her to bed.

Next day I set off for Callard's Dingle. It was a way nobody would choose to go with snow deep on the ground, for it lay over bleak, high pastures, with northerly slopes, bitter cold and drifted up. But seeing I was on a good errand, I began to sing, out on the bare pastures with none to hear.

'Open the gates as wide as the sky . . .'

And there by the farm, in a little fenced field, what should I see grazing under a dark pine wood but the white bull that Kester saved from the baiting? I stopped and looked at it a bit. There it was, not dead nor maimed, its nice white coat in good case, and looking as contented as if it was just come to heaven, and all because of Kester.

He'd kept his promise and paid the money, and then given the bull back to Callard for his children.

'If you ever come to think bull-baiting's bad, I'd lief you told 'em so,' he said, 'but not agen your conscience.'

Now Callard was a very honest man, and he felt bound to make some return, whether or no, so he took the matter up in good sadness. Jancis said afterwards that it was very amusing to see him gather all the children together round the hearth, sitting on their little stools, of an evening, the baby also being there on its mother's knee. And Callard ud say very loud –

'Bull-baiting's bad!'

And his missus in that melancholy voice of hers would repeat –

'Bad!' like the Sarn echo.

. Then all the children would sing out, like a nest of birds –
'Bull-baiting's bad!'

And times the baby would give a guggle, and times he'd
stay quiet, considering, like. There was only one disagreeing
voice, and that was old Granfer Callard's, which was very
high and trembling. He'd call out –

'No! No! It inna bad. It be a right good merry old
sport!'

But nobody listened to him, for he was getting very
simple. He came to the door when I knocked, and called
out to his daughter-in-law –

'It be that there long thin young 'oman, Maria. The
witch woman.'

'Well, bring her in, feyther-law.'

'Come thy ways,' he says. 'Her'll be down when the baby
gives over hollering. I do wish I'd got such lungs as hisn. I
be very middling. Very middling I be. Can you do cures?'

I said no to that.

'Oh! I thought Beguildy's learnt ye. A very sinful man
is that. Soaked in sin like a sheep in raddle. It wunna be
any manner use for 'im to yammer at the doors o' Paradise
and say, 'Wesh me and I shall be whiter than snow.' For
I tell ye not the Judge of all could clane 'im, even if He
could spare the time to it. Ah! A wicked old man is the
Wizard. I do believe he lives by sucking folks' life away in
the mid of night. Ah! sucks their blood, he does. They
seyn he goes to the churchyard and digs folk up to steal
their bwones and grind 'em for his spells. They seyn he
fetches little children whome in his bag, and makes a meal
of 'em. Oh, he be the wickedest man since Punty Pilate,
no danger!'

By this, the elder children were roaring with fright, and
Missis Callard called out from the top of the stair –

'Feyther-law, what be saying now? Hold thy noise!'

Mister Callard came in then, and said I'd best take pot-
luck, seeing it was tea-time. So when we'd had our tea, I
told them about Jancis.

182

'So 'er run away!' says Mister Callard. 'In this weather. Well, by gum!'

'Gum!' says his missus.

'Broke her time!' says Callard.

'Time!' says his missus, sorrowful.

'Nobody ever broke their time when *I* was a lad,' said the old man. 'They darstna. They'd have been put in the stocks.'

'And you be sure it inna anything to do with Weaver?'

'Weaver!' says Missis Callard, grievous.

'Weaver! Weaver!' shouted the children, and it seemed to me as if they praised his name.

'I be as sure of that as I'm sure that I breathe,' I said.

'And she's promised to your brother?'

'Ah. They'll be wed come Harvest Home.'

'Then,' says Mister Callard, 'the missus shall give the girl a trial.'

'Trial!' echoes Missis Callard in a hopeless sort of way, as if she thought that was what Jancis would be.

They agreed to take Jancis for six months, and to give her three pound, which was a deal for them to offer. So I went back in high feather. Next day Gideon said we could have Bendigo, so I drove Jancis to Callard's, stopping at Beguildy's on the way, to break the news to the old man.

Oh, dear me, but he was in a passion And the worst of it was, that he blamed it all on to Gideon, who had nought to do with it at all.

'I'll be even with that brother of yours for this,' he says. 'Ah! A very aggravating man. His dad was the same. I couldna plan out anything or set my hand to any work but he'd come and knock it down, tiddly-bump. And young Sarn's the same. Look at the way he's let and hindered me over the young squire!'

But Missis Beguildy was pleased.

'And you shall come whome at the end of hay harvest, Jancis,' she said, 'to make your wedding clo'es. And the wedding shall be at Michaelmas. The Glory roses'll be in their second blooming then, and you shall have 'em for your nosegay.'

'I tell ye,' says Beguildy, 'as Sarn shanna take her. You can tell un so from me, Prue Sarn. Thwarted I wunna be. I've cursed the man by fire and watter, and cursed he'll surely be. Tell un neither with the ring nor without it shall he take my wench.'

'Well, good day to you, Mister Beguildy,' I said. For I thought it was time to drive on.

'Prue,' said Jancis as we drove through the water meadows between Plash and Callard's Dingle, 'what for did ye knife Grimble's dog and take on the way you did about Weaver?'

She looked up at me with those big blue eyes of hers, and I beat Bendigo cruel so as to be busy about summat. The poor old nag gave a half look round, and my conscience pricked me, but what was I to do?

'Folk be saying it was a very out-of-the-ornary thing for a girl to do for a stranger. Ah! even as far as Grimble's they knew it was you, though neither Grimble nor the missus told 'em, for they didna like to speak of it, being beaten over it. But everybody knows in all the country round by this.'

She kept on looking and looking at me, and the red-scarlet was burning like fire in my cheeks. I kept on thrashing Bendigo, and we went over the tumps and marshy bits at such a wallop as never was.

Jancis gave a little laugh, very knowing and aggravating.

'Poor owd Bendigo's done nought,' she says.

'I want to get there,' I answers, foolish-like.

'Oh, I'll be bound you'll get there,' she says. Then she was quiet for a bit, though she watched me all the while.

'I wonder,' she said after a time, 'what Weaver ud think if he knew?'

'He couldna know,' I said. 'He was in a swound.'

'He met hear tell! And I wonder that he'd think if it came to his ears that Prue Sarn had foughten for un like a tiger?'

'He'd think nought. Everybody do know *I*'m sorry for the afflicted.'

'Well, but he inna what you'd call one of the afflicted, Mister Woodseaves inna. He's the best wrostler in these parts, and a right proper man.'

'He was afflicted when Grimble's Toby got 'im by the throat, wunna he?'

'Ah. But why must it be Prue Sarn that did save him? And why must she take his yead to her bosom so kind and all? Not but what he's got very nice brown hair, and silky. I was used to notice it when he was writing the letters for me. And that Felena thinks so too. She does fairly tarment him, market days.'

'What a brazen piece! What does she do?'

I was glad to turn Jancis on to summat else.

'O she goes to the house, and leaves a great basket of mushrooms, or a frail of wimberries, or maybe a bit of mutton, if shepherd's killed a sheep. And if she meets him in the road, she'll look at un with them green eyes and smile as sweet as an October nut. And one night when shepherd was drunk and they were late starting whome, what must she do but go in the dusk and sing a wild song outside his window.'

'What did she sing?'

'O, she sang –

'A vargin went a-souling in the dark of the moon.
A soul-cake! A soul-cake!
O give it me kindly and give it me soon.
A soul-cake! A soul-cake!
The young man he looks from his window so bright.
Here's a vargin come wailing in the dark of the night!
Now what'll you give me for a soul-cake, my maid?
My body, my body for a soul-cake! she said.'

And I call that a right down improper song, dunna you, Prue?'

'What did *he* think of it?'

'I wouldna demean myself to ask him. But she's a very wild woman, is Felena. She'll 'tice him and tempt him to a fall if somebody dunna keep her off. But I want to know what I be to say to Weaver if he asks me why you were so busy a-saving of him.'

'Say nought.'

'Nought's no answer.'

'It's all he'll get.'

'The way you stood over the fellow like one of the angels at Eden gate, with that great knife!'

'It's none of your business if I did.'

'Ah. It be.'

'For why?'

'Because I love ye, Prue.'

'Thanks be to goodness, we're at Callard's,' I said, as we came into the fold, and the house door burst open and out came the five children, Granfeyther Callard, Missis Callard and the baby, like bees from a skep.

The last thing Jancis said afore I drove away was –

'I shall be bound to send for Weaver soon.'

'Whatever for?'

'To write me a letter to Sarn.'

'Why, you be only a tuthree miles from Gideon now. Whatever do you want to write a letter for?'

'It's none of your business if I do,' says she, very mim, and laughing to herself, 'which is what you did say to me, Prue Sarn!'

Chapter 5: *Dragon-Flies*

FROM the time when Jancis went to Callard's Dingle, through the spring and summer, there is nothing written in my book saving of my own special concerns, such as

the progress I made in reading hard books and the thoughts
that came to me in the attic. These, as they had no bearing
on the lives of others at that time, are not of any interest,
and I will not weary you with them. Gideon went to
Callard's Dingle every Sunday, and worked like three men
in between. I ploughed furrow for furrow along of him,
and dug spade for spade. Our farm was rich with corn.
Never afore or since did I see any fields in our part of
the country in such good case, for it was a year of sweet,
growing weather, with enough rain to swell the grain and
not enough to make it ackerspire. Sunday after Sunday
I saw Gideon, on the way to Callard's, stop and lean over
the gate at the top of the sloping meadow, where you
could look over the whole place, like a miser with his gold.
And now and agen I went with him, and was glad to see
such a glowing content in anybody's face, but a deal more
glad since it was Gideon's, that was seldom what you met
call a happy face. When he'd gone striding along, whistling
pretty near out loud, I'd sit a while afore going back
to Mother. I'd think to myself that when he was wed
to Jancis, the corn and Fortune knocking at the door,
then at long last he'd whistle out loud. I got a great longing to hear that, for it seemed to me an unhealthy sort
of thing for folks to whistle or sing or speak to their mommets
all the while.

'Come harvest!' I'd think. And I'd begin to dream of
being as beautiful as a fairy.

It was a great delight to me, apart from the thought of
all this, to look at the standing corn and see it like a great
mere under the wind. Times it was still, without a ripple;
times it went in little waves, and you could almost think
the big bosses of wild onion flowers under the far hedges
were lilies heaving gently on the tide; and times there was
a great storm down in those hollows, like the storm in
Galilee Mere, that the King of Love did still. So I watched
the grain week by week, from the time when it was all
one green till it began to take colour, turning raddled or

abron or pale, each in its kind. And it shone nights, as
if there was a light behind it, with a kind of soft shining
like glow-worms or a marish light. I never knew, nor do
I know now, why corn shines thus in the nights of July
and August, keeping a moonlight of its own even when
there is no moon. But it is a marvellous thing to see when
the great hush of full summer and deep night is upon the
land, till even the aspen tree, that will ever be gossiping,
durstna speak, but holds breath as if she waited for the
coming of the Lord. I make no doubt that if any read
this book it will seem strange to them that a farm woman
should look at the things about her in this wise, and indeed
it is not many do. But when you dwell in a house you
mislike, you will look out of window a deal more than
those that are content with their dwelling. So I, finding
my own person and my own life not to my mind, took
my pleasure where I could. There were things I waited
for as a wench waits for her sweetheart at her edge of
the forest. This rippling and shining of the corn was one,
and another which came about the time of the beginning
of the troubling of the water, was the marvellous sight
of the dragon-flies coming out of their bodies. We had
a power of dragon-flies at Sarn, of many kinds and colours,
little and big. But every one was bound in due season to
climb up out of its watery grave and come out of its body
with great labour and pain, and a torment like the torment of childbirth, and a rending like the rending of
the tomb. And there was no year, since the first time I
saw it, that I missed to see this showing forth of God's
power.

I went down by the mere to gather honeysuckle wrathes
to bind besoms. And being sad in calling to mind what
Miss Dorabella had said, for besoms ever made me think
on it, and seeing that the troubling of the water was even
now beginning, with a slow gentle simmering all over the
mere, I thought I would go to a place I knew where there
were always mort of dragon-flies, and take comfort from

seeing them coming out of their bodies. Dragon-fly, I say, because I doubt some wouldna know what our name for them meant. We called the dragon-fly the ether's mon or ether's nild at Sarn, for it was supposed that where the adder, or ether, lay hid in the grass, there above hovered the ether's mon as a warning. One kind, all blue, we called the kingfisher; and another one, with a very thin body, the darning-needle. Mother was used to tell Gideon that if he took dog's leave or did other mischief the devil would take needle to him and use the dragon-flies to sew up his ears, so he couldna hear the comfortable word of God and would come to damnation. But I could never believe that the devil could have power over such a fair thing as a dragon-fly.

That was the best time of year for our lake, when in the still, hot noons the water looked so kind, being of a calm, pale blue, that you would never think it could drown anybody. All round stood the tall trees, thick-leaved with rich summer green, unstirring, caught in a spell, sending down their coloured shadows into the mere, so that the tree-tops almost met in the middle. From either hand the notes of the small birds that had not yet given up singing went winging out across the water, and so quiet it was that though they were only such thin songs as those of willow wrens and robins, you could hear them all across the mere. Even on such a burning day as this, when I pulled the honeysuckle wrathes, there was a sweet, cool air from the water, very heady and full of life. For though Sarn was an ill place to live, and in the wintry months a very mournful place, at this one time of the year it left off dreaming of sorrow and was as other fair stretches of wood and water. All around the lake stood the tall bulrushes with their stout heads of brown plush, just like a long coat Miss Dorabella had. Within the ring of rushes was another ring of lilies, and at this time of the year they were the most beautiful thing at Sarn, and the most beautiful thing I'd ever seen. The big bright leaves lay calm upon the

189

water, and calmer yet upon the leaves lay the lilies, white and yellow. When they were buds, they were like white and gold birds sleeping, head under wing, or like summat carven out of glistering stone, or, as I said afore, they were like gouts of pale wax. But when they were come into full blow they wunna like anything but themselves, and they were so lovely you couldna choose but cry to see them. The yellow ones had more of a spread of petals, having five or six apiece, but the white ones opened their four wider and each petal was bigger. These petals are of a glistening white within, like the raiment of those men who stood with Christ upon the mountain top, and without they are stained with tender green, as if they had taken colour from the green shadows in the water. Some of the dragon-flies look like this also, for their lacy wings without other colour are sometimes touched with shifting green.

So the mere was three times ringed about, as if it had been three times put in a spell. First there was the ring of oaks and larches, willows, ollern trees and beeches, solemn and strong, to keep the world out. Then there was the ring of rushes, sighing thinly, brittle and sparse, but enough, with their long, trembling shadows, to keep the spells in.

Then there was the ring of lilies, as I said, lying there as if Jesus, walking upon the water, had laid them down with His cool hands, afore He turned to the multitude saying, 'Behold the lilies!' And as if they were not enough to shake your soul, there beneath every lily, white and green or pale gold, was her bright shadow, as it had been her angel. And through the long, untroubled day the lilies and their angels looked one upon the other and were content.

There were plenty of dragon-flies about, both big and little. There were the big blue ones that are so strong they will fly over the top of tallest tree if you fritten them, and there were the tiny thin ones that seem almost too small to be called dragon-flies at all. There were rich blue kingfisher flies and those we called damsels, coloured and polished in the manner of lustre ware. There were a good few with clear wings of no colour or of faint green, and a tuthree with a powdery look like you see on the leaves of 'rickluses. Some were tawny, like a fitchet cat, some were rusty or coloured like the copper fruit-kettle. Jewels, they made you think of, precious gems such as be listed in the Bible. And the sound of their wings was loud in the air, sharp and whirring, when they had come to themselves after their agony. Whiles, in some mossy bit of clear ground between the trees, they'd sit about like so many cats round the hearth, very contented in themselves, so you could almost think they were washing their faces and purring.

On a tall rush close by the bank I found one just beginning to come out of its body, and I leaned near, pretty well holding my breath, to see the miracle. Already the skin over its bright, flaming eyes was as thin as glass, so that you could see them shining like coloured lamps. In a little, the old skin split and it got its head out. Then began the wrostling and the travail to get free, first its legs, then its shoulders and soft wrinkled wings. It was like a creature possessed, seeming to fall into a fit, times, and, times, to be struck stiff as a corpse. Just afore the end, it stayed a long while still, as if it was wondering whether it durst get quite free in a world all new. Then it gave a great heave and a kind of bursting wrench and it was out. It clomb a little way further up the bulrush, very sleepy and tired, like a child after a long day at the fair, and fell into a doze, while its wings began to grow. 'Well,' I says, with a bit of a laugh and summat near a bit of a sob, 'well, you've done it! It's cost you summat, but you've won free. I'm in behopes you'll have a pleasant time. I suppose this be your Paradise, binna it?'

But of course it couldna make any sign, save to go on growing its wings as fast as might be. So there I stood, with my armful of wrathes, and there it clung, limp on the brown rush, in the golden light that had come upon Sarn like a merciful healer. I was wasting my time, which was deadly sin at our place, and I turned to go. But just as I turned, there was a bit of a rustle, and there stood Kester Woodseaves.

I made to run away, and indeed I'd have jumped into the mere sooner than he should see me. But he put his hand on my shoulder, and for all it was gentle, it was a wrostler's hand, and not to be said no to.

'What? Oot run away? Why, Prue Sarn?' he said.

I hung my head and wished I was the dragon-fly. I said nought.

I gave a despert pull, but it was no manner use. He only laughed.

'I do think,' he said, in the voice that made its own summer, 'that to be a very funny way to treat a chap as comes to thank ye kindly for saving of his life, Prue Sarn, to take off the like of that'n, and try to jump in the lake!'

His hand sent such a throbbing through me that I could scarce stand.

'What were you looking at when I came?' he asked me.

'The damsel fly, coming out of its shroud.'

'Once out,' he says, 'they're out for good. It costs a deal to get free. But once free, they never fold their wings.'

'No,' I said, 'and some of 'em go so high, I think, times, they might flitter right into heaven.'

'We'd all like to do that, I'll be bound, if we could choose our heaven. I'm not very choice of golden streets myself. And I'd like my heaven afore I die.'

'And what ud it be?' I asked him. I was so interested, I declare I'd clean forgot my curse.

'I'm not quite sure yet,' he says, 'but come a year, maybe, I'll know.'

'There's a long while,' I says, mocking at him, 'to be hiver hovering, choosing your bit of paradise.'

'Could you think of yours sooner, Prue Sarn?' says he.

I looked at his green coat, which made him a very personable man, and I fixed on a place on the left side, just betwixt the sleeve of it and the breast of it, where I'd lief lay my head, and I said –

'Ah. I've thought of mine.'

'Oh! Well, what is it?'

'I said as I'd thought of it, Mister Woodseaves. But my thoughts be my own.'

He laughed. Then he says –

'You can write a dommed good letter, Prue.'

'They were Gideon's letters.'

'I take it very kind in Sarn to tell me to change my stockings when they be wet. It inna often you find a man as thinks of such things, and Sarn least of all, I'd have said.'

He let me have the full light of his eyes, and I hung my head and found nothing to answer.

'And the sewing work, and the damson cheese and the pickle at half market price, well, I tell you, it fairly bowled me over, for I'd heard Sarn was a hard man, very near in a bargain, asking nothing and giving nothing. And then for him to offer me those victuals! I must have misjudged the chap cruel.'

But by this I'd remembered that the stockings were in the letter I wrote for Jancis after she ran away. So I said, it was Jancis mentioned stockings.

'Oh, yes, so it was!' he says. 'I liked that letter. A very nice girl, that. For whoever wrote the letter, she made it up, of course!'

He looked at me again, and I found nought to say.

' "I be more choice of him I love than of all else in the world beside!" That's a woman worth summat to a fellow,' he went on. 'And, "I love him past telling, and shall to the end." And in especial that about, "spend my life any time very willing, and die for you by bite of dog or any way, my dear." I liked that. But when I come to think of it, 'twas Sarn said that to Jancis Beguildy. What a lover the man must be! You must be main fond of him, Prue Sarn.'

193

'Oh, yes,' I said, all in a flush, 'I be.'

'Indeed yes, and only what you should be. Good feeling he has, too, about the choice of texts, and Jancis the same. For that text, "The Maister be come," was in the letter Jancis wrote to me, as well as in the one Sarn wrote to Jancis.'

'Only natural,' I said.

'I'm coming to Sarn's love-carriage, and I'll be bound to thank him for his kind thoughts about the sewing and the damson cheese and the pickle,' he said.

'Oh, dunna!' I cried out, knowing how angry Gideon would be.

'There's a grudging girl,' he says, 'not wanting her brother to be thanked.'

He had a look of satisfaction on his face, as if he'd found out what he wanted to know.

'Well, it's no use ifting and anding any more,' he says. 'You wrote the letters, and you made 'em up. And all I can say is, the chap you were thinking of when you said the things you did say is a lucky chap, whoever he is.'

'I hanna got an acquaintance.'

'Dear me! That's pity, to my mind. But anyway, you've got a friend. You write in your book, when you go back, that Kester Woodseaves is your friend till Time stops.'

I thanked him very kindly for that, and then he said, should we go and look for some more dragon-flies coming out of their shrouds? So we did, and had a tidy bit of talk, one way or another, about this and that. We watched the dragon-flies take off from the tops of the rushes, and we saw the water simmering in its troubling, and the lilies looking at their angels.

But it was a long time before I remembered to say, how did he know about my book that I wrote in? For it seemed I couldna remember anything very well when he was by.

'Well,' he says, 'maybe a bird told me. Or an old ancient woman like a little bird.'

194

'But how did you get to know all the other things you do seem to know about me?'

'Well,' he said, 'there's a tuthree people know you, Prue. And there's few know you and dunna love you. And I expect I've been leasing in their hearts a bit. And I think there's not much that I dunna know about you, Prue.'

There was rest in that saying. And oh, the summer in his voice, then and always! I forgot the time and all. Yes, indeed to goodness, I forgot milking time! But when I saw the light of evening long upon the mere, and heard the evening breezes lifting up the leaves in the forest, I turned to go. Then he said –

'There's a thing I'm bound to ask you.'

He stood looking straight into my eyes, for we were almost of a height, though he was a little the taller.

'What for did you do all you did for me that day at the baiting?' he said. 'What for did you stand above me with the knife, and run to Lullingford and all, to save me?'

There was a deep silence, with only the lifting of the summer boughs, the lapping of the quiet water. How was I to answer? Yet he would have an answer, I could see.

Then I thought, seeing the lilies looking at their angels, how I'd called myself Kester's angel at the baiting.

'Why, it was only that I was your angel for that day,' I said at long last. 'A poor daggly angel, too.'

'If you're ever wanting an angel's situation, you can send to me for a written character,' he said, and though his words were merry, his eyes were as grave as grave could be. And then, as we said good night and I turned home, he called out after me – 'Not so daggly, neither!'

And I could hear him laughing in the wood.

BOOK FOUR

Chapter 1: *Harvest Home*

NEVER in all my days did I see a corn harvest like that one. We started swiving, that is reaping, at the beginning of August-month, and we left the stooks standing in the fields till it should be time for the love-carriage, for the weather was so fine that they took no harm. It was the custom, if a farmer hadna much strength about him, that he should fix on a day for the neighbours to come and give a hand in the lugging of the grain. But up to that time, the weather being so good, we worked alone. It was up in the morning early, and no mistake! Such mornings as they were, too, with a strong heady sweetness in the air from the ripened corn, and the sun coming up stately as a swan into the vasty sky that had no cloud. Mother was very peärt and lively, what with the hot weather, which was good for the rheumatics, and the thought of the easing off of the work which was to come when the harvest was gotten in. She'd be up and about at five, getting us our breakfast, and then off we'd go, with only just enough of clo'es on to be decent, and with our wooden harvest bottles full of small beer. We always had a brewing for the rep, that is, the reaping. This year we brewed a deal more, for there be all the neighbours to find in victuals and drink at the love-carriage. Looking back, it always seems to me that there was a kind of dwelling charm on all that time. Gideon was more contented than I've ever seen him, for there were two things that contented him, namely, to work till he dropped, and to finish what he set out to do. To see all his farm set with these rick stooks, sound and ripe, with never a sign of the weevil nor of mildew nor the smut, was very life to him. He was all of a fever to get it safe in stack, but we were bound to wait till the day fixed. Jancis was to come on that day, to help in the leasing. And it seemed to me as she ought to go atop of the last load with blossoms about her, like the image they were used to set up there, for she seemed a part of the harvest, with all that pink and gold.

As for me, I went all dazed and dumb with wonder. To think it was true, 'The Maister be come!' To think as he'd looked at me and hadna hated me! To think as all that time we spent in the midst of the painted dragon-flies by the mere was true, as true as daily bread! When I called to mind the things he'd said and still more the things he'd looked, I was like to swound. Dear to goodness, how I did sing, those early dawns, when the dews lay heavy after a ketch of frost, and the corn rustled and stirred in the wind of morning!

When we went out, the leaves of the late-blooming white clover would be folded tight, and the shepherd's hour-glass shut. I'd watch them, in the minutes I took for rest, opening soft and slow like timid hearts. Then Mother would come with our nooning, creeping over the fields in her black like a little sad-coloured bird, and some-times singing *Barley Bridge* in her old, small voice, that yet was sweet. Then after the noon-spell, through the long, blazing evening (for with us all the time after noon is called evening), I'd watch the shepherd's hour-glass shutting up again, and the white clover leaves, folding as the dews came. We took turns to go whome and milk, then we'd have our tea in the field, and at it again. All the while I thought of Kester, as would soon be working at the coloured weaving in the great city. But when my heart said he was working for me as well as hisself, I hushed it, saying that it was but his flaming look that made me think it, for he hadna said it, and so it was only that the wish fathered the thought. But I did dream of the fifty pounds I was to have, a great fortune, it seemed. And

I did plan how I'd get to be cured as quick as might be, so when Kester came back after this time away I'd stand afore him with as proper a face as even Felena, though I hoped not so forrard.

At last the day of the love-carriage came and a tremendous blue day it was, with a sky like a dark bowl, Worcester china colour. We'd got fifty people coming, no less, counting the women-folk. I was up afore dawn getting all ready, setting the china, both ours and what we'd borrowed, on the trestles in the orchard, helping Gideon to put the casks of beer in the yard, ready for the men to fill their harvest bottles, and fetching water from the well for the tea. The orchard was a sight to see when the trestles were set out (for I could put all ready with no fear of rain on such a day) with the mugs and platters of many colours, and the brown quartern loaves, and the big pats of butter stamped with a swan, and the slabs of honeycomb dough cakes, gingerbread, cheese, jam and jelly, let alone the ham at one end of each trestle and the round of beef at the other. Even Gideon didna begrutch the food on this day. For it was one of the laws you couldna break, that at a love-carriage everybody must have his bellyful.

It was very early when the waggons began to roll into the fold, with a solemn gladsome sound, and each with its own pair of horses or oxen. Each farmer brought his own men and his own waggon, and sometimes he brought two. The teams were decked out with ribbons and flowers, and some had a motto as well, such as, 'Luck to our Day,' or 'God bless the Corn.' It was a fine thing to see the big horses, with great manes on their fetlocks, groomed till they shone like satin, stepping along as proud as Lucifer, knowing very well how long the waggoner had been a-plaiting their ribbons. The oxen were good to see, also, for their horns were all bedecked, and about their necks were thick chains of Sweet William and Travellers' Joy and corn. Miller came among the first, with his gig and the old coach horse, the best he had, poor man. And very good work they did, too, for it's surprising what a deal you can get on to a gig if you put a set of wings on top.

It was time for me to go and give the folks welcome, so I got Miller's Tim to mind the trestles, and left him with a big meat patty, sitting at the top of one of the tables, with half the patty in one cheek, ready to drive away birds and cats and dogs, and even goblins out of fairyland, after the patty. The ox-driver from Plash had dizened his beasts up proper, with bulrushes nodding on their horns, and there were Sukey and Moll each riding one. Their mother wasna coming till late, and they were wild as mountain finches. Then came Felena, riding the shepherd's rough pony, with the panniers to put her leasings in. When I saw those green eyes of hers shining like jewels in her brown face, all flushed with summer, and the long, slim shoulders of her, and that red mouth, I almost hoped Kester would forget to come after all. Missis Beguildy and Jancis came, but Beguildy wouldna. The cousin from Lullingford that got the toothache so bad came, and his missus. Then there were Callards, all packed in a great harvest wain, and a net over the five children, so that they looked for all the world like little calves on the way to market. Granfeyther Callard sat by his son, dressed out in his best snuff-coloured coat and his beaver hat, for all it was so hot. There was a posy in his hat, which he waved like a lad as they came creaking in at the fold gate, shouting –

'Harroost! Harroost! Never was such God A'mighty's weather!'

He always said harroost, it being the old way of saying harvest. Then came Sexton, tall and black, a bit sour, but the best man of his age with a pikel anywhere round. Missis Sexton had a vast apron of blue gingham, with pockets for leasing, and it made her look bigger than ever. It did seem a blasphemy to speak of her leasing, as if

Solomon in all his glory had put on an apron and gathered up the ears.

Tivvy was dressed out very grand, as often was the way of girls at such '*dos*' as this, for a '*do*' was a thing that came but seldom, and where else but church, where all but bonnets was swallowed by the pew, could you show your gown with the flounces, or your gown that was cut low?

Tivvy had a straw bonnet with quilled muslin under, a sprigged gown cut low with a rose at the breast, white stockings and new black sandal-shoes. Jancis was pretty past telling in her blue poplin and a sunbonnet, and Sukey and Moll had tight frocks of white cotton with red roses sprinkled on them.

The Callard children ran about like a clutch of chickens when you empty 'em out of the basket, but Miller's Tim was as mim as a mute, feeling so grand to be trusted with all the feast to mind. Missis Miller and Polly, I may say, came first of all, and there was Miller's man as well, and Sexton's Sammy, a queer, long lad like an eel, with twice as many teeth as he wanted, and a power of texts in his head that ud fly out at you on every excuse, and hit you like a startle-de-buz will on a summer evening. It seemed as if all the texts his dad had ever read had lodged in his big head, and so he'd always got one pat.

'Pray ye therefore the Lord of the harvest to send down labourers into His harvest,' he says. But the publican from the *Mug o' Cider*, whose missus was looking after the bar so he could come, Gideon being like to be a good customer in the future, catched him up very quick.

'Dunna begin the prayers till I've had a quart, lad,' he says, 'for they might be answered, you being Sexton's lad, and I'm welly parched.'

The men gathered together by the beer barrels, and as more came, they went and got their beer. Towler came, and shepherd, Felena's maister, a tall, brown man, all bones, striding with his long kibba, which is a stick of six foot or so, to walk with, held about the middle.

'Well, shepherd!' pipes up Granfeyther Callard, 'han you seed the sun dance yet, Easter morning, on thy mountain?'

Shepherd took no notice, for being with the dumb sheep so much, he was pretty near as silent as the miller, though not quite, for nobody could be. But the father of Moll and Sukey said –

'Nay, but 'tis his missus sees the moon dance, midsummer, as we know well.'

'When she dances with the devil!' screeched Sukey.

'And not the devil only,' says Missis Sexton.

Felena didna seem to care. She was standing by me, and she whispered that she'd liefer dance, whoever it was with, and be jimp and souple, than be as stiff as a tombstone like Missis Sexton.

'She brought him up into the high place of Baal, Numbers twenty-two,' said Sammy. And after that there didna seem anything more to say about it.

Gideon came up to settle each man's work, and he looked right well in his nice clean smock, well broidered, with the sleeves rolled up to show his great arms, and a pikel over shoulder.

'Now, Gaffer!' pipes up old Callard. 'What bin 'e going to give I to do?'

'You shall go atop of the waggon I serve,' says Sexton, 'if ye promise to take as quick as I chuck.'

There was a laugh, for nobody ever liked the job of settling the sheaves Sexton heaved, he being the quickest heaver anywhere round, and never tiring.

'Oh,' says Mug of Cider, 'we'll put you on the leader of the foremost waggon for a lucky image, wunna we, lads? You can holler *Haw-woop!* and *Jiggin!* and be a sight more use than any of us.'

The old man took this as a great compliment, and nought would do but his son must help him up there and then.

'Well, lads,' says Gideon, 'we'd best be shifting if we're to bring the harvest whome this day.'

'Harroost! Harroost!' calls out old Callard. *'Haw-woop!'*

Obedient to the word, the lead-horse went forrard, and all the waggons and carts moved slow past the house. Mother stood on the door-sill, nodding and smiling, and saying –

'Thank you for us, I'm sure! My son Sarn'll be obleeged to ye.'

So we went out under the blue sky to lug home the corn, the big waggons with solid wheels rolling over the stubble, Granfeyther Callard shouting *'Jiggin!'* when he meant *'Haw-woop!'* being quite tipsy with enjoyment, and causing a great confusion, the horses not knowing what to do. The rest of us followed on, strung out over the fields in bright colours, children and dogs running hither and thither, while in the rickyard the men told off to make the stacks put the logs in place ready for the stacks to be built on, got all prepared against the first waggon came back loaded high with grain, and then stood leaning on their pikels, talking over the work of the coming day, each man as busy about the planning of it all as if the harvest was his'n, and each man as glad of the grain as if he was to have the selling of it. For that was the manner of the love-carriages in time past.

In the noon-spell I went up to the high pasture, to see if there was any sign of Kester. He was coming across the far meadows, by a field path, and I stayed so long watching him, who was all the world to me, that they'd started work again before I went back. It was a pretty thing to see, in such a place, on such a day. The farm being all under corn now, it looked like a boss of gold in the dark woods and meadows around. And all the bright colours of the women's gowns, the creamy smocks and a tuthree coloured shirts of the men, the shining horses and deep-coloured oxen, the yellow stooks with blue shadows under, the towering yellow loads on the wains, made up such a picture as you wunna often see in a lifetime, anyway in these days.

It was merry to hear, also. The voices rang so sweet in the thin, still air. I could hear old Callard's *'Haw-woop!'* and *'Jiggin!'* and the other men's shouts, and Jancis laughing out high and sweet at summat Gideon did say, and the children crying out, 'Mother, I've gotten two pinnies full now!' 'Mam, I've found six ears together!' From the rickyard came the far calls of the rickmakers, and, times, a pigeon cooed in the deep woods, where the mere lay like glass, and, times, a jay would scold, or a woodpecker laugh out. Never a cloud was in the sky, nor any hint of trouble in the little airs that stirred in the leavy hedges. And there, two fields off, one field off, and now in the same field, was the man I could never think about but in those words, 'The Maister be come.'

From a long way off he saw me, and waved his hat, so that the well-shapen head I did love was bare, with the dark hair just so upon it, that you must long to stroke it.

I came down from the high pasture and stood beside Gideon's waggon, knowing that Kester would come to get his orders from the maister of the day.

There was some chaff, Kester being so late.

'Weaver's forgot the day and come to-morrow instead!'

'Dunna be so forrard, Weaver, come on Plough Monday!'

'He bin late, but he bin full of power and might and young blood,' said old Callard, for nobody of that family would ever hear a word against Kester.

'The last shall be fust, and the fust last, Matthew twenty,' says Sammy.

'Luck to the day, Gaffer!' Kester called to Gideon.

'And thank you kind for coming,' answers Gideon.

'What be I to do?'

'Ever done any harvesting?'

'Ah.'

'Can ye pitch?'

'Ah.'

'Well, then you take my place a bit while I go the round, oot? Sexton's tother side from you, and he's a terrible

quick pitcher. But you canna be too quick for young
Callard and Towler.'

'But mind not to push pikel too fur when the load be
low,' called old Callard, 'for I mind once a fellow did that,
and he stuck it right into the chap atop. Ah! like a piece
of toast on toasting-fork he was, poor fellow, and hollered
so that the team bolted, ooth the pikel still in.'

But Kester did very well and made toast of none. His
eyes would laugh at me now and again, and once, when
the empty waggon tarried, he came where I was leasing,
and said –

'You still go frommet me a bit, I see, Prue Sarn. It mun
be toerts, not frommet.'

I put the ears this way and that way, but no words came.

Then he said, slow, with a laugh at the back of his voice,
but with a cosseting sound as well –

'There, there, my dear! None shall touch you now!'

All the strong life of the man was gathered in his eyes,
and blazing full on me. So he'd heard! Folk do sometimes
when they seem nigh dead. He'd heard and remembered
the words I'd said when his head was on my bosom and my
heart was all rent with love. What could I say? Nought.
Where could I hide my burning face, that his eyes did so
dwell on? Nowhere at all.

'Hi, Weaver!' they called. 'Waggon be come and we be
hindered for ye!'

'I never knew a mother's love, nor yet a sister's, nor yet a
sweetheart's.' He said it ever so softly, but despert earnest,
so that the words burnt in. 'But if I had, I should have
forgot 'em all three when you said those words to me, Prue
Sarn!'

With that, he turned sharp and went back to the waggon.

What a day that was! Gold? I should think it *was* gold!
I leased and leased, and it was just as if every armful was
some precious, heavenly treasure. Nearly all the fields
were clean and bare when we had our tea under the hedge
shade, for it grew no cooler as the shadows lengthened,

being one of those mid-September days when all the gathered warmship of the summer seems to be spent and squandered in love of the golden grain.

The sun was low in heaven and the harvest-beer low in cask when Mother banged the tray for me to come and help with the urns for supper. They were loading the last waggon, and I told Tim, who'd been a good, faithful watcher, that he could go to the field and ride home atop along with the other children, in the triumph. Then we brought out the urns, and the cask of home-brewed, very strong and good, and set about cutting up the meat and bread.

We heard 'em shouting from the fields, and in a while there it came, the biggest waggon, with Jancis's white oxen and the oxen from Plash lugging it, Granfeyther Callard driving, all the children on top, and Jancis with them, waving green boughs and bunches of poppies, and Gideon, looking taller than customary in his smock, walking glad and solemn beside the load.

Deary me, how the tears do spring! Tears like Mother and I shed then, for the joy of it all, and other tears, for what came to pass after. For if in the mid of that great golden day you'd sent a sough of wind, and a mutter, and black clouds running up the sky, and darkness and thunder and forkit lightning, it couldna have been worse nor less expected than the storm that broke on us so soon.

The waggon came on, and all the people followed, singing and shouting, till they came to the gate of the rickyard.

There stood Parson, with Mother and me close by, to bless the corn.

'People!' he said, 'let us give thanks for daily bread!'

And all the people said –

'We give thanks unto the Lord.'

'God bless the corn and the master of Sarn,' says Parson, 'and may his good deeds return unto him as doves to their mountains.'

'Amen!' said the people.

'Missis Sarn bids me say that the feast is spread in the orchard, and all are welcome,' said Parson.

Gideon stepped forrard.

'The harvest's whome, friends, and thank ye kindly,' he said. 'Let every man who's lent a hand claim task work of me from this on, till I've paid my debt.'

We sat at the trestles in the long light of sunset. At least, the company did, but we at the urns were kept busy enough and hadna much time to sit down.

'Well, Weaver,' says Mug o' Cider, 'I hear tell as they're making it pretty warm for ye, for stopping the bull-baiting. But I bear no grutch, I'm sure.'

'Nor yet me. I like a man that likes a dawg,' says Towler.

'Nor yet me,' says Mister Callard from the next table.

'But there's some not to hold nor to bind,' said Mug o' Cider. 'I hear 'em in the bar, nights. Oh, I say nought! Landlord's a dumb dog with pricket ears. Ah! That's landlord. But they mean ye no good, Weaver. It'll go hard but they'll take thy work away if they can. And if they can do a spite to you and yours, they ool. They've worked on Squire, too.'

'I know, thank ye kindly all the same,' said Kester. 'It was Squire I was hindered for to-day. He wanted to buy my cottage. Nothing would do but he must buy it. He knows very well that if he did he'd soon turn me out of the place, for all the rest belong to him or friends of his'n. Offered me a deal of money, did Squire.'

'Shall you consider it over?'

'Dear to goodness, no! I shall bide.'

There was something very pleasant to me in the way he said that. It was as if he builded a tower of refuge afore my eyes. He met go for a little while, a year even, but for his life-long he'd bide. And it was only fifteen mile away, and less as the crow flies.

206

'And *you'd* best look out, too, Prue Sarn,' says Mug o' Cider. 'Grimble took it very ill, you knifing his dawg. Not but what you did it well, I must say. I'm sure any farmer as kills his own meat ud be glad of ye or you met go for a doctor's mon and do right well.

'Mine said she couldna believe it when Prue Sarn drave the knife in,' went on the landlord. 'Thought she'd seen a ghostly vision, her did. Said a feather would have knocked her down, her did. Which shows it must have bin pretty bad, for it inna easy to knock the missus down, she's like a bouncing ball.'

'I do wish I'd been there,' said Sukey. 'I'd knifed the dog for ye in a minute, Mister Woodseaves. What did I give ye at the Beguildy's love-spinning, Mister Woodseaves?'

'Play kiss in the ring with us after, Mister Woodseaves!' says Moll. 'You kiss right well, I know!'

Felena leant forrard across the narrow table.

'Oot play?' she said. 'Oot play, Weaver?'

Just then there was a call from the next table.

'Husht, husht! Sexton's going to say a few words.'

When Sexton spoke, the four walls of the church seemed to grow up round you, and you could smell the damp, musty smell of it and hear the flies plaining in the windows. For whether he was reading, 'He took unto him a wife and begat Aminadab,' or 'The golden bowl be broken,' or speaking at a harvest supper, it was all the same.

'Friends,' says Sexton, 'we've had a good day. I'm sartin there's not a man among us as hanna sweated proper, even Granfeyther Callard has, I'll be bound.'

'Oh, ah! I sweated right well!' calls out the old man, very pleased.

'And now we be enjoying good victuals and drink, and after that a game or two –'

'The people sat down to eat and to drink, and rose up to play, Exodus thirty-two.'

This was Sammy.

Sexton looked very angrily at his missus, as much as to say –

'Stop Sammy!' and she said –

'Husht, Sammy! Feyther's speaking. Dunna you forget as you can only call to mind other folks' words, but Feyther makes it all up new as he goes on.'

She settled down again to watching Sexton, for all the world like a cat watching a whirring wheel.

'I say we've had a good day, and Sarn's had a good harvest, and I ask ye for why? Because he's industrious, people, and his sister's industrious, and his mother's industrious. You couldna find in ten parishes a more industrious family. Not like some I could mention, as never do a hand's turn, coddling about with old ancient wicked books. Ah! There's some I could mention, as I dunna see the face of here to-day, that a bit of work would be the saving of. Well, neighbours, we all know as God helps those that help theirselves, and when we look at all them grand ricks of grain, I'm sure we see it's true. And we wish you well, Sarn. And I'm in behopes the young woman'll be industrious too. For I hear tell the next randy we come to at Sarn is to be a wedding. And may it bring more prosperation and not less, though of course we may think our thoughts, knowing where she's from and what's bred in the bone'll come out in the flesh –'

But fortunately there was a stir when he got to that, and a call from the other tables –

'There's two riders at the gate.'

And there was the young squire, and Miss Dorabella with him. They rode across the orchard, and the young man called out, 'Give you good evening, folks, and luck to the corn!'

For he was ever hail-fellow-well-met with all men, I'll say that for un, and it made him well liked.

Miss Dorabella seemed quite to forget she'd quarrelled

with Gideon. She drew up by his table and smiled, sparkling her black eyes.

'Well, Sarn,' she said, 'you've worked your will with the farm, I see. You've got a desperate good crop. Are you going to offer us a drink of harvest beer, to drink your health?'

I could see she admired him for a strong man, which he was. I never met but one stronger. And I could see that the Squire had told her to make it up with Gideon, and very likely sent young Mister Camperdine to see she did it, for it was common property that she'd sarved him wi' sauce at the *Mug o' Cider*, and the Squire couldna afford to lose a man that was like to do well. Gideon looked at her straight and sullen, but she kept on smiling for all that, a bit conquering and a bit pleading. Then they gave her up the best pewter measure full of ale, and she says –

'Health and prosperation, Sarn!'

Then she tossed it off, for she could drink ale with any man, and in those days it wunna so long since ale was a lady's only breakfast drink. Then she gave back the measure and leaned down, holding out her hand, stripping off the grand gauntlet, and she says –

'Your hand, Sarn!'

Well, he was done then, for he couldna refuse a lady's hand. So he took it in his great fist, and young Mister Camperdine nodded, as if to say she'd done enough now, and she put on her glove again. All the while I saw Jancis looking at her in a way that meant she was frit of her, and also that she couldna abide her. But looking at Miss Dorabella, with that sort of stony handsomeness she'd got, and then at Jancis, so soft and pinky-sweet, it didna seem to me that Jancis had much to be afraid of. They gave young Mister Camperdine some ale then, and when he'd wished well and drunk it, he said –

'I thought maybe Beguildy was here, but I don't glimpse him.'

Missis Beguildy stood up and curtsied.

'No, sir, he inna here, though he should be. And you'd best not look for 'im at home, sir, for I doubt you wouldna find 'im. But if you come to-day's a week –'

I thought that was right clever of Missis Beguildy. She wanted to give Gideon and Jancis time, and to keep the young gentleman away as long as she durst, while she thought how to manage Beguildy.

'Right!' calls out the young fellow as they rode off.

'To-day week, and mind Venus is there!'

Jancis began to giggle at that. She always did at any mention of the silly affair. And it seemed so funny to her that he should be enquiring so anxious after the very woman his cousin had sarved wi' sauce, and she at table all the while. But I crouched down on the bench, to seem short, and not to let him see my shape, so that Jancis went off into a fit of laughter again, and said I looked for all the world like a broody hen. We had some sport together over the young squire. Then up came Missis Beguildy, very put-about, wondering what to do with Beguildy till the wedding day was safely come. All of a sudden she thought of summat, and laughed and slapped herself till I thought she'd be took ill.

'Dear now, I've thought of it!' she says. 'I'll ask my cousin from Lullingford, as is here by the mercy of God, to send a message to my maister this very night, to say as hers is took ill (I mun think what he's to have. Summat cruel bad!) and as there's no cure but the old famous cure, to eat seven loaves baked at one baking by the seventh child of a seventh child, and she's to offer good money (you can pay after you be wed, Jancis, for you'll be having butter-money or summat) and off he'll go, dang-swang, to look for a seventh of a seventh, and it'll go hard but we'll be in peace till Michaelmas.'

'Oh, Mother,' says Jancis, giving her a kiss, 'you'd ought to have been a great general to ride along with Lord Wellington and lay traps for Frenchmen!'

It was all fixed up before the games and dancing began,

and I felt sorry for Beguildy, till I remembered what a wicked old man he was, wanting to sell his child unwilling.

By this it was near dark, and the moon rising, big and raddled. They got together a dozen fellows, mostly middle-aged or old, to whistle for the dancing. They danced in the rickyard, among the stacks of golden corn, sweeping up the straw with besoms first. Old Callard had been chosen for a whistler, and very proud he was, for being the oldest he chose the tunes and set the measure, and so he could feel that all the merry life in a manner depended on him, which is pleasing to old folks.

'*Barley Bridge!*' he says.

The pretty tune sounded out clear on the quiet air.

I was standing under one of the stacks, watching. It was a gay thing to see. Gideon was dancing, holding Jancis close and strong. Missis Sexton was sailing about, and Felena too, jimp as a fairy. Even Mother made shift to dance a few steps.

The twelve were whistling like a nest of throstles, sitting in one of the empty waggons –

'Open the gates as wide as the sky . . .'

when Kester found me.

'So that's where you be,' he said. 'Not dancing?'

'No.'

'For why?'

'I amna like other girls.'

He considered that. Then he said –

'Well, I mun be going. I'm off to prentice myself for ten months to learn the coloured weaving in London Town. Then I can do piecework at home, and care nothing for Grimble and his gang. Coloured weaving brings in a tidy bit, and I'll send it by coach every few months.'

'When'll you be raught back?' I said as if I was drowning.

'I'll be back for next August fair, and I'll come and talk with you a bit then, Prue Sarn.'

'Maybe you'll forget.'

"I dunna think so.'

'Well, God bless ye,' I says.

'And you.'

He turned to go. Then he turned back.

'But it's foolish in you not to dance,' he says. 'A wench with a figure like an apple-blow fairy!'

He gi'd a little laugh and went.

So he knew about Venus! Oh, I was ashamed and dumb-founded! I was angry with Jancis too, for she must have told him, though she never would confess it, but giggled and said he must have noticed my nice shape through my clo'es, so that I was more ashamed and vexed than ever.

Mother was tired and wanted me to help her to bed. After, I looked from her window on to the rickyard, that had been void, but for one big haystack, all peopled now with dark shapes. As I stood there, Gideon and Jancis suddenly came round the corner of the house, and as they went by, slow and seeing nought but each other, I plainly heard Gideon say, 'Nay, Jancis, I'll make sure of what's mine. To-morrow night when your father's gone, come down and let me in.'

I didna hear her answer, for they were past the window then, and besides, I drew back, for I canna abide an eaves-dropper. So that was in his mind! He couldna trust his dear love even for a sennight. I thought, well, maybe it was no harm, for they would be wed so soon. And indeed, whether it was agen the church or no, I was bound to be glad that Gideon should show any human feeling. Times, he seemed like a frozen man. When all were gone, and the chattels fetched in out of the dew, it was getting on towards dawn. So I went up to the attic and wrote in my book. But first I took a sheet of paper and put down in very neat writing.

'A figure like an apple-blow fairy.'

"Twas me he meant,' I said over and over, "poor Prue Sarn!'

And a glow began in my heart, warm and pleasant as a

gledy fire. For what is there in this earth, or in heaven, if it comes to that, like the knowledge that you've found favour in the eyes of him that is your dear acquaintance, and the Maister? I left off wondering what he thought of my hare-shotten lip, for indeed it seemed he thought of it not at all. I called to mind a thing he'd said while we watched the dragon-flies, about sin. He said if you thought of it rightly it just wunna there. It was gone like the shrouds of the dragon-flies when they'd wrostled free. What did you want to go hunting about after the shroud for, when you could look at the bright fly? Maybe that was how he thought of me. My poor hideous lip was, as it were, my sin, though a kind of innocent wickedness. It was my sin, and all the rest of me was my righteousness, and my glory, and the way I made him glad. I cried a long while for very joy, and such a rushing happiness went through me as seemed to make all the blood in my veins new, and I felt as if it was so pure and strong it might even cure me of my ill. There was some truth in it, too, for my lip did never look quite so bad from that day.

Morning came fresh and sweet, and the rooks went streaming out across the windy sky, to our stubble, with sleepy, contented caws, falling scattered here and there. On the way to milk I stopped by the rickyard to give thanks for the corn. Why then in that hour did I think of those words, 'The precious bane'? Why did I think of that which men will garner with their harvest, and treasure, though it is as fire-grass in a haystack? Why did a cold boding horror stir in my heart, where all was gay and warm, as a catch of frost will strike in your garden plot of an autumn evening, when the dahlias are at their proudest – wine-colour and clear gold, every quill in place, blooming high above the wall, with bees about them – so that in the morning all is winter-sad?

Chapter 2: *Beguildy Seeks a Seventh Child*

THAT very evening, so Jancis told us next day, Missis Beguildy gave the pretended message, and the day after the love-carriage Beguildy set out, full of importance, with his ash-wood kibba, to find the seventh child and bring back the bread. I said it did seem a shame to deceive the poor man so, but Jancis said, 'No danger! It makes him happy, and we'll give him the money if he finds the seventh child, so what more is to do?'

She was looking as pretty as a pink, was Jancis. She stayed a bit, to help in the washing-up, and then she sat in the kitchen while I worked, sewing a seam in her wedding clo'es. After tea when she was going, Gideon said –

'Mind you dunna forget!'

She coloured up as pink as codlins-and-cream, and ran along the wood-path. After supper Gideon said, careless like, 'If I be late, Prue, and you want to go to bed, put the key over stable door.'

I said I would, and no more. But I saw him shaving hisself very particular, and putting on his Sunday stock, so I knew that whatever date parson met have got fixed for the wedding, the wedding was now, and I fetched a rose for his coat. He looked very bashful over that, but I said that when a fellow went to see his girl so soon afore the wedding he must always wear a flower. That seemed to make it all right, thinking I guessed nought, and off he went, whistling loud and clear, up the wood path where the leaves were turning rusty, and sighs were sounding here and there, and the airs breathing autumn, and the brown cobs falling with little thuds for lads to play conquer to their own let and hindrance. Sad, and very sad I thought it in the wood path when Gideon's tall figure was passed away, and the mere lapped, and the boat was knocking on the steps, and an owl hooting. Why was it so sad, I wondered, when the wedding was fixed so soon, and the glory roses blooming,

corn safe housed, and in my own heart the Maister come?
Yet there was that about the evening which you feel when
summat has died. I went the rounds to see if all was well.
Mother was asleep, brown and small and peaceful in the
big bed. Bendigo was in stable, very comfortable, for he was
old and nesh, and we fetched him in before October. All
was well, and I wondered what the harm was, that I felt
in the air. I was to know afore long, though for a little
while things kept on as usual. Every night I put the key
in the stable, but said nought. Every morning Gideon's bed
was all tossed and tumbled, but I knew very well he hadna
slept in it. He whistled about the place as merry as any
other man, not under breath any more. I was glad for
him, and glad to be making ready for Jancis. They were to
have the guest chamber, which, not having been used for
many years, was in very bad repair. So I'd bought a few
rolls of cheap paper out of the butter-money, and I was
papering it unbeknown to Gideon. Mother was in the
secret, and she'd come and clasp her hands and say, 'Looks
a pretty paper! Doing it right well you are, my dear.
Roses and all! Roses be lucky to my mind. Your Aunt
Dorcas had roses in her bride-chamber, and not one
of her children ever died, nor ailed, nor cried. I mind
she made a joke over that. "Neither die nor cry," she
says. I hope Sarn's wunna cry much, for I canna bear
to hear a child cry. Sarn ud roar ever so, it was awful
to hear un. Beat on the cot, a would, summat cruel.
Mun always get what a wanted very quick, but if it
tarried, he wouldna forget, he'd cry the day long, but
he'd get it.'

I'd got the paper on, and I was about putting a bit of
glazed calico round the dressing-table when Missis Beguildy
came rushing to our place, like a wild woman. It was
such pleasant weather too, with little birds in the new ricks
and the first apples falling. It was early in the morning
when she came. I'd been churning. I hadna seen Gideon,
for he'd taken a crust out into the field where he was

ploughing. I was in the dairy when Missis Beguildy rushed in.

'Oh, my dear!' she cries out. 'Oh, my dear, the worst as could happen's come to pass.'

'Goodness me, what?'

I was frightened to see her face.

'He comed back!'

'Who? Not Mister Beguildy?'

'Ah! No less. And all going so well. Him away till a fortnit anyway, I thought. And the two of 'em so sweet together. I didna think Sarn could be so fair spoken to anybody as what he was to me, and Jancis like the Queen of the May. "Mother," she says, "I be more gladsome than I thought any could be." Ah, and your brother too. It eased him to see that his doubts and fears about young Camperdine were nought. If I hadna let un come he'd a thought the young man was at our place. 'Twas the only way. The more any body wants a thing, the more they do think others want it. But seeing all was fair and square, he was fair and square too. "Mother," he says, for indeed it inna long till I shall be afore Him above and all the blessed angels, "Mother, leave me bide the night over from now on, till we be wed. Soon, it is," he says, "or I wouldna ask it. And her's willing." So I gave them our room, and slept on Jancis's box bed in kitchen. I put the best dimity counterpane on their bed, and the best sheets, without a patch, and a tidy bit of drugget on floor, and I killed a fowl and made a nice bit of bread sauce, and left 'em to their supper, pleasant and to theirselves afore the fire, and stayed out till they'd done, though they did say as nice as nice as I mun sup with 'em. But newly wed is newly wed, ring or none. And when they were abed I'd tidy the place and wash up. And I'd just done, and I was setting afore the fire thinking of the time when I wed Beguildy, and what a proper young man he was, though you'd never think it, and deserve my thoughts he didna, the grutching, wicked old man. I was setting there very peaceful, and thinking

216

I must draw the bolt and rake the fire out, when there was a little sound without, and in came Beguildy. I could ha' dropped on floor.'

'Well, missus,' he says, 'where be Jancis.'

'She be asleep,' I says.

'And since when did ye give the wench our room and sleep in box bed?'

With that he rushes in, and there they were. 'Twas hell let loose, and no mistake. He put such a curse on Sarn as I never heard nor shall hear.

'And for all you've crept in the like of this, you shanna have the wench in wedlock,' he says.

'You canna stop it,' says Sarn. 'No power in the 'orld can stop it now.'

'Yet stop it I will,' says the mester. 'Hanna I cursed ye by fire and by water? Hanna I told ye you were born under the threepenny planet and canna keep money? Hanna I said you'll be poor in life and die in the water? Eh?'

'Well, it's a pity for ye, seeing you be a wise man and all, to be put in the wrong,' says Sarn, 'but harvest be in and I be a rich man.'

'You binna a tenth nor a hundredth part as rich as young squire. His pockets be crammed ooth French money,' shouts Beguildy. 'You shanna have my girl, Sarn.'

'I've got her, seemingly,' says Sarn, as calm as calm could be, and that drave Beguildy right out of mind. He puck up the blunderbus as he keeps by the window ready for the fox, and he went for your brother with the butt end.

'Dear to goodness!'

'You may as well say that, Prue Sarn. I screeched and Jancis screeched, and I ran in from the kitchen, for I'd kept out, thinking Sarn met not like it, him being in his night-shirt, and as fine a man as you could wish, but not wanting to cause any awkwardness more than already. But afore I could get in, Sarn knocked mine flat on floor, and a lay like a log and none deserved it better. For a very curst man is Beguildy, and obstinate, and bearing ill will

217

year after year. I do believe the root of the matter is your dad asking him for that crown when he'd made mind up it was to be a present. Ah! Though mine he is, I canna but say he's a terrible man to bear a grutch. Well, Sarn knocked un flat, and he says, "Take his feet, oot, Mother, and we'll put un in kitchen. For whether he's dead or quick, I'll not be disturbed any more this night." Ah. He said that. And he says, "Swing for it I may, but I wunna be disturbed this night." Cold and quiet as a frozen mere, but a terrible man to rouse, is your brother. So I doused mine with water, and I gid him some spirits, and in a while he come round, but I took the precaution to tie him to the bed afore that. He struggled cruel, but it was a good rope and I fed spirits to un regular, and in a while he calmed a bit and quietened, and then slept. So in the morning your brother went, and I untied the mester, and when he woke up I says, what fetched him back? So he says, ill news travels fast, and he supposed he'd got ears, and he hadna but just got as far towards the mountains as Mallard's Keep when a man told un Sarn slept at our place now. Interfering meddlers, folks be! So I got him a bit of breakfast and he went out. Quiet as quiet he be, so I've come to warn ye, for when he's quiet-angry he's deadly.'

I said, what harm could an old man the like of that do, and especially as we knew all his spells and what-nots were but foolish games? But it made no difference, and she only kept on saying there was harm brewing, and God send the wedding day quick, and she went off home as wild-seeming as she came, wringing her hands, with wisps of hair blowing in the stormy wind. For there was a real tempest blowing, that had been rising for two or three days, and it blew up the loose straws and the chaff in the rickyard till the air was full of them, dusty and choking. Out in the field I had to go close up to Gideon and shout afore I could make him hear. There was a roar in the treetops like the sound of weirs after the snow melts, and a howling in the chimneys that made you glad of four walls and a roof. I said to

Gideon when we were at our tea, did he think it would blow the tops off the stacks? But he said no, they were well weighted. It was only two days now till the dealer came to price the grain, and only three days after that till the wedding. Knowing this, and being easy in mind about Beguildy, since he'd taken no harm from the blow, I listened to the wind very contented, and made some rounds of toast, and thought about Kester. For I do think there's nothing makes you feel so contented as a roaring wind in the chimney when all's well. I said should we go to bed early, and Gideon said we might as well, seeing we'd worked hard and the harvest was in. So we went at eight, and I fell asleep in a minute with the sound of the loud, dry tempest in my ears.

When I woke, sudden, I thought, 'It be the Judgment!' There was a great light and a roaring, very dreadful to hear, and knockings and cries out of the night. I lay there, mazed, saying '*Our Father*' as fast as I could, and wishing I'd been more regular at church. Then I heard Gideon's voice calling from window, and other voices below, and one was the voice of Sexton's Sammy. This comforted me in my foolish fear, for I felt as if Sammy would be able to think of a text, and mouth it too, even on Judgment night. For night it still was, and early too, since we found out after that we'd not been abed much more than two hours. Gideon came rushing past my door, shouting for me, so I got up and put on my clo'es, for I supposed that whether it was the Judgment or not I'd better wear them, though in the pictures the redeemed go in their night rails. But I did feel that I must wait to get to heaven afore I could be at my ease to stand afore Sexton's Sammy in my night-gown.

I ran downstairs and out, and then I saw. I thought even the end of the world would have been better than that, for then we'd have been provided for, with no more harvests to get in nor money to gather with pain and labour. It would be the same for all in that hour, but this was for us only, and crushed us as a waggon wheel crushes an ear of wheat.

For it was the corn burning that made the roaring noise. It was the harvest, all of it, the whole garnering of all those years of work, the very stuff of Gideon's soul, and our future. It was no great comet nor flaming star raging across the sky to herald in the end of all, no trumpet of an archangel pealing and whining along the black night betwixt the trembling worlds. It was only the corn. Only all we had! Only that which was to make a kindly man, a loving man, of our Gideon, since having it he would leave slaving by day and dark, and making us all slave, and would work only like any other man. Only the corn, that meant a bit of comfort for Mother, a bit of hope for me. Only the corn, that would give Jancis dear children, and the place of wife by fireside, and a bit of love, maybe. Oh, my soul, it was the corn! I clung to the rickyard gate, and my hair was lifted in the fierce-hot wind. There were black figures running in the red light, most like a picture of hell, but they were nought, and less than nought. The vasty roaring wind went on, taking the fire with it. I could see that the thing must have started with the barley, that was on the west of the rickyard, whence the wind was coming. There was no barley now. Where it had been were two great round housen made of white fire, very fearful to see, being of the size and shape of the stacks, but made of molten flame. There was no substance in them, and it was marvel how they stood so. Now and again a piece of this molten stuff would fall inward with no sound, and there could be seen within caves of grey ash and red, sullen, smouldering fire. So it will surely be when the world is burned with fervent heat in the end of all. It will go rolling on, maybe, as it ever has, only it will be no more a kindly thing with mists about it, a pleasant painted ball with patterns of blue seas and green mountains upon its roundness. It will be a thing rotten with fire as an apple is rotten when the wasps have been within, light and empty and of no account. So

was our barley, falling inwards with no sound, as though
one went here and there within, unseen. It was a worse
thing to see than if it had fallen down in a heap, for being
yet a stack, it seemed like a jest of some demon, saying –
'Well, what is to do? There be your stacks of barley! Make
barley bread and eat.' I looked at those two abodes of
demons, of the roundness and height of our good barley
stacks, and I remembered the barley, oh, the sweet barley,
rustling in the wind of dawn! I called to mind the ploughing for it, in such good behopes, and sowing of it, between
the sowing of the winter wheat and the sowing of the
summer wheat, Gideon and me walking up and down
the fields with the bags of seed slung over shoulder, or
with a deep round lid to hold enough of seed for one cross-
ing of the field there and back, and swinging out our arms
with a great giving movement, as if we were feeding all
the world, a thing I dearly loved to see. For reaping,
though it is good to watch as be all the year's doings on a
farm, is a grutching and a grabbing thing compared with
sowing. You must lean out to it and sweep it in to you, and
hold it to your bosom, jealous, and grasp it and take it.
There is ever a greediness in reaping with the sickle, in my
sight. There is not in scything, which is a large destroying
movement without either love or anger in it, like the
judgments of God. Nor is there in flailing, which is a thing
full of anger, but without any will or wish to have or keep.
But reaping is all greed, just as sowing is all giving. For
there you go, up and down the wide fields, bearing that
which you have saved with so much care, winnowing it
from the chaff, and treasuring it for this hour. And though
it is all you have, you care not, but take it in great handfuls and cast it abroad, with no thought of holding back
any. On you go, straight forrard, and the bigger your
hand the better pleased you are, and you cast it away
on this side and on that, till one not learned in country
ways would say, here is a mad person. For it would seem
as if you were feeding all the birds of the country, since

221

there was always a following of rooks in the furrows, and starlings, and many small birds, which would be very unprofitable chickens.

It is a pretty thing to see the golden seed tossed in the air with sunshine on it and the light spring wind scattering it here and there; or if it is winter wheat, then it will be, very like, a still brown day with the mellowness of old beer in the colours and the scent of the air. I was always ready for the sowing, though Gideon did not care about it, and indeed would often seem to begrutch casting the grain from him, and would sow too thin and so waste land and labour. I thought of all this, and of the fair evenings when we had walked forth, Mother and me, to look at the young barley pushing up bright and sparse, then thickening, till the brown earth was all greened over, and springing taller and brighter, stiff and pointed, and then softening and lengthening yet more, with the wind running in it like a boat furrowing the water and finding a voice at last, and a song, and sending up its green, plaited ears to swell and ripen, till at the end they stood perfect as if the Lord had but that moment lifted His hand from them, all made of purest, clearest gold. Gold leaves, gold stalks, gold knops for heads, and these knops bearded thick with gold as well. Yet it was an innocent gold, and not that gold which is called the bane. Oh, how I could mind it, on those still Sunday mornings when I went to the well, and would set down the buckets for a little while and go out into the corn fields that lay beneath the vasty pale blue peace of the sky like creatures satisfied and at rest! There would be small birds about, making low contented cries and soft songs. There would be a ruffling breeze, and rooks far up the sky, and a second bloom of pale gold flowers on the honeysuckle wrathes against the blue. There would be warmship that lapped you round, and the queenly gift of the scent of corn. What other scent is like it? There is so much in it, beyond other sweets. There is summer in it, and frost. There is water in it, and the heart of the flint which the corn has

222

taken up into its hollow stalks. There is bread in it, and life for man and beast.

All these thoughts, moithered and bewildered, came to me as I clung to the gate with the parching wind upon my face, too stunned to move. There are misfortunes that make you spring up and rush to save yourself, but there are others that are too bad for this, for they leave nought to do. Then a stillness falls on the soul, like the stillness of a rabbit when the stoat looks hotly upon it and it knows that there is no more to be done.

The fire was in the two biggest stacks of wheat now. It had gone upon them and they were not. Soon they would be as the barley was. They were good stacks, those, of a solid squarish oblong, and as high as might be with safety, for we had such a harvest that we could only make room by having the stacks high. It was good wheat too, long in the straw, and no touch of mildew. It had taken the most time of all both to sow and to reap, and in the lugging it had the biggest waggons all day. And now it was gone! It was a great mound of fire with the black shapes of two stacks in it, and soon the fire would be passed on and there would be no more sound, but just two grey-white housen for demons, with baleful red gleams in the crumbling passages within. There were more stacks of wheat by the hedge, but the next to the blazing stacks was the oats. The lovely oats, so pale and fine, like ferns for a lady's table!

They were so sweet, the oats, so very fine and fair, like midsummer grasses come golden. I did ever love the oats best of all. And suddenly I was all mother to the oats. The fire met have the wheat and the barley, but it should not take my oats. I clomb over the gate and ran where the little figures moved. I caught Gideon by the sleeve.

'You mun save the oats!' I screamed. 'Oh, save the oats, as is so fair and fine!'

But he said nought. He was working like a madman, and I saw that it was the oats he was trying to save, the oats and the stacks by the hedge. He and Sammy were digging

223

trenches between the blazing stacks and these, to fill with water.

'Where's Tivvy?' I said, for now I was come to myself I wanted all the help there was.

'Gone for Feyther,' said Sammy, sweating and groaning over his space, for the fire was gaining on them.

'Shall I take Bendigo and go for help?' I said. 'Or shall I get the buckets and begin fetching water?'

'Ah, that?' says Sammy. 'Do that, for help ud be too late, a power.'

Not a word did Gideon say. He was stricken with a dumb madness, but he worked like ten men. What with the horror of mind and the stress of labour and the great heat of the fire, the sweat ran down his face in a river and his clo'es were as if he had been in the water. And being so wet, and so near the fire, he went in a cloud of steam, which had a very strange look, as if he had been put under some curse or was already in hell.

I loosed Bendigo and the oxen and cows, such as were lying in, and they went pounding away into the woods, half crazy with fear. I woke Mother and told her she must dress and come to the mere and dip while we made a chain for the buckets, to send them from hand to hand. I got together all the pails and buckets, and thought it seemed a pitiful thing that with all that great mere full of water we could only slake our fire with as much as we could get into our little buckets. And I've thought since that when folk grumble about this and that and be not happy, it is not the fault of creation, that is like a vast mere full of good, but it is the fault of their buckets' smallness.

Mother came with me like a child, very mazed and quiet.

'Must I dip now, Prue?' she said.

'You can begin now, and have all the buckets ready,' I answered. 'But the time when you must dip your best will be in a tuthree minutes when we come.'

'Now, Sarn,' says Sammy, 'you mun leave digging and come for water.'

224

For though it may seem a thing not to be believed, all that awful night, though it was Gideon that did the most of the work, it was Sammy or me that gave the orders. Gideon would go at what he was set at in a frenzy and go on after it stopped being any use, working like an ox at the threshing floor. He threw down the spade when Sammy spoke, and came with us to the mere. Mother was toiling over the dipping. She looked smaller and smaller as the trouble thickened about her, like a person that had eaten some fairy stuff to make her not able to be seen. She seemed no more than one of those little brown birds that will light down by the water for a while in their journeying and then be gone, nobody knows where.

'Now here comes Feyther, thanks be to the Lord,' said Sammy. He was a good lad that night, was Sammy, and while the fire lasted he never said but one text, and that a very temptuous one, 'Burning and fuel of fire,' though he must have thought of no end of them.

Sure enough there was Sexton bursting through the wood, and Tivvy not far behind, and an angry voice crying on the wind a long way back, that was Missis Sexton, who misliked being by her lonesome.

'Now,' says Sammy, 'Feyther can go in the rickyard, chuck on the water to dout the fire, Tivvy can gather the empty buckets as fast as he throws 'em down, and run back to Missis Sarn with 'em, and you and me and Prue'll run with full ones. I did think we might make a chain and pass from hand to hand, but we be too few, Sarn.'

Gideon spoke for the first time.

'I never,' he said with a wild, pale face, 'never had much strength about me, only me and these two.'

And with that he put his arm across his face as he was used to do when he was a lad and things went badly wrong; and cried.

Ah, I tell you it was a thing few would have cared to see, a great strong, masterful man like that, crying like a little lad.

'Now, now, Sarn!' says Sexton, shocked as we all were,

225

'Now, you munna take on. The Lord gave and the Lord hath taken away.'

At that Gideon came to himself.

'The Lord?' he says. 'No. It wunna the Lord! It was Beguildy. When we've douted the stacks I shall fetch un and roast un.'

No words of mine can tell you the awful way Gideon said that. I wanted to ask how he knew, if he did know, but there was no time for words. We were running to and again with two full buckets each, which, after an hour or so, is enough to try a strong man, leave alone a woman. Water-carrying is an easy job if there's no hurry and you can use a yoke. But to run stumbling through a roasting heat, which we did for most of the journey, and to know that if you tarried the oats would go, and maybe if you didna tarry, was enough to take the spirit out of anybody. The oats did go. The fire leapt the ditch and all, and there was a new, tremendous blaze. I lost heart after that, and though I ran, it was with no hope.

'Oh, I be so tired,' said poor Mother. But I couldna let her rest.

'If we canna save it,' I said, 'you'll never get free of tending swine, Mother.'

So she bent her poor old back again, standing half in the water, in spite of the rheumatics. The cry went up to save the barn, for if the barn was lost, the house was lost. At that, Mother left dipping for water, so I was forced to get Tivvy to do it, and we had to bring back our own empty pails. I looked up once, and there was Mother fetching things out of the house. I looked at them after, and there was her sewing and the copper fruit pan, and a sampler she did when she was little, and Father's picture cut out in black paper, done by parson's brother-law, who was part foreign. People thought he must be simple to play with scissors and paper like a child, though they owned that he did it very well, and said that being part foreign he knew no better. Though Mother had been so mortal

226

feared of Father in life, she treasured this picture in the queerest way. So there it was with the other things and six pots of damson cheese, and Pussy in a basket.

It was only at dawn, when the wind dropped and a fine, quiet rain began to fall, that we got the fire under. At least, it had burnt itself out, and we managed to save barn and house. The red light was gone from the sky and the burning from the mere. For all night it had seemed that the water in the mere was turned to fiery spirit, and was burning too. Everything was there, confused and topsy-turvy, the red and yellow flames, the smoke, bellying in the wind, the white-hot stacks, hollow and canting, the farm and the barn and our little black figures like mommets in the tumult.

Not long after it was over came Missis Sexton, who had suffered frittening of Bendigo, that came snorting and trampling through the wood so that she thought it had been the Black Huntsman. There were many hollow trees about the Sarn woods, they being old forest land, so she crept into one, and stayed till the light began to come. And then, once in, she could not get out, for she was more than ornary stout and also had so many clo'es on, and though in the stress of fear she squoze herself in, it was not easy to get out again in cold blood. But when she did come, she soon got us all some breakfast, and indeed we were in need of it, not only for what was past, but to face the day.

'Why, look's Tivvy and Prue white as ghosses!' she said. 'And you, Missis Sarn, should be abed, and to bed you shall go when you've had bite and sup. And as for you, Sarn! Why, man, man, you fritten me worse than Bendigo, indeed to goodness! Now then, where's ours? Draw up now, draw up, take bite and sup, people!'

She said it just as she said, 'Take your places for the game of Costly Colours.'

'But what I'd lief know,' says Mother, 'is how Sexton and Sammy knew our ricks were afire?'

'I knew,' said Sammy, 'because Tivvy and me were

227

coming back latish from the mill, and we saw Beguildy coming along very quiet and sneaking this way. So I says to Tivvy as we'd follow, for I've been keeping an eye on Beguildy a goodish while, he being a wicked old man and the power of the Lord far from him. By their fruits you shall know them. And it seemed a funny time for him to be coming to Sarn, he being one for early bed always. So we followed on slow, keeping a long way back. And just as we came to the end of the wood there was a tremendous blaze from the far corner of the rickyard, and in a minute Beguildy came running up wood path, so we only had just time to hide. As soon as he was past, we did run to the rickyard, and it was the little stack in the corner, and just by it was this.'

Sammy held up the lid of Beguildy's tinder box, which everybody knew well, for he'd put his name on the inside of the lid in red paint, being proud of his writing.

'What a fool, to drop un!' says Missis Sexton.

'Nay, Mother,' says Sexton, 'Beguildy's no fool. 'Twas the hand of the Lord took the tinder box lid off'n un and chucked it there for Sam to see. Ah, so it was.'

'In the hand of the Lord there is a cup, Psalms seventy-five, eight,' said Sammy.

'Only it wunna a cup,' giggled Tivvy, who was always sillier when she was excited, ' 'twas the one-half of an old iron tinder box.'

' 'Tis the curse!' moaned Mother. 'He did curse my son Sarn by fire and water, and this be the first. Dear Lord knows what the second'll be. 'Tis the sin you did eat, Sarn. There's bin harm on the place ever since you did it. Ah, ever since my poor maister died in his boots the place has been ill to live in, very ill it's been, what with the pigs and the rheumatics and the everlasting ploughing, and now all gone, as if it hadna been.'

'Ah, fire's a greedy feeder,' said Missis Sexton.

'I will consoom them in a moment, Numbers sixteen. This great fire will consoom us, Deuteronomy five. Fire

228

consoomed the palaces of Benhadad, Jeremiah forty-nine,' said Sammy.

'Three texes at a birth! Good lad, good lad!' cries Sexton.

'Only it's Beguildy did ought to be consoomed,' remarked Missis Sexton.

'And the awful thing about such wickedness,' says Tivvy, 'is that it's in the blood. It goes on from father to child. You'd never know when it ud break out. I wonder at you, Mister Sarn, I do, to be thinking of taking the child of a viper in wedlock. I never did like the Beguildys, Jancis in especial.'

'Indeed to goodness, the girl's right!' cried out her Mother, and Sexton added –

'What's bred in the bone'll come out in the flesh.'

Gideon looked around, with a grey lined face, like an old man's. He was never the same again after that night. You canna knock an ox on the head with the mallet and then expect it to be just as it was. He made to speak, but the words were slow in coming. Just then there was a trampling and traversing without, and Bendigo trotted past the window.

'Ha!' says Gideon, and makes for the door.

I knew what he was going for, and I rushed after him. By good fortune the cows were coming back from the wood, making soft mooing plaints that it was long past milking time. So instead of pleading for Beguildy I said – 'Look's cows coming, they'll be stanked if they inna milked.'

'Ah, you mun mind not to let 'em get like that'n,' Missis Sexton cautioned from the room. 'A brother-law's cousin of mine had the best herd ever you saw. Cheshire, he come from. Grand cows they were, and never ailed, and plenty of everything there was in that house, good milk and butter and cheese, and buckets and buckets of skim for the pigs, and fine fat pigs they were, and a fine fat man my brother-law's cousin was, and a fine fat woman he'd got for wife, and twelve fine fat children.'

I may say that Missis Sexton, being so fat herself, always judged folk by it, and if they were thin they might as well never have been born, in her sight.

'Ah,' she went on, 'they were all as fat as butter, filled the pew at church to bursting, until the day he let the cows get stanked. Ah! That was a bad day for 'em. There was no prosperation after. The cows dwined and the pigs dwined, and in a bit the family dwined too, and in a little while, of all that fine fat family there was nought left but fourteen miserable rails.'

Tivvy was in a fit of giggling, for her Mother's stories 'most always made her laugh, though many's the beating she had for it.

'Milk first, lad,' I says to Gideon, 'and go to the Stone House after.'

God forgive me to deceive him so, but I wanted to save him from the sin of murder. No sooner was he in the shippen, milking, than I took Bendigo to the door and cried out to Sexton to mount and ride, and take Sammy too, for Bendigo could carry both as far as Plash, and to take Beguildy and march him off to the parish constable at Lullingford all in a courant, and save him from Gideon. For if he was locked up Gideon couldna get at him, and he'd only suffer what was right according to the law.

'I see,' says Sammy. 'Let me fall into the hand of the Lord, and not into the hand of man. Two Samuel twenty-four. Ah, we'd best go, Feyther.'

'Will Jancis and Missis Beguildy go to prison too?' enquired Tivvy.

'Surely to goodness no! They've done nought. In fact Jancis be a very tidy wench, and if she'd had the right spirit in her, and meekened her soul and gone softly in good sadness, I dunno but I'd have taken her in wedlock myself,' said Sammy.

They only got off just in time, for Gideon came running from the shippen, crying upon them to stop.

230

'They'll take Beguildy to prison,' I said. 'You munna have murder on your soul, lad, things be bad enough without that.'

'It would have eased me,' he answered with a strange look. 'It's all dammed up within. Choking, choking me. 'Twould have eased me to kill un. I'll never mend of it now.'

'But you couldna kill the father of your wife-to-be,' I said.

'Wife? What wife?'

'Why, Jancis! You'll be wed to Jancis come a week now.'

'What?' he says, with a wild, fierce look. 'Do ye think I'll wed with the devil's daughter? I tell ye, if it was to save my life and all, I'd never wed with her. Nay, I'll never see the wench again, not of choice, not unless she do force herself into my company.'

'Gideon, Gideon! Dunna say it! Oh, Gideon, there be things in life as is better than money and that'n. Leave be, lad! It inna meant for us to be rich. Let you settle down and be content, and marry the poor child as loves you so well, and if so be money comes, all the better. And if so be it dunna, none the worse. But deny the poor girl marriage after what's took place, you canna. Your heart canna be as hard as that.'

'It is. The granite mountain, quartzite, b'rytes, inna as hard. If you leave that girl come nigh me, I'll tromple out her life like I would a clothes-moth's. And so I warn ye. Rotten. That's what they be. Like father like child. A fause smiling face, but any minute, any minute she met burn the place to the ground. I shouldna wonder but she fetched the flint and tinder for un last night. Camperdine may take her and welcome. I make him a present of her.'

'But, Gideon, you've bin as good as wed to her this last week. And suppose there was to be a baby, what then?'

'A baby? What? My child and hers? I tell ye, if any such thing come to pass, I'd strangle it. Hark ye, their blood's black.—Foul, foxy, vermin. That's what they be. They're not fit to live. Thanks be to God, folks can swing for arson. I'll see he swings for it. And you tell the girl to keep away from me. It'll be the better for her.'

I durst say no more. What could I say, when the human kindness in my poor brother had been scorched up in the fire and was not? Only a fool will dip and dip in a dry well. He looked a deal taller as he stood there, with his back to the dark driving woods, where the rain was lashing now, that would have saved all last night, where the autumn storm was moaning, and the dry leaves churning and boiling in the air as the weeds will in the mere at the troubling of the waters. His clo'es yet clung to him, all scorched and darkened with the fire. His face was grimed, so that the lines that had not showed were very clear to see, and there were more lines, I was sure, since last night. His eyes, that were so cold, like water, blazed with hatred when he thought upon Beguildy or any of hisn, but at other times his face was blank and dim, like the face of one without hope, spent and foredone, a lost face. I said, should we dig taters, for I thought maybe it would be a bit of comfort, to think he'd got summat. He came without a word, and worked hard and well, but every now and again he'd stop, and look about him strangely at the chill, silent mere, the overcast heavens and the stormy woods. It seemed to me that the spirit of the man was like a bird with a broken wing. And at noon, when I went to get our meal, he missed to come when I banged the tray, and I found him in the rickyard, where the heaps of ash yet smouldered, lying upon his face, as still and hard of hearing as a dead man, and indeed I do think his heart was dead from that time.

Chapter 3: *The Deathly Bane*

'Tis hard, and very hard, to write of the wintry time we went through after that night of grief and bitter woe. For when the quill has traced out good words of a kind meaning, it irks it to make them sad and evil. But sad and evil that time was, and there is no use in gainsaying it. For many days after the fire, the work on the farm stood still, as it often will after a death. Gideon's one thought was to get at Beguildy, or if not that, to make him suffer the utmost of the law. Missis Beguildy was forced to give up the Stone House, for the landlord didna want a man there who burnt ricks, nor his folk, so he made the excuse of the rent being late to turn them out. Everything was sold, and Missis Beguildy and Jancis went off to Silverton,where Beguildy lay in prison waiting for the assizes, with only what they stood in. At least, poor Jancis didna stand, for when she heard the dreadful news of what Gideon had said, which I told her Mother to break to her as best she could, she fell down on the floor and stirred neither hand nor foot, nor spoke a single word. They carried her to the waggon from Plash Farm, which was to take her and her mother away, and they say she lay there like a broken flower. Maybe it was as well, for if her strength hadna gone from her she'd have tried to see Gideon, and I do think he'd have struck her down in his bitter smouldering rage. It seemed to ease him to hear of their misfortune, and when the day came for them to go, he went off to a place in the woods where he could see the waggon pass by, and stood there looking down upon it, with the sullen farm labourer driving, misliking having anything to do with folk in such evil case in men's sight, and poor Missis Beguildy sitting in the waggon all aged and wild, and Jancis lying on some straw at the bottom, like a white waxen image. I know, because Miller's Tim was in the wood at

233

the time, and he came running to me, frit out of his life, pretty near, to tell me all about it.

'Oh, Prue Sarn, I was in the 'ood after a tuthree nuts,' he says, 'and I saw Mister Sarn a-walking by lonesome, very glooming and drodsome, and I was feared, so I did hide in a tree. And Mister Sarn went under the boughs of the big beech, where the road through the wood comes by. And in a while there was a rumbling, and I saw the waggon from Plash, and Missis Beguildy crying and taking on awful, but I couldna see Jancis. So I clomb the tree to see if she was in the bottom of the waggon, and there she was. She did look like a dead maid. Oh, she did look like the picture in the church of the little maid as was dead in the house when they fetched the Lord in, and He says "Rise you up!" He says. Only He hadna said it to Jancis. And I was feared, and I came down quiet from the tree, and I saw Mister Sarn staring down upon the waggon, for you do know there's a bit of a bank just there. And his face did frit me so that I made to run off, only then he stirred, so I kept quiet for fear he might come my way. He gloomed upon the waggon a long while, till the rumbling went ever so quiet, and wunna no more than the noise of a startle-de-buz when it be gone past, and then there was no sound at all, save the noise of a throstle banging a conker on a stone. And Mister Sarn did lift up both his fisses and did shake 'em after the waggon, and oh, Prue! his face was like the face of the Lord Jehovah in Feyther's book, when his anger was not turned away. Then he went away, slow, looking upon the ground, and the throstle went on banging the conker on the stone, and I runned to you.'

And that was how the properest man in our countryside did see the girl of his choice go, a girl like a water-lily bud, as loved him right well.

I said to myself, 'It be the bane. Oh, it be the dreadful bane.'

But after that Gideon seemed more at ease in himself.

And I think it was that he had mistrusted his own heart, being afraid that if Jancis came to him he'd give in. And his purpose was not to give in, but to begin all over agin, and go straight forrard to his fixed end and aim.

The morning after they'd gone, he fetched out the ploughs, and came to the kitchen door and called to me as I was making gruel for mother, who was abed again, and had been ever since the fire, taking nought but gruel or a posset, and he said –

'Come and start of the big field, oot, Prue?'

I thought it was best not to give him a nay-word at all, so I said, Ah, I'd come. I took the gruel to Mother and said should I get Tivvy to come and sit with her a bit now and again, seeing we were starting on the ploughing. And she says –

'Oh, that bitter old ploughing! And maybe all the corn'll be burnt like-the last. No wedding, nor house nor china nor nothing, only the pigs to tend again come the spring! But maybe I wunna see the spring. I'm very middling, Prue. You mun get the doctor's mon to me, I doubt.'

And indeed her poor hands were very thin and shrunken, and her small face browner and thinner, and she seemed more like a lost bird or a trapped creature than ever, and more in fear of Gideon.

'Dunna let him come in till I be better,' she'd say. 'Dunna let my son Sarn come and make me feel as I'm a burden. He dunna love me. He'd lief I was dead and sodded.'

And she'd lift up her hands, beseeching.

So I got Tivvy to come and mind her, and all that winter of dark weather, dark within as well as without, we ploughed, turning over the stubble of that good harvest we'd lost. We were poorer than ever, and things didna prosper so well as they had, there being no heart in us. There were Tivvy's meals to find as well, for though she came for love, being sweet on Gideon, yet we had her victuals to find, and she was a very hearty feeder. The doctor's man cost a lot, also, and the worse the weather was, the more he charged. About the New Year there was a bitter cold spell, and ice on the roads, so his horse came down and broke its leg, and we had to pay summat towards that. Things seemed to go from bad to worse, for Gideon kept me so hard at it, driving plough, that I was forced to leave the dairy work and the fowls and pigs to Tivvy, and she was ever a bit flighty, and careless, so folks began to complain about the butter, and the fowls laid badly, and the pigs began to look thin and unkind, and Tivvy thought of nothing but to make herself look pretty and temptuous for Gideon. As January went on the weather got worse, and we had a heavy fall of snow, and Mother was so bad one night that I was forced to send for the doctor's man again. At least, send I didna, for nobody would go, the snow being deep. There was nothing for market, the cows being dry all but one, and eggs scarce. So Gideon didna go to Lullingford, and I made up my mind to go on Sunday, when even Gideon didna plough, and once at Lullingford I could send word to the doctor by the Silverton coach. This I did, and a weary day I had of it, and a sad day also, passing the empty house of Kester Wood-seaves, and thinking maybe some ill might come to him in the great city, or he might meet a lover there, and so come no more to Lullingford. But I was glad of this weary day after, for there be times when the only comfort a body has is the remembrance of hardship borne for somebody dear.

When the doctor's man came after a good few days, he was forced to bide with us some time, on account of the badness of the roads. This irked Gideon, for the expense of the food and also his nag's keep. He was the more put out because the doctor's man gave a good account of Mother, for he seemed to think she should have been at death's door afore I called the man to come from so far away. I mind we were sitting round the hearth, late on a wild night, with hailstorms taboring on the window, and a good clear fire that we were mighty glad of. The doctor's man was a pleasant-spoken person, round and short and ruddy, with a bright red colour on his cheeks that looked as if it had a good glaze over it. He was always rubbing his hands, as if the last patient had pleased him very well, but you could never tell from this how the person had prospered, for he'd rub his hands as much over a corpse as over a quick person, and indeed, I sometimes thought, more. He was rubbing them while we talked about Mother, though not so much as he did when he told us of poor Missis Beguildy, who had ailed more and more ever since she got to Silverton, and was now said to be going into a decline. It wasna that he was an unkind man, or wished folk harm, only naturally it was more interesting to him if they were took for death than if they were only a little ailing.

'Missis Sarn'll pull through now. Nicely, she will,' he said.

'Oh,' says Gideon. 'Her'll pull through, will her?'

'Ah. And last a-many years, I shouldna wonder. A wiry old lady! Tough, for all she's thin and nesh-looking.'

'How many years?' says Gideon.

'Oh! It's hard to say. Doctor might be able to, but of course I be only like his 'prentice. But it might be as much as ten, easy. Ah. I should say ten. With care.'

'Ten years!' Gideon said it in a very strange way.

'Ah, but you mun cosset her.'

'Ten years, and always like this?'

'Oh, ah! Her'll be bedridden, winters, and may be all the year round later on.'

'And she'll be no more use?'

'Use? Why, what use could she be?'

'And you coming over a tuthree times every winter, I suppose?'

'Oh, ah, if you send for me,' says doctor's man, taking a pull at his ale and helping himself to another piece of bread and cheese, which made Gideon scowl.

'Whenever be you going to clear supper, Prue?' he says. 'I've had my bellyful this long while.'

'Oh, but you're such a poor eater, Sarn,' Tivvy cries out. 'It's wonder you're not clemmed. You want a wife to cook for ye and sarve up temptuous dishes. Chitterling puffs, now. They're as different from plain chitterlings as heaven from hell. I made some Sunday was a week, and neither Feyther nor Sammy spoke a word all day after, they were that contented in their innards.'

'Oh, dear me, I do wish I wunna a married man,' says the doctor's chap. 'Ah, in good sadness I wish it!'

'If you wunna, it would be no manner use,' said Tivvy pertly. 'I like a big man.'

Gideon took no notice, any more than he did of the chitterling puffs.

'A very big man,' went on that forrard little piece, 'and dark. Big shoulders, big 'ands, arms with great big lumps of muscle and sinew, big feet, strong legs –'

'Why, missis, you be giving a list like the list in the Song o' Solomon,' says doctor's man.

'And hard,' went on Tivvy, taking no notice, but fixing her eyes on Gideon, 'hard and never tired, lusty and lungeous and ill to thwart, but a good lover, ah, and fiery, and not to be gainsayed by the girl he's a mind for. That's the man for me! Ah. That's the man Sexton's Tivvyriah would be a right good missus to, with no other thought but to save and scrape and scrat to do his will and make him rich.'

'Well, you should have been a lawyer, Missis, so you should,' says the visitor, 'and if you dunna get what you want, may I be bottled in spirits like a tadpole!'

But Gideon never lifted his eyes to Tivvy at all, only sat and glowered till she'd gone to bed. Then he said again –

'And she'll last for years, always ailing, but lasting on?'

'Ah. Indeed to goodness! Creaking doors, you know. But you mun see you keep her pulse strong. There's the danger. If it wunna kept strong, she'd very likely go off quiet and sudden before you'd time to say sarsaparilla. Keep the pulse strong and she'll be as merry as a robin.'

We talked a bit more, and then Gideon said he was going to look the stock afore turning in.

'The brindled longhorn's very middling,' he said. 'Seems to be in a fever all the while. Heart's like to burst sometimes. I suppose a dose of foxglove ud put her right maybe?'

'Ah. Foxglove'll lower the pulse as quick as anything. But you mun be careful. Be she a young cow?'

'Going four.'

'Dunna give her too much, then. When things get old and worn out they canna stand much of it.'

When the visitor was gone to bed, and Gideon back from the shippen, he sat down, hopeless-like, and said —

'Her means dying.'

'What, Brindle?' I says.

'Ah. Seems like that old devil's put a curse on me all right.'

'It's only the weather, and Tivvy being a bit careless, and me so busy at it, ploughing.'

'And there's Mother,' he said, 'as was used to help a bit, no use and less than no use. A heavy burden! We'll never pick up now she's like that.'

'Dunna let her know you think it,' I said.

But the very next day, when I took her supper, there was Gideon standing in the mid of the room, talking very loud, and Mother like a frittened mouse.

'Well,' he was saying, 'you be very middling, Mother!'

'Ah, I be ailing, Sarn,' she says, with her smile.

'It mun be a sorrow to you that you canna do a hand's turn.'

'Ah. It be, Sarn. But come the warm weather, I'm in behopes to see to the broody hens and the rest of the fowl. Ah! And the ducks and the cade lambs.'

'But not the pigs?'

'Well, if Tim could mind 'em a bit longer I'd be glad. It does make me so rheumaticky, down by the water there.'

239

'It's a big expense, giving that great lad his tea every day.'

'I know it be, and I'll be as quick as I can getting better, Sarn.'

'I shouldna think life's much of a pleasure to you, ailing so.'

'It be weary time and again, but in between I'm pretty comfortable.'

'What with the rheumatics and the cough and the sinking feeling, I should think you'd as lief be in the Better Land.'

'When it pleases the Lord to take me to the Better Land, I mun go without complaint, but I'd liefer be in life, for life I do know, and the worst of it, but the Better Land I dunna know.'

'You know there's no coughs nor rheumatics there, nor sinking feeling.'

'Nor chimney corners nor cups of tea,' she says, 'and I doubt it'll be too grand for me, Sarn.'

But Gideon, standing in the mid of the room and talking very loud, said –

'You'd as lief be dead as quick.'

He went away then, but every evening he went in again and talked in the same way, which seemed a pity to my mind, for though he might mean to cheer her up, and though folk never seem to think it matters what you say to the sick, yet it seemed to me melancholy talk for a poor old ailing woman. But at last, one evening at the end of March, in a spell of wet, muggy weather, when the rheumatics were very bad, she said, when he came to what he always ended with – 'I should think you'd as lief be dead as quick –'

'Well, maybe I would, Sarn.'

And that seemed to content him. He left off coming every evening, which eased Mother, for she was more in dread of him than ever nowadays, so that even Tivvy noticed it. I thought when April came in, things seemed to be going better, Mother being more cheerful, though still very weak. I got on better with my work, being free of worry, and Mother seemed quite happy with Tivvy. We were working harder than ever, and my clo'es hung about me, but I didna mind that. I was sowing the big field with wheat, while Gideon went on ploughing. It was grand out there in the fresh of the morning, with purple shadows on the wet earth, and the sun rilling up beyond the woods, and Sarn Mere like pale blue crackled glass with a light behind it. Times, the sky would be all pale blue too, with larks hanging in it. Times the big white clouds, like new-washed and carded wool, stood upon the tops of the budding trees. The bright colours made me think of the coloured weaving, which I supposed Kester would have pretty near mastered by now. Though no word had come, since Christmas, of his doings or his well-being, I felt in myself that all was right with him. At Christmas the Silverton coachman had left a little packet for me at the *Mug o' Cider*, and when I was raught back to the attic I found within a bit of cloth woven in two colours, and a letter.

LONDON TOWN.

Christmas.

DEAR PRUE SARN,—

This is to wish you well as it leaves me. I can do two colours now, as you see by pattern. The women here are poor things, pale and small, mostly fair, and not a real melting dark eye among them. I was bid to a banquet at the house of an alderman that is a weaver. There was a young wench sat by me that had spared her bodice-stuff but not her blushes. I called to mind a dark stone chamber, and young Camperdine's face in the shadows, and a woman that did what she did for loving-kindness and in bitterness of spirit, but did look like an apple-blossom fairy all the same, and did light a fire in one chap as will be very hard to dout. And so a happy Christmas and a good New Year from

KESTER WOODSEAVES.

241

I may say that letter was in rags by April, as if the mice had been at it.

I had sent him a letter for Christmas also, and this was it.

SARN.

Christmas.

DEAR WEAVER,

Please find herein a lockram shirt. If you wear it, they say you'll take no harm from the smallpox or other ills. I wove it and made it of hemp, and said a good few old righteous charms over it, but no unrighteous ones. I often call to mind the day we watched the dragon-flies, at the time of the troubling of the waters, when the lilies were in blow. So farewell for now, and God send you happy.

Yours obediently,
PRUDENCE SARN.

The seventh of April being a very clear-coloured morning, I called the weaving to mind, and so, as I went up and down the field sowing the bright seed, I sang *Barley Bridge.*

> *'Shift your feet in nimble flight,*
> *You'll be home by candlelight.*
> *Open the gates as wide as the sky,*
> *And let the king come riding by.'*

Would Kester ever come riding to Sarn from London Town? I wondered. For the fair, he'd said he'd come, at the time of the troubling of the waters, when the lilies were in blow all along the marges of the mere, looking at their angels, and when blue kingfisher-flies and the bright, lustre-coloured damsels were coming out of their shrouds.

I was thinking thus, when I looked up, and there was Tivvy, coming running in a great courant, all distraught.

'Come quick, Prue!' she said. 'Her's took very bad. The tea didna agree. He says, give it her strong, he says, for it'll do more good the like of that'n. So I did. And she

242

said it was a bitter brew. But she drank it. And in a while she went ever so quiet, and I couldna hear her breathe. And then she gave a guggle and whispers –

"Go for Prue." ’

I was only just in time to kiss Mother, who was all shrunken down in her pillows. She whispered –

‘A bitter brew!’ and smiled, and caught her breath, and was gone.

After a while I says to Tivvy –

‘Where’s that tea?’

But she’d thrown it away.

‘Gideon,’ I said, ‘was there bane in that tea you did tell Tivvy to give Mother?’

‘Now what do I know what Tivvy did give to Mother?’ says he.

‘Oh, Sarn, you did know?’ cries Tivvy. ‘You said, "Give it her strong," you did.’

‘Hold your tongue, you little liar,’ shouts Gideon, ‘or I’ll thank you to tell Prue what you and me were doing in the loft, Sunday’s a week.’

With that, Tivvy went as red as fire, and hushed.

I could make nothing of them. I sent for the doctor, to see what Mother died of. And he said, were we in the habit of giving her *digitalis*, a strange word that I didna know, but he spelled it out for me, and I wrote it down. So I said no, I’d never heard tell of it. So he says, ‘Foxglove! Foxglove!’

‘Foxglove?’ I says. ‘No. Whatever should I give her that for?’

‘What indeed?’ he says, looking at me very sharp.

‘What do puzzle me, sir,’ I says, ‘is what Mother died of. She was beginning to pick up so nice.’

‘That’s what I want to know, too,’ he says.

‘Maybe we’d ought to have a Crowner’s ’Quest, sir?’ I says.

‘Oh, you’d be willing to have an inquest on the body?’

'Why, yes, indeed, if it was right and proper.'

'Well, if you're willing to have it, there's no need to have it.'

He was a very peculiar man. I couldna make him out at all.

'I was doubtful,' he says. 'But if you're willing . . . It's nothing but old age, I expect. They go like that in the spring sometimes. And it's a great trouble and expense, an inquest . . . all just for the flicker of a doubt . . . and can't do the poor woman any manner of good . . . so, if you're willing, we won't bother with an inquest.'

I could make neither head nor tail of that. But remembering that Doctor was an educated man, I left off trying to understand him. For there's as much of a mystery about an educated man, that's been schooled and colleged proper, as there is about the Trinity. So, being busy over the funeral and all, I thought no more about him, but I grieved sorely for Mother, because as she lay in coffin she did look like a frozen bird, foredone with winter.

Chapter 4: *All on a May Morning*

IT was quieter than ever at Sarn without Mother's quiet ways. I missed her a deal more than if I'd depended on her, for it's the folk that depend on us for this and for the other that we most do miss. So the mother is more let and hindered lacking the little creatures clinging to her skirt than she is when they be there, for she has no heart for her work. So in the lengthening April days I'd often sit and cry, calling to mind her poor little hands uplifted, and her way of giving me a right good welcome when I came in tired of an evening. There was only Gideon and me, and Tivvy now and again. The work went on the same as ever, though there was a sadness about it all. Gideon never went into the stackyard but he cursed Beguildy, who was still in prison, with no sentence fixed. We'd heard nought of Jancis nor her mother for a good while, nor had there been another letter from Kester. The market began again. I mean, we began to go again, having plenty to fill the stall. One of us would go, and the other would mind the farm, and I heard that every time Gideon·went, Miss Dorabella would come and buy summat. Indeed it was already being said that she was sweet on Gideon, and I could only hope it wouldna come to the Squire's ears. I didna wonder at her being partial to Gideon, for indeed he was a fine, strong man, with a deal of character and power, and very good to look at, and there were few young gentlemen about Lullingford at that time, what with some of them going to bide in London, and some never coming back from the wars. Gideon never said anything to me, but I could see he was flattered at her liking, and I thought once when she came to our door for a drink of milk, that his hand shook a bit when he gave her the cup. But if he was thinking of her, I'm sure it was only the lust of the eye, and youth, and the wish to get on, and not love, such as he felt for Jancis. I didna believe he'd ever love anybody again, since that early love had been poisoned – for indeed the bane seemed to have got into it as it had into everything. But there was no doubt he was very taken up with her, and when it wasna Miss Dorabella it was Tivvy. He didna care a farden for Tivvy, but he was ready to take all she'd give, as many another young man would, especially after such an upsetting of his life, and the losing of his dear acquaintance. He seemed to want to be out along with Tivvy when he wasna working, as if he was restless, and he couldna bear to speak of Mother. This seemed curious to me, for he never appeared to care much about her in life. I mind when May Day came, and we were starting for the market, for the things must be sold, mourning or not, I said I called to mind just where Mother

245

stood to send us last time. And Gideon gave a bit of a start, and looked, nervous like, at the place I pointed to, almost as if he thought she'd come again. And sometimes I noticed that he'd look across at her chair, anxious and brooding. This troubled me, for it was so different from his usual ways. In all else he was the same, and the farm was the same, and the mere, and the spring. May came in warm and splendid, and the buds and blades, the opening petals and the blown petals, the wafts of sweet air and the storms of warm rain drove on over the country as in every other year. The blackbirds kept up their charm the day long, and the cuckoos were at it from four or five in the morning. Out went the coots and their young across the mere, the dippers made their well-roofed house, the wagtails played beside the water, and the heron stood watching his long shadow in the glassy lake, as if he wondered how soon it would be as long as the steeple. The lily leaves lay green and bright, like empty boats, for the time of lilies was not yet. The young leaves on the forest trees lengthened and broadened, the grass grew long and began to ripple, the corn sprang quick and bright. The Lent lilies in the meadow wilted, and the bluebells came, like smoke bellying up the slopes of the woods. All was made anew, and the brighter the colours were, the more I thought of Kester and his weaving, and the more unkind I felt it to be on my part, to be glad of the spring, with poor Mother in her new-made grave. There came a day in the very mid of all this fine May weather, when the thorn trees along by the mere were so thick-set with blossom that they laid a solid wall of white in the water at their feet. Though it was noon, the charm of bird-song was nearly as loud as it was at dawn, for in May they never seem to weary. We were in the kitchen, having our dinner afore going out to finish earthing up the taters. Tivvy was helping, as she often did now, though she got but little thanks from Gideon, who would brood all the while, and frown, and start up sometimes as if he heard a voice.

The kitchen was pleasant after the heat outside, for it was an early year. The sun lay in quiet patches along the quarries, and the lilac outside, just past its prime and the sweeter for it, sent a strong freshness through the open window.

Something went past the window, and there was a little soft tap on the door. It reminded me of the time when Jancis ran away and came to our door in the snow. I went to open, and there she stood, Jancis, white as a ghost, leaning against the doorpost, with a shawl wrapped about her, and in the shawl, as I could just see, a baby no bigger than a doll.

'Why, Jancis!' I says. 'However in the name of goodness did you come?'

But she only looked past me, as wild and as white as any mermaid in the old tales, peering after her mortal lover.

She gave me neither word nor look. She gave Tivvy no glance even. We wunna there for Jancis in that hour. She just slipped in, like a wreath of mist from off the winter mountain or a drift of blossom from off the summer trees, or a white woman from under the mere. She'd got on the gown she was used to wear for randies, torn and crumpled but still white, and though it didna set her off as well as the blue one, it did, with the white shawl, make her look like a floating spirit out of the air, as she went across the kitchen. There she was, all of a heap at Gideon's feet, and she had set the baby on the floor in front of him, as he sate in the big arm-chair at the table. And the table being set out with food, and he at its head, and Jancis there upon the floor, it did make me think of that story in the Bible when Jesus was at a feast, and some poor person came and asked summat, and was chid, and did up and say that not even the dogs need lack their crumbs. It was as if all the good of life was outspread there on our oaken table, till it creaked under the weight. There were the fruits of love, there was the homely bread of daily kindness, and the cup to quench all thirst, and salt to make

247

life tasty, and all the lesser pleasures that do make life a good, sweet thing in the living. And Gideon had the helping of them. Sarn of Sarn Mere was the maister of that feast, and he might say, if he would, 'Here, let me heap thy plate, and fill up thy mug!' Or he might begrutch it all.

Jancis was kneeling in the patch of bright sunshine, and she seemed as the snowflake when the day turns to a thaw. In the ticking of one moment she might be melted clean away. I called to mind that day in the dairy, when she came in behopes that Gideon might ask her to wed there and then. I called to mind the night I wished her well when Beguildy was gone to look for the seventh child and the time I saw her coming toërts me between her white oxen, like a lady of old time that has been a long while dead. I remembered how she'd sung *Green Gravel* that Christmas when she ran away, and how the light from the window was green upon her face, and how she was used to say –

'O, I wanted to play *Green Gravel!*'

All the things she'd ever said or done seemed to be lapped around her as she knelt there with her golden hair all loose about her shoulders. That she was so pale, all white and gold, and that Gideon was so dark, and darkly clad, made it seem yet more as if she came from some other world, and the baby also, for it was white too, and its tiny head, where the wrapper fell aside, was covered with a light yellow down. There was no look of Gideon in it at all. It wunna like a real baby, but like a changeling that came into being in the mid of a summer night on the petal of a lily flower. Oh, it was a strange baby as ever I saw! I leaned against the doorpost with the tears rolling down my face, and so that I shouldna sob out loud I promised myself to give Jancis the best meal ever she had, so soon as this should be over, and she should have a new-laid egg from the slatey game hen, whose eggs were worth a mint of money for setting, she being a prize bird. Though why it should please me so to think of her eating it, when a common egg would have been quite as nice, and bigger,

I dunna know. And I promised myself that the baby should have the best wash ever, for indeed it looked as if it had rolled in the ashes. And oh, dear me! how I'd stuff it with milk, and how I'd dress up the old rush cot, and make a little counterpane, and then put the well-stuffed baby to lie in the sun and sleep! And in time it would lose that wisht, awful look, so ancient, as if it knew all there was to know, and didna like it. I wanted to see it with a great big tossy-ball of golden cowslips. And all the while Tivvy sat by Gideon with her mouth fallen open with surprise, and looking almost as frittened as if she'd seen a ghost.

Gideon was like a stone man. There was no feeling in his face at all, neither pity nor anger. All that was over-past, it seemed. It was like an old tale that he'd forgotten, and Jancis was chief lady in that tale, but why she was, and who she was, and what she did was all out of mind, because the tale was lost to his remembrance. Once, at Christmas, maybe, if she'd come, he'd have knocked her down, very likely, in his anger. But then he might have kissed her after. Now he neither struck nor kissed.

All he'd felt for her had died in the fire that night of September, and the sin of the father was visited upon the poor girl. For when Gideon's eye fell on her, he saw his burning ricks, and in her blue glance there were the red reflections of fire, as you will see on some clear morning the last wild smoulderings of the thunderstorm. That was all she meant to him now. And though his hatred of Beguildy was as savage as ever, he had no feeling at all for her, neither hatred nor desire, nor even lust, much less any love. Miss Dorabella had seized upon his mind, and Tivvy had satisfied his body. There was no place for Jancis. There he sat, in our old kitchen, so quiet, yet so full of whispers, so full of the remembrance of all the Sarns that had been here, from Tim, with the lightning in his blood, to Father, passing out from life in a dark snoring after a fit of anger. I thought of Mother spinning there day after day, whirring like a little lych-fowl. I thought

249

of all the other Sarn women, and of myself, striving and slaving for the bane. And it seemed that the bane was like some plant, such as the catch-fly, that does wile living creatures into its banqueting hall, spreading a great feast and see! when they are in, she catches them and grips them, and binds them, ana trammels their feet, so that they cannot go. There was a heavy sweetness from the day-lilies in the border that made me think of death chambers. I wished Jancis would say summat and get it over, whether for good or ill, so that I might the sooner set about the babe. But she didna, and time went on and on. Outside there was Sarn Mere standing up afore me like a mirror framed in some precious green gem work. There was no sound but the saddish charm of the birds near and far, and the wandering hum of a bee that came into our kitchen, and, misliking it, blundered out again.

Then Jancis lifted up her head and looked at Gideon. 'Sarn!' she said. And again, 'Sarn!'

As she said it, I got the feeling that there were many listeners, leaning down out of the air, crowded together as close as the petals of a white peony, waiting to hear what should come of this meeting.

She clasped her hands and set her blue eyes upon Gideon, seeming to leave the baby aside for a while, as if he should speak up for himself later.

'Do you mind, Sarn,' she said, 'how we used to play *Conquer* with the big pink and white snail-housen down by the water, and you nearly always won, and I lost? Do you mind how I wanted to play *Green Gravel?*'

Her faint voice stopped a while, and a strange thing happened, for as I watched her it seemed to me as if many voices, a long way off, took up the words of that old song and sang it right through, in parts, as is the manner of singers in our country-side. For if anybody sings at all, he or she can sing parts, the people being all very fond of music and having it grained into their souls. So I heard it, with the grace-notes of the trebles and the rolling of the bass voices, and the altos and the tenors taking up the words and playing with them, and all, as it were, making much of the song, and speaking for Jancis through it. Very low and far it seemed, yet rich with many voices.

> *'Green gravel, green gravel, the grass is so green!*
> *The fairest young lady that ever was seen.*
> *I'll wash you in milk, and I'll clothe you in silk,*
> *And write down your name with a gold pen and ink.'*

What it was I heard, I never knew. Parson said it was my busy imagination playing about the past. I canna say. Only, in my imagination or in reality, I did hear it, in very truth, a part song, well sung and tuneful, with every note clear and each part intertwining as it should, but all a very long way off.

'Do you call to mind the even when you saw me under the rosy light, Sarn, when you were coming back from Lullingford ooth the sheep? And the day we found the canbottlins' nest in the spinney, and fourteen young uns in it, and you kissed me once for every canbottlin?'

Still Gideon made no sound, nor stirred.

'And when I ran away, and Prue took me in, you did say to me, standing in the mid of this very kitchen, "Give us a kiss, wench!" And in the dairy once you said I looked as if I was made of may and milk. And at Callard's, that evening I held the baby while Mister Callard made 'em all say, "Bull-baiting's bad!" do you mind how Granfeyther Callard said all of a sudden, "I see two babbies in her arms, ours, and hers as is to come!" And the harvest dance, when they whistled so well, and we danced?'

A quiver went across Gideon's face at the mention of that harvest, and I wondered at Jancis speaking of it, till I saw that she'd forgotten the cause of Gideon's quarrel with her. All she knew now was that he didna love her, and the reason was neither here nor there.

'And when Feyther went to look for the seventh child

251

and you came, and we were so sweet together? Ah! Even that morning after Feyther came back we were so, and you said "Come five days, my little dear!" And I said, "God send you happy!" And since that, Sarn, I hanna set eyes on you till this hour.'

Still Gideon made no sign, so she laid her hand on his arm.

'Do you mind it, Sarn?' she says.

'Ah!' he said, indifferent, 'I mind it, but it was long ago. Time out of mind.'

'But the babe wasna. Here be the babe, Sarn! Yours and mine.'

She held the child up as if she'd put it on his knees, but he waved it away.

'A boy!' says Jancis. 'Not a girl, to cumber you with women. A boy, to mind pigs for ye ever so soon, and in a few years he'll be driving plough. Ah. I reckon he'll be a good lad to you, and work well and gather in twice as much as his grandad scattered abroad.'

The poor babe stirred, as if it felt the heavy burden.

Gideon looked at it, as if when it touched his life's aim it could be seen, though invisible at other times. Then he gave a short, cruel laugh.

'That?' he says. 'You offer me that to help me? Thank ye! Why, if it lives, which I doubt, it'll never be no good but to coddle about in the house and feed on soft food.'

And as if it knew that it hadna passed the test, the poor mite set up a wail. At this Gideon pushed the table aside and got up. He went to the back kitchen door, that being the nearest way to the kitchen garden. At the door he stopped a minute.

'Best go back where you came from,' he said. 'You binna wanted here, neither the one nor the other.'

With that, he shut the door and went out.

Jancis stayed where she was, seeming mazed and dumb-foundered. A pale feather borne along the air, a lily petal wandering on the water, couldna be as lost as she was then. I ran to her, and lifted her and the babe to the settle, for indeed she was so light, it was pity to feel her lightness.

'Now, lookye,' I said, 'never a word shall you speak till you've had a bite and sup! Put the kettle on, Tivvy, there's a good girl, the while I warm some milk for baby.'

Jancis said nought, but in a little the tears began to steal down her cheeks. She took a sup of tea, and then I asked her how she got here.

'I walked,' she said, 'and poor baby was so heavy. You'd never think to look at him, what a weight he was to lug.' I knew he scarce weighed more than a good fowl, and so I knew also how weary poor Jancis must have been, to feel so small burden so heavy.

'Whatever was your mother thinking of, to let you walk?'

'Mother's dead.'

'Dear to goodness! I be sorry for that,' I said. 'She was a right nice woman.'

'There's kind!' says Jancis, but without any heart in it.

She was like one who, in the game of *Costly Colours*, has risked all, playing the card called *Costly*, and lost it. She was out of the game now, with nothing more to gain or lose. I didna like to mention her dad, and she said nothing about him.

'Well, your home's here,' I said. 'You know that, Jancis, my dear.'

'My home canna be here if Sarn dunna love me, Prue.'

'Ah, but it is!' I cried out. 'Though I did swear on the Book to obey Gideon like a 'prentice, a wife, and a dog, yet this day I shall gainsay him. You'll lie in my bed tonight, child. You and the little un will sleep at home from this time on.'

She gave a little sad smile, as if to say, 'I wonder!' and lay holding the babe. But now Tivvy, who'd been looking more and more sulky, burst out –

'And will she sleep here indeed, Prue Sarn? I do think not! Maybe you dunna know as I'm going to wed with Sarn myself. Ah! He's got to wed me for my sake and for his own as well.'

Jancis had opened her eyes and was watching her with a look like a Wise Woman's I knew once, who could tell you your own thoughts.

'I know it ud be as well for you, Tivvy, if he did wed with you,' I said, pretty dry and sneering, for I never could abide Tivvy, and that's the truth, 'and I reckon he'd best not be too long about it, neither, and you Sexton's girl and all! But the thing is, will he? And I'm pretty sure he never will. I'm sorry for you, Tivvy, and I'd never have said a word afore Jancis, only you began it.'

Tivvy's face was scarlet, but she didna flinch.

'I said, good for him as well as for me,' she answered.

'I canna see,' I says, and God forgive me for being so sharp with the girl, 'how it ud be good for Gideon, *in any way*, to marry you.'

'Oh! Well, I'll soon show you,' she says.

'He did love Jancis once, Tivvy,' I told her. 'And she was his dear acquaintance and his wife, all but the ring.'

She took no notice of that.

'I'll tell you why it ud be good for Sarn to marry me,' she said. 'Foxglove tea! That's why.'

'Foxglove tea! Are you crazy, Tivvy?'

'Everybody knows as I know nought of yarbs. Everybody knows Sarn gave the cow foxglove leaves. You and I know that the doctor said your mother seemed as if she'd had foxglove.'

She spoke slower and slower, leaning forrard with her hands on the table.

'Everybody knows, Prue Sarn, that your brother thought Missis Sarn a burden. Everybody knows he does want to get on. And *I* know, and if he dunna marry me pretty quick everybody else 'll know too, what was in the tea he made for his mother and told me to give her strong.'

'What was it?' I said, with a sickness at the heart.
'Foxglove!'

She snapped out the word like a bite. I knew it was true.

'I can prove it,' she said, 'because as it chanced Mother had come to bring Missis Sarn that night-rail she'd been sewing for 'er. And when I came down from giving Missis Sarn her tea, I poured a cup for Mother, there being some left, and Mother said in a minute, 'This is foxglove tea.' Ah, Mother knows right well what Missis Sarn died of, but she'll never mouth it to a mouse if Sarn weds with me.'

'I'll never believe it!' I cried out. But Tivvy says –

'You will. You believe it now.'

And I did. Jancis did, too. She gave a little moan and whispered –

'It was foreboded, Prue! It was to be. I've no home now, Prue, no home on all this earth. Neither baby nor me's got anywhere to go. What shall us do, baby?'

The baby, being spoken to and being well content with the meal it had just finished, gave a milky smile. Jancis shut her eyes and seemed to care no more what anybody said.

But Tivvy came to the settle, and she says –

'If you stop the night over, we'll publish it all abroad, Jancis Beguildy!'

And then I be sorry to say my temper was out, and I rushed at her and boxed her ears right well.

'Go!' I says. 'Go, you cruel wench, afore I maul you. I never hated afore. But you I hate. How dare you be so curst to that poor child? You may settle with Gideon what you both do. But when you come over the door-sill, out go I. And for this day, out go you!'

And I may say she went pretty quick, very startled to see meek Prue Sarn in such a temper.

'Now lie you still, and rest, my dear,' I said, 'while I go to Gideon.'

'No. Dunna werrit Sarn, Prue,' she says. 'But I'll rest.

255

Ah. Baby and me's both in need of rest. We'll take a good long rest, Prue. And thank you kindly for all.'

Out I went. There was Gideon, working like seven. I do believe those unkind words he said to Jancis were but his way of brazening it out to his own heart. I do believe there was a seed of love there even then, and if it hadna been for Tivvy it might have pushed up and flowered. I was never one to hiver-hover over things, so I walked up to Gideon and said –

'Tivvy says you gave Mother poison. Be it true?'

'By gum, that wench wants a good hiding!' says Gideon. 'And if she forces me to wed with her, that's the bridegift she'll get.'

'You *did* give her foxglove tea to give Mother, then?'

'Mother told me she'd liefer be dead than quick, and she was a burden.'

He never tried to soften it nor deny it, for that wasna his way.

'Well, you be a murderer, and I've done with you,' I said.

'You swore to do as I said.'

'Murder cancels all vows,' I answered.

'I dunna want Tivvy here. She's no manner use.'

'Seemingly you canna choose,' I said. 'It's Tivvy or hang, as far as I can see. I'd save you if I could, for you be my brother, when all's said, and I like you right well, too. When you've worked along of a person, furrow for furrow and spade for spade, as long as I've worked with you, lad, you do like the person right well, unless you hate him. And you I canna hate, though I've been trying to the last few minutes. Gideon! What for did you do such a wicked thing? Indeed to goodness you mun repent in dust and ashes, and think of nothing else at all, or the devil 'll certainly put his mark on you, so you'll come to no good in this life, and go to the lowest hell in the other. Your own mother, Gideon!'

But all he'd say was –

'She said she'd liefer be dead than quick, and she was a great burden.'

'Well, I'm going, and so I warn you,' I said, in a passion.

'I'm in behopes you'll stay over hay and corn harvest,' he answers, as cool as cool could be, just as if he'd done no wrong at all, which I believe in his own sight he hadna.

'No,' I said. 'Fix up with Tivvy.'

'She's no use in the harvest. She's so bone-idle.'

'I'll stay till she comes, and no longer,' I said. 'And I wouldna promise that, only I know she's in a pretty taking to get wed quick. I be right down disappointed with you, Gideon, on every count.'

'You've no right to be. What have I done? Put an old woman to sleep as wanted to sleep. And as for Tivvy, she as good as asked me to.'

Calm? Oh, he was as calm as the mere when it was frozen deep.

'And what about Jancis?' I burst out. 'What about that poor mommet of hers that you've brought into the world? They're neither old nor forrard.'

For answer, he pointed across to the blackened floor of the rickyard, and said –

'You know whose child she is.'

Then, under breath, he said, as if he'd forgotten me –

'But I did love her once.'

So I left him to his thoughts, and ran back to the house, calling out as I opened the back door –

'Here, Jancis, my dear, I've brought the slatey hen's egg to beat up in milk for you.'

But no one answered, and when I came into the kitchen the settle was empty.

I ran across the fold and out through the gate by the mixen into the road, into that good road the Romans did make, so many a year ago. And yet, to the mere, that long while was but a little, for though it had been troubled

257

two thousand times since then, so Parson said, yet it had been troubled uncounted thousands of times afore, and would be again, till the world and all shrivelled like the cast-off body of a dragon-fly. I ran along the road in the strong heat, and the sandy earth shone in the light, and the shadows were short and very dark. I ran round the first corner, that came soon, and the next, and even the next, in case she'd walked faster than I thought. But there was nobody on the road, no white and gold mother with a white and gold mommet. Only the camomile, in clumps on the banks, was their colour, gold and white, and as I ran the strong scent of it caught my heart. I thought maybe she'd gone up to my room to wash baby. I ran back, calling and searching high and low. But there was nobody in the house save Pussy, who looked at me, sad, and ran into every room a bit in front of me. I looked in the barn and the loft and the shippen. Why I should think she was there I canna say, only I was getting despert eager to find her by this. I ran up the wood path, in case she'd had a fancy to walk there, where Gideon so often went to send her on her way home. I ran on and on, calling till the wood-pigeons flew up with a clattering noise, but nobody answered. Only the forest stood about me. Only the varnished kingcups were yellow round the edges of the mere, each clump of blossoms multiplied by two in the clear water, and the walls of thorn-bloom lay there, white and green. A lost and lonesome feeling crept over me. I went to Gideon in the garden at the back of the house.

'I canna find Jancis,' I said.

'I told her to go back where she came from,' he answered with the same manner of speaking as he had afore, brazening it out.

'She couldna do that,' I said, 'for she's gotten no money and her mother's dead, and what's come to her father only the assize court knows, seemingly, for she dunna. She walked all the way from Silverton, Gideon. She hadna

258

any money for the coach. All those weary miles she walked to come to you. And how did you make her welcome?'

He said nought to that, but went on with his work.

'You mun come and look for the poor girl,' I said. 'Now. This instant minute, you must come. You must think of somewhere else to look. Oh, think of somewhere else quick, Gideon! For I canna. And if we canna think of anywhere else, there's only –'

With a great shudder I pointed to the mere.

'What!' he said, very angered. 'What, you'd fritten me, would ye?'

He smote the spade into the earth as if there was an enemy hid there, and came with me round the house and the buildings. Then he set off up the road, saying she might have got a lift, which made me afraid for his wits, seeing that there was nobody to give lifts on that road but us and the ghostly chariots that people said you could hear, nights, rolling and grinding along the old road. But in a while came back, finding no sign of Jancis.

'We must drag the mere,' I said. 'We needna go far, I doubt. She'd soon be out of her depth, being so little and small. And she'd no time to walk far. She must have gone in by the caus'y here.'

For, as I said afore, this broad stone caus'y that the Romans made ran from just in front of our house down into the village at the bottom of the mere, where the bells did play, they said, of an evening.

And it turned out that I was right, for there, just where the caus'y went into the water, was one of baby's boots. I'd noticed that the ribbon was out of it, and that it was nearly off, and would have been right off if this un had been like other babes, kicking and laughing to feel its own might. But it was only a poor silly waxen creature, and so, doubtless, the boot stayed on till it felt the cold water, and struggled to find itself dying as it never did to find itself living.

259

They lay there in a bed of lily leaves, and we took them up without a word and carried them within. I washed them and dressed them in white, and we laid them on Mother's bed, and I mounded it up with flowers, white lilac, and thorn, golden day-lilies and golden cowslips, that the child should have made into tossy-balls in the time to come.

All the while, Gideon said nothing, nor did he look much at them, but went on with his work about the place.

But the neighbours came all the three days afore the funeral, from near and far. For the coming back of Jancis, and the child, and the drowning, made such a tale as hadna been in our part of the country, where things go on middling quiet, even in the memory of Granfeyther Callard.

They came and looked at her, and the women cried, though in her life they'd been hard as flint to Jancis. The younger men stood a while, saying nought, looking down upon her as if they were fain of her.

'The sins of the fathers,' said Sexton, making an oration over those two, 'and not only the sins of the fathers, for it's no use to be mealymouthed, people, and though it be sad to say it, the poor wench was no better than she should be, for the child wunna born in wedlock. No, people, it wunna even a barley child, for there was no ring in the case at all. We dunna know who the man was,' he went on, looking at Gideon in a way that showed he knew right well, and meant to say unless Gideon wed with Tivvy, 'we dunna know that, but what we do know is, *where she came from*. We know who was her feyther, neighbours. We know she was sired by the devil's odd-man. We know that the burning of the ricks was as nought, yea, and less than nought, compared with the things he did secret and unbeknown. What's come to pass was only what we had to expect, for what's bred in the bone will come out in the flesh, dear souls.'

260

'By their fruits ye shall know them, Matthew seven,' added Sammy.

Then, looking down upon the two golden heads a good while, as you might look at some rare bird you'd never see again, he said to himself and so low that I only heard because I was nighest to him –

'They were lovely and pleasant in their lives, and in their death they were not divided.'

And he catched his breath a bit, forgetting chapter and verse.

Callard's children came two by two, to view the bodies. And as they stood at the foot of the bed after, looking on the babe in the crook of its mother's arm, suddenly they cried out all together, as they were taught to do about the baiting –

'Oh, look's pretty! The little mommet!'

And Miller nodded his head three times, as if to say, here were two kit-cats, where they should be.

Then Grandfeyther Callard stood out, and he said –

'Two funerals in a month! It do make me think of the days when the great sickness was on the land, and we as were quick were weary of the buryings. And strange it is, friends all, that these two should be dead, when their ages added together dunna amount to near thirty years, while I number one-and-ninety years and yet I've so far missed to catch the plague that ravens through this bitter old world the ancient plague of dying.'

Still Gideon said nothing. But the night afore we took them to the churchyard I heard him stirring, and being afraid that in a sudden horror of the spirit he might do himself a mischief, for though a slow, quiet man in daily life, he could be, now and again, hasty of a sudden, I went to see what the matter was.

He was standing beside the bed. As I went in he had just stretched forth his hand and lifted in his great brown fingers the plait of golden hair, so thick and fine, that was

261

ever the pride of poor Jancis. When he turned at my coming, he was like a lad taken in a fault, hanging his head and muttering, as if it should explain his act, which indeed it did –

'I did love her once.'

Chapter 5: *The Last Game of Conquer*

IF it had not been that Parson said I must be careful to write all, and leave out none, since to know all made folks kind, but to know a part made 'em worse than if they knew nothing, if it hadna been for that, I'd never have tried to write of those three months at Sarn betwixt the time of the death of Jancis and the time of the troubling of the waters. For there are some things so hard to write of that even a great scholar might boggle at it, and I, though I can do the tall and the short script, am not anything of a scholar, and words be hard to find for some things. I think, times, that in our mortal language there are no words for the things that are of most account. So, when those things come upon us we are struck silent, and can but feel and feel, till our hearts are like a bursting dam. Maybe, in the life yonder, that already I begin to glimpse on the edge of this world, we shall find the proper words. But not yet. So, if I fail in what I've set out to do, you must pardon what I canna help, and fill up the glats in my speech with the brushwood of your own imagining.

The strangest part of that time was the silence of it. Gideon had always been a silent man, but now he was as bad as the miller. He'd come and he'd go, but not a word would pass his lips. And sometimes he'd stop all of a sudden, as he went about his work, as if he'd been struck of a heap by summat. His thoughts, I guessed it to be. Then he'd straighten his shoulders, and mighty shoulders they were, and go about his work again. I thought it would pass in time, and as nothing was settled between him and Tivvy yet, I made up my mind not to leave the poor lad all alone, but to bide still for a while. Tivvy was in a fix, for she was determined to have Gideon, and yet she was so mortal afraid of the frittening, for the frittening is said to be very bad in a place where mother and babe die together, that she durstna set foot our side of the mere at all. So there we were, in a thick, cruddled silence, that grew ever more and more solid like freezing water or souring milk. Save for the birds, that minded their own affairs and took no thought of us, there were no voices uplifted at Sarn. Evenings, when they hushed, it fell so still that I could hear Gideon's boat, moored just by the beginning of the caus'y, knocking and knocking with small, reminding taps. And, times, in the kitchen of a night, when Gideon was out, working late at the hoeing of the young corn or at the haying, I'd hold up a bit of tasty victuals to Pussy just to make her mew. And I'd say, 'There, now thee's mewed! Good Pussy!'

When he was in, Gideon was as dumb as the crowned, save that once, on a night of bright moonlight when we were having our supper late after haying, he leaned forrard of a sudden and said –

'Did ye see that?'

'What?' I says.

'Why, somebody went by the door, in a white gown.'

But it wasna till July, in a spell of very thundery weather, hot and still and gloomy, that his strangeness came upon him in good earnest. I was sitting in the doorway, to get what air there was, for it drew off the mere, evenings. I was carding wool, and the white of it, heaped up on my black, made me look like a magpie, I thought. The lilac leaves were limp with the heat, and the mere like hot lead

263

to look at, with the tall thick trees around it, carven out of iron. All round the marges of the mere were the lilies, lying on the heavy water, their small white buds shining. Not a bird spoke, for all were in their coverts, since the heat was so great. Even the water-birds stayed among the reeds, and the boat had given over knocking on the steps, as if the day was fixed now for the passenger to come, and there was no more to do till then. Suddenly Gideon came round the corner all in a sweat of haste, with the brummock in one hand and his hedging gloves still on, for he was busy at the hedges between hay and corn harvest. He stopped when he saw me, and put hand to head, and then broke out in a passion –

'What for do ye sit there the like of that, making game you're Mother?'

'I never made game to be Mother,' I said. 'Whatever ails you?'

'Mother was used to sit there and card wool. I thought you were Mother.'

'Well, I couldna help that,' I said. 'But what did you come round the corner in such a courant for?'

'I was pleaching the big thorn hedge, and she came upon the top of it, all in white.'

'Who came upon the top of it?' I asks, impatient.

'Jancis,' he says, as quiet as could be, not as if he was saying anything strange, but just as he might speak of seeing Tivvy or Polly Miller. He said no more, but went back to his work, though he gave up the hedge. He'd never argue at all about what he saw but just say he saw it, and that was all. The next time was when he was hoeing in the big wheat field. He came into the house, very hasty, with the hoe and all, and said he'd seen Jancis ploughing with her two white oxen, in the barley field, and the child sitting up on the nighest ox.

'Now look you, Gideon,' I said, 'you mun leave thinking of Jancis, or you'll be possessed. And a man possessed is pretty far on to madness. You just think of getting on,

264

and scraping and saving as you used to, and dunna think of Jancis or Mother till you're more settled in your mind.'

'I dunna think of Jancis. She just comes.'

'Well, set your mind on other things and she wunna.'

'What things?'

'Why, getting rich, and getting the house.'

'What for?'

'For the same reason you began of it. Because you want it.'

'I dunna want it now.'

'But why? You wanted it so much, you poisoned Mother. You wanted it so much, you gave the nay-word to Jancis. Let alone all the things you did afore, you must have been pretty well clemmed for it to do as you did.'

'Well, I dunna want it now.'

'What for not?'

'Summat went out of it when I did see 'em in the water.'

'Well, think of Tivvy, then. She'd like to go to the Hunt Ball, I know.'

'I wunna take up with Tivvy. I'd liefer swing.'

'Miss Dorabella, then. She's sweet on you. Take up with her, and she'll spend her money to save you from Tivvy.'

'Dorabella's abron. I like a fair woman. Little. With blue eyes. A woman like may and milk.'

'Well, think of me, then. Be a bit of company for me now and again.'

'But you be going.'

'Not till you're more settled in mind, lad. I'll stop on a bit, if you'll keep a cheerful heart, and not call old grief to mind.'

But it was no use. In less than a week he came in all of a hurry and said –

'She's at it again.'

'What, ploughing?'

'Ah. And the barley field's as bald as a coot.'

265

'It's bad seed,' I says, 'that's what it is, Gideon. It's because you had to buy instead of putting in our own.'

But my heart was heavy, and I couldna see what the end of this would be. I even wished Tivvy would come.

It got to be the usual thing for him to say –

'She came again in the wood to-day.' Or he'd say –

'Look ye! There she is, drawing in to the caus'y. There! Now she's coming up the caus'y, dripping wet. There! Now she's gone.'

Once he said she beckoned from the boat. But it was always out of doors he saw her, so the house was a kind of refuge, and when he suffered that strange fear, in he'd come, and be more himself. I was glad he never saw anything in the house. I was glad, too, that he never heard anything. It was like as if, being smitten to the heart with the sight of her in the water, he'd lost the power to choose what he *saw*, but could still choose what he heard. And then at the beginning of August month, when the corn was just on ripe, he came in and said she'd been singing *Green Gravel* across the water.

'The sound comes in here,' he said, anxious. So I shut the window.

'Best put some wool in your ears,' I said. For indeed it was pitiful to see a man like Gideon trembling at a gleam of white in the hedge or an echo across the water. So he put wool in his ears and we got on pretty well through the first part of August. Then, it was the evening afore the fair at Sarn Mere and many of the booths were already set up. We sat down early to our supper because there had come a letter from Miss Dorabella, brought by one of their men, with news in it about Beguildy. So I opened the letter and read it to Gideon, and he took the wool out of his ears to hear; and what it said was that they'd let Beguildy off light, because he'd had great provocation on account of his daughter.

'Domm!' says Gideon. The blazing hate in him burnt up afresh at hearing of the light sentence, and I almost thought it might cure him of seeing things. But in a little while he fell into his melancholy again, and said he'd seen Mother in the oak wood, where the pigs were.

'Now, dear to goodness,' I said, 'it was nobody in the world but Miller's Polly. She's getting a big girl for her age, and Mother was but little.'

'No,' he said. 'It was Mother. They bother me, Prue.'

'There, there!' I said, patting him on shoulder like a child. For indeed when he spoke of his haunting, he seemed as weak and full of fear as a child in the dark.

'Now see, it'll all come right,' I said. 'You must be well plucked and not mind. You was used to be so fond of *Conquer*. Well, now you must play *Conquer* with your own thoughts.'

'But he only looked at me as if he didna understand, and said –

'What she didna like was me speaking unkind of the babe. Very touchy, mothers be, about their babes.'

We sat quiet a bit, and then he said, all of a sudden –

'Hark ye! She's singing *Green Gravel*.'

He listened a long while, though I could hear nothing.

Then he leaned forrard and said she was coming up off the caus'y toërts the house. His face broke out in a sweat, as if he was feared out of his life. But indeed the weather was enough to make anybody sweat without that, it was so hot and dank at once, the worst weather of all at Sarn, which never had much air, being down in a hollow, and which was always damp from the water. On an evening such as this, the walls ran down with water, so that the whitewash shone as if with the tracks of many snails. Over the mere a mist was rising in trails and wisps, white as wool, thickening and gathering into clotted heaps towards the mid of the mere. Sometimes a wreath of mist would be drawn out like a scarf, and other times it would stand up in the shape of a woman, but wavering upon the air. It seemed to me it might well be one of these ghosts of mist that Gideon had seen. For they rose and sank about the caus'y all the while, as the light airs on the water took them. At Sarn in August there were always heavy mists night and morning, and this was out of the common bad, because we'd had thunder-rain the night before, and a day of brooding heat after it. Bad, I say, because I never could abide mist, and we had such a deal of it, so that sometimes it blotted the farm and the woods and the church right out, as if the mere had turned to milk and risen up and drowned all.

'Hark!' says Gideon. 'Can you hear *Green Gravel*?'

So strong was his mind, and so much it had the mastery over mine, that I almost thought I did hear a wailing song. And then, without any warning, sitting in the big arm-chair with a set, yearning face, like a man enchanted, as I do think he was, Gideon began to sing the song himself. He held up his right hand, solemn, like parson giving the blessing, and he looked out through the doorway toërts the mere and the caus'y and the slow, white, curdling mist. He sang as if some power was on him that made him. You could see he was bound to sing. He had a rolling voice, a fine bass it was; and though he began very softly, it strengthened as he went on, till the music seemed to master the place. And the way he made that childish song mean such a deal! – all the love he'd had for Jancis, and how he'd wanted her to have everything so grand, and go to the Ball like a lady, and all the fear and pity of her ending. It seemed as if he was easier in mind, after having, as it were, given in and so made peace. Still watching the door, he says –

'Here's Jancis. Soused with water she is, out of the mere.'

So I said I saw nothing.

'Why, look's the water dripping off her gown!' he said.

'See there, and there, where she goes! Sogging wet she is, by gum!'

268

He pointed to the floor, and indeed there was water in all the little hollows in the quarries, as if the mere had found a way to soak up through the floor. So I said, yes, I saw the water in the hollows of the quarries.

'Hark at the mud in her boots sooking! Muddy, the mere is. See now, how slow she comes – slow, like she used to walk when she spun with the big wheel. She walks slow because her clo'es are so heavy about her. It's uphill and agen the heart for Jancis, with the mommet to carry all alone.'

Then he said, worried –

'I wish I hadna mocked at the babe.'

A long while went by. The sounds in the room were less than on the evening Father died. It was as if Sarn, all the live part of it, us and our beasts, the trees full of birds, and the wood ways with wild creatures in them, had sunk to the bottom of the mere where the village was. I was beginning to believe all Gideon said, which was not so very different, after all, from many a tale of frittening we'd heard.

'Look ye now!' he muttered. 'She's going toërts the dairy door. There, she's gone! 'Twas in the dairy I gave her the nay-word that time afore she went to Grimbles. There now, she's coming back. Her yellow head does shine so, she makes me call to mind that wandering light at Lullingford New House.'

He was leaning forrard staring down the dimmery passage that led to the dairy.

'There, look's the wet floor!' he said. 'It's like as if she'd brought the mere in along of her. I never thought she'd come in the house. A castle's easy kept when none comes against it. But now –'

He looked down at the wet quarries a good while.

'Why, she's gone!' he said then. 'Like a golden bee sailing away on the air, and singing as she goes. Look's pretty!'

He stayed brooding a long time. Then he got up and told me he was going to see to the stock, for the evening

269

was well on to night. He said that in his usual way, and I thought the frittening had lifted from his mind. But as he went out, he turned, and looked at me just as he did the night Beguildy went to seek a seventh child, and said –

'If I'm late, put the key over the stable door.'

I thought, no, if he was out so much as a half-hour, I should go after him. Indeed I almost did then. Summat told me to go. But it seemed so queer when he was only going to see to the stock, to run after him. So I stayed where I was and began looking in Beguildy's book, that I bought at the sale, and in the Bible, to see if I could find any cure for such bewitchments. I hadna been reading more than half an hour, if so much, and I suppose it was about nine o'clock, though it seemed later because of the muffling mist and the silence, when all of a sudden there was a taboring at the door, and in rushed Miller's Tim and Polly too.

'Oh, Prue, Prue! we'd just brought the pigs along, being late because the black un wouldna come out of the rushes, and we'd put 'em un yard, quiet, for fear Mister Sarn ud be angry with us for being late, and we were looking for glow-worms under the orchard hedge, when out comes Mister Sarn. So we hid. And looking from under the hedge we saw him, standing by the water, with his head stooped forrard a bit, like a horse with the staggers. And I told Polly what I heard Granfeyther Callard say. "Sarn?" he says, "Oh, Sarn's known frittening of the beautiful bogey out of the mere, and he'll never be his own man again." And while I was whispering that to Polly, Mister Sarn lifted up his head and seemed to look all around at everything, only there was not much but mist. Then he turned toërts the caus'y, going like a chap in his sleep, and went down the caus'y to the boat, and untied the boat, and got in and took up the oars, and rowed with big strokes away from the farm, straight out where the caus'y went, to the mid of the lake. So we ran round to see if we could get a blink of him, but he was in the mist. The noise of the oars

270

went on for a while, and I wished I was in the boat. But in a bit I was glad I was on dry land. The sound of the rowing stopped.'

'Ah. Dead as dead it stopped,' said Polly.

'We held our breath to see if we could hear aught, but no! It was like the text parson learned us last Sunday, "There was silence over all the land till the ninth hour." Oh, it was solemn.'

'You should have come to me then,' I said. 'But quick now! What else?'

'Why nothing else at all,' says Tim, 'saving a great splash. I never heard such a splash, not even when the brindled calf fell into the water.'

'Ah. Dear to goodness, it *was* a splash!' says Polly.

'Then it went quieter and quieter, and we held breath and listened, but there was nought. And I did call on Mister Sarn's name, but none answered. And I was feared and so was Polly, and we ran to you.'

The boat! I must get to the boat. I ran down to the caus'y, tearing off my skirt, but there was no need to swim, for the boat was coming back, since the air drew from the other end of the mere, sending the currents toërts us, and these currents were stronger at the time of the troubling of the waters. A dreadful thing it was to see that empty boat come stealing in, slow, slow. I catched it and got in, taking up the oars which Gideon had unshipped, for even in this hour he couldna do anything slipshod or careless. I pulled out, calling to the children to run for Sexton, he being the nighest. They were soon gone, and glad to go. And I rowed out to the mid of the lake, feeling in the water with the oars, looking here and there, and calling his name, though I knew all the while it was too late. I was still rowing and calling when I heard Sexton shout from the shore.

'Me and Sam will go while you rest a bit,' he said. 'But we'll never find Sarn. You canna drag the mere out there. It's too deep. None were ever found that went in there.'

They rowed away, and as they came toward the middle of the mere, I heard them singing, as we'd sung over Father long ago –

> '*Your good deeds and your bad, dear man,*
> *Afore the Lord shall meet.*'

Only they left out about the turf at head and foot, for the water was his grave. Ah! The whole of that great stretch of water wasna too much to make the grave of a man as strong as that one. The mile-long mist that lay upon the place wasna too grand a shroud. For though he was wrong, and did evil, and hurtid folks with his strength, yet he never did meanly, nor turned out bad work, nor lied. 'The granite mountain, quartzite, b'rytes,' he said once to me, speaking of his own hardness. And he was like them all. He could no more give in than the granite can crumble like sandstone. And now he'd played his last game of *Conquer*, and what he played with wasna one of the big pink-and-white ones, but his own life.

And since the other player was one that none can ever hope to conquer, it shivered into brittle fragments in a moment, and so Gideon Sarn lost his last game.

Chapter 6: *The Breaking of the Mere*

THAT was a night of grief and fear which nothing in life has ever made me forget. Sexton and Sammy, after a vain search, went home, I was alone under the coverlet of fog, in that place full of ghostly footsteps. I said a prayer for dying men. Then I sat hour by hour beside the fire, in that dim slothfulness of the spirit which a great sorrow or a great amazement will bring. It was the strangest Wake

Eve I'd ever known, and the most grievous night of all my life. I thought how Gideon forbade me to go down into the water as folk did of old time, and be cured of my ill. And now, see! he was gone down into the mere himself, to be cured of his own curse. Then I thought of golden Jancis, and the little babe, and Missis Beguildy, and Father and poor Mother, all dead too. It seemed Death had been very busy at it, swiving among us. Ah! It was a bitter watching, for I ever liked those I cared for to be in good case. A year back, there was Jancis chosen for the sport called Heaving the Chair, for which the prettiest girl was always called out. There she was in her blue gown, I minded it well, with a crown of summer flowers on her head and a posy in her hand, lifted high in the chair by two strapping young fellows, while the rest came by, one by one, to see who she'd choose. All the young chaps were in it, but only one girl, so you may guess there was a deal of heart-searching over who'd be chosen.

They gave her a posy, and one fellow held a basin of water, and when she'd chosen her chap, she dipped the posy in the water and smote his face with it, which made everybody laugh.

And Jancis had chosen Gideon, of course, and he'd waited till the very last, because it pleased him to see all the others turned away and to know he wouldna be. And she smacked his face well with the posy, and gave her sweet, tinkling laugh, and then he lifted her down, which was part of the game, and gave her a kiss, which wunna. And I thought now, how untoërt a thing it was that she should have soused his face with water, as if in token that she should baptize him in the mere, 'ticing him to his death, and that it was the coming round of the fair day that had been the last straw. So I sighed, thinking – 'we be all His mommets, and He orders the play.'

I called to mind also how Gideon won the guinea for whistling best and clearest. He could whistle very well, and also he could keep his face straight in spite of all the fooling of the merry-andrew, who tried to make them laugh. For if Gideon was at the making of money he took it in such good sadness that nothing in the world could even make him smile. Beguildy whistled well also, but his best chance of a prize was always the yawning match, in which Granfeyther Callard ran him very close. Beguildy would come to the fair, though it angered Sexton, who persisted in saying it was a festival of the Church, and not for wizards, and who made himself very busy about everything, as if he was chief man.

Thinking of all this, I was sick at heart, for what is there more grievous than calling to mind old, merry randies? Then you say, 'Ah, this one or that one was here then.' And you remember how you were so strong in your joy, you could even be merry over jests that played upon great and solemn things. You call to mind how such an one said, 'A goose walks over my grave!' and laughed. And you remember that the one who said it has been under the sod a long while. So the thought of last year's fair set me crying, though the drowning of Gideon didna. Indeed, it was out of the ornary strange, his dying, and not like the common lot, for he neither died in his bed nor by violence, but went into the mist of his own will and wish, and then was not. And that we never found him seemed to me only a rightful ending to a life which so cut itself adrift from all pleasant, feckless human ways and doings. He belonged to none, seemingly, for he gave the go-by to his nearest kin. What he had most truck with was the earth and the water from which he was building himself a life to his mind. Rock, and troubled water, heavy earth, trees groaning, yet unyielding in the storm, all these he was kin to, though he didna love them. He took hold of them, browbeat them, made them his'n. And in the doing of it he fell, as it were, among thieves, for they took hold of him and made him their slave. It seemed to me he couldna die like other men, and be sodded, and lie in six feet of soil, and have a name-stone. No. He must have a large room and be free of all, roaming at will in the troubled currents of the mere, in the mid of his own farm and his own woodland. How can you cry for such a thing as this? Can you cry about a thunderbolt or a cloud-burst? No. It was only when I remembered those few times when he gave in that I could cry for him, as when I called to mind how he put his arm across his face at the fire, and sobbed.

All that night I thought of him, and the dark was full of cold fear, and a horror gathered about the place, it seemed so lone, as if it didna belong to the world at all. I knew I couldna spend another night there, and I began wondering what to do with the live stock, since nobody else would set foot here after such doings. No, not if it was ever so! Sexton refused out and out, and if he wouldna, nobody would. Not a soul would buy the place, and though I could leave the fields we'd laboured on to go back into wood and heath, yet the live stock must be seen to as long as it was there. Yet I was determined to bide there no longer, but to flee away as they did from the cities of the plain, not for any fault in the place, but for what Gideon had made of it. I'd shift to-morrow. But what to do with the beasts I couldna think, for if I asked anyone even so much as to water them, they'd say, 'No, no, missus, there's summat to be seen there.'

At last came the blessed dawn, and the mist lay like a vasty shining cloud on the place, but as the sun swam up, full of power and warmship, not to be gainsayed, the mist came loose all in a piece, and lifted slow, till there was a space betwixt its under side and the mere, where the coots swam, like bees running about between two boards. Then one half of the tree-trunks came free, so that the forest seemed to be mounded up with snow. It lifted and lifted, and at last went into the sky, and failed amid the clouds of dawn. Then the clouds faded, and there were only the proper heavens, blue as bird's eye. As soon as the mist lifted, I saw that the mere had broken in the

275

night, and the water was thick and troubled, simmering all over, so that the lilies were stirred as they lay anchored. When the blessed sunshine came, a way out came also into my mind. It was fair day. There'd be a sight of people here. Why not take the creatures to the fair, and make a pen, and get somebody to sell them? They could go cheap. Ah. That was it! So when I'd fed the stock, and milked, I fetched all into the fold, to be ready, and tidied the house, drawing the curtains, and set out to Sexton's to ask if I could put up a pen and bring the beasts, and get the crockman to sell them by auction, as he sold his wares. Sexton didna care about it much, but seeing he knew he'd got no authority, and the fair being held in our wood, he could do no else than agree. Tivvy looked very spitefully at me, for she wanted sore to be missus at Sarn, not to speak of her being sweet on Gideon, and she seemed to blame me that all had gone wrong. But I'd no time to waste, for already the first waggons were coming to the fair ground. It was still the custom then to deck out a waggon for each village with flowers and boughs, to bring the people. Or sometimes the young ones would walk, the men and women in separate companies, singing as they came. But they went back two by two, men and maids. They were setting out the booths when I went by, spiced ale and the ginger-bread-babies Moll liked, mint cakes and pebble brooches and combs to stand high in the hair. A woman had lit a fire and was getting ready the huge bowl of hasty pudding for the trial, which could eat it hot quickest. The waggons rolled along the wood ways with the same sound as at our harvest home. The folk chattered like a lot of jays, until they came to the fair ground and heard the news about Gideon. I could hear when each waggon heard tell, for a hush fell on all. Then I suppose they thought, well, they were a-nigh the church, that was on holy ground, and the accursed place was at the other end of the mere, so they took heart and began to chatter again. I saw Mister Huglet

276

and Mister Grimble, thick as thieves, and they scowled at me as I went by.

All along the wood-path there was a great stirring of dragon-flies, and the lustre-coloured damsels looked grand, sailing over the crimson bosses of dragon's blood, that is the wild geranium. I thought, 'The wind lifts in the branches, the lilies be in blow, the dragon-flies be coming out of their shrouds, but Kester Woodseaves has forgot me.' For by this he was to have raught back. And why should he remember a woman with a curse upon her, a hare-shotten woman, in danger of being accused of witchcraft? No, he wouldna call me to mind again. He'd take up with that young woman he spoke of that didna spare her blushes.

When I got home, I gathered together all the sheep and pigs, the cows and oxen, and drove them, riding upon Bendigo, to the fair. By good fortune they were all fain of me and went where I told them. Then I went back and put the fowl and ducks, the geese and turkeys in boxes and hampers, and wheeled them on the barrow. I'd left them shut up, to catch them the sooner. The people stared when they saw me riding through the wood with my flocks and herds afore me, for the creatures made a great stir baaing and grunting and mooing, misliking the woods. And as we went there we all were in the troubled water, dimly shadowed, and I thought how we had been reflected there when we buried Father. Then, all the fields and barns, fold and shippen, being void of life, I put Pussy in a basket and locked the door. And I thought, now the ghosts could have the place, yes, all of them, even as far back as Tim, that had the lightning in his blood. My vow that I took to Gideon was cancelled now. I'd no more to do here. What should I stay for, with nobody to ask a hand's turn of me? I was for the road. What road I didna know, but I thought it would be lonely. I'd packed a few things to leave with Miller, for him to take to Lullingford, else, I had what I stood in, and the old

277

Bible, and my book. So I set forth from the farm, where Sarns had been time out of mind. It was hard to leave the fields I'd laboured so long upon, but it would have been harder to stay. I shivered to think how the church spire would point across the water at the haunted house this night, lying over that deepest, darkest plaçe where Gideon was.

They were selling the things by the time I got back to the fair, with a pewter tankard to put the money in. So, not wishing to have part or lot in the merrymaking, I sat down on the churchyard wall to wait till all was done and I might go. The bidding was pretty brisk, for the beasts didna carry any curse, folk supposed, though they did come from an ill place. Sexton bought Bendigo, and Moll's father bought the oxen for his maister. Callard had some of the cows, the other things were bought up in good time, and I gave Pussy to Felena, because I thought she had a good heart, though not much respectability – or maybe it was because of that.

She said –

'Do you get tidings of weaver, Prue?'

'No,' I said. 'We've not heard this long while.'

'He's one in many,' she said. 'Ah! He does seem to me to be of other stuff than we are. As if he came from afar. Do you mind how we played *Costly* for weaver's soul, you and me? But I doubt some fine madam in the city's catched his soul by this.'

All the while, as we talked, and as I sat lonesome on the churchyard wall, I was ware of black looks cast at me, side-glances, a pushing out of the lips, and lifting of shoulders, and some would draw away a bit as I passed. I wondered what this might be, for though the old tales about me had gone on growing in the lonely farms, as I knew, and though a misfortune is enough, times, to turn people against you, as if they thought it was the hand of the Lord meting punishment for sin, yet it didna seem to me enough to explain the looks I got, which did cut me to the heart, for in them I saw hatred. I ever loved my kind, and as I once said, I was like one standing at the lane ends with a nosegay to offer to the world as it rode by. But instead, it rode me down. Ah! On this day of mid August, in the time of the troubling of the waters, it rode me down.

I was considering, and wondering what to do, for I was waiting for some people who were driving to Bramton, and would take me, and so I should be part way to Silverton. If I went now, I'd get no lift, and besides, the money couldna be counted till it was all in so the crockman could take his pay of so much in the shilling. On both counts I was bound to wait.

Missis Miller came up, quiet, and said she'd been there since the first and she'd heard a deal said about me, and the whispers were started by Grimble and Huglet, here one and there one, saying this and that, with a nod or a wink, maybe, or a shaking of the head, and, 'Pity. A tidy young woman, too!' Or, 'Summat should be done about it. Parson ought to see about it.' So the talk got fixed on me, she said, and no sooner did they tire of speaking of the manner of Gideon's death than they'd start of me. The younger ones had been brought up on tales of how I roamed the country at night in the body of a hare, and had a muse under this very churchyard wall. Miss Dorabella's words at the *Mug o' Cider* had stayed in people's minds, and then the fire had fixed on us the idea of a curse, for though Beguildy did it, yet 'twas thought the Lord wouldna have suffered him to do it at a righteous farm. Then the drowning of Jancis made things ten times blacker, and Gideon's death put the last touch to it. There was something here that the folks couldna understand. The only cause for all the misfortune that they could see was the curse of God. There must have been a Jonah in our ship, they thought. And as Mother had always been liked, and Gideon thought pretty well of, as a man bound to get on, it seemed to them that I must be the one that called down

279

the curse. They'd reasoned it out slow, as we do in the country, but once they came to the end of the reasoning they were fixed, and it would take a deal to turn them. This was the reason for the hating looks, the turnings aside, the whispers. I was the witch of Sarn. I was the woman cursed of God with a hare-shotten lip. I was the woman who had friended Beguildy, that wicked old man, the devil's oddman, and like holds to like. And now, almost the worst crime of all, I stood alone. I may say that in our part of the country, whatever happened in other parts, it was thought suspicious to stand alone. This might be because in those lost and forgotten farms in the mountains and the flooded lands about the meres, where in the long winters the winds would howl around the corners of the house like wolves, and there was talk of old terrible things – men done to death in sight of home; the fretting of unhappy ghosts at the bottle-glass windows that once they owned but now were the wrong side of; the dreadful music of the death pack; the howl of witches such as I was said to be, riding with blown leaves upon the gale; the threat of gentlemen of the road who had long lain at the cross-ways – nobody could choose to be alone, and nobody without good reason would condemn another to be alone. Therefore, if you were alone you were as good as damned.

I canna tell you what a sinking of the heart all this gave me. For to one that can feel the love and hate of others flowing about her without word spoken, and who can only do well in warmship of the soul, even a little mis-liking is enough to nip the blossom.

'Now,' says Missis Miller, 'I know what it's like, a bit, for mine's said to be under a curse, and cause he gives, indeed, but you dunna, and I say, "Beware of Grimble!" He's fause, is Grimble. Huglet's all of a roar, but you know what he's after. With Grimble you dunna. He'll drop a word here and a word there like thistledown, and you see nought and think nought, but dear to goodness, what a crop of thistles! And I doubt the thistles be all up and just about in blow.'

While she was yet speaking, Tivvy darted up to me, all in black, for she'd given out that she was promised to Gideon and she says.

'You boxed my ears, Prue Sarn! Now see!'

With that she jumped up on the wall and shouted out –

'People all, I'll speak this once and no more. A wronged woman I am. Sarn was promised to wed with me to-day's five months, and it's five months gone that I should have been Missis Sarn. For Sarn did love me right well. But *she* stopped it. Prue Sarn stopped it. For she put me in such mortal fear, I couldna come near the place. Clouted me, she did. And she being a witch, I was afraid of her. She wanted to be missus there, seesta! Couldna abide anybody else to have a say in things. And see what's come to pass! She's missus there altogether now, and the very next day after my poor Sarn's death she sells all. Oh, she's a heartless piece! There's no wickedness she wouldna do. Five months I'd ought to have been Missis Sarn, but for her. She's so strong, because she's a witch!'

I was astounded at the furious way she said it, till I remembered that she was expecting a love-child, which was ten times worse as she was Sexton's daughter, and what Sexton would do when he knew was awful to think of, and so Tivvy must have somebody to put the blame on. But no sooner was she finished than up gets Grimble. There he stood, with his long nose pointing down as if he was considering, among all he could say, what he'd fix on.

'People,' he began, 'this is a solemn day. In this here water lies a fine farmer. Ah! A man as would have made a mark on Sarn. Look at the ploughing he'd done! Bound to be rich, he was. Promised to a tidy young woman, too, and a righteous, for we know that her brother can come as pat with a text as any man even in the memory of Granfeyther Callard.'

'Ah. That's righteous!' calls out the old man from the cart where he sat. 'But old Camperdine could run him pretty close, the one as Beguildy had in bottle, I mean. Ah! He was a good un with a text when he was in liquor! I've heard him roll 'em out till you wanted a yard-stick to measure 'em. But when he was sober, not a text would he say. Very bawdy he was then. But in liquor, oh, indeed to goodness it was a miracle!'

'As I say,' Mister Grimble went on in his reasonable voice, 'her brother can mouth a text, her father's Sexton, her mother's Sexton's married wife, so it stands to reason she's a good young woman. And you've heard what she said. I tell you, what she says is true, and more than true. Now listen. Since birth Prudence Sarn's been a woman smitten by the Lord. What she does she canna altogether help, being in the power of Satan. That's why she roams the land, as we know. That's why she was friend to Beguildy, and learned all his wickedness off him, for like finds like. That's why she puts her eye on this one or that one, a child or a beast, or a field of corn, it's no matter. It dwines, whatever it is, dwines and withers away. Or she'll as soon kill outright. What did she do to my dog, as was worth a deal to me? Ah! And darker things yet. Blacker and blacker. What did her mother die of? People, she died of foxglove tea. Poisoned. Sexton's missis is my witness. Who nurses a sick mother? Her daughter. Well, people, what do you say to that?'

There was a muttering in the crowd, a pushing and stirring to look at me, where I sat, struck dumb with astonishment. But nobody said anything as yet. Country folk dunna condemn in a hurry. They were ready tinder, but the flint wunna put to it yet.

'And darker,' says Grimble. 'But first let Missis Sexton and Tivvyriah Sexton stand up and say in one word if it be true. Now then. Aye or no?'

'Aye!' said both together.

'Now, why did that feckless young creature, Jancis

Beguildy, and her poor child, meet their deaths in the water? Who was alone in the house with them when it took place? Prudence Sarn! Why was Jancis irksome to the witch? Because she knew things. She knew the devil's tricks that were played betwixt her father and the witch. And as she'd no money, she came to threaten to speak unless she was well paid, and that Prudence Sarn wouldna do. So, when nobody was there but the weak, nesh little thing, trammelled with her baby, and Prue Sarn, who's as strong as a man, Jancis Beguildy met her death in the water.'

There were murmurs again, but it would need more than the death of the wizard's daughter, who was in ill odour, to rouse them.

'But there's worse,' said Grimble. 'When Sarn took up with Tivvyriah, his sister didna like it. She wanted to keep on being missus. She wanted no other woman about the place. She'd got rid of her mother on that count. Ah! Liefer would she have no brother, friends, than have a married brother.'

A sigh went through the crowd, which must have numbered three hundred souls, all told, for it was a big fair. 'What did she do?' Grimble went on, and the hate in his eyes when he looked at me was awful to see. 'Why, when dusk drew on and the mist rose, and Sarn was dipping water for the beasts, she did push him in, and then took the boat out to deceive Sexton, having put such dread upon the miller's children that they durstna say the truth.'

He waited a minute for the people to understand. Then he said –

'Hare-shotten! A witch! Three times a murderess!'

And on the instant Huglet roared out –

'Suffer not a witch to live!'

The flint was set to the tinder. A howl went up. There were cries of –

'Tromple on her!'

'Stone her!'

283

'Let her drown!'.

There was nobody to speak for me, except such as would not be heard. Sexton was gone home. He was a fair-minded man, and I think he'd have stood for me. Most of the people were strangers. Some were neither for me nor against me.

Felena pushed her husband forrard, telling him to speak for me, but they shouted –

'Thee's in danger of damnation thyself, shepherd! How do ye pay yer rent?'

They came on me like the rising of a winter flood. They sent some to the church for the ducking stool. And still the voice of Huglet went roaring on.

'Suffer not a witch to live!'

I do think I fainted for very terror, for I knew no more, till I felt the chill water, and came up gasping, feeling the ropes that tied me to the ducking-stool and hearing the roaring of Huglet, which seemed like the blaring of some great demon.

Chapter 7:

'Open the Gates as wide as the sky,
And let the King come riding by.'

I CAME to myself, and opened my eyes, wondering what the great trompling was, and thinking it was Bendigo got loose. Then I remembered that Sexton had taken Bendigo away, so I looked to see what it might be, for all the waggon horses had been taken back to Plash Farm for the day. I looked up, and straightway I thought I must have died, and be now in Paradise.

284

There, looking down upon me from his nag, with a dwelling gaze so blazing with life that, if I hadna been sure the other way, I should have thought he loved me, was none other than Kester Woodseaves. Older-seeming he was, a little, and his face even cleaner cut than afore, as if the soul had been busy chiselling at it. As for his eyes, all the light of heaven was in them, not to speak of a very pleasant touch of the old Adam. They took me in from head to foot, and I was at rest. Ah! tied to the ducking-stool, in such sad case as no self-respecting woman could choose to be seen in by any man, let alone the man she loved, I was yet at rest. I cared for nothing now. I werrited about nothing. Kester was here. Kester had gotten things in hand. What could ail me? Such was my faith, that though three hundred people, more or less, were set against me, and only Kester for me, yet I knew that I was safe. I could have turned on my side and gone to sleep on that ducking-stool as if it was a feather bed, so comfortable I was in my mind.

'Well,' says he at last, 'well, Prue, my dear, you be in poor case!'

And he gave a little smile, as much as to say, 'But not for long!'

'I be,' I answered, and my voice was all of a tremble with joy, 'in very poor case, Kester Woodseaves.'

He gave a look round, and then beckoned to Felena. She darted forrard as if she was his slave.

'Untie those, 'oot?' he said, pointing to the cords.

As she was doing it, she whispered –

'I dunna care what they do to me. I'll work his will. A man to die for!'

'Is there any fellow here friend to me enough to catch a holt of my nag a minute?' he asks.

Callard called out –

'I will, and welcome.'

Afore he got off, Kester looked all round, and he says –

'Well, you were having a fine randy, I must say! Last

285

time it was a little white ox. Now it's a woman whiter than lily. I know very well who's egging you on.'

Some hung their heads, but most were angered to have their fun stopped.

Kester went up to Grimble.

'You and me's had ado afore, Grimble,' he says. 'You're too mean and twisty to be treated as a man. If you dunna like the treatment you get, you can fight me any time you like. But you're only good enough to laugh at. Your nose is too long, Grimble. It stirs about in everybody's business.'

And with that, he gave Grimble a tremenjous blow on the nose with his fist, and Grimble roared so, being a real coward, that the people couldna help but laugh.

Then Kester went to Huglet and he said –

'You're above board all right. You dunna do things secret. Man, I could hear you hollering even to Plash! Oot wrostle?'

Now, for all he was so big, Huglet didna want to wrostle. He hiver-hovered over it a good bit, for he knew Kester was a right proper wrostler. But many of the people knew nothing about Kester, and wouldna have cared if they had, for they only wanted a good day's sport. This was what Kester had reckoned on.

'A wrostling match!' they called out, quite in a pleasant humour again, though what they'd be after, nobody could say.

'Haw-woop!' cries out old Callard, pretty well beside himself with excitement, and the children, seeing Kester and remembering their lessons, folded their hands very primly over their stomachs and sang out –

'Bull-baiting's bad!' which would have made me laugh if I hadna been so uneasy in mind about Kester.

'A ring! Make a ring!'

'Ah, chaps, there's a nice smooth bit of turf there,' says Kester, pointing to a place close by the water. So they made a ring there. Kester stripped off his coat and weskit, and Huglet took his off unwilling. There were some hasty wagers made. Then they set to at it. I thought Huglet would crush every one of Kester's bones, but no! Kester was hard, and a practised wrostler, and when Huglet seemed to have got him safe and sure, he was out of his grip, ready to start all over again. A tuthree times Huglet bore him back till his one shoulder very near touched the ground, but each time he wrostled free, sharp and sudden, so it was only a *foyle*, and didna count. I was in a terror all the while that Huglet by his great strength would break Kester's back, and I could see he'd dearly like to, for he'd forgotten everything but hate of the man who'd twice robbed him of his sport. I wondered why Kester didna try, by some feint, to get him down, but Felena whispered –

'He's got summat in mind, Weaver has. He's tarrying for summat.'

All the while Kester kept edging nigher to the water, and I wondered at it, for the mud was very slippery there.

Then, all in a minute, it was done. Though how it was done I never knew to this day. Kester said it was a new throw he'd learnt in the city. Anyway, in the blink of an eye, Huglet was flung, not only on to the ground but clean out in the water. He went in souse, and when he struggled out, which he did with a deal of difficulty, for he'd gone all his length and the mud was very sticky, there was such a roar of laughter that he blenched. And indeed he was a comical sight. Miller, who stood by, smiled for the first time in anybody's memory, as if to say, 'Another kit-cat in the water!'

Kester stood a minute, breathed with the tremenjous heave, getting his wind. Then he took the rein from Callard, put foot in stirrup, and was in the saddle.

'I'd lief,' says Felena, low, 'I'd lief be on that saddle afore you, Weaver.'

I never saw such worship as was in her green eyes.

But he took no manner notice.

287

'Prue!' he said.

I rose up.

'Did I say at the harvesting at Sarn that it was to be toërts or frommet?' he asked me.

'Toërts.'

I could only whisper it.

'Come here then, Prue Woodseaves!'

He stooped. He set his arms about me. He lifted me to the saddle. It was just as in the dream I had. And, as in that dream, Felena looked up, imploring, and he took no account of her, and the noise of the people sank away, the laughter, and the curses of Huglet and Grimble, the clapping of the Callard children and the high voice of Granfeyther Callard telling of a wrostling match nearly a century ago. All sank, all faded in the quiet air. There was only the evening wind lifting the boughs, like a lover lifting his maid's long hair.

'Tabor on, owd nag!' says Kester, and we were going at a canter towards the blue and purple mountains.

'But no!' I said 'It mun be frommet, Kester. You mun marry a girl like a lily. See, I be hare-shotten!'

But he wouldna listen. He wouldna argufy. Only after I'd pleaded agen myself a long while, he pulled up sharp, and looking down into my eyes, he said –

'No more sad talk! I've chosen my bit of Paradise. 'Tis on your breast, my dear acquaintance!'

And when he'd said those words, he bent his comely head and kissed me full upon the mouth.

· · · · ·

Here ends the story of Prudence Sarn.

288